1819-1861 Desmos

Old Toney and his Master

The abolitionist and the land-pirate - founded on facts - a tale of 1824-1827

1819-1861 Desmos

Old Toney and his Master
The abolitionist and the land-pirate - founded on facts - a tale of 1824-1827

ISBN/EAN: 9783337120771

Printed in Europe, USA, Canada, Australia, Japan

Cover: Foto ©Andreas Hilbeck / pixelio.de

More available books at **www.hansebooks.com**

OLD TONEY AND HIS MASTER;

OR,

THE ABOLITIONIST AND THE LAND-PIRATE.

FOUNDED ON FACTS.

A TALE OF 1824-1827

BY DESMOS.

NASHVILLE, TENN.:

SOUTHWESTERN PUBLISHING HOUSE.

1861.

TO THE

HON. J. D. B. DE BOW,

THIS WORK IS MOST AFFECTIONATELY

Inscribed,

AS A MEMORIAL OF THE

AUTHOR'S PERSONAL REGARD AND GRATITUDE FOR MANY FAVORS CONFERRED;

AS A TESTIMONIAL OF

HIS UNFLINCHING PATRIOTISM, HIS STERN INTEGRITY,

HIS UNTIRING PERSEVERANCE UNDER DIFFICULTIES APPALLING TO OTHERS;

HIS NOBLE AND UNSELFISH PHILANTHROPY;

BUT, ABOVE ALL,

HIS MANLY INDEPENDENCE, AND DEVOTION TO THE CAUSE OF THE SOUTH,

WHOSE INTERESTS HE HAS SO LONG AND SO

FAITHFULLY ADVOCATED.

DESMOS.

PREFACE.

MAY the reading of these pages touch the heart of the reader, as the writing of the largest portion of this work touched mine, so that my eyes were often blinded by my tears. And the reason why my own heart was so deeply affected, kind reader, is because the facts herein recorded are so true, and so near home. *For there is scarcely a chapter written of either of these three books, which does not contain a great fact.* The whole book is, in truth, a compilation of facts, many of them disconnected, it is true, which the author has attempted to interweave as artistically as the delicate nature of the circumstances would admit. This work may, therefore, more properly be considered a *history* than a *fiction.*

It is true that names of persons and places, of dates and scenery, have all been altered or suppressed, for obvious reasons, but these alterations do not affect the value of the truths themselves, nor should they, because they are tangible facts, touch less deeply the reader's sympathetic heart.

Kind reader, bear with the faults of the work, whatever in your opinion they may be, and look only at the good which is intended. For although it may be regarded as an attempt to represent the *inner life* of

(vii)

the slave and the slaveholder, and the infamous character of *some or most of those* who have operated *secretly* at the South as engineers upon the so-called "Underground Railroad," yet the author has had a higher and a grander object, that of representing the Christian's faith in times of tribulation and distress, and to show that God "will not always chide, neither will He keep his anger forever," but He "tempers the wind to the shorn lamb." It strives also to inculcate the truth that God is his avenger. Why then, should he himself seek to avenge his own wrongs, since God will "bring him out of all his troubles."

As a politico-religious work, therefore, I lay this book, with an humble heart, but a hopeful spirit, as an offering—the one part upon the altar of my country—the other, upon the altar of my God.

                                              DESMOS.

LAWTONVILLE, *April* 10, 1860.

TABLE OF CONTENTS.

BOOK I.

1*   (ix)

CHAPTER IV.

CHAPTER V.

CHAPTER VI.

CHAPTER VII.

CHAPTER VIII.

CHAPTER IX.

CONCLUSION.

OLD TONEY AND HIS MASTER;

OR,

THE ABOLITIONIST AND THE LAND PIRATE.

––––––•••––––––

BOOK I.—CHAPTER I.

THE lamented Colonel Shelton was one of those lordly Southern planters who possessed many thousand broad acres of fertile land, which extended not for miles only, but many leagues away; and who counted his slaves not by tens, nor scores, but by hundreds. And when I use the term "lordly," I mean not in regard to wealth only. I have reference to that princely generosity and magnificence which characterizes very many of our best and noblest spirits. For when was the complaint of the poor man unheeded? when did he go away empty-handed when his necessities demanded relief? what agent of a benevolent or religious society ever had just cause of complaint against the liberality of Colonel Shelton? "Is the object of your agency a worthy one?" was the only inquiry which ever presented itself to his mind. No matter if the agent came from the North, or the South, or the East, or the West; or even if he had crossed the broad Atlantic in quest of pecuniary aid, it was all one to the benevolent-hearted Colonel, for he recognized the cosmopolitan principle that man

(13)

is the same everywhere, and his wants must be supplied. With the liberal spirit of the philanthropist, he lavished the almost countless treasure that a beneficent Deity had given him upon all alike who presented their petitions to him. While upon the European mendicant he bestowed alms to the amount of five or ten dollars *per capita*, his donations to colleges and to church edifices were as high as ten, and even fifty thousand dollars.

But the reader is not to suppose that Colonel Shelton was a religious man; at least in the common acceptation of the term. For, while he was charitable, and kind, and generous almost to a fault, he had never attached himself to any particular denomination of Christians, but welcomed them all to his fireside, while upon each he dispensed his favors with a bounteous hand. His idea was, that if religion be *love*, then it would be unkind and unchristian not to love all who professed the name of Christ; and if his wishes could have been gratified, he would have rejoiced to see erected one grand and glorious temple, like that at Jerusalem in its character, though grander in its proportions, beneath which all the followers of Christ could assemble at least once a year, and hold an annual jubilee, where all differences should be reconciled, and no discord nor jarring note should be heard in God's Tabernacle!

Colonel Shelton had also been a military man in the fullest sense of the term. His was no honorary title bestowed by some governor of the state, or purchased by a hotly-contested election. He had won his military honors by hard blows administered upon the British foe in the memorable war of 1812; and, in other contests, had fought bravely by the side of that gallant chieftain, General Andrew Jackson.

But although his eye used to flash and flame at the sounds of battle, and his strong sword-arm grew red to the elbow with the blood of his country's foes, and his war-cry was as terrible as the angry thunder, yet, now that the battle was over, and peace had resumed its sway, his kindly loving

blue eyes were as gentle as the dove's; while his voice of
encouragement and love would ever draw the timid to his
side, and make the innocent prattler run joyously to seize
his hand, or climb upon his knee.   And where was the poor,
bruised heart and broken spirit who did not find in him a
kind friend who could sympathize with him in his woe and
sorrows?

If the reader likes the character of Colonel Shelton, surely
he will be as much interested in his family.   For, among
all the queenly women of earth, where could be found a single
one more queenly in her native dignity, more gentle in her
deportment, more affable, and loving, and kind in her disposition, than Mrs. Shelton, the wife and noble matron?
Her large, black, and lustrous eyes would swim with tears
at a tale of distress; and when her noble husband had given
all the pecuniary aid which, in his judgment, he thought
the circumstances of the case demanded, she, like a kind
soul, would not let the applicant go until she had done
something herself for the relief of suffering humanity,
or the advancement of God's cause throughout the earth.
Her private purse seemed inexhaustible; and, as her husband
used jocularly to say, "She must possess a gold mine somewhere! for how else could her few house-servants at their
odd moments make cotton enough to produce so much money!"

But the Colonel well knew, nor did his wife attempt to
conceal the fact from him, that when she had spent all the
money which her house-servants had made from the rich
cotton-patches contiguous to the house, she felt that it was
not only her right, but her duty, to take from the common
treasury as much money as would supply her deficiencies.
But her "pin-money," amounting usually to three or four
hundred dollars, was not spent upon herself, nor lavished
with foolish indulgence upon her children.   Was there a
poor woman dying and in want of some little delicacy; were
there orphan children who needed clothing or education,
Mrs. Shelton did not wait to consult her husband, but was

off upon her errand of mercy the moment the cry of distress was borne to her ears.

Nor did she do these deeds of love to be praised by men, or stand unrivaled among women as a sister of charity. In silence and alone she often labored in the cottage of the lowly; propping up the head of the dying patient, and preparing, frequently with her own hands, a pot of gruel, when there was no one present capable of performing correctly the menial office.

But in the hut as well as in the palace, she seemed ever the same—an angel of light and love, dispensing her smiles upon the gay and the happy, and shedding copious tears of sympathy with the sorrowful and distressed. The spirit, too, which actuated her charity, was that inculcated in the Bible, "not to let the right hand know what the left hand doeth;" thus doing her alms in secret, because she wished not that "they should be known of men," but to God only. In doing so, however, her secret deeds of charity became their own trumpeters; for how many hearts sent up their fervent prayers for blessings on her head! and how many tongues longed to proclaim to the whole world the timely aid which her sympathetic heart had brought their homes, and had made happy their humble firesides! And how many a strong and sturdy yeoman, a thankful husband, or a grateful father, has felt so like choking, that it was with difficulty he could utter a "God bless you, madam!" as she turned away from his cottage to enter her carriage in waiting, after having sat all night by the bedside of the poor, bedridden wife, or the dying child.

"God bless you, madam! may you never want a friend!" and, "God bless you, dear Mrs. Shelton!" was heard upon every hand, and uttered by hundreds of grateful hearts. "God bless you, madam!" was echoed by the woods, and warbled by the birds, and wafted by the breeze, as incense to the throne of God! "God bless you, madam!"—the "God bless you" of the poor, and the miserable, and the

dying, and the distressed, was the sweetest music on earth
to her. It soothed her wearied spirit to slumber ; it filled her
dreams with bright visions of the poor in glory, encircled
by the arms of Jesus ; and she thought in her wakeful
moments, "If he said, 'Blessed are the poor,' how sweet
it is to have their blessing, and to hear their sincere, and
so oft-repeated, 'God bless you !' uttered in prayer for herself to the God of the poor !"

Nor did the Colonel ever object to the active benevolence
of his dear wife, of whom he was not only fond, but proud
—yes, proud that he possessed so noble a wife, "whose heart
was in the right place," as he used to say with a benignant
smile; "for it was in her head ! and when the *heart* is in
the *head*, it is not so apt to be led astray by sinful passions."

But if the hearts of Colonel Shelton and his truly adorable
wife were made happy by the blessings of the poor and the
needy, God had blessed them yet more in the love and devotion of their children, who seemed to regard their parents
as something more than human ; and to whom they looked
up with that filial adoration which is so rare, and yet so
lovely, to be seen in any of the rising generation.

If Ella was their beautiful and most fragrant rose, which,
growing up as a vine, had wound its tendrils around their
hearts, and, like the perennial ivy, clung every day with still
greater tenacity to the strong hold which she maintained
upon the love of her dear father and mother, Langdon, their
brave and chivalric boy, was none the less an object of
admiration and respect, as the young and graceful sapling
which had grown from the acorn cast from the boughs of the
noble and the sturdy old oak standing in grandeur by his
side. If the daughter was the image of her mother, in all the
refinement of her heart and the graces of her person, Langdon
was fashioned after no meaner mold, and stamped with an
image no less imperial than his noble father. Like his
honored sire, honor and honesty were stamped by the Deity

in broad and legible characters upon a brow where Truth
sat enthroned in all her majesty. While he possessed not
a rival in the chase, or in other manly sports, and while his
hand was "*as steady as a die*," that he was considered a
"dead shot," yet who so ready to lend a helping hand to
a fellow-companion in distress? or whose heart would shrink
more from inflicting injury upon others?

If it be true that, as a general rule, Southern youth are
humane and kind, and seem to vie with their fathers in acts
of hospitality; and if it be a foul slander that they are
recklessly dissipated, and profligate, and abandoned, preferring the midnight brawl and the dangers and heartless-
ness of the hateful duello to the quiet enjoyments of the
domestic fireside, and the generous emulation of their worthy sires in their deeds of love and their acts of humanity;
if, among the many worthy associates of Langdon Shelton—
those brave, and chivalric, and honorable young men—his
noble spirit towered above them all; while his acts of generosity and disinterested benevolence outstripped them all
in the race of humanity as he used to do in the chase, when
his splendid steed bore his impetuous rider far away over
"brake and brier," leaving his companions in the distance,
as he met the stag at bay, and encountered, single-handed
and alone, the monarch of our Southern forests;—yet there
were none who envied his superiority, while all delighted
to do him honor.

Langdon Shelton was not only the pride of his father and
the idol of his mother, but the admiration of all who knew
him. He was too far superior to all his associates to be a
subject for envy, while his frank and loyal countenance, his
magnanimous acts and princely favors, had drawn to his side
a host of ardent admirers. If he had a foe, he knew it not;
and so numerous were his devoted friends, that he was just
the brave youth and impetuous rider to head a troop of
gallant spirits, at a moment's warning, to repel invasion,
whether from the North or any other quarter. As to *insur-*

rection — a *servile insurrection!* — that is an obsolete idea,
which has ceased to disturb the brains or agitate the hearts
of all save the visionary, or the cruel and the wicked! Yes,
the day has long since passed away. There was a time,
long ago — when our slaves were pure-blooded Africans,
fresh from their native desert, and wild as the Bedouin;
when they were not yet *christianized*, *humanized*, and en-
lightened,—when apprehensions of an occasional outbreak
were felt, and when caution was necessary to be observed.
But that day has passed; and if the youth of our land are
ever called to arms in defense of their homes and their domestic altars, it will not be to repulse the attacks of the
slave, but to hang with a halter those incendiaries who seek
to tamper with the deep-rooted affections which must forever exist between the master and his bondman.

Langdon Shelton—O! how his father loved the boy, just
springing into the dignity of manhood's estate! How his
mother petted and tried hard to spoil her darling—her only
boy! How his companions gloried in his excellencies, and
tried in vain to rival him in his prowess; his skill in the
use of fire-arms, or the management of the horse! How
his angelic sister looked with tenderest love upon her manly
brother, and ever welcomed his coming with one of those
winning smiles that caused his heart to leap with joy, and
made it bless God that he had lived to feel how happy he
could be in answering the greetings of the fairest and loveliest of sisters. How the neighbors praised him; and how
the young and lovely maidens smiled at his approach; while
the hearts of many beat quicker, and their cheeks blushed
deeper red, becoming incarnadine with the tell-tale taint of
love, as he saluted them with the graceful ease of the courtier, but with all the fervor of the ardent devotee at the
shrine of youthful beauty and virgin innocence! But, O!
last, not least, how the humble, the tried, the devoted slave
gloried in his young master. How great his homage; how
unselfish his love! He could have kissed the ground upon

which Langdon trod, and licked the dust from his feet, not through servile fear—no, no!—but through the same spirit of adoration with which he would have licked the polluting dust from the sandals of a Divinity.

"God bless you, my masser! You da your farer and your murrer own chile!" And the "God bless you, masser," of the African sounded in the ears of young Shelton wherever he went; whether at his own home or the homes of his companions. For is it not true that another man's slave invariably loves his fellow-slave's master, once his character is established for goodness, and generosity, and genuine heroism? For there is a spirit of chivalry inherent to the African as well as to the white man. He loves and worships heroism—the heroism of the white man, whom he regards as a superior being in proportion to his reverence for his character for goodness, and the outward signs that he possesses a noble soul. He loves a deed of daring when performed by his master, and looks with admiration upon him as a superior genius in proportion as his headlong temerity makes him stand aghast with consternation at what he regards as invincibility and indomitable courage. He imagines that his own idolized master, backed by that master's brave friends, could not only conquer all his foes, be they few or many, and come from whence they may, but that, single-handed and alone, he could put to flight a host with no other weapon than a sling, or that with which Samson routed the Philistines. He loves to feel and to see all this, and more, in his master, and glories in him as "the bravest of the brave;" looking with the same kind of admiration, and even awe, as did the Cossacks upon Murat when he rode up to their very front, and scattered the host of his annoying foes with the simple words, "Disperse, ye reptiles!" But, *above all*, the African slave loves generosity, liberality, a *giving* spirit, more than all other kind of spirits, except, perhaps, *ardent* spirits. The man who pays no attention to their wants, or rebukes their begging for "a piece of tobakker, masser!"—or, if he does not himself make use of "the weed," fails to throw to the wayside beggar a sixpence or a half-dime for tobacco money, will hold no place in his "heart of hearts," and hear no "God bless you, masser!" ringing in his ears from morning until night.

No wonder that Langdon Shelton was so popular with the negroes of the neighborhood—his father's, as also every other man's; for it was his invariable rule never to refuse, but always to give, often unasked, some little trifle—a cigar, or a piece of tobacco, or a "bon-bon," to make glad the heart of the faithful negro.

But let us return to Colonel Shelton, around whom and his family the interest of our story must center for a while, and in whose fate the reader must already feel somewhat interested.

A man of wealth, and possessing a spirit of boundless liberality, it is not surprising that he should have kept an open house for the free entertainment of all comers. Surrounded by all the comforts and elegancies of life, with a truly palatial residence, and numerous domestics, none could better afford than he to accommodate the wayfarer and the traveler, without charge; while, of all the hospitable entertainers on Carolina's soil, there was not one who welcomed his guests with more cordiality, or who possessed, in so high a degree, the art of making his visitors feel perfectly at home. Not only were the high and the low, the rich and the poor, the learned and the ignorant, all alike made welcome by the hospitable owner of the mansion, but even the servants themselves seemed to possess the spirit of accommodation and urbanity which characterized their master; and the case was unheard of when the stranger, whether on horseback or foot, was refused a night's lodging because the house was too crowded and there was no more any room! Indeed, it grew into a proverb, that Colonel Shelton's house could never be so entirely filled up that not another guest could find a lodging beneath its capacious roof. Whether

"prince or peddler," it was all the same. The welcome of
the one, if more cordial than that extended to the other,
did not prevent the latter, at least, from enjoying a good
bed, nor feasting upon the very fat of the land.

But, at the present time, the guests assembled at the
Colonel's are invited for a special object. They are his
neighbors and friends, mostly, who have gathered for the
purpose of a deer-hunt. It has been long talked of, and some
have even come from the city, by special invitation; while
there are a few volunteers who have come unasked, but are,
nevertheless, treated by the Colonel and his son with the
same kindness and courtesy as though they had been invited
guests and princes of the blood royal. Among the latter
was a young man of a thick-set and very muscular frame;
possessing a bushy head of black hair and a keen, hawk's
eye, which seemed to follow you wherever you went. He
was dressed in a genteel suit of blue cloth with brass but-
tons, then fashionable, with long spurs upon his heels, a
hunter's horn and powder-flask around his neck. He had
evidently come armed and equipped for the hunt, of which
he had heard so much; for the Colonel had numerous deer
within his fences, which had kept them as completely as if
hemmed in by a stone wall or a park.

There were several others who had come of their own
accord, and had been duly acknowledged as members of
the party. But this particular young man was most welcome, although uninvited, because he was a bold and a fearless horseman, and a splendid shot. The brave old Colonel,
who had been trained in a military school, loved at all times
to see a bold equestrian, or to witness a splendid shot; but
more especially in the chase, when some of the warlike
spirit of the soldier was kindled into action by the cry of
the hounds, the shouts of men, or the bugle-blasts of the
hunter's horn.

The reader has not, perhaps, discovered anything, save
the expression of the eye of Stephen Stevens, who afterward

became notorious as a land-pirate, and suffered upon the
gallows for the double crimes of murder and negro stealing,
oft repeated, and of which he made confession when about
to die. But although the spirit of evil was inherent to his
nature, and deadly mischief was rife within his heart, he
had not yet been guilty of any crime against the "majesty of
the law," either overtly or secretly committed. His opportunity had not yet come, but it was coming soon, and would
be but the "beginning of the end."

We will not attempt to describe a deer-hunt at the South,
which in no respect differs from a deer-hunt in the West,
or anywhere else where the deer are wild and fleet, the hounds
fierce and bloodthirsty, and the huntsmen dashing, adven-
turous spirits. Suffice it then, to say, that it was an exciting
and a successful chase, and that more than one antlered head
was laid low in the dust. At a signal from the Colonel, who
has pulled out his heavy gold watch, the driver, who beats
the bush and urges on the hounds with his lash, which he
pops with peculiar skill, accompanied by cheering words,
which the well-trained dogs understand—the driver, with
his bugle to his lips, now sounds the "return home," or
"recall," which summons the scattered party to the central
point. It is time now to convey home the noble game which
has been killed, and to partake of that sumptuous repast
which has been prepared with no illiberal hand, and to which
the entire party are most cordially invited.

They had traversed but half the distance from the hunt-
ing ground, a gay and a merry cavalcade, when their merri-
ment was suddenly suppressed by their wonder at seeing a
messenger approaching at a rapid gallop from the direction
of the Colonel's residence. He was a black man, mounted
upon a strong horse, taken fresh from the pasture. The
object of his mission, therefore, must be one of urgency.
As he pulls off his black velvet cap, he reveals a head of
hair which rivals in its whiteness the unspotted snow; and
seems more like freshly-ginned cotton, which has been con-

verted into a wig, than the natural covering of a human
being's head. He bows low his venerable head, even to his
horse's mane, as he salutes his adored master with the same
kind of obeisance which an officer of the household would
make before an Oriental prince. As the venerable old man,
of more than sixty years, raises his head, and looks Colonel
Shelton in the face, his lip trembles slightly; for he feels
in his heart that he is the bearer of sad news, although he
does not as yet know what is precisely the nature of the
intelligence contained in the note which he slowly and solemnly withdraws from the breast-pocket of his coat, cut in
military fashion, which he has taken good care to button
up to his chin. As he is engaged in leisurely unbuttoning
his coat, as if reluctant to bring forth the dispatch, sent
in haste by his mistress, the Colonel takes occasion to remark :

" How now, Old Toney! I thought that you were too un-
well to join in the hunt. What brings you hither at this
time? You seem as solemn as though you had just come
from your wife's funeral. Has any one been attacked with
sudden illness during our brief absence?"

" No, my dear masser," replied the old man, with a long-
drawn sigh ; " dey is all well, t'ank God, at home. But dis
note from my missis, dat I lef' at home a cryin', will reveal
to your comperhension what am happened. I don't know
what de matter egzackly; but I 'fraid de bank is broke, or
somet'ing wuss dan dat! for a young man is come all de
way from Charleston to see you on puppose."

While Old Toney—whose only employment was that of
looking after the boys who attended to the horses, or, in
other words, chief hostler—was making these remarks, Colonel Shelton had read the few, brief lines contained in the
note, which he crumpled with desperation in his hand, while
he uttered a deep, deep groan, and the single word " Ruined!"
which was spoken almost between his clenched teeth, so that
it was unheard by those around him. His friends saw enough,

and understood enough by that groan, which sounded to their ears something like a smothered sob; which, taken in connection with the spasmodic twitching of the facial muscles, revealed the intense agony which had rent his soul.

They were, nearly all of them, his sincere and devoted friends, who loved him, not on account of his great wealth, but for himself alone; for the many noble qualities of his head and heart. Indeed, several of that company were near and dear relatives; while, with the exception of two or three, all were allied, in some way, by the ties of consanguinity or intermarriage with some one of his family, of whom he was the acknowledged chief; and something akin to the old love and veneration of a Scottish clan for its venerated chieftain characterized the feelings of those who followed Colonel Shelton in silence to his home.

There was no gay laughter now, no merry joke, nor joyous hunter's chorus. In solemn silence, as a funeral procession, or a band of soldiers bearing their wounded or dead comrade upon a litter, they followed their leader, who rode a little in front, with his head bowed and his eyes upon the ground. A single time he reined the chestnut stallion, upon which he sat usually with the grace and attitude of a hero, and confronting his friends, who had checked their horses also so suddenly that some of them fell back upon their haunches; then, with a bitter smile so unusual to him, he said, in slow and measured accents, and with suppressed breath, "Gentlemen, this is our last hunt together!" But in a moment he recollected himself, and recovered his habitual self-control.

His friends felt that there was an awful mystery in these words, but they dared not question him as to the signification of the mission which he had so lately received. They respected his grief too much, while their innate delicacy and refinement prevented them from obtruding upon his secret sorrows by useless and impertinent questions. They felt that, when the time came, he would, of his own accord,

2

consult them as friends and advisers; or, at least, reveal
to them the nature of his sudden calamity. For a great
and heavy calamity they well knew it must be; for, otherwise, this brave old soldier, who had heard the war-whoop
of the Seminole in the everglades and forests of Florida,
and the shouts of the British at New Orleans, such a man
would not be so deeply moved by any light or trifling circumstance. They made no reply to the words which he had
spoken so defiantly and with so much bitterness; not as if
addressed to them so much as to some invisible fate or iron
destiny, which he feared would crush him with its weight.
They followed him, in mournful silence, to his home, and'
entered the spacious hall two by two, in double file, as
trained soldiers following a dead comrade to his last resting-place; or, rather, as if entering his home to look, for
the last time, upon the face of the dead, and then to bear
him away in his coffin.

CHAPTER II.

WHEN Colonel Shelton entered the large hall into which his guests had followed him, he seemed to recover from the self-abandonment and abstraction into which he had allowed himself to fall; and re-assuming his old style of urbanity, and with a bow and a smile, he bade his visitors to be seated and make them-selves at home until his return, for it was necessary to see a gentleman from Charleston, who was then awaiting him in the library.

"Gentlemen, pray excuse me for a few moments, until I have attended to a little business of importance. My son Langdon will do the honors of the house during my absence from the room. Langdon, my son, see that the gentlemen are provided with everything which they need.·

"George!" speaking to one of the servants, "tell the but-ler to hand out some wine, and brandy, also; and be sure that the gentlemen are provided with fresh water and clean towels. Excuse me, messieurs. Au revoir!" and bowing as a courtier at the palace of the Tuilleries in the days of Louis XIV, the polite old Colonel left his guests in charge of his son, and, perhaps, what many of them liked better still, in company with the butler's wines and French brandy.

But the reader must recollect that this was more than thirty years ago, when it was the fashion of the day for everybody, no matter whether layman or divine, not only to *invite*, but to *insist* upon all alike to participate in "a

friendly glass" with his neighbor. Indeed, as alcohol had
been called, by a celebrated French chemist, the elixir of
life, the "*aqua vitæ*" by which the lives of men were to be
lengthened out to an indefinite period, it was considered in
those days as not only an innocent, but a very necessary
beverage, and regarded even by medical men of the highest
authority, as a prophylactic, or preventive against diseases
of almost every form. If one was sick, he must certainly
drink brandy in order to get well; and if he was well, it
would be folly to get sick when one could so easily keep well
by a little timely correction of any unseen or unfelt disorder.
If he was cold, he ought to take a little "to warm his in-
nards;" and if he was *hot*—burning up with fever, or almost
melted by the sultry heat of summer—then there was no
other way in the world; not even ice was supposed to be
half so good a refrigerator as old Cognac or Bordeaux, etc.
Indeed, ice, "*dry so*," without the addition of Cognac or
Monongahela, was condemned as a promoter of cramps, and
decidedly colicky.

Some of my readers may be astonished to hear that their
grandfathers, and even grandmothers, drank so much, and
yet lived long enough that they, or their fathers and mothers, should ever have been born? And their dear old grandmothers, too! Did they use brandy? Yes, both inside and
out! They rubbed it upon their bodies, to prevent and
cure rheumatism; they rubbed it upon their faces and their
children's faces, to take out freckles and clean off the tan;
they rubbed their head and feet when they got wet; and
they were sure to saturate the hair with ardent spirits of
some sort, when there was any hair-cutting. And upon
each and every occasion when they rubbed a little on, they
poured a little in. In short, never was there a little baby
born in those days that ever grew fat or ceased to squall
without the aid of brandy, which was consumed, in eating
and drinking, from the cradle to the grave. And when we
use this latter doleful expression, we do not mean to say

that the baby never grew up to manhood's estate, nor became old enough to be the reader's grandfather. By no means. For they were a ruddy and a hardy race, and we are told that there were fewer downright drunkards, and fewer cases of "*delirium tremens*," in those days—in the olden time—than now. The reason to be assigned for this is, that their "liquors were a pure article," which *can not be obtained now*, and were unadulterated by noxious and most deadly drugs, which themselves intoxicate, and produce death in so many different ways.

While we have been indulging in these reflections, so natural to the occasion, and while the numerous guests of Colonel Shelton are taking their brandy or their wine at the sideboard which stands in the hall, and then quietly falling back and betaking themselves to their ablutions, so necessary after a day's hunt, the Colonel himself is engaged in earnest conversation with a handsome young man, who has arrived from Charleston as a special envoy from the President of the bank then most prominent in that ancient and honorable city.

Let us enter the library also with the Colonel, and conceal ourselves behind the drapery of a large window, that we may understand the nature of the visit which has brought this confidential agent of the bank so unexpectedly to the peaceful home of Colonel Shelton.

As we said before, he was a handsome young man; and, judging from the lines of thought written upon his brow, you might suppose him to be twenty-seven or eight, or even thirty. But he was much younger—not more than twenty-three or four—but possessing such decided abilities that the bank regarded him as one of its ablest officers. He was reclining upon a sofa when Colonel Shelton entered the chamber, and seemed to be very much fatigued by the severe horseback journey which he had performed in haste over a rough road; but he immediately arose, and, with a pleasant smile of recognition, extended his hand to grasp

the Colonel's with a warm and fervid pressure. Nor did he
release his hold until he had said, "I bring you sad news,
Colonel!" and the smile vanished as his lip quivered, and
his voice trembled with emotion.

"I have received a hint from my wife," replied the Colonel,
with perfect composure, "that my friend Johnson has failed,
and as I am his indorser to a large amount, I presume you
have come to apprise me of the fact. Is it not so, Mr. Herbert?"

"Alas!" replied the young man, in a tone of the profoundest melancholy. "You must be prepared for the worst,
my dear Colonel Shelton. Not only has Mr. Johnson failed,
but Mr. Rivers also; and upon both their paper your name
stands indorsed for large amounts, sufficient, perhaps, to
sweep away your entire property, unless counter-arrange-
ments can be effected."

The old Colonel's eyes did not fill with tears, nor did the
muscles of his face quiver or twitch convulsively now. His
nerves were braced up for the issue, and his heart beat
steadier, as the danger of bankruptcy began to stare him
in the face. Just as in the time of battle, when the whistle
of the rifle-ball and the music of the cannon's roar began to
be heard loudest, and the conflict grew hottest, he used to
straighten himself up in his stirrups, and then settle himself slowly in the saddle again, ready and in waiting for the
coming time when individual action and personal prowess
should be necessary; or as the sailor, who sees the storm-
clouds swooping down upon him, makes ready for the gale
by stripping each mast and every spar of its canvas, while
the helmsman lashes himself firmly to the helm; so, too,
Colonel Shelton was already looking the storm-wind of adversity in the face, and making preparation in his mind to
meet the calamitous events which had burst with the suddenness of a thunder-storm upon him.

His composure astonished Mr. Herbert, who looked upon
him now with the same admiration as he would upon a hero;

but more especially when he heard the Colonel coolly remark, "I thank God it is no worse! and I only hope that
my property will sell for enough to meet the demand against
me. Sit down, Mr. Herbert, and help me to make a few
calculations; they can all be made in a few moments. Have
you an accurate memorandum with you of all the bills likely
to be protested, or which have already fallen due?"

"I have them all here," was the reply of young Herbert,
who drew forth a large leathern pocket-book, from which
he abstracted Colonel Shelton's account current and a memorandum of his liabilities to the bank.

"The president, with the kindest considerations for your
welfare, and the sincerest sympathy in your distresses, delegated me not only to condole with you, but to offer you a
reasonable extension."

"I am sincerely obliged to the president for his kindness,
Mr. Herbert," replied the old Colonel, with a slight quivering of his voice, "but it is useless—I might say, madness—for the mariner to keep his sails spread when his bow
is turned toward the rocky shore, and his keel already begins to scrape against the strand. No, sir; it is too late to
''bout ship' now; and to put on more canvas would only
drive the poor hull harder against the lee-shore, and splin-
ter it into a thousand pieces, and, perhaps, bring desolation
and death upon others. No, sir; if I must sink, let me
sink alone. If I must break to pieces, let me not be the
means of breaking others also."

"I honor your sentiments, Colonel Shelton! Indeed,
yours is the very reply that the president was apprehensive
you would make. But consider, my dear sir, a moment!
Could you not work out the debt in the course of time?"

"Nay, nay! my dear, young friend! I am too old now
to begin life anew! I would only involve myself deeper and
deeper in difficulties from which my children could never
extricate themselves. I feel unwilling to involve them in
my troubles. Far better that they should start the world

poor, and without any show of wealth, than to begin life
under such heavy embarrassments as would be entailed upon
them as my only legacy. I shall sell my property to the best
advantage, and if there shall be anything left, why, then it
will be mine and theirs. And if everything shall be swept
away, I can then feel the same consolation which Henri
Quatre felt when, driven a wanderer from his throne, he
exclaimed, ' *We have lost all but our honor !* ' "

Herbert clasped the old man's hand in his, and bowing
his head low over it to hide his emotion, dropped a warm,
fresh tea" upon the Colonel's hand. It was the irrepressible
feeling of a generous and a manly soul; the warm gushing
from his heart's deep fountain of affection for the man whose
daughter he loved with the idolatrous love of idol-wor-
ship.

"Come, Herbert!" said the old Colonel, almost gayly,
"let us to business. This is my field-book, and on the first
pages are recorded all the names of my slaves, old and
young; and here are plats and grants which will tell to an
acre how much land I possess."

He drew from his mahogany secretary a large field-book,
in which he kept a diary of all his farming transactions,
meteorological, and other observations, anything and everything worthy of comment or notice. It was a book from
which the scientific man would have gathered much valuable information, and which would have been prized, perhaps,
even at the Washington or Greenwich Observatory. Upon
the first dozen or more pages had been recorded, in a plain
and legible hand, the names and ages of all his slaves upon
his several plantations. These, upon being counted up carefully upon each page, made a sum total of about five hundred
souls; which, valued at four hundred dollars *per capita*, would
make the sum of two hundred thousand dollars only. But the
land and bank stock owned by Colonel Shelton would make the
sum amount to about five hundred thousand dollars. This
was a very large estate in those days, and but few individuals

could lay claim to so much landed and negro property. But as large as it was, it would not cover all of Colonel Shelton's present indebtedness. By an accurate calculation, there would be an apparent deficiency of fifty-six thousand dollars! This seemed to worry the good Colonel more than the actual loss, at one fell swoop, of more than a half million of dollars. But he was relieved from his embarrassment by young Herbert, who saw his distress, although he had said nothing.

"The bank has received from Mr. Johnson sixty thousand dollars, as the proceeds of your crop this year. This has been placed to your credit, so that it will leave you a balance of four thousand dollars, should you determine, at all hazards, to sell immediately."

Joy now lighted up Colonel Shelton's eye. He seemed to have forgotten that he had ever sent any crop to market; or that he had any other resource whatever than his land and negroes.

"Then," said Colonel Shelton, exultingly, "it is all right. I trust that my dear wife and children will help me to bear the loss, since, with these few thousands, we can retain Old Toney and his family. Indeed, my dear Herbert, it was not so much the loss of property which moved me so when I first received the intelligence of poor Johnson's failure, as the heart-breaking scenes through which I must pass in tearing myself away from my servants, who love me more as a father than as a master, and for whom I entertain now, at this dreadful moment, a feeling more akin to that which binds me to my children than the selfish feelings of the master to his slave. But I thank God that I am so circumstanced that I can provide for them all good and pleasant homes, and kind masters, who, perhaps, will treat them even better than I, as hard as I have striven to do. Ah! sir, once before I had to pass through an ordeal something like this. It was when I left the army, and laid down the sword, which had been drawn only in my country's defense. My

2 *

brave soldiers—those veteran warriors who had fought by
my side in many a bloody contest, and whose blood had
been so often commingled with mine that we grew at last
to be like kindred—were all drawn up in line, ready to
receive their discharge, and to hear my farewell adieus.   I
attempted to speak to them, but I could not. My heart
was too full, and my tongue could not utter a single word.
I could only weep and sob like a child, as I leaned upon
my blood-crusted sword; and was forced at last to wave
with my hand the farewell which my lips could not utter.
Then was seen such a sight as was, perhaps, never witnessed
before.   The gray-headed old warrior was forced to sit down
upon the grass, for his emotions so overcame him that he
had no power to stand up in the ranks; while even the
younger and more vigorous spirits were bent as bulrushes
before the storm of grief, which oppressed them so that they
were compelled to bear heavily upon their muskets for support.   There was not a dry eye either among the officers or
the men in my regiment, and we separated as brothers in
arms, who should meet no more in this world.   Such, sir,
was the sad ordeal through which I was destined to pass at
the end of the war; and sad must it be again at the close
of my pilgrimage on earth."

Herbert could offer no word of sympathy to that benevolent and wounded heart; for he was a Southern man, born
and raised among slaves, and hence he could appreciate the
feelings and understand the endearing ties which bind together the master and his slave.   He well knew that there
was no other feeling which could outrival this, save the love
of the husband and the wife, the parent and the child.   He
knew that the loving, faithful negro would lay down his life
for his master as readily as the brave soldier who bares his
broad chest to the saber thrust which is aimed at his general; and that, on the other hand, the kind and affectionate
master would not only defend the life of his slave at all
hazards, but sacrifice great things for his comfort and hap-

piness. Herbert, we say, knew all this, and more, which the purest philanthropist of England or the North could never know, unless he had been " to the manor born." He held his peace, therefore; for he had no sympathy to give, no word of comfort or counsel to offer. He preserved the same kind of mournful silence which men maintain when standing, and with heads uncovered and arms folded upon their breast, they render silent honors to the dead heroes and statesmen who are lifeless in the grave.

But the silence of several moments was interrupted at length by Colonel Shelton himself, who asked, in a mournful tone :

" But tell me, Herbert, about my poor friend Johnson. Poor fellow! The blow must come with the crushing, desolating force of an avalanche upon him; for, unlike me, his nerves have not been hardened by the exercises of the camp, and blunted by the rigors and sterner duties of the soldier. His poor and helpless wife, also. She has not been, like mine, accustomed to witness suffering and distress at the bedside of the dying, and in the lowly cabin of the poor, or the home of the negro. Accustomed to the fashionable life of a city, and reared from the very cradle in all the affluence and splendor of an aristocratic home; vain and proud; must she not sink beneath the sudden weight of her misfortunes? From the bottom of my soul I pity her, and lament that I have not the means left to prevent her from feeling too keenly the sharp, keen pangs of poverty."

Colonel Shelton groaned audibly at the picture of distress which his own imagination had painted and held up in bold relief to his mind, of the future woes and sorrows of another. But the generous, whole-souled man never once thought of the probability, that the picture he had drawn for another might, by reversing the easel, prove a likeness of himself, or an overshadowing of the woes in reserve for the cherished idols of his heart.

"But I have not asked you, Herbert, how it came about? How have poor Johnson & Rivers managed to fail? For I confess that I had indorsed for them so often, in return for similar favors—had felt so certain that they were as impregnable as the rock of Gibraltar—that I must confess to a little curiosity concerning the manner in which their ruin has been effected. Of one thing, however, I feel certain, that their *honor* will be untouched, and that the foulest tongue could not impeach their integrity, or malign the rectitude of their intentions."

"You but do them both simple justice, my dear sir. The merchants of Charleston will mourn their heavy losses, and weep over the mercantile ruin of men who have stood so long among us as beacon-lights of wisdom and sterling integrity, but whose lights have been toppled down from their perch by the fierce gales of this financial year. Thus far, sir, it has never been the case, and God forbid that it should ever be so, that the finger of scorn has been pointed at one of Charleston's noble merchants; nor can the tongue of the foul-mouthed calumniator say, 'He has failed full-handed, and at the expense of his creditors.' No, sir; we have earned the envious title of hard-working, honest men, and we hope ever to maintain it."

Colonel Shelton smiled joyously at the enthusiasm of the young man, but he did not interrupt his remarks by any ill-timed phrase or exclamation; and Herbert apologized for not having answered more satisfactorily the question which had been asked him in regard to the failure of Mr. Johnson, in whose fate Colonel Shelton seemed most deeply interested.

"Excuse me, Colonel," said the young man, "for not replying to your inquiry sooner. But we Charlestonians are all so deeply interested in the welfare of each other, that the success of one is as much the cause of general gratification, as the ruin of another never fails to fling a gloom and heartfelt sorrow over the entire community. We are rivals in the career of wealth and mercantile glory; but so far from attempting to push each other down in the race, we are more apt to help each other on, once we have fairly got ahead, and see that the goal is won for ourselves."

"That is right and proper, my young friend. I admire the spirit of the Charlestonians. I regard them as the noblest race of merchants on earth. Even their *Jews* seem to deal fairly, and to lose their peculiar characteristic in the mercantile atmosphere of Charleston. But, in my estimation, Johnson stood noblest among the noble. And Rivers, too, was ever ready to lend a helping hand to the young man of energy and promise."

"Yes, sir; what you say of the one is equally true of the other. They were both honest, honorable men; and when they failed, they lost all but their honor. But the causes of their failure have been the result of a train of unforeseen circumstances and casualties. In the first place, the severe storms which have prevailed this year, and which will make the year 1824 ever memorable, not only on account of the great destruction of the cotton crop, but because numerous vessels and valuable lives have been lost upon our coast. These storms, I say, have been the means of breaking into pieces many a noble house in Charleston, Savannah, New Orleans, New York, and Liverpool. Whole fleets of vessels, laden with cotton for Northern and European ports, which had been sent out by Mr. Johnson, and Mr. Rivers also, were broken into a thousand fragments; some upon the Florida reefs, some upon the coast off Cape Hatteras, while others were dashed to pieces upon the banks of the Bahamas. These heavy shipwrecks ruined, of course, many of our staunchest insurance companies, and their failure to refund has fallen back upon the buyers. Mr. Johnson and Mr. Rivers had both been filling immense orders for Northern and European factories; and some of these factories failed for large amounts before the cotton consigned to them could possibly have reached the European markets. But, perhaps, as grand a cause of the commercial disasters which have only begun to be felt, and which must, in the end, scatter ruin and havoc broadcast over the commercial world, is due to the heartless policy of the Rothschilds, who are responsible, to a vast degree, for the woes and lamentations which will be soon heard rising from all parts of our land. They, sir, while seated in their easy arm-chair, have set in motion the ball which is destined to roll on and on with increasing velocity, gathering in its weight, and increasing to immense proportions, until, like a mighty avalanche, it shall sweep over the precipice, and level to the ground many a fair fabric which has hitherto stood upon a firm basis, and withstood the shock of many a desolating crisis. Yes, sir, I repeat it : the Rothschilds are responsible for the ruin which begins to stare our merchants in the face, who, as yet, have seen but half way to the end. This is, in my conception, but the beginning; the fearful end is yet to come."

"You surprise me, my dear Herbert," exclaimed the Colonel, who had been listening with great interest to the narrative, and to the eloquent tones of his young friend, whom he foresaw would occupy a prominent position before the world one day, if no unforeseen misfortune befell him to cast a cloud over his prospects. "How has all this happened? and in what way are the Rothschilds so deeply responsible for the woe and distress which your imagination has so fearfully depictured?"

"Why, sir, this may be explained to your satisfaction in a few words. Know, then, that the Rothschilds had agreed to lend to the Czar of Russia from three to five millions of money; whether dollars or pounds sterling I am not prepared to say. England had been using this sum, but had determined to pay it back as soon as the payment became due, without asking for any further extension of time or use of the funds. Indeed, I am told, that on account of a rupture of the friendly relations which had previously existed between the Rothschilds and the English minister, on account of England's jealousy toward Russia, and the consent of those Jewish arbiters of European destiny to lend Russia money without obtaining first the consent of England to the transaction, the wrath of the British Lion had become so aroused, that they forced back the money upon the Rothschilds much against their will, although they begged and entreated that it should be retained only three months longer. 'Not another hour!' exclaimed the minister, who coolly handed them a check upon the Bank of England for the whole amount, to be paid in gold or silver, as they might desire; 'not another hour! England is poor, very poor! and the Czar is rich. I understand that contrary to the *known*, if not *expressed*, wishes of England, you have agreed to furnish the Emperor of all the Russias this very sum, the loan to take place within three months. Send it to him at once. England needs it no longer!' In vain did the Rothschild beg, and entreat, and whine. In vain did he wring his hands and say he had no use for the money, which would lie idle upon his hands, and remain dead capital for three whole months. This would be ruinous! It would be positively a waste of the precious metal, which would become so rusted from want of use that it might stick forever to their fingers. His entreaties were all in vain. England refused positively to retain the money any longer, and Russia did not want it until at the expiration of three months. In this dilemma, the great money-king conceived an idea of sending a half score or more of agents over to America, whose instructions were to buy up every bale of cotton they could find, and hold them all long enough to induce the belief that the raw material was not only in great demand in Europe, but that the late storms had cut short the cotton crop to a much greater extent than was at first supposed. These agents stationed themselves *incog.* at New Orleans, Mobile, Charleston, Savannah, etc., and in a little while had all the cotton which had been brought to market under lock and key in warehouses rented for the purpose, and which seemed to be waiting there for orders for shipment to European ports. Not the slightest suspicion was entertained of any unfairness or immoral proceedings, and men knew not that they were sleeping over a volcano which would soon burst with the suddenness of a bombshell in their midst! The result was, that when legitimate orders came for supplies of cotton, scarcely a bale could be found; and the article which seemed to be so scarce, ran up from fourteen to thirty cents. I am told, sir, that all of your first and best cottons were sold, at the opening of the season, at from thirteen to fourteen cents per pound; while a few bales of your "store cotton," which was filled with dirt and trash, actually was disposed of to a Northern manufacturer at the enormous sum of eighteen to twenty cents. But look, sir, at the infamy of these wretches, who, because they possessed the power, determined to wield it secretly to the utter ruin of thousands of honest men who had hitherto prospered among us. No sooner had they established those fictitious prices, and created this false demand, than, little by little, they let out their hidden merchandise; and as soon as they had sold their last bale, and had sucked, as vampires, the last life-drop from our most honored merchants, they immediately set sail for Europe, laughing in their sleeves at the stupidity of the Americans, who could be so easily cheated upon their own ground, and pocketing with glee their ill-gotten gains. It was the most monstrous piece of ingenious rascality which has ever been practiced upon the commercial world, and merits the scorn and eternal indignation of generations to come."

"Monstrous!" exclaimed the Colonel, partaking of the indignation which seemed to burn and flash from the eyes of Herbert. "The villains ought to be hung! But come! There is the dinner-bell. My friends are waiting; and you yourself must be hungry as well as fatigued."

Colonel Shelton passed his arm through that of Mr. Herbert and led him from the library to the large hall, or entrance-room, in which the numerous guests were still assembled.

"Gentlemen," said the Colonel, "allow me to introduce to you all my friend, Mr. Edgar Herbert, from Charleston."

The gentlemen all rose from their seats simultaneously, and most of them came forward and cordially grasped his hand; some expressing their regrets that he had not arrived soon enough to participate in the day's sport.

"Come, gentlemen," said the Colonel, after the salutations were over, "come, let us in to dinner, which is full late, for the sun is about setting."

The old Colonel led the way with a smile. But his countenance became suddenly overcast, and a cloud of melancholy, and even positive distress, settled upon his brow as he entered the dining-saloon, and a servant, approaching, said in a low tone:

"Misses beg you fur 'scuse um, sah. She say she can't come to de table, 'cause she got a berry bad headache; and Miss Ella, too, sah. She got headache, too."

"My poor wife and Ella! what will become of them?" said the Colonel to himself in a low voice, which he supposed no other ear could hear; while a groan, but ill-suppressed, escaped from his anguished heart.

But there was one who heard that groan, though he may not have heard all the words which had been employed to express the deep sorrow which was flung like a pall over the heart of the old soldier. But as the pall is removed from the coffin only that the coffin may be placed away in the grave, thus hiding more effectually from the light of the sun the face of a loved one, so, also, the gloom which had begun to overshadow the soul of Colonel Shelton was destined to grow deeper and deeper, so that never a glad smile should rest again upon those finely-formed lips; and the light of his eye should grow dimmer and dimmer, until he should have fought his last battle on earth, and been conquered by the grim warrior, Death!

CHAPTER III.

THE party which surrounded that long table would have been a convivial one had not their spirits been depressed by witnessing the sadness which sat upon the features of their host, who was usually so cheerful that no one could feel otherwise than happy in his presence. But how could they be gay when the genial smile was no longer upon the lips of the man whom they loved so well? They seemed to feel that in his unexplained, and, to them, unknown future, there was a sad, a dreadful mystery, which both shocked and amazed them. They were not the men who could joke or laugh aloud in the presence of dead hopes and blasted prospects. As soon would they think to revel in a charnel-house, or to laugh and to sport in the chamber of death, as to intrude now their witticisms, which they felt would be as ill-timed and out of place as at a funeral. Save the occasional clatter of a knife and fork, and now and then some casual remark addressed to a neighbor in an undertone, there were no other sounds to interrupt the solemn festival, which, so far from being like a carnival of rejoicing, was rather like a feast among the dead. Even the well-trained servants moved noiselessly upon tip-toe, as if afraid to disturb the thoughts of their beloved master, who ate his meal in gloomy abstraction, as if unconscious that he was seated at the head of his own table, and surrounded by numerous guests, all, or nearly all, anxious concerning his welfare.

But when the meal was ended, and the cloth removed from the table, the Colonel seemed to recover from his abstraction almost in a moment; and, leaning over the table, he addressed a gentleman, who, judging from the formation and expression of his features, would be readily taken to be a near relative.

"Tom," said the Colonel—but checking himself immediately, and turning his eyes upon the entire company as if about to address each individual separately, he added, "Gentlemen, I am not ignorant nor unconscious of the fact —at least I flatter myself that you all feel a deep interest in my welfare ; and that a very natural curiosity has been excited in your minds in regard to the sudden arrival of Mr. Herbert, whom I believe some of you know to be the confidential agent of the bank at Charleston. Gentlemen, it is my painful duty to gratify your curiosity now in a few words. By certain heavy failures in Charleston I am nearly, if not completely ruined—hopelessly, irretrievably ruined !"

"Ruined !" cried several, in a breath. "Impossible ! you have overestimated your losses, Colonel."

"No, my dear sirs ; the case is too plain. Mr. Herbert and myself have already carefully made all the calculations, and we have ascertained that it will take all my property to pay off the notes upon which my name has been indorsed, or they must otherwise be protested, and my name become dishonored. This can not, shall not be. For my own honor's sake, and that of my children, I must sell my property immediately, both lands and negroes. And as I desire you all to consider yourselves as in family conclave assembled, I wish, for my own sake, but more especially for the happiness and interest of my poor negroes"——

The Colonel's voice here faltered, and it was some time before he could proceed further; but he recovered his outward composure after a few moments, so that when he resumed his remarks a careless observer, entering the room a second or two afterward, would never have supposed that the stern old soldier had been nearly overcome by his emotions of pity and of love toward those dependent beings whom God and Nature had placed under his care almost from his own and their infancy. None but those who have been placed in similar circumstances can tell how much effort it cost even a veteran soldier to choke back the sobs which well-nigh convulsed his frame.

"But," he added, after a pause of several minutes, uninterrupted by a single sound, "for my servants I feel even more than for myself or family; for we can bear it better. It is true, I know, that my friends at this table are, unitedly, able to buy them all; and that they will thus be provided with good and kind masters, who can afford, perhaps, to treat them even better than I can possibly do. In the hands of either one of my relatives I feel satisfied that their physical wants will be attended to, and they will lack for nothing. My friends, I know that you can furnish my poor slaves with as good homes as the laborers upon English or Northern soil; and it is not from any apprehension of neglect or ill-treatment—for the master's interests, aside from the dictates of humanity, require that he should treat his slaves kindly—but it is because ties of long standing must suddenly be ruptured; and with some of them, I fear, it will be like snapping their very heart-strings asunder. And already I can imagine the scene of woe, and hear the lamentations which will soon fill the air, so that this entire plantation will become a place of mourning, where there was contentment and rejoicing before. God have mercy on me and them, and enable us both to bear the separation."

Colonel Shelton could no longer restrain his feelings; and hiding his face in his hands, he shook as an aspen leaf, and became so convulsed by his great grief, that the table fairly shook beneath the weight of his elbows, which were pressed hard upon it. The fountain of his tears had burst forth; and the strong man of iron nerve and heroic heart was bowed in sorrow, as a bulrush is bent down and pressed hard to the earth by the blast of the tornado.

There were few dry eyes in that company; but one of his friends brushed hastily away his flowing tears, and remarked:

"My dear Colonel, this may be all needless apprehension; and I trust that, after all, you will not be forced to so sad an alternative as the sale of your property. Can not some arrangement be effected, by which you may be enabled, in the course of a few years, to pay off both principal and interest?"

"Alas! no. I am too old now, as I have already replied to Mr. Herbert, who, in the kindness of his heart, made a similar suggestion, which I know his judgment could not approve. No, no, my friends; I am resolved to sell at once. Excuse the weakness, if it be a weakness, which I exhibited just now, and attribute it not to vain regrets. Come, tell me who among you will buy my property at the market value?"

"If you are determined to sell immediately, my dear Colonel, I will buy fifty of the negroes, and land in proportion," said his cousin, Mr. Thomas Shelton.

"And you, Walters, must purchase at least one hundred."

"I have no desire to increase the number of my slaves, Colonel Shelton; but to gratify you I will take them, and do the best I can toward them," was the reply of Mr. Walters.

While these business arrangements are being effected at the Colonel's table, we must call the reader's attention to another scene, which he can not fully comprehend unless he has been an eye-witness to a similar one. The news of Colonel Shelton's embarrassments, and his sudden determination to sell his property, had flown like wild-fire throughout the entire plantation, so that a large crowd of negroes had already collected together under the oak trees in front of the house; while the entire steps and front piazza were filled with anxious servants, who had come in haste from their quarters, eager to know the worst, and to hear the truth from their master's own lips, if it were possible that their "own dear masser could have the heart to sell them to anybody." Old men stood in gloomy silence, with arms folded upon their breasts, like sable princes defeated in battle, and forced reluctantly to submit to their destiny; while old women sat upon the steps, or upon the floor of the piazza, rocking their bodies to and fro, moaning most piteously. It was hard, very hard, for servants such as these to give their kind master up. The younger ones could do so more easily, for with them love had not grown into an eternal habit. Impressions, however strong, could be more easily erased from their elastic minds, and their pliant will could be more easily molded to the pleasure or caprices of another owner. But with the old it was different. Many of them had ceased to labor for Colonel Shelton, and were no more regarded as field hands, subsisting entirely upon his bounty, and humored to the gratification of almost every whim; although, had they lived in a free state, necessity— WANT, *stern*, *unrelenting* want, a harder master than any Southern planter could be—would have stared them in the face, with constant, imperious look, and commanded them, in harsh tones and taunting words, to labor or to die.

"You are not too old to work, old man—old woman. It is a shame that one who can walk as erect as you, who are so little bent with age, should beg for your daily bread. Surely you can do something. Go and work for your living. It is a thousand pities you were not back upon a Southern plantation, or in the heart of Africa. Go. I love to look upon a free man, it is true, but I despise to see a beggar. But above all beggars, I despise to *see a nigger, who was born to work, holding out his hand for alms.* You ought to be ashamed of yourself, and feel willing to die, rather, with your hoe in your hand." Such would have been the conduct of many of the pseudo-philanthropists of the North and England toward these poor old men and women, who said themselves that they were too old to work, and had, of their own accord, laid down the hoe and left the cotton-field several years before. Colonel Shelton had scolded some of them a little, while at others he was compelled to laugh at the persistent obstinacy with which they declared that they could no longer endure the least labor; that they were superannuated; worn out before their time; and fit for nothing more than to sit, with clasped hands, and pray that their "good, blessed masser might live a thousand years."

They were old men, it is true; but few of them were older than Colonel Shelton himself. They had grown up with him from boyhood; had played and wrestled together a thousand times; hunted, fished, ate together, and even had slept side by side. Not from a plate had they shared the same food, but from an earthen vessel, or a common iron pot, in which the food had been prepared. Yes, their hands—the one as black as the ace of spades, the other as white as snow—had met together, and had touched, in brotherhood, in the same dish; while wearied by the fatigues of a coon hunt, they had nodded, when boys, around the camp-fire until their heads had touched—the silky ringlets of the aristocratic son of an aristocratic father had touched the woolly, kinky hair of the African boy.

Does the author exaggerate in the least? Will not many a Southern man confirm the statement that, if they have had no such experiences of their own, they can at least remember these in the juvenile history of some of their old friends and acquaintances? Many can testify that this is no fancy sketch, and that the love which had existed from boyhood between Colonel Shelton and his old negroes is not an isolated or anomalous fact.

But if this is true in a thousand instances, what shall we say of the affection which existed between Colonel Shelton

OLD TONEY AND HIS MASTER ; OR,

and Old Toney. It was like the love of foster-brothers who
had tugged at the same paps, and had drank from infancy
at the same fountain. And was it not a literal fact? Had
not Colonel Shelton nursed from the breast of Toney's black
mother? Had they not gone to sleep in her arms, and been
rocked in the same cradle? How, then, was it possible to
rupture the ties—ties so indissoluble—which existed between
such a master and such a slave? Could all the John Browns
of the universe bribe or force the one to do aught of injury
to the other? Could countless thousands, could the promise
of freedom—not for the narrow space of a lifetime, but a
liberty which should last through eternal ages, seduce Old
Toney's love, or tempt him to commit treason? Let future
facts in Old Toney's history answer the question. And when
Old Toney's life has been studied and his true character
comprehended, let the Northern fanatic understand that his
case is a complete and final rebuke to his fanaticism; that
his voice gathers accumulative strength, and grows louder
and louder, as echoes after echoes roll upward from thousands and myriads of faithful slaves, until the whispering
voice of one man, a slave, has swelled into the awful voice
and stern rebuke of a god.

What! men, like Old Toney take up arms or be bribed
to commit treason against the master whom they love?
Sooner far would they hang to the nearest limb, as high as
Haman, the man who would dare to insult their instincts
with such a proposition! Old Toney had fought by the
side of Colonel Shelton, and had done brave work in more
battles than one. He had been his kind master's body
servant, as well as foster-brother, from boyhood. In Florida, he had scalped many a Seminole, whose scalps he still
retained and exhibited with pride to the "rest of the niggers," as trophies of his individual prowess, and as proofs
that he was not afraid of the red man. At the battle of
New Orleans he had headed a party of blacks, who charged
the British so impetuously, and with such savage shouts as

did the Turcos and Zouaves the Austrians in the late Italian war. General Jackson, with the genius of a Napoleon, knew how to render available every circumstance, and to adopt every means, however *outré*, which presented itself to his hand. His purpose was to conquer the enemy, and it was immaterial to him *how* he succeeded in his designs, whether by the sword and the bayonet, in decency and military order, or pell-mell and "rough and tumble," by cotton-bags, or the "*niggers*" who had *made* the cotton.

But the victory of the eighth of January was not due to the protection afforded by cotton bales, as has been falsely stated by the English historians, and frequently indorsed by American writers themselves. How, we ask, could cotton-bags secure a victory? They might serve as a redoubt, and prove an impregnable wall of defense against the bullets of the foe, but they could never charge upon the enemy and force him to retreat to the water and fly for shelter to his boats. Old Toney could testify, if still living, that he himself "had helped to lick de British;" that when General Jackson placed arms in the hands of the slaves, in the city of New Orleans, he himself had been foremost in the fight, and had driven the British to a hasty and inglorious flight.

It was in that memorable battle, in which Old Toney had borne himself like a sable hero, that the faithful old servant had lost an eye; it was his left eye; but the loss of the one had only seemed to strengthen the vision of the other. It gave to his countenance a peculiar expression; a kind of wide-awake cunning, as if he was always on the *qui vive*. He seemed to say, in plain language : "You see dis eye shut enty. Nebber mind; I can open 'um if I want to; you better look sharp; I no 'sleep. 'Fore you can say Jack Robison, dat same eye will open and scare you wid his look, same as he scare de British when he poke his bayonet into 'um, 'cause I make 'um take to de water same like a mink."

Poor Old Toney! He had been listening at the door of
3

the dining-room to the conversation which passed between
his master and his guests. He had heard Colonel Shelton
say that it would take *all* of his property to pay his security
debts ; but he did not know that there was a mental reserv-
ation of himself and his entire family. Old Toney groaned
in spirit when he heard that single word *all*, which sounded
to his ears more like a funeral bell, which, though struck
with the faintest touch — a whisper — seems to peal loud
enough to be heard by the corpse as it is borne onward to
the grave. Old Toney leaned heavily against the door-sill,
and pressed his hand hard upon his throbbing, aching heart.
He turned away mournfully and went into the piazza, where
numerous other servants were assembled, and stood still for
a few moments among them, overcome by his own and his
fellow-servants' great and overwhelming sorrows. Their
mournings sounded like the requiem which the dying Indian chief sings for himself, as he lies down to die alone in
the forest, and gathers the dry leaves which lie scattered in
profusion around him to cover up his war-scarred body from
the curious eyes of men.

But Old Toney felt it to be his duty to speak to his
brethren "a word of comfort" and consolation in his way.
He was no preacher, but he had often exhorted them, at
their religious meetings, to do their duty as faithful servants to God and their master. But now he moved among
them as a priest, scattering incense upon the right hand and
on the left ; heaving aloft his smoking chalice, not in hope,
but in despair ; not as if invoking the blessings of Heaven
upon his people, but imprecating the wrath of an offended
Deity.

"Weep on, my breddren !" said the old man ; " yes, weep,
till your tears be dry ! Weep, till your heart break and
bust open ! for you got no masser now ! Your Masser Shelton loss to you now, and you may hang all your harps on de
willow, same like de Philistines hang dere's at the Walley ob
Baca ! Weep on, weep on, my childrens ! 'Let your woice

be heard to earth's remotest bounds!' as de preacher say.
Cry loud and long, and let no man spare himself! Fly to de
mountains and let de rocks fall upon you to hide you from
dat great and dreadful day when de Son ob man cometh!"
By this time, Old Toney had worked himself and his entire
audience into a sort of phrensy, half natural, half religious.
The noise had become so loud as to disturb the gentlemen
in the house, and it was at this time that Colonel Shelton
had sent for Old Toney, in order to request him to preserve
order in the piazza. Old Toney had approached his master
from behind just at the time when he said:

"It will take all of my property, except Toney and his wife,
Old Rinah and their children, to pay the demands which will
soon be due. I can retire to a small farm, which I think I
can buy for three thousand dollars, which lies not far from
here. By the by, Langdon, you must start early in the morning for Georgia, and take Old Toney with you, in order to
receive just that amount—three thousand dollars—which
Mr. McPherson wrote me, some time since, was ready for me.
With this amount to pay down for a farm, by industry and
economy, Old Toney and myself can manage to support the
family in a plain way, I hope. I am not ashamed, gentlemen, to work; and, old as I am, I feel not only able but willing to encounter the rigors of *honest poverty.* Labor, so far
from being a curse, in my estimation, was the grandest
blessing conferred upon man. 'To earn your bread by the
sweat of your brow,' instead of driving men to despair,
should buoy up their spirits with hope, and fill their minds
with victorious energy. Hard work brings the sweetest
sleep; a sleep sweeter than all the anodynes of earth can
give. Labor! I can assure you that, so far from despising,
I love it. It dignifies a man in proportion as idleness sinks
him into degradation and contempt. I have ever loved and
respected the honest, hard-working man. Indeed, I have
labored in some way all my life; I have worked with both
brain and sinew. But I can assure you that, while the brain

may discover treasures and rear edifices for the good of
others, its weariness brings no sleep, but rather wakefulness
and injury to health and happiness. O! give me the sleep of
the hard-working, conscience-free, independent laborer, who
depends on God alone for his daily bread, and feels and
believes in his soul that 'the Lord is his shepherd, he shall
not want.'"

Old Toney had not remained long enough to hear all
the remarks of Colonel Shelton upon the dignity of man-
ual or bodily labor. He had heard them expressed often
before, in even warmer and more eloquent terms. They
were his own sentiments; for, above all things, he despised "a lazy nigger;" and so necessary was active, vigorous action to his very existence, that he would have died
from dropsy if he had folded his arms as the sluggard, and
refused to labor any longer because he was getting old. He
must be doing something. Untold, and without an order, he
saw not only to the horses, in his capacity of chief ostler,
but flogged the boys, by way of exercise, if they neglected
their duties; especially if the Colonel's saddle-horse was
not curried as clean as a penny and rubbed as bright as "a
spang new silber dollar."

If his mistress wanted a tree or a shrub set out, or removed from one place to another, Old Toney felt that no
one could perform that office so well as he; for if "a common nigger" did it, the tree was sure to die or grow crooked.
He felt, therefore—had always felt and said it, but now
he was assured—that he, and he alone of all the host, with
his entire family, would still be retained as the servants of
Colonel Shelton; and that, with Old Rinah and all her children, they would constitute a small but happy household in
some quiet nook. Why, then, Old Toney's joy knew no
bounds; and *then,* at that particular moment, he felt that
Colonel Shelton could no more do without *him* than he
could do without his brave old master. His heart beat
stronger than it had done a few moments before. His eye,

that single eye, like a lone star set in the blackest azure,
twinkled with brightest luster.   His step grew more elastic,
and he felt some of his old Samson strength—the strength
of his young manhood returning, with a tingling sensation to
his muscles, and bracing up his old bones, which seemed, just
before, ready to crumble into decay—he stepped forth into
the piazza, and trod upon its planks no more like a solemn
priest, but like an emperor whose autocrat could impose
silence upon the universe.

"Hush up your cryin', you foolish niggers! What you all
cryin' for? I tell you all, you is only worryin' masser, and
doin' yourself no good! Hush up dat racket, I tell you,
or I'll see if I can't mek you cry for someting on turrer
side ob your face!"

But just then Old Toney seemed to remember that he had
not only encouraged, but ordered them to weep and to howl
until their lamentations should be heard to earth's remotest
bounds.   It was with a show of leniency, therefore, that he
added, in condoling tones:

"I is berry sorry to part wid you, my breddren and
friends—berry sorry, indeed.   But circumstance to cases,
observation to consequence.   Weep not, my breddren; weep
not as dose who hab no hope.   You will see your ole masser
and missis berry often.   I don't tink ary one ob you will
be more nor ten mile, or mebbe fifteen mile, from my house.
You can come to see me whenebber you wants to; always
berry glad to see my old fellow-serbants; and I berry sure
my ole masser will nebber dribe you from his door, and say,
'Go 'long, you good for nuttin' ting! you black nigger! you
only come fur tief!'   No, no.   My masser and me is all both
above dat.   Den hush up, my friends, and dry your eyes,
and let us all sing dat good ole hymn so suitable fur dis
weepin' and wailin' occasion:

> "'When I can read my title clear,
> To mansions in de skies,
> I'll bid farewell to ebbry fear,
> And wipe my weepin' eyes.'"

Then was heard music which few in this world have been privileged to hear. We have heard your grand concerts at the North, and some of the greatest musicians which Europe has sent to our shores, but the music of more than a hundred voices, in perfect unison, of those dark sons and daughters of Africa, as it rose upon the stillness of the night air, while it was louder than the tallest, grandest organ, was sweeter than the sweetest-toned harp ever touched by the hand of the most skillful master. O! that was music worth a pilgrimage to hear! It was the voice of nature blended with the most cultivated, sweetest tones of art; untaught by any master musician, they were, nevertheless, a well-trained band. With no gamut or music-scale learned by rote and squalled aloud with the jarring discord of cracked reeds, these poor, grief-smitten, music-loving people, in their simple melodies, their plaintive airs, their wailing requiems, stand unrivaled by any other people on earth. The music of the Indian is monotonous—the song of the African is the song of poetry and pathos. Very many of them are improvisators, and express impromptu, by sweet sounds, the feelings and varying emotions of their souls. And now, upon this particular occasion, the deep bass tones, like the swell of the organ, in perfect unison with the flute-like notes of the women— the tenor, the alto, the treble, and the bass often heard upon different octaves, but all in perfect accord; causing one to compare it in his imagination to the song which rolls up unceasingly from the angelic choir. Who, we ask, could refuse to listen? Who would stop his ears? Who could fail to be enraptured at such melody as this?

Herbert could not resist its influence. Although accustomed to the boasted musical soirées of Charleston; although he had heard the finest soprano and contralto voices which had ever floated upon the air of his native city, he thought within himself that he had never in his life heard music before. He rose from the table, and passing through the parlor beyond the hall, stepped out into a small veranda which looked out upon the scene. He stood with arms folded upon his chest and listened with rapt attention until the music ceased. Then he could not resist the impulse to exclaim with enthusiasm, "Grand! glorious!" He heard a half-suppressed sigh at his side. He started and turned his head in the direction of the sound, and saw Ella Shelton standing by a column alone in the moonlight. She had been weeping, and a stray moonbeam which glanced through the foliage of a large old oak-tree reflected upon her pale cheek, and caused the tears, as they flowed from her eyes, to glisten and glitter like so many rolling, liquid diamonds.

"Pardon my intrusion, my dear Miss Shelton!" exclaimed the young man, as he extended his hand cordially to the beautiful girl, whom he had seen for the first time since his coming, although they had often met before, and known each other even from infancy. Herbert had loved and worshiped her from a boy with the idolatry of the man who worships the woman he loves, and falls down in adoration at her feet as before a divinity. He had never told his love, because it was too big for utterance, nor had ever an occasion offered so fitting as the present. He did not release her hand, but held it pressed in his nervous grasp. His pressure, though strong and manlike, was not painful to the delicate, fairy little hand of Ella Shelton. Its warmth was even pleasant and genial, and seemed to dissipate the coldness of her fingers, which had become chilled by the painful anxiety which had weighed like a chilling iceberg upon her heart ever since she had heard the sad news which Herbert had brought from the city, and her father's determination to meet his security debts by an immediate sale of his property. She was not a coy nor a prudish maiden, who shrinks from the touch, or fears to feel the warm and manly grasp of a noble heart. Her tiny white hand, therefore, soft as velvet, and white as the snow-flake, lay in his as a wounded bird taking shelter in the stranger's nest. And when Herbert again

spoke, almost in a whisper, "Forgive me, my dear Miss
Shelton, if I have thoughtlessly intruded upon you at an
unpropitious hour,"—she replied, in a sweet voice:

"My father's friends are always welcome to me, Mr.
Herbert. You are guilty of no intrusion. Your presence
is most welcome."

"I thank you kindly for those words. Would that my
presence were so welcome that my image could never be
effaced from your heart. Ella! dearest Ella!" exclaimed
Herbert, in the low, deep, but distinct tones of earnest,
manlike devotion, "we have known each other from childhood, and my love for you has grown with my growth and
strengthened with my strength. The love of the boy, which
some may have regarded only as one of the vagaries of childhood, has attained to the Herculean proportions of something mightier than the love of ordinary manlike affection.
Ella, dearest Ella!" and Herbert's voice trembled from the
intensity of his passion, so long suppressed, but which had
burst forth for the first time in words, "I love you with
all the ardor of which a strong nature is capable. Can
you love me in return? Do not say 'nay;' do not utter
a word of denial; for, O, it would crush out my young life,
and wither, as the breath of a sirocco, all my budding hopes.
Only say that thou wilt be mine."

There was no answer to this passionate appeal of the
lover, but a single pressure, slight, but irresistible, and most
expressive, which, in the life of young and ardent lovers,
like the signs and the grips employed in Freemasonry or
Odd Fellowship, is felt only by him who understands the
sign, and has received the true password. That touch, slight
and tremulous as it was, sent a thrill throughout his entire
frame, and, in a moment, the beautiful girl was clasped with
a passionate, almost phrensied love to his breast.

"Say, Ella!" exclaimed Herbert, with a wild energy,
which was the result of excessive joy, "say that you love
me! Let me hear your voice! Speak but a single word!

Whisper it in my ear, though it be but as the faintest echo of the öolian harp, and I will bless you with a heart's best, greatest love, which has been treasured up for you alone from my earliest recollection!"

Ella answered the eloquent appeal of her lover in low tones; but the murmur of her words, as they escaped her coral lips, like the murmur of the purling brook over the pebbly strand, though low and soft, was distinct enough for his attentive ear.

"I love you, Herbert!" she whispered. "You, and you alone, could be worthy of all the love of my virgin heart."

"God bless you for that saying, Ella, and may Heaven bless our future with happiness and peace."

"Amen!" said a voice behind; and they started abashed at the sound, but recovered from their confusion in a moment, as they recognized Old Toney, who had been standing for some seconds just behind them, indulging that irresistible curiosity of the negro, which, while contemptible in a white man, and in him is looked upon with abhorrence, as indicative of a mean and groveling spirit, in the slave is not regarded as eavesdropping; for the eavesdropper conceals himself, and slinks with shame from discovery, thus confessing to himself his own heart's treachery and meanness.

Old Toney had not come to listen to the conversation of the lovers, or to pry into their secrets. But when he found himself in their presence, and beheld their attitude, he felt interested—deeply interested in the answer which his young mistress would make to the earnest appeal of her devoted lover. He felt so sure of her virtuous instincts, that he was certain that the man whose love she would accept must be worthy of her choice. The man who could be worthy of his young mistress, in the estimation of Old Toney, must be equal to a prince himself, or even to a divinity.

Hence he not only felt satisfied, but rejoiced in his soul at the successful issue of Herbert's wooing; and he felt

3*

toward the young man a degree of pride and admiration, as he looked .upon his broad chest, still heaving from the effects of his powerful and overmastering emotion, putting him in mind of his old master's when he used to snuff the smell of battle. Old Toney felt toward young Herbert even more than pride and admiration; for already his heart began to warm with love toward the object of his mistress's love, and to feel a sort of kinship—a sort of fatherly feeling. If young Herbert had courted his own daughter, and was destined to become his son-in-law, he could not have had half the love which he already began to feel toward the young man who would, perhaps, one day be his master, and take the place of Colonel Shelton, when the old soldier should be called to give up his life on earth and take his seat in heaven. His son-in-law! Bah! Old Toney would have spurned the amalgamationist from his presence with loathing and abhorrence, who was base-born enough to make such a proposition. Old Toney was a very aristocratic old negro, and thought a great deal of himself. He belonged to an aristocratic gentleman, and he was, by consequence, a member of the same school. Old Toney would have thought his aristocratic blood eternally disgraced, if his daughter should so far forget her dignity and stoop so low as to marry any white man, even though he might be a member of Congress. For a gentleman, he knew, come he from where he may, could not so far forget his dignity as to taint his blood by mingling it with that of the negro or any other race; while his own daughter, he hoped, was too proud to marry a low white man.

But these were not Old Toney's thoughts at the time; they are only the reflections of the author—reflections derived from a positive knowledge of the negro character, and an intimate acquaintance with Old Toney himself; for the old man had made just such observations before, with a flashing eye and a lip curling with contempt.

"Mass' Herbert must 'xcuse me for disturbing his happiness at dis time," said the old man, with a bow and a scrape of the foot. "I said 'amen,' 'cause I could n't help it. I berry glad, masser, to know dat you and my nyung misses lub one anurrer. You hab my free consent to your matrimony. I gib you leabe, masser, and I gib you joy, too."

"But what is the object of your coming here at this time, old man? for I suppose that it was hardly without design."

"I beg your pardon, Mass' Herbert. My old masser, Colonel Shelton, sen' me here for tell you he want to see you a little while."

Colonel Shelton's object in sending for Mr. Herbert was simply to inform him that all preliminary steps had been taken, and that on the morrow the necessary papers would be arranged, by which he could place in bank the notes of other responsible gentlemen, both as collateral security and as payment or liquidation of his own, when they should have arrived at maturity.

"But come, gentlemen, what say you for bed? for the hour is late, and Langdon must start early in the morning for Georgia; for I shall need all the money I can lay my hands upon which is rightly my own. Langdon, my boy! you had better go to bed at once, so as to make as early a start as possible. Gentlemen all, let's to bed; and may you have refreshing sleep and pleasant dreams. But where is Mr. Stevens?" asked the Colonel, in some surprise.

"Mr. Stevens' gone, sir," answered a negro boy, who was holding a candle in his hand to light a gentleman to his chamber.

"Gone! how long since?"

"About an hour ago, sir," replied the boy.

"And without any formality? Ah! well, it is all right! He would have been welcome to remain all night. But I confess there is something in that young man's countenance which I do not like. He is a bold rider and a good shot, however, and he may, for aught I know to the contrary, be a good friend; but I fear he would make a bad enemy."

CHAPTER IV.

THE next morning Herbert rose at an early hour, and went down to the stables to see how his horse looked after a hard ride on the previous day. He found Colonel Shelton and his son already in the horse-lot.

Langdon was already mounted, and was shaking hands with his father.

"Ah! Mr. Herbert, you are an early riser," said Langdon. "I am glad you are up; for otherwise I should not have had the pleasure of shaking you by the hand once more."

"Which way do you go? Across the Savannah river?"

"No; I understand that it is very bad crossing, even on horseback, and that most, if not all, the flat-boats have been swept away by the freshets, and have not as yet been recovered. The alternative is either to cross the river in a canoe, and foot it all the way down, or ride to the Ohaties, or May river, and get some one of those accommodating sea-island gentlemen to send me around to Savannah in a row-boat."

"And I presume that, as you have no desire to have your feet blistered up by a long walk of sixty or seventy miles, you have concluded to make good the reverse of the old saying—'The longest way round is the shortest way *from* as well as *to* home.'"

"Yes, that is my intention," replied Langdon, with a smile.

"But you will have a very lonesome ride by yourself. Do you go alone?" asked Herbert, with interest.

"No, Old Toney goes with me.   My father seems to forget that I am nearly twenty-one, and that I am old enough
to take care of myself.   Come, old man, bring out your
horse and mount.   It is time we should be moving and on
the road."

Old Toney was · just then leading his horse out of the
stable door, and replied himself to Langdon Shelton's last
remark, by addressing himself to Mr. Herbert.

"No, Mass' Langdon ain't old enough yet to take care ob
himself, widout me.   He is nyung yet, masser, and ain't
sowed all ob his wild oats.   He ain't up to all the ways ob
de world, and do n't know how fur steer a boat, and, derefore, my masser and me concluded dat, on de whole, it would
best for me—Old Toney—to go 'long wid him.   Mass' Langdon know berry well how to guide a hoss, but to steer a boat
am a berry different t'ing."

"Old Toney is right, Langdon," said Herbert, with a
smile.   "The up-countryman is indeed like a fish out of
water when he goes upon the 'salts.'   He is a regular curiosity to a sea-islander, a land-crab, and, in attempting to
manage a helm, would cause the boat hands 'to *catch more
crabs*' with their *oars* than they ever caught, perhaps, with
their *hands!*—even if he had the good luck to escape running aground, or capsizing the boat in rough water."

"Well, well! I suppose you know best. Good-by, old
fellow. Good-by again, father."

"Good-by, Langdon," and "God bless you, my son," were
the only words spoken by Mr. Herbert and Colonel Shelton
to the young man, who passed out of the gate followed by
Old Toney on his coal-black horse; and Colonel Shelton
and the bank officer were left alone in the lot.   It was a
good opportunity to unburden his mind, and, difficult as
was the task, he determined to speak to the Colonel upon
the subject nearest his heart.   But as eloquent as Herbert
could be at other times, he found it difficult—far more difficult to express himself in the simplest terms, than he had

ever found it in all his life before. He could only stammer forth the words, "Colonel Shelton, I love your daughter, and am loved in return. Can you consent to our union?"

"No, no! my dear Herbert! not now, not now!" said the Colonel, with emotion. "I have just lost all my property. Do n't let me lose my daughter so soon. She will be, for some time to come, one of my greatest comforts."

"I did not mean, sir, in asking your consent to our union, to propose marriage at this time. May I hope, however, that at some future period, when you can spare her better than now, I may claim her as my bride?"

"Herbert, my boy," said the old Colonel, with emotion, while the tears trickled down his furrowed and sun-burnt cheeks, "if you will promise me that, Ella shall be yours. God bless you, Herbert. I have loved you from the time you were a boy, and I do not think there is a young man on earth whom I could love more as a son-in-law. You can have Ella, if you promise not to marry her now."

But let us make haste to follow Langdon and Old Toney, before they are out of sight and are too far to be overtaken; for it is our design to take the reader along with them, that he may see and understand something of the characteristics of the salt-water negro, who, like the water-dog, lives in scarcely any other element; for, although amphibious, he seems to prefer the water to the land. You might as well cut off his head at once, as to attempt to move him from the salt water, where he was bred and born. "In de up-country, masser, you can't see nothin' 't all—no water, no fish, no crab, no oshter, not nothin'. Ow! me no want to lib in de up-country."

But if the sea-island negro loves the salt water, he dreads one inhabitant of the rivers and creeks more than anything in nature. It is not the shark, with which he could do battle upon vantage-ground, but the alligator—the terrible alligator. But it is not that he dreads his teeth, sharp and

powerful as they are; nor his mighty tail, which he can
sweep with the force and destruction of a leviathan. It is
with a superstitious awe that he regards the beast, insomuch that he shudders, and shakes his head, and would turn
pale if he could, at the very mention of his name. This is
doubtless a superstition brought from Africa by their fore-
fathers—the Africans—who ingrafted their religious belief,
to a great degree, upon the minds of their children. The
African, as well as the Hindoo, worships the crocodile,
regarding him as a wrathful deity, whose anger must never
be provoked, and always appeased. Hence they fling their
helpless children, and deformed or crippled, into the jaws
of the monster, who devours them before the very eyes of
the devotee, and then goes away satisfied and appeased, as
the poor, ignorant savage vainly imagines.

It was this superstition, so abhorrent to our nature, that
became ingrafted upon the mind of the sea-island negro,
who retained, in a modified degree, the erroneous impression that the alligator was to be reverenced and dreaded as
the harbinger of evil tidings and the forerunner of calamitous events. To see him lying like a log, floating upon the
water, is bad enough, but to speak of him in any way—to
call his name aloud, while in a boat and upon the water,
can not be tolerated; and the luckless wight who should
mention irreverently the name of the foul beast would be
threatened, if not actually put out of the boat upon the
nearest marsh, unless he had a protector strong enough to
defend him. With such a superstitious crew—a half dozen
able-bodied men—did Langdon Shelton and Old Toney take
passage for Savannah from the landing of Mr. Stearly. The
boat was a good one, and swam the water like a duck; but
never did she go so fast as when the oar-hands were singing some lively boat-song. These songs are usually the
impromptu words of a leader, who makes them as he goes.
They seldom or never rhyme, and can not be dignified even
with the title of blank verse. They have but little sense or

meaning in them, but they have a lively, cheering effect, especially when heard at a distance.

But, besides the cheering fact that the flood-tide was itself bearing them rapidly toward the city, they were in a gallant boat, of whose speed they felt as proud as the boy who pats the victorious racer upon his mane. The boat has no mane, it is true, but as they approach nearer and nearer to the city, see how the foreman straightens up, and, rowing with one hand a while, pats the gunwale of the boat, and then, turning round slaps his neighbor's oar with the other hand, exclaiming, "Come brudder, come, come! pass um on, pass um on!"

Now is the time for a song, such a song as will inspire and give new life and power to the muscle which was half weary before. And these are somewhat like the words which the foreman sung, as leader of the sable band. He sung them usually in a low, plaintive tone, and was answered in quite a different style by a cheering chorus of voices, which might have been heard across the waters for many miles:

Foreman.—My masser gone to Boston.
Chorus.—   Yo! he! ho!
Foreman.—My misses gone to Charleston.
Chorus.—   Yo! he! ho!
Foreman.—My masser is a blessed man.
Chorus.—   Yo! he! ho!
Foreman.—My missis is a lubly 'oman.
Chorus.—   Yo! he! ho!
Foreman.—God bless my masser.
Chorus.—   Yo! he! ho!
Foreman.—Mek de vessel sail fast.
Chorus.—   Yo! ho! ho!
Foreman.—Let my masser come home.
Chorus.—   Yo! he! ho!
Foreman.—God bless my masser.
Chorus.—   Yo! ho! ho!
Foreman.—He gib poor nigger belly full.
Chorus.—   Yo! he! ho!
Foreman.—I want to see my misses.
Chorus.—   Yo! he! ho!
Foreman.—My misses she is berry kind.
Chorus.—   Yo! he! ho!
Foreman.—She will bring my Chris'mas.
Chorus.—   Yo! he! ho!

Now, be it borne in mind, gentle reader, that Mr. and Mrs. Stearly were both at home; neither the one at Boston, nor the other in Charleston. It was, therefore, a purely imaginative composition, improvised as do the Italians, and possessing, from the accounts of some travelers, about as much poetry and pathos as many of the impromptu songs of the gondoliers at Venice. All that was said and sung, at least by this sable poet, came from his heart, which was full of joy, because he was not only nearing his journey's end, but was going to town; and what negro's heart does not beat faster as he sees the tall spires of the city which he is approaching? Especially was it the case with these boatmen now. For did they not well know that young Shelton would give them all presents and grog-money? for was it ever known, since the days of Noah, that a young man should go to town in a fast-rowing boat and not treat the boat hands?

But the joy of the boatmen was converted into grief in a moment by an ill-timed exclamation of Langdon Shelton, who cried out, with enthusiasm:

"There swims an alligator! Would that I had my rifle here!"

The song ceased; the strongly-braced muscles of the oars-men relaxed; their sable countenances fell; and their woolly heads drooped upon their breasts. Shelton, ignorant of the superstitions of the salt-water negro, had incautiously, imprudently, mentioned that dread name—the name of the river god, whose wrath would be surely kindled against them.

"Ow! masser! enty you know dat word should n't be talk on de water?"

"What harm is there in speaking of an alligator, I should like to know?" exclaimed Shelton, with surprise.

"Bad luck, masser! berry bad luck! No good can happen to de man dat take his name in vain."

"Foolishness! foolishness!" cried Old Toncy, who was seated on the stern-seat, behind his young master, who

reclined upon the platform, which was covered with two or
three buffalo robes. "Boys! I am older dan you," said the
old man, with fatherly pride and dignity, "and I am, derefore, able to teach you some t'ings dat may do you good.
When I was a nyung man, I used to hab silly notions myself. But I hab seen a great deal in my time, and I 'speck
I know more dan most niggers in de up-country, 'specially
dan salt-water niggers, who am berry ignorant as a general
rule. My old masser, Colonel Shelton, is a berry smart
man—almost as smart as General Jackson, who licked the
British. Dat is to say, he *helped* to lick dem; aldo' he
could n't 'a done it widout me and my masser to help him.
Now, when I was to New Orleans, I see a great many alli-
gators—de biggest kind; one ob them could swallow a Sab-
'nah riber alligator at one swallow! Well, a succumstance
happened to me, when I was out on de Massissip, which
cured me complete ob all my old foolishness 'bout alliga-
tors; and as we got two or tree miles to go yet, I will tell
de story in as few words as possible. Well, you see, it was
just after de great battle of New Orleans, when General
Jackson, and Colonel Shelton, and myself, and de rest ob
us licked de British, for we all helped to lick 'em; and I
reckon we licked 'em till dey stayed licked dat time; for
we licked 'em all clean into de water, and sent 'em back to
dere big gun-boats as fast a passel of otters scared off a
riber bank. It was in dat great battle dat I loss dis lef'
eye; not to say I loss it complete, 'cause I can see out'n
'um if I wants to. But den, you see, it was berry sore for
seb'ral days, and I could n't open de lid, which was all
swell up some like a bee-sting. I was berry tired ob de
camp and de city, and Colonel Shelton gib me leabe to go
and walk in de country, to get de fresh air. So I walked
and I walked, mile arter mile, mile arter mile, forgetful ob
what I was about. But I was wake up sudden like from
my wisions, by a slap on my leg, cowallup. De blow happened to be a light one, or, please God, it would 'a broke my

leg; for de blow was gib by the tail-eend ob a alligator's
tail. You see de way dat happen was dis: de alligator was
lyin' on de lef' side ob de road, and my lef' eye was all
shut up—bung up so dat I could n't see 'um good; and I
t'inks if de t'ing had been de debble, he would 'a know better how to strike; he would n't 'a tried to do a t'ing widout
doin' it right. Don't you tink so, Brudder Cæsar?"

"I dunno, Uncle Toney; mebbe de good Lord unjint ee
tail jis 'bout dat time," said the foreman, shaking his head.
"I dunno, Uncle Toney."

"You shake your head, enty? Berry well. I will prove
de t'ing still plainer to your dull onderstandin'. Well, sir,
when I feel de blow, I gib one spring dat way, and please
God, I jump right where de good Lord would hab it; for if
I had a jump de udder way, I would a jump right into de
alligator's mout'; and den, hoss, dere was some tall runnin',
I can tell you. I do n't mean to say dat I run any more
dan de alligator; for mebbe I would n't 'a run if de alligator
had n't run too. 'T was a reg'lar race, you see, and 't was
'pull Dick, pull debble' who should git to de fence fust. If
I was always a leetle ahead, him bein' right arter me—close
'pon my heels—I had often yerry that if you run crooked,
and run fas', de alligator could n't cotch you. But 'taint no
use. De alligator can run crookeder dan you can—some like
a sarpent. Well, boys, to make my story short, I got at last to
a fence which was close to de water, and I climbed on de rail
like an old coon takin' to a tree. But, please God! Mass'
Langdon, would you beliebe it? dat alligator could climb
as good as a squerrel! I was dat scared dat I could n't
move, nor even jump ober de fence, but sot on de fence like
a coon on a tree, lookin' down on de monster. De alligator
climb up same like a man! He come right at me! He most
eat me up! I fall off de fence wid fear! De alligator crawl
ober and come straight at me! I was den lyin' on de ground,
and I could n't move! His two eyes shine into mine like
two coals ob fire! He opened his big mout', and showed

his two long white rows ob hard ivory! T'inks I to myself
just den, 'If you *will* eat me up, eat my hand fust.' So I
poked my right hand into his mout', and, please God! de
alligator nebber could open his mout' any more!"

"How was that, old man?" asked young Shelton, who
seemed very much interested in Old Toney's narrative.

"Why, you see, Mass' Langdon, de way ob it was dis:
when I fall off de fence, I was holdin' on to the rail—de
top rail; and in my scare, a piece ob de rail, 'bout twelve
or eighteen inch long, broke off in my hand, and I did n't
know it at all. When, derefore, I poke hand in de alligator mout', I did n't know dat I had a fat lightwood splin-
ter, 'bout two inch t'ick and most two feet long, grasped in
my hand. Dat succumstance saved my life. It was de good
Providence ob a mussiful Fa'rer dat persaved my life from
de jaws ob de alligator. Masser, you know de good book
say dat de Lord locked de mout' ob de lions, so dat dey
could n't hu't Daniel, de prophet; and he locked dere
mout's by shuttin' dem *down!* But alligator mout' lock
tudder way; he lock by keepin' um open. Well, de alligator roll and tumble and bellow like a mad bull; but what
could he do? Nothin'. I jist stan' up on my feet and
laugh at 'um till I could n't laugh no longer, and I only quit
'cause de cussed t'ing got so tired dat he could n't roll and
pitch and tumble any more. When dat happen, I goes
right up to 'um, and catch 'um hold by de stick in his mout'.
I pull berry hard and strong, like a man pullin' a jackass
down to de water agin de jackass' consent and free will;
but at last I got 'um to de water and dere I drowned 'um.
Yes, masser, 't is a fac' trut'! I duck 'um wid his mout'
wide open, till I drowned 'um as easy as a puppy. When
I seed *dat*, I loss all my respek for de alligator, and ebber
since I talk 'bout 'um much as I please, in de water or out
ob de water. He is a stinkin' cuss any way."

The last stroke of the oar was given as Old Toney concluded his narrative, which his young master knew to be

true, for Old Toney never willfully exaggerated, for a man may be a good story-teller and yet a man of the strictest veracity. As soon as the boat was made secure to the wharf, Langdon stepped from the boat, followed by the faithful servant, and ascended the steps leading from the water's edge. Crossing over a wide, sandy area, "under the bluff," he ascended step after step of dark-colored stone, until he became weary in the ascent, but at length succeeded in reaching "the Bay,"—a broad, sandy street, with two rows of mammoth trees, called "Pride of India," growing in the center. These trees formed, in those days, a splendid commercial avenue, where the business men of the city walked and talked, and where many a grand scheme had its origin which would make some future merchant prince, or mar the fortune of those who had already obtained that position and power which wealth confers.

Those grand old trees! how beautiful they looked when in spring or summer-time they were dressed in all the glory of their verdant foliage! But they were not in bloom when Langdon Shelton looked upon them as he leaned against the iron railing near the Exchange, to recover his breath from the fatigue of his ascent. Old winter had shorn them of their glory for a brief season only. Who could have foretold that the storm of '56 would lay nearly all of them low, while scarcely a single one would be left standing which was not so scarred, and bruised, and battered by the storm as to render its removal necessary? Those grand old trees! they are passing away, even as the ancient, and honorable, and grand old men of the Revolution; and the times still later, of which we are writing, are passing away and giving place not only to younger men, but to men of other climes. Let them pass away—the trees and men—and let others take their place; but let them not be forgotten. Just here let us shed a tear as tribute to their memory; a tear over the graves and the graveyard of those venerable men whom we knew and loved in our infancy and boyhood. A tear over

the spot where those noble old trees once stood, and beneath
whose cool shade we have played the gambols of the child.
Grand, dear old trees! the spot which knew you once shall
know you no more. Grand, glorious old men! but few
remain to tell how great, and good, and kind, their prede-
cessors to the tomb once were.

As soon as Langdon Shelton had somewhat recovered
from his fatigue he went straight to the counting-room of a
commission merchant on the Bay, whom we shall call Mr.
Hartwell. He was an old acquaintance and friend of
Colonel Shelton; and he could impart to Langdon all
necessary information which he needed for the further
performance of his journey. Mr. Hartwell insisted that
Langdon should take a couple of his own horses instead of
applying at the livery stables, as he had intended doing.
After some persuasion, which amounted finally to a per-
emptory command, the young man consented to the proposal.
Old Bob, who had swept the floor of the counting-house and
had occupied the post of cotton-sampler from time imme-
morial, was called up by Mr. Hartwell, and ordered to take
Old Toney with him and saddle immediately a couple of
horses, for Old Bob was chief ostler as well as cotton-
sampler. A half-hour afterward Langdon and Old Toney
had left the city, and were on the broad highway, or
stage-road, leading to Augusta. Nothing worthy of notice
occurred on the road to Mr. McPherson's, who was the
gentleman to whose house Langdon was going to receive a
sum of money amounting to between two and three thousand dollars.

"I am truly glad you have come;" said the old man, who
was crippled with rheumatism. "I have been wanting to pay
your father a long time; but the old Colonel is so rich—
indeed, never seemed to value money as other men—that I
wonder he has sent you at all."

"Ah! sir!" said Langdon, with a sigh; "my father is
rich no longer. He has been compelled to sell all of his

large property, with the exception of Old Toney and his family, amounting in all to ten negroes, old and young. This number of slaves, and the few thousands you are so kind as to offer to pay him now, constitute all the property of my once so wealthy father. It is the property of a poor man, sir, but, thank God, of an honest one. In the act of selling out so promptly to prevent his notes being protested in bank, he has left his son a richer legacy than could have been procured from all the mines of Peru, or the rubies of Golconda. And God giving me strength, sir, I shall repay him for his noble act. I trust in God that the son may prove worthy of such a sire."

"Spoken like a brave young man," exclaimed old Mr. McPherson. "Your metal has the right sort of ring. I do not doubt, sir, that if you live long enough you will prove not only an honor to your father, but the country."

"God grant it," said young Shelton, solemnly, and in fervent tones.

"Amen! I say," exclaimed Mr. McPherson. "We shall need, by and by, strong men; smart men; inflexible men; men with a head and a heart, too; sons with such sires as yours; men such as I predict you will become one day, with God's blessing upon you. The slavery question is beginning to worry us; but at present only 'paper bullets of the brain' are used as weapons. The day is coming, young man. I am no prophet, nor the son of a prophet, but I can see the handwriting upon the wall, which may be illegible to others—and as Lochiel was warned by the seer, I, also, an old man looking into the grave, warn the generations to come that the evil day is not far off, when they will be compelled to stand by their arms, and with sword and bayonet to defend their firesides and domestic altars."

"From whom do you expect such evils?" asked young Shelton, in a moment of abstraction; "from the Indians?"

"No, sir, not from the red man, but from our Northern brethren; from white men; from Anglo-Saxons like our-

selves, who will be a more terrible foe than ever the Indian
could be.   The Indian will burn your home, it is true, and
scalp your women and children ; but his race is soon run.
For when the white man rises up in all his might, he can
crush with his heel the head of the viper, whose impatient
tail only will writhe, and make manifest its former life
through the remnants of a few scattered tribes.   But, sir,
should an intestine war prevail, it would be a war wherein
'Greek meets Greek;' and the clash of steel and the roar
of artillery will never cease to be heard until the North
and the South, in their last death-struggle, shall lie locked
in each other's arms.   An internecine war will be a war of
extermination, which shall redden not our rivers only, but
the broad Atlantic itself shall become so tainted and so thick
with human gore, that vessels of commerce can no more sail
upon its bosom than a bird can fly over the Dead sea, or a
horse swim upon its bituminous waters.   Trade, which is
already beginning to assume such vast proportions, and to
become such a splendid edifice, will become a wreck of
scattered ruins; and, amid the fallen piers of the Temple
of Commerce, leveled to the earth by the ruthless hand of
fanaticism, the future statesman and patriot will stand weeping, like Marius amid the ruins of Carthage, and mourning
that his own or his brother's hand had wrought such woe
and desolation!"

Langdon was astonished as he looked upon this old man,
whose plain, hard features and home-spun clothes gave no
evidence of scholarship or superior training.

"He reads—he thinks," said Langdon, mentally.   "If
such are the men of our plantations, and even small farms,
what giants will our future statesmen be!   The men of the
South have a high destiny before them.   God grant that
the fruit of promise may not be plucked from the national
tree before it has reached the age of maturity and attained
to its period of ripeness."

"Amen!" said Mr. McPherson, with an energy which

startled young Shelton, so that he stepped backward and
looked at the old man with surprise depicted upon his
countenance. He knew not that he had been speaking
aloud, and that his thoughts had gradually assumed the
shape of audible words, which were both heard and appreciated by his auditor.

Mr. McPherson would have been a "fire-eater" if he had
lived in the present day; he was only an observer then—a
sharp, shrewd observer—watching the smoke and the peb-
bles which were now and then puffed out by the infant volcano, which he foresaw was destined to become a tall,
burning mountain, whose rumbling would be heard all over
the American continent; whose shocks would be felt in
distant Europe, and whose burning lava might roll from its
lofty hight to sweep away Liberty and the Constitution,
brotherly love, commerce, everything which a free people
could think worth having or striving for.

Mr. McPherson's predictions are fast becoming verified.
Humboldt says he saw, in South America, an old man seated in
front of his cabin smoking a pipe. In the distance, and apparently but a little way off, was a volcano then smoking and
casting out stones and melted lava, which rolled down its sides.

"How long has that mountain been smoking, do you suppose?" asked the traveler of the old man.

"Ever since I was a boy," replied the South American.
"I can remember when it was but a little hole no bigger
than the bowl of my pipe, and puffing out a little column
of smoke in regular puffs, as if blown by a bellows by some
óne concealed in the bowels of the earth. *Then*, its smoke
rose no higher than this which curls from my pipe ; see
how black and thick it is now! Then, it was no bigger
than an ant-hill, and only grains of glittering sand and peb-
bles were puffed out from its tiny mouth ; *now*, see to what
a lofty hight it has attained, and how its smoky peaks look
down with contempt upon the clouds. It casts forth peb-
bles no more, but mighty stones."

4

"Astonishing!" said Humboldt; "such a mountain the work of a few years only!"

As rapid as was the growth of that mountain, no less so has been the volcano of Abolitionism. But, as the old man had sat for so many years before his little cabin, watching its growth unharmed and as indifferently as he watched the smoke which curled from his calumet, let us pray God that we of the United States may see this political volcano die out, and its internal fires become quenched as that of South America. For, as Humboldt's volcano afterward became extinct, and as no lives were ever lost by its eruptions, let us sincerely hope that the prayers and tears of brotherhood commingled at the national altar, and gathered in a mighty reservoir, shall be poured down the smoking crater of Black Republicanism, until they shall extinguish the consuming fires which rage in the heart of the mad Abolitionist who would light the torch of civil war.

CHAPTER V.

ANGDON was so interested in Mr. McPherson's society that he did not attempt to return to the city
until the afternoon of the next day; for he did not
reach Mr. McPherson's until some time after dark; and
as he was very much fatigued by his journey, he had
slept to a very late hour of the morning. It was not until
twelve o'clock, therefore, that he had finished the moneyed
transactions which had called him into Georgia, and as
dinner was upon the table by one o'clock, Mr. McPherson
pressed him to remain, and so engaged his attention that
it was some time in the afternoon before he left the house of
his hospitable entertainer.

But now shaking Mr. McPherson by the hand, Langdon
mounted his horse and rode toward the city in a rapid gallop,
with Old Toney close behind him in the rear. They had
been riding in this way for several miles, until they reached
the celebrated Jasper Spring, two or three miles from Savannah, on the Augusta road. It had been a spot fatal to
the life of more than one man; for here Sergeant Jasper,
with a single fellow-soldier, had shot down the British
guard, to whom had been intrusted several valuable American citizens as prisoners. In the distance, Jasper and his
friend had built several fires equidistant, to resemble the
camp-fires of the American army. Then, creeping silently,
and with cat-like tread upon the foe, Jasper and his friend
fired upon the enemy, and rushing in with clubbed mus-

kets, dashed out the brains of some who resisted, and made
prisoners of the remainder. Imagine the astonishment of
the British, when they afterward discovered that the supposed camp-fires were only deceitful lights, kindled by their
two daring captors, whose plan was to impose upon them
the belief that the fires which they saw were the camp-fires
of the American army, and that the two men who had sprung
so suddenly upon them was only the advance-guard of the
avengers of liberty, hurled as a thunderbolt in their midst.

The heroism of Jasper is a household word among us, and
his history had been known and read with delight by young
Shelton. He had not forgotten to ask Mr. McPherson where
was the locality, and was surprised to learn that he had
passed by the very spot the day before, where one of the
most dashing, heroic deeds had been performed, during our
struggle for independence, which has ever been recorded
upon the bright page of history. Langdon was now approaching this celebrated spring, which, in itself considered,
possesses no ordinary attractions to the traveler. But, for
the name of the thing, and because the gallant young Carolinian loved a heroic and a chivalric deed, whether performed
by the lowly or the great, he had determined to dismount
as soon as he had reached the wayside fountain, and drink
a deep draught of its cooling waters, even as Jasper had
drank deep at the fountain of liberty.

With this patriotic intention, and with such thoughts as
these revolving in his mind, he had checked his horse when
a few hundred yards from the spot where he supposed the
spring to be located. He had been told that it was on the
left side of the road as he returned to the city; and that
he would know when he was approaching it by a deep bay
which either gave rise to, or was formed by the spring.
Shelton had already reached the spring, and was looking
down into its limpid waters as they purled upward and then
passed into the bay. Old Toney was just behind his young
master, and was about to rein in his horse, also, when he

heard the sharp click as of a pistol set on trigger; and his
horse taking fright at the noise, or at some object in the
bushes, reared and plunged, and then dashed off at full speed
with the bit in his mouth. It was in vain that Old Toney
pulled upon the reins; the frightened animal could not be
restrained; nor did he recover from his fright until he
reached that part of the city now occupied by the Central
Railroad Depot, which was then one of the suburbs, and
known as "Yamacraw."

Old Toney then, and not until then, succeeded in turning
his horse's head, and rode back under whip and spur, fearing
nothing for himself, although he dreaded everything for
his young master. That a robbery was contemplated by
some one concealed in the thicket he did not doubt; that
a murder had been committed, his instincts of affection caused
him greatly to fear. As his horse dashed off at full speed,
and before he had even attained the distance of fifty yards,
the report of a pistol had rung upon the air, causing his
horse to make a longer leap, and to give a wilder snort of
terror. Who had fired that pistol? or was it the click of a
shot-gun which he had heard? and was it the faint echo of a
barrel of small caliber, loaded with bird-shot, and fired just
then at some feathered songster by some truant boy?

A thousand conjectures rushed into the mind of the old
negro; all acting as so many spurs to his haste, and lending
strength to his arm. But if before he had not strength
enough to hold in the frightened courser, he lacked the
power now to urge forward, as fast as he desired, the jaded,
panting steed; and he arrived at the Jasper Spring only at
an ordinary hand gallop. There were no signs of his master
there, and his horse was gone. But a little way up the road
Old Toney discovered several drops of blood; and as he
traced these, as he used to do a trail of blood upon the leaves
and grass of the Cherokee and Seminole war-fields, the old
veteran halted as he saw, with amazement, just before him,
quite a pool of blood; and there was the spot where he felt

convinced the body of his dear young master lay. He sat down upon the grass by the roadside and wept and sobbed as if his heart would break. Then, as if resolved to discover the murderer, and avenge the death of his young master, he rose from his cool, damp seat, and followed the tracks of the horse. He saw no more blood, and then he turned back and stood again by the crimson pool. He could trace the red drops backward, but he could find none either upon the right hand or the left. Again he mounted his horse, and, followed the fresh trail of the animal which his master had rode. But in a little while he came to other roads and other tracks; and night had settled down so fast that he could no longer distinguish any signs. He determined, therefore, to return in haste to the city and inform Mr. Hartwell of the melancholy circumstances, and secure his aid in discovering the fact whether a murder had, in reality, been committed. But his jaded horse carried him back to the city much slower than he wished, and to his distress of mind was added the discomfort of a pelting rain. The lightning flashed and blazed in broad sheets as very rarely blazes beneath a Southern sky. The thunder rolled and rattled like the united reports of a thousand cannon. Peal after peal, and flash after flash, burst forth from the dark bosom of the angry cloud, as though Jehovah, in his wrath, was rebuking the sins of wicked men. But, by all this storm, Old Toney was unmoved by any unmanly fear. Although he might feel awful in the presence of his God, and with the conviction firmly riveted upon his mind that his young master, whom he so tenderly loved as his own offspring, had been most foully murdered at the Jasper Spring; although these circumstances might fill his mind with awe, yet the brave old negro had no fears for himself. Old Toney, in common parlance, "had heard it thunder before." He had seen the fire-flash of artillery blaze through the thick smoke of battle; and had heard the terrific war-whoop of the Indian savage screamed in his ears with diabolical energy, and issuing, simultaneously, from a thousand savage voices. He had seen blood enough shed in his lifetime to swim a horse, or, perhaps, to float even a man-of-war vessel. But all the sounds and sights combined of the most bloody contest he had ever witnessed, had never made him tremble so as when he stood, for the first time, by the little pool of blood which his instincts told him was no other than the blood of his dear young master. Nor could he easily recover from the panic and the grief with which he was so deeply affected by the sight of that crimson pool.

When Old Toney reached the residence of Mr. Hartwell it was late at night, and though drenched to the skin the rain had ceased to fall. With difficulty had he succeeded in arousing any of the servants; and it was not until repeated knocks and loud calls that he at length gained admittance into the yard. Old Bob himself answered the summons, and was surprised to see the jaded condition of the horse, who seemed to be both thumped and wind-broken, and could scarcely drag one foot after the other.

"What you been do to my hoss, man, for mek 'um so? You got no better manners den to go and borrow a hoss, and den ride 'um to det?" said Old Bob, as Old Toney led the animal into the stable.

But Old Toney answered not a word to this complaint, which, at another time, he would have resented as an insult offered to his humanity. His heart was too hardly smitten with grief, and too well-nigh broken to take umbrage at any indignity which was offered him now. He felt that he was willing to be trampled upon and rolled in the dust. He would have regarded it as a friendly blow, and would have blessed the hand that had laid him in death by the side, or at the feet, of his master's corpse.

"Would to God I had died for him!" he thought within himself, and groaned so deep and loud that Old Bob, as provoked as he was, started in amazement.

"What de matter, Old Toney?" said Old Bob, in tones

of sympathy and curiosity combined; "something seems
to be a weighin' on your mind. Tell your brudder what de
matter."

"I want to see your masser, Mr. Hartwell," was the only
reply of the old man, whose whole manner as well as the
very inflections of his voice seemed shared by the mourning
spirit within him.

"My masser can't be seed! He is fast asleep in his bed,
and would n't be woke up dis time o'night for nothin' less
dan a dollar and a half, or mebbe a dollar, if it's gib to
me!" was Bob's answer, as he drew himself up with all the
dignity of a cotton sampler.

"I *must* see your masser *now*—dis minute!"

"Dat's easier said dan done, old man. I tell you I can't
wake 'um up unless it be a case ob life and det."

"It *is* a case ob life and det, as you say! My nyung
masser, wat went wid me, has been murdered on de road"——

"Murdered! You do n't say so! Who kill?" exclaimed
Old Bob, with consternation in his countenance, which was
now lighted by the gleam of the lantern, as its light flashed
upon his sable features.

"I do n't know who did it," was Old Toney's reply; "but
I know dat God's almighty vengeance will obertake de guilty
and bring de murderer some day to the gallows. May God
punish de wretch who killed my Masser Langdon."

The solemn tones of the old man's voice, coupled with
the awful nature of his communication, filled Old Bob with
a feeling of mysterious awe, and he felt a chill creeping
over him, which increased to such a degree that his teeth
fairly chattered and clacked together as though the spirit
of the murdered man had suddenly appeared before them.
Curiosity and cunning have been said to be the most striking traits of the negro character, and doubtless they are
prominent characteristics of his nature. But the most
marked and prominent features of the African, which have
been thus far so feebly portrayed, *are* his *superstition* and his

fidelity to his master. He believes in ghosts, and trembles at his own shadow when any startling circumstance reminds him that the hour has come when the troubled spirits of the departed walk forth in unrest from their graves. That hour had now arrived, and it was natural that Old Bob should draw closer to his companion, and even take him affectionately by the hand.

"Come, Brudder Toney," said he, coaxingly, "let's go to masser and tell 'um all about it. My masser is a berry kind man, and I know he will be as sorry as me when you tell him de perticklars."

Mr. Hartwell was easily aroused from his slumbers, and, on hearing the statement of Old Toney, lost no time in sending immediately for a magistrate. The nearest magistrate lived but a little way from Mr. Hartwell's, and he came very promptly at the summons of that gentleman. A constable was afterward sent for, and after hearing the story, several times repeated, of Colonel Shelton's old servant, they determined to take him along with them, to see if they could discover any traces which might lead to the detection of crime, if crime had indeed been committed. As soon as the day dawned, therefore, the party sallied forth in quest of evidences of guilt; and, as a matter of course, they were led by Old Toney to the Jasper Spring, on the Augusta road.

"Here, sir, my nyung masser sat upon his horse. It was de berry last time I ebber saw him."

Old Toney's voice trembled so that he could scarcely articulate the words. He beckoned to the three gentlemen to follow him on a little further. He had dismounted from his horse at the Jasper Spring, and the three gentlemen did likewise. They followed after the old man on foot, leading their horses, also, by the bridle; and when Old Toney reached the spot where had once been the pool of blood, he added, "And here"—— but he could say nothing more. The fountains of his soul were all opened again, and the old man's

4*

heart seemed to bleed afresh. He sunk down upon the
grass as before, or, rather, as if he had been pressed down
by the invisible but irresistible pressure of some giant
phantom's hand, than as if yielding to a natural impulse.

Mr. Hartwell was greatly moved by the unmistakable evidences of the old man's grief. He pulled his handkerchief
from his pocket and held it to his eyes; and when he removed it from his face, his eyes were red with weeping.

But neither the magistrate nor the constable seemed to
be at all concerned by the distress of Old Toney. These
men of the law seem to possess iron hearts, and to be heed-
less of suffering when they are called upon to act in their
official capacity. Doubtless some of them may feel as men,
or would do so, if they allowed themselves to be controlled
by their natural instincts. But they steel themselves against
all emotions, and seem, at least to others, not to feel, while
oceans of tears may be falling in their presence. If they
weep not in the court-house, however distressing to others
may be the circumstances, they would not weep now, when
they saw nothing to weep about, as they supposed. Indeed,
so far from weeping, the constable even smiled, and stooping
down, examined closely the spot which had been indicated by
Old Toney as the place where he had seen the blood. He
examined it long and very attentively, but saw nothing to induce him to believe that there had ever been any blood there.

"This is a pretty tale you have been telling us, old man,"
said the suspicious and hard-hearted constable. "I am
afraid you have been telling us a lie, and have brought us
upon a wild-goose chase."

"Me tell you lie, masser?" said Old Toney, rising in astonishment. "Why, masser, as old a man as I is, Colonel
Shelton nebber said sich a word to me before."

"Well, then, show us the blood," said the constable, with
some degree of excitement and mortification at the dignified
rebuke of the old negro.

"Why, masser, how can I show you? God has wiped

out wid his tears de murderer's mark. I do n't know wedder to spare de guilty wretch a little longer, or wedder de
good Lord's heart was so filled wid grief at de sight ob my
nyung masser Langdon lying in his blood. All I know is
dat de rain poured down in torrents such as I nebber see
before, and it has washed clean away de last sign ob my
poor masser."

The old man could say no more, but sobbed out again
as if his heart would certainly break this time; and surely
none but the hard-hearted or the narrow-minded could, for
a single moment, doubt the sincerity of his grief. Mr.
Hartwell did not once doubt it; but the law has a hard
heart and a narrow mind in regard to the innocent; it is
only tender and broad and comprehensive in reference to
the guilty. It is true that the law has a maxim that "it
is better that ninety and nine guilty persons should ·escape,
than one innocent man should suffer." This reads beautifully, and sounds humane in theory. But when the innocent man—the purely innocent—the man whom our natural
instincts and moral perceptions declare to be innocent—let
such an one come within the grasp of the law, and how it
delights to clutch him and hold him fast, if only for a
little while, just to let him feel grateful to the law for having *proved* what he knew before—how very innocent he is.
If a rogue, who has stolen a hundred horses in his time,
is put in the prisoner's box, why, then, the law is so very
merciful that she could not hang or imprison *him ;* and, ten
chances to one, she convinces not only the jury, *but the villain himself,* that he never had committed a theft in his life.
But let the evidence be circumstantial only ; let there be
suspicion breathed against one, be he never so innocent,
and see how hard is the effort to stain and defame the unfortunate man, who is either too innocent, or not guilty
enough, to excite or deserve the mercy of the law. This
fact can be explained only upon the principle that there is
"honor among thieves," and a wonderful fellowship in ras-

cality. For, while the law would rather that "ninety and nine guilty persons should escape," she would gladly hang the innocent man to make the number an even hundred.

No wonder, then, that the constable smiled when he should have wept, as did the generous-hearted and noble-minded Mr. Hartwell, when he looked with sympathy upon the sorrow-smitten old negro.

As Mr. Hartwell returned with the two myrmidons of the law to the city, they conversed together in low, but very earnest tones. Old Toney, who followed them in the rear, at a distance of ten or twelve paces, knew not that the conversation concerned himself alone; and that the burden of the argument urged by the constable, and assented to in silence by the magistrate, was, that in all probability a murder had been committed; but that, inasmuch as Old Toney had pointed out no guilty party upon whom the law might take recourse, suspicion must necessarily attach to himself until he was proved innocent.

"What else must we conclude?" said the constable, who was backed even by the usually silent magistrate, who seemed to depend upon his minion as the owner of a bloodhound depends upon the keen scent of the animal to follow up a trail which he can neither smell nor see himself.

"What else must we conclude?" said he, in reply to Mr. Hartwell's entreaty to let Old Toney alone, and let him return to his master; for how could it be possible that Old Toney should be guilty of the murder of his young master, Langdon Shelton? "Will you vouch for his integrity upon your own personal knowledge? Do you know anything yourself of the negro's antecedents?"

"No! I never saw him before. But I know Colonel Shelton too well to suppose that he would intrust his son to the care of a servant of doubtful character."

"That may be all very true, as you say, Mr. Hartwell. But the law is very plain, indeed, upon this *pint!* If a man is suspected, the law thinks he ought to have a chance to clear himself and prove to the world that he is innocent; for the law *holds him guilty until he proves the contrary!*" The crafty constable regarded himself as the representative of the law and the guardian of her honor. If *he* suspected him, of course the law, in his person, suspected him also! Verily, the law is made up, at best, of persons and personalities, and the only thing grand or glorious about her is that which the lawyers and judges, who are the priests of her altar, themselves admit—her "glorious uncertainties!"

Mr. Hartwell knew but little of the law, and cared less about it. He had never studied its technicalities, nor committed to memory its dogmas. He did not perceive, therefore, that the constable had stated, perhaps ignorantly, the very reverse of a proposition; and had reversed a rule which would be a "poor one if it didn't work both ways!" Nor did he perceive the innate selfishness of the man who could worry and distress the feelings of another for the sake of gain; for the constable was all the while thinking that he had taken a disagreeable ride for nothing, and was likely to receive no fee nor reward for his faithfulness in attempting to ferret out a secret offense committed against the law. Had he unbosomed himself to Mr. Hartwell, and plainly said that he was only after a fee, Mr. Hartwell would have cheerfully paid him his demand to release Old Toney from his grasp; but this, of course, the constable was too cunning and worldly-wise to do. Hence he said, in continuation of his previous remarks:

"This, sir, is our safest plan. If we should do any other way, we might render ourselves liable."

Mr. Hartwell was a mild as well as a kind man. Indeed, are they not almost inseparable—mildness and kindness? He made, therefore, no further objection to a course which he foresaw, almost from the beginning, was a foregone conclusion founded upon nothing but ignorance or blind prejudice. He yielded in silence, just as the man of superior information yields to the boastful assertions or vain teachings of the ignorant, or the artful pretender, who attempts to convict the man of learning of being a fool while he is himself the wiseacre.

When the party had returned to Mr. Hartwell's house, breakfast was already upon the table, and the magistrate and the constable were politely requested to sit down and partake of the morning's repast. This is a meal which usually consumes but a few moments, and which most men eat either sparingly or in a hurry. But quicker than usual did the constable swallow his meal, and nudging the magistrate with his elbow, he said:

"Come, John, make haste and write out your warrant for a commitment, for I must be going."

"Will Mr. Hartwell favor me with a pen and ink?" said the magistrate, bowing his head politely to Mr. Hartwell, for he possessed more native refinement than the constable, and he added:

"This, sir, is only to be on the safe side. Of course, there will be no further proceedings against the negro until his master arrives from Carolina. You will, of course, write to him?"

Of course, sir, immediately, and by a trusty messenger. Walk in, sir, to the library; my secretary is at your service."

The warrant for arrest and commitment to jail was soon written out against Old Toney, and placed in the hands of the constable, who put it into his pocket, and, without any further ceremony, walked down into the back yard, and calling forth Old Toney, who had ensconced himself in the kitchen, said, in those startling, harsh tones, which only a constable or a policeman can assume:

"You are my prisoner; come along with me to jail."

"To jail, massa!" exclaimed Old Toney, in amazement. "Me go to jail? Wha' fur?"

"Never mind what for; you will find out by-and-by. Come along!" and he seized him rudely by the arm to lead him away.

It was just at this precise moment that one of the boat-hands who had rowed them to town—it was the same one who had led the stroke-oar, and whom the reader remembers as the author of the very poetic effusion and impromptu boat-song recorded in the first part of the previous chapter—Cæsar, approached Old Toney with a sorrowful countenance.

"Uncle Toney," said the simple-hearted negro, "I yerry ebery t'ing, and I berry sorry for you! But enty I tell you so? Your nyung masser would n't beliebe *me;* and you gone, like a foolish old man, and mek bad wusser! You ought to 'a hab more sense, Uncle Toney, fur go and talk dat bat t'ing name! I tell you, no good! Berry bad luck will always follow a man who talk dat wicked t'ing name, on de water 'specially!"

Old Toney did not make any reply to this taunt or reproof. He drew himself up with dignity—with the dignity of an old king who is deserted by his former courtiers, and spit at and reviled by his enemies, who heap reproaches upon him for his extravagance or pretended crimes. He made no remonstrance to the order of the officer; he neither admitted nor denied the reproof of the boatman. In silence he followed his-harsh captor to the city jail, which then stood alone upon "the common" in stern solitude and gloomy isolation. It was a large, and a dingy, and a very cheerless-looking brick building; and as the large door of one of the rooms opened and swung back upon its hinges to admit the prisoner, and as the jailer turned the large key in the huge lock, and Old Toney felt that *he was, indeed, locked in from the world!*—shut up in a prison for no crime whatever—*then*, Old Toney could n't help admitting to himself that "the salt-water nigger was more than half right," to say the least; "*it was berry bad luck to say* 'alligator,' and *mebbe*," he added mentally, "*to t'ink 'bout 'em, too! Please God, I do n't t'ink I will ebber call de name ob dat t'ing again!*"

Poor old man! The superstition of his earlier life, which had been almost eradicated by his daily intercourse with his intelligent master, had returned upon him with ten-fold power, from a single fatal coincidence. There was proof now, tangible proof, that it was no chimera, no vain nor foolish precaution to avoid the mention of a name which had brought him a great deal of bad luck, and had overwhelmed him with trouble. The cold, damp walls of his prison, and the grated bars of his window, would every day admonish him that "*it was, indeed, berry bad luck to call de name ob dat t'ing.*"

CHAPTER VI.

AS soon as Old Toney was carried off to prison, Mr.
Hartwell very considerately sat down and wrote a
kind letter of condolence and sympathy to Colonel
Shelton, which he placed in the hands of his own
faithful old man, Bob. Every Southern planter (and
even merchant) has at least one faithful old servant. And
by this we do not mean to say that he has *but one;* but
that this particular servant is, *par excellence,* the very prince
of all faithful servants ; standing, in the estimation of his
master, a head and shoulders taller than all the rest ; out-
rivaling far the devotion of the affectionate spaniel, and
receiving, in return, an unselfish love, greater even than the
undying attachment of the Arab chieftain for his winged
steed of the desert.

Mr. Hartwell, who thought he possessed such a treasure
in Old Bob, knew how to sympathize both with the master
at a distance and Old Toney in the jail. While he sent,
therefore, condoling words by his special and trusty messenger, upon whom he could rely with confidence, he did
not forget to visit the old negro in prison, to minister to
his temporal wants, and to cheer his almost broken heart
with words of hope, that his master would soon arrive in
the city and liberate him from his place of captivity and
confinement.

Old Bob took the place of Old Toney in the boat, which
he steered in safety to the landing of Mr. Stearly ; and

taking Old Toney's black horse, he rode, in a brisk trot, for the up-country. But he did not ride as fast as Old Toney rode that stormy evening, when, maddened by the sudden and unlooked-for loss of his young master, he seemed like a mad hippogriff, urged onward by a single and undivided influence.

If Old Bob could feel for Old Toney in his distress, he could feel also for his horse ; and with the vain-glory and exultant spirit of the Pharisee, who said, " I thank thee, Lord, that I am not as other men, extortioners, unjust, adulterers," Old Bob added, in spirit if not in substance, " and not even as horse-killers." For he patted Old Toney's coal-black steed upon the neck as he came to a running stream, and encouraged the animal to drink to his heart's content ; speaking in a peculiarly coaxing tone, but using language which the horse would have construed into a downright insult if he had understood all the words employed in the vocabulary of the Anglo-African dialect.

" Old Toney berry hard on horse, enty ? He kill my horse to Savannah, enty ? Berry well. Me no gwine to hu't you for pay. Old Toney in jail now, you know. I better man to horse dan Old Toney. Old Toney broke my horse bellows, so ee let out all de wind. Nebber mind ; I can mend yours if ee git broke. But I wont broke 'um. Old Bob ain't hard on a horse. Aldo' I say it myself, I t'ank de Lord I is better dan most niggers."

Thus soliloquizing, Old Bob jogged on much slower than before, as if determined to prove to the horse's entire satisfaction the truth of his remarks ; and to convince him, by the pleasantness of the journey, that he was indeed a better horse-master than his sable rival now lying in the city jail at Savannah. Now, be it known, that the Southern negro is famous for his soliloquizing propensities. He talks to himself upon all occasions ; talks to his horse in the plow ; talks continually to his team in the wagon ; talks to the trees of the forest ; talks to the winds as they howl

and rage aloft ; to any and everything he talks, whether of
animate or inanimate nature—whether to beast or to fowl ;
whether to the fishes or to the senseless stone. It is all
the same to him what the object is ; he talks to it for company ; or, if for nothing more, to while away the tedious-
ness of a lonely hour. Not that he ever feels lonely. O,
no ! He has thoughts enough, and fertile resources enough
to prevent him from ever feeling lonely. But if he should
happen "*to get the blues*"—which, according to his physical
organization, or, rather, epidermic constitution, would seem
to be an impossibility—why, then, it would be the easiest
thing in the world for him to lie down and go to sleep ;
thus forgetting all his troubles, not in "*five minutes,*" as
we usually say of a man who is a ready sleeper, or "by
the time his head touches the pillow," but in the "twinkling of an eye," and, as it often seems, *a good while before
he has even made up his mind to sleep at all.*

When the negro is tired of himself or the world, therefore, and tired of soliloquizing, or singing, or whistling, he
can go to sleep, whether standing or lying down, whether
riding or walking. And this is what Old Bob now did as
he jogged along, nodding to the trees with the stateliness
of the "black knight" upon his coal-black steed, bowing
to a Saxon host, with waving banners, whom he had come
from prison and exile to claim as his own, and whom they,
in return, would acknowledge, as the "Cœur de Lion" whom
they adored. We do not mean to intimate, by any means,
that the simile is a perfect one ; or that, as Old Bob's head
leaned far back toward the crupper, and then returned
slowly until it touched the horse's mane, that the trees, in
return, waved their branches and shook their green tops
like so many banners rustled in the air. We mean simply
to intimate that Old Bob nodded and slept with a *vim*
which no other than a negro can imitate in slumber.

Some one—no matter who—has said, "It is God who
steeps the mind in Lethe, and bids us slumber, that our

bodies may be refreshed, so that for to-morrow's toil we
may rise recruited and strengthened." But surely Old Bob
needed no rising up from his slumbers, for he had never
got down, and "recruited and strengthened" his energies
as he went along. Thus "recruited and strengthened," he
arrived, on the second day after his departure from home,
at the residence of Colonel Shelton, who was already beginning to feel anxious at Langdon's delay.

But if the old Colonel's heart was overwhelmed with
sorrow as he read the first part of Mr. Hartwell's letter,
informing him, in the most cautious terms, of the uncertain
fate of his son, and sympathizing, in heartfelt expressions,
in a parent's anxiety, great was his indignation also, when
Mr. Hartwell informed him that Old Toney, his faithful
Old Toney, whom not only he and his family, but every
one else in the community loved and reverenced, and whom
he thought everybody else in the world ought to love and
reverence also—that his tried and trusty body-servant—the
man who had fought by his side as a fellow-soldier, and
through whose courage and by whose strong right arm his
life had been more than once saved from the uplifted tomahawk of the Indian savage. O! it was too bad to doubt
such a man. And so great was Colonel Shelton's indignation, that if, at that moment, he could have seized that
meanest of all men, a mean constable, he would have torn
that off-cast "limb of the law" limb from limb, and flung
his quivering flesh to the dogs to spurn, or snuff at with
up-turned noses of contempt. The indignation of Colonel
Shelton was good for him just at that crisis, so trying to
his heart's best and holiest affections. It prevented the
lion-hearted old Colonel from dying, at that moment from
the effects of so sudden and overwhelming a calamity; for
even the lion-hearted Richard of England died at last of
a wound inflicted by a poisonous arrow ; and the invincible
Achilles perished from a simple puncture in the heel. But
the brave old Colonel had received a deeper, broader, more

frightful wound than they; for his was a wound of the heart, which even time would not, could not heal. But while his heart was bleeding inwardly with grief for the loss of his son, it was boiling outwardly with rage at the indignity offered to his old servant Toney, by his false imprisonment. He lost no time, therefore, in mounting his horse, and pushing in haste for Savannah, to liberate, as soon as possible, his old friend and fellow-soldier.

When Colonel Shelton reached the jail, in company with Mr. Hartwell, and was led by the jailer to the prisoner's cell, he saw Old Toney, with a sad countenance and over-burdened heart, leaning against the damp wall of the prison. The sight of the brave old negro, who had fought and shed his blood for the liberties of his country, and the aspect of his woe, so overcame him that he forgot himself entirely; forgot all the dignity of his aristocratic birth; forgot the wide difference existing between them as master and servant; forgot the presence of Mr. Hartwell and the jailer; forgot everything in that moment but the predominant impulse of his noble, god-like heart, and, flinging himself into Old Toney's arms, which, just then, were outreached, as if imploring for mercy and pitying love, the white man's heart beat and throbbed against the black man's, acknowledging that, although they were bond and free, there was a tie of brotherhood—a strong and adamantine chain, which was so indissoluble that it could only be severed or dissolved by death.

Yes, hear it, ye so-called philanthropists, who would shrink from the touch of the black man and think it pollution!— ye who would refuse to sit down by his side and give him wholesome advice and friendly counsel, but who will stand off at a distance, and poke into his hand a pitiful dime or a sixpence stuck into the end of a "ten-foot pole!"—ye who hate and curse the master, and preach *at the slave*, but can never know the wants, nor love the Ethiopian *as a man*, come, look at this scene—this prison scene. It is no fan-

cied sketch, no highly-colored picture, which overdoes the
thing. It is a scene which we have witnessed more than
once in seasons of affliction and distress. It is a scene
which many a Southern man has witnessed, and to which,
perhaps, some of our Southern members of Congress can
testify. Behold Colonel Shelton—that brave, that refined,
that accomplished scholar and dignified old gentleman—
weeping like a child upon the breast of his slave! With
their arms twined around each other, they are sobbing as
two brothers long separated, and but now united. They
are weeping as two wrecked and broken-hearted mariners
over the broken hull and splintered masts of a once gallant
bark. They are weeping as only the proud, but grief-smitten parent and the loving, doting foster-father can weep,
when, standing front to front, they cross hands over the
grave of a dead darling who was dear to them both—the
legitimate parent and the foster-father.

But let us not dwell upon this scene, so painful because
so true. It is enough to say that, although not a very common or every-day scene, simply because great occasions do
not often arise, and though the bowl may be several times
cracked at the fountain, it can be broken but once, yet such
scenes have occurred before, and will occur again, although,
perhaps, but once in a life-time, and only when the heart is
breaking beneath the mountain load of its sorrow. *Colonel
Shelton's heart was already broken.*

When Colonel Shelton had again recovered his habitual
outward control, he took Old Toney by the hand and led
him out of the prison. He asked no permission of the
jailer, and paid none of his bills; nor would he have
deigned to notice them. With the imperious tread of the
conqueror, and the stern look of the emperor whose autocrat is law, he went forth from the prison walls, followed
by Old Toney. Only once did Colonel Shelton express
himself in terms of indignation while at the jail. It was
while standing on the steps for a moment preparatory to

bidding adieu, with his accustomed courtesy, to the jailer, who was himself a kind-hearted man, for there was a tear of sympathy in his eye, which Colonel Shelton observed and appreciated.

"That constable," said the Colonel, addressing himself to Mr. Hartwell, "and that magistrate, must be a couple of fools, or arrant scoundrels."

"Perhaps they are one and the other—the magistrate and the constable," replied Mr. Hartwell.

"Nebber mind now, masser," said Old Toney, who felt called upon to make a last thrust—a home-thrust at his false accusers. "Nebber mind," said he, with a lip curling upward with scorn. "'Tain't no use to fret ober it now; we must mek' allowance for dem. Dey only Georgy Buckra. Georgy Buckra, masser, ain't like we Ca'lina Buckra."

Old Toney forgot entirely, in addressing Mr. Hartwell, who was as kind and as gentlemanly and refined as his master, that he was addressing a thorough-bred Georgian, who gloried in his native state, and felt a peculiar pride in the growing prosperity of his native city; a pride equal to that which the most patriotic son of the Palmetto State feels when he treads again his native soil, after an absence of many months or years, and a weary wandering in the land of the stranger, and says in his heart of hearts:

"Yes, my native land, I love thee,
Home of the free and brave!"

But Mr. Hartwell understood Old Toney perfectly, and smiled pleasantly, for he knew that the old negro meant that a mean rascal who claimed to be a Georgian, was not half so good as a thorough gentleman who claimed to be a Carolinian; and to this, Mr. Hartwell as cheerfully would assent as Old Toney.

But Old Toney made no explanation to Mr. Hartwell, nor did he think any apology necessary to that gentleman, who, in addition to other kindnesses, shook him by the hand as

he stood upon the wharf just below the Exchange, expressing his regrets at the treatment which he had received in
Savannah, and hoping that the fresh air of the country would
soon restore him to his former equanimity and cheerfulness.
Old Toney thanked Mr. Hartwell for his kindness, and declared that he could never forget him while he had breath
in his body. But when he reached the water's edge, and
before entering the boat, in which Colonel Shelton was
already seated, he pulled off both his shoes very deliberately, and shook all the sand out into the water. After
brushing very carefully the soles with his coat sleeve, he
held his shoes up toward the Exchange, and looking at the
face of the dial, as if addressing it as the living representative of the city of Savannah, which could both see and hear
him, he exclaimed, with a solemnly indignant look and a
threatening frown:

"You see, you enty; dey is clean as my hand; I shake
de berry dust off my feet agin you. May Old Toney never
see Georgy state as long as he lib in dis sinful world."

And to make good his words, and that never a doubt
might be raised upon the subject, Old Toney deliberately
sat down and washed his feet at the river dock; and no
doubt they needed an ablution, and helped to cool down his
wrathful feelings.

As soon as the old man took his seat in the bow, the
boat was pushed from the wharf, and Colonel Shelton and
Mr. Hartwell waved to each other their last adieus. They
were the last that Colonel Shelton ever waved to his faithful old friend; for if they meet again, it will be no more on
earth, but in heaven.

CHAPTER VII.

THE women of South Carolina, during the Revolution, were famous for their courage and endurance under difficulties and dangers which even "tried men's souls." There were heroines those days; but their spirit has not died out from the hearts of their daughters. The heroism of '76 became infused into the daughters of '24 and '25, and still continues in the noble women of 1860.

It is a great mistake to suppose that our Southern women are a lazy, inactive, good-for-nothing set, who do nothing but read novels and lie down all day in the summer, fanned by a slave, as we read of the Turkish harems. We know that Northern writers who have seen but little of their habits of industry, have painted them, whether in admiration or contempt, as indolent and dreamy, and requiring a great deal of "waiting on" by their numerous servants. This may be true in very many cases, but they are rather exceptions to the general rule than otherwise. The notion that the men and women of the North are more energetic and industrious than those of the South, is absurd, and false, in fact. The Southern lady requires no more "waiting on" than the Northern lady with equal wealth and command of servants, or "helps." The only difference is, that the one sometimes requires the aid of her *black servant*, while the other calls upon her white serf. The difference, therefore, exists, not in reality, but in the distinction of color; and if there are "lazy women in the world, they may be

5

found in one land as well as another; just as glorious women may be found at the North as at the South, in England, or in France.

Let the Northern reader, to understand this statement— an honest and a truthful one—enter the new home of Colonel Shelton, who was, but a short time since, one of the wealthiest magnates of the land. Behold him now in his new home. His numerous slaves have all been apportioned out among his relatives and friends. They have all found good and kind masters, and are as contented as they can well be away from the old master and mistress in whose ownership they had spent so much of their life. For, be it known, that the African slave, if he has been faithful, never forgets his old master and his old home; for around them both his fondest memories cluster. His early attachments are the most in- dissoluble bonds to his existence. While he may love and serve, ever so faithfully, his new owners, he can not forget his old master. But what slave could forget such a master as Colonel Shelton had been? and what friend could dishonor the friendship of such a man? And now, when he met any of them occasionally on Sabbath days, or all of them at quarterly meetings, when they assembled from the planta- tions for many miles, around a certain church, which the old Colonel himself usually attended, then his eye moistened, and his lip quivered, when his old slaves gathered round him, with their old love unextinguished, and said, " Huddy, (for, how do ye,) my masser? God bless you, my masser!" This was always a painful spectacle even to the by-standers; and it was, as often as it recurred, a mighty struggle, on the part of Colonel Shelton, to keep back the sobs which well- nigh convulsed the old soldier's heart.

Colonel Shelton's family, so greatly reduced in numbers, consisted of his wife and daughter, with ten slaves. These were Old Toney, with whom the reader is already partially acquainted, his wife, Old Rinah, and eight children. Old Rinah's eldest child was a powerful, strapping fellow, about

six feet high, and had been named after his father. He had
been consequently called " Young Toney " from the cradle,
and, although upward of forty, was called Young Toney
still, that is, Toney Jr.; and would, in all probability, be
called Young Toney to the end of his life, though he might
live a hundred years, or, at least, so long as his father lived.
Through these pages, at all events, the man of forty shall
be Young Toney still. Besides Young Toney there was a
younger son, about twenty-one or two, whose name was
George, who will figure a little hereafter ; and two bronzed,
or mulatto girls, resembling in complexion their mother ;
the one, about nineteen, and the other, seventeen ; the eldest
called Lucy, and the youngest, Fanny. Old Rinah, herself,
was a bright mulatto ; and not only Lucy and Fanny were
of light complexion, but nearly all of her younger children ;
only " Young Toney " partook of the nature and ebony hue
of his old father.

Lucy was a young married woman, whose husband lived
upon a plantation a few miles off ; and every Saturday
evening, and sometimes twice a week, or even oftener, he
came to see his young wife, whom he loved devotedly, and
was proud of her accomplishments ; for she could dress
equal to her young mistress, and usually wore several more
rings, all pure gold, which had been either purchased by her
needle, or had been given to her by her mistress and her
friends.

But as fond as Lucy was of finery, Fanny far surpassed
her sister in her love of display ; and well she might, for
she was, indeed, a beautiful girl, with a figure as faultless
as her elegant young mistress ; and, as all pretty girls, she
was vain of her beauty, and loved to set off her elegant figure
to the best possible advantage. Be it borne in mind, gentle
reader, that there were no *hoops* those days ; for that article
(whether expensive, or otherwise, deponent saith not) of a
woman's dress is of very recent origin. But although there
were no hoops then in use, yet there were any quantity of

bustles, pads, etc.; and women looked well, because we were
accustomed to their style, and what would seem very unsightly
now, seemed very sightly, and even comely, then. While
it must be confessed that it was difficult for a slab-sided
woman to appear otherwise than slab-sided, or for a fat and
corpulent woman to appear otherwise than fat and corpulent,
it is equally true that a woman of elegant figure could
exhibit her natural shape to the very best advantage, to the
admiration of the beaux, and the envy of the belles, especially
those who were so fortunate as to be shaped like a Venus
or a Daphne. We are not going to say a word *pro* or *con.*
about hoops, but let them be as they are, a thick drapery
which conceals from our view many a lovely, glorious madonna; but, on the other hand, a friendly vail to hide the
deformities and shocking disproportions of many a Medusa,
in form, if not in features.

But in the year 1825, the period at which we have arrived
in the course of our narrative, there were no hoops to hide
the roundness of Fanny's figure, which very much resembled
the graceful outlines and nymph-like proportions of Ella
Shelton; and when her back was turned toward you, and
she was dressed up in one of her young mistress's splendid,
and but little used, silk or satin dresses, and had on her
last winter's bonnet, which Ella would herself trim with
new ribbon, or re-adjust the old, with ingenious skill, to suit
the latest style—when, we say, Fanny's back was turned
toward you, and she was thus dressed up in her silks and
her satins, and her jewelry of purest gold, the natural inquiry would have been, " What elegant lady is that?" And
how astonished would the Englishman or the Yankee have
been to hear the response: "Elegant lady—fiddlesticks!
That is Miss Shelton's maid!"

Fanny loved and was as proud of her young mistress, as
Ella loved and was proud of her beautiful servant. They
were just the same age, and had grown up together from
childhood. Old Rinah had rocked them to sleep often side

by side in the same cradle, and they had together tugged
at the same paps, and been nourished by the same milk;
while, from Mrs. Shelton's own snowy bosom Fanny had,
more than once, and full many a time, imbibed pure, unadulterated, aristocratic blood. But, notwithstanding all
this, Fanny knew her place, as a dutiful servant, and never
took any undue liberties, which Miss Shelton would have
repelled with a hauteur and a queenly dignity, in just such
a way as she would have repelled the advances of a pert and
insolent snob, or would-be lady of doubtful character and
uncertain social position.

The farm which Colonel Shelton had purchased contained
over a thousand acres of fertile land, and, at the present
day, would be a little fortune itself, when land has advanced
at the South in value from one or two dollars to ten, thirty,
fifty, and even one hundred dollars per acre; and slaves from
four hundred to one thousand, or even fifteen to eighteen
hundred dollars per capita. In 1824, Colonel Shelton, who
was then one of our most successful planters, made scarcely
one bale of cotton to the hand. But it is true that his crop
was greatly injured by the storm which prevailed that year,
his usual average being from two to two and a half bales
only. Now, in 1860, farmers not possessing any more skill,
and upon the same soil, make from five to ten bales, and
think they are doing a poor business at that. Thus, where
fifty bales of upland cotton were produced by the labor of
from thirty to fifty hands, the same number of laborers
will raise from two hundred and fifty to four hundred and
upward of bales. Verily, slave labor has injured the South
at an amazingly fearful rate! Thus, while the South has
grown rich and independent by the enormous increase in
the number and weight of her cotton-bags, she has built
up Northern manufactures, and made our brethren of the
North our rivals in wealth and prosperity. The entire Yankee nation is the most singular people on the face of the
earth—a very peculiar people indeed; for while they grow

rich themselves, they make every one else rich with whom they have trade and commercial intercourse. Thus, while the South has built up Northern manufactures, and made the entire North rich and powerful also, the North and South combined have so helped England by their immense trade, as to save her from bankruptcy and utter ruin, with which she was threatened a quarter of a century ago.

But it is not our purpose to philosophize now; let facts and figures speak for themselves, and let us return to the family of Colonel Shelton, who found themselves in a new situation and a new home; a situation, if not one of absolute poverty, at least widely removed from the affluence and splendor in which they had lived all their lives before. They were now compelled to occupy a humble, but no less honorable sphere, although their new home was not lighted by gilded candelabras and chandeliers sparkling with prismatic colors, nor its humble walls frescoed and painted by skillful artists and designers.

The present home of Colonel Shelton was a very different one from that which he had formerly occupied in his days of independence and prosperity. It was a plain log-cabin with four rooms, to which he added a wing, to be used as a library, where he kept his books, and sat and read, as had been his custom during his former life. But as plain and humble as was their new home, did Ella Shelton and her mother repine, and fret, and scold because God, in his mysterious providence, had thought proper to alter their mode and style of living? Far from it. Instead of being unhappy and morose, they were positively as cheerful and as happy as they well could be under the melancholy circumstances; and but for the absence of Langdon, whose fate was shrouded in tragic mystery, and Colonel Shelton's gloomy countenance, which was seldom lighted up by a smile, they would have been cheerful, and even gay. But as sad as the circumstances were, Ella could not sit still except when at the harp or the piano; for she had

retained these two favorite instruments; and often the hearts
of the servants, her chief auditors now, were made glad by
her sweet songs and the delightful tones which were struck,
with the skill of a master, from the chords of that sweetest and most ancient and honored instrument, the harp.
Upon the piano she played beautifully, it is true, and used
to run very gracefully her taper fingers over its ivory keys.
But upon the harp she spoke the language of her soul, and
expressed her feelings in an audible voice, and with an
accent such as angels may employ. It was sweet to hear
those notes—that voice, which rivaled the voice of the fairy
nightingale; and that deep-toned harp, which could awake
the echoes of the forest, and float high above the stillness
of the night air, or sink to the coaxing whisper of an angel
wooing its brother or sister angel with its whisper of love.
Whose ear would not be unstopped to listen, with ravished
attention and breathless delight, when Ella Shelton played,
con amore, upon her sweet-toned, heaven-strung harp?

But as fond of music as was Ella Shelton, the reader
must not suppose that she was always running her fingers
over the keys of the piano, or seated with her hand upon
her harp. There was much of her life spent in motion and
active exercise. Never a garden had graced that log-house
before; for it had been occupied by ignorant and unlettered
people, whose want of refinement was evinced by the neglected appearance of all the premises. Now, however, a
flower-garden was thought to be an indispensable append-
age to the dwelling, as rude and as uncouth as it might
seem. Young Toney was therefore called upon to fell, with
his strong, brawny arm, a few tall pines, from which beautiful, straight white slabs were obtained, and these he carefully and securely wattled in until he had inclosed a space
sufficiently large for a handsome flower-garden and shrubbery. The flower-garden was laid off by Ella's own little
hands, assisted by Fanny, who rendered her mistress important aid by her taste as well as by her superior strength.

When the ground was all laid off into squares, and octa-
gons, and heart-shaped, and a hundred other figures, and
when George had been called upon with his brush and fresh-
white lime to whitewash the palings, and when the house
had been made clean and white as the driven snow, both
inside and out, and when Young Toney had also inclosed
a vegetable garden for Mrs. Shelton's amusement and the
benefit of the entire family, both white and black, and when
the peas had been planted and were growing finely, and the
beets and the Irish potatoes were up, and the mustard and
the kale almost fit to be eaten, then spring had come, although only the latter part of February; for the spring comes
early at the South, although this was one of the earliest and
most propitious.

And if, when the spring comes, even the old man feels
his tread grown more elastic and springy, and thinks with
pleasure of his boyhood's days, and with pride of his young
manhood's prime, when his heart beat strong and his eye
burned with the fire and energy of hopes which had never
yet been blasted; if all nature becomes rejuvinated, and
the birds chirp gayly, and the trees bud forth joyously to
array themselves in their gorgeous green, and gold, and
crimson, or parti-colored attire, what must be the feelings
of the young and the innocent, who look upon Nature so
smiling in her aspect and captivating in her altered appearance, when Spring, like a delighted little goddess, seems
to be clapping her hands with merry glee at the discomfit-
ure of Old Winter, who retires, all wrinkled with frowns,
before the onward progress and *jubilante deo* songs of this
goddess of the seasons?

Ella Shelton could no more resist the influence of this
happiest of all happy springs, than could the birds refuse
to sing, or the leaves to expand, and the flowers to burst
forth and bloom in all their beauty. Although a sigh often
heaved her chest when she thought of her absent lover,
who was seldom indeed absent from her thoughts, as most

loving maidens similarly situated can testify from their own happy experience; and although whenever a thought of her poor lost brother would cross her mind, as too often, for her peace, she was thus afflicted, so that her merry laugh would end almost in a wail, and her song, though trilled never so sweetly, would die away into the low and mournful notes of the turtle-dove that has lost its mate, yet still she laughed, and still she sung, and moved as a humming-bird from shrub to flower; and with industry and energy unabated by her secret sorrows or her altered fortunes, she planted and arranged her garden with all the tasteful care of a Turkish lady adorning with elegance her boudoir for the reception of her absent lord.

Who could have supposed that in so short a time so much could have been accomplished? Who could have recognized the new home of Colonel Shelton, which, under the hand of tasteful and ingenious females, presented an appearance so pleasing and so different from the dingy and cheerless aspect which it formerly wore? If Colonel Shelton never once thought of the contrast, but only grieved for his lost son, and if Mrs. Shelton was resigned to her lot, Ella Shelton clapped her hands and exclaimed with joy, that it was indeed "a love of a cottage!" and she had a thousand times rather live in it than to dwell in the great old house, which was so lonely, unless crowded always with guests.

The jessamines were blooming, and the air was loaded with their perfumes, and filled with the fragrance of the wood-bine, when one day of the first week of March, Ella determined to go out into the woods to gather some of those native flowers to adorn her large flower-vases and decorate the mantle, as did the ancient Teutons their family altars. Fanny went with her, and they had strolled some distance from the house, when suddenly they discovered, among the thick bushes, a little boy and a girl, about fourteen or fifteen, culling flowers also. They were clad in plain homespun, but Ella thought she had never looked upon a face so beau-

5*

tiful and so angelic in its expression, as seemed to her then
the face and features of that rustic girl. She went close up
to her and saluted her kindly; but when her little brother
took her hand in his and guided it forward until she could
feel the hand of the stranger, Ella Shelton's eyes became
suffused with tears, for she saw that she was blind. But
although the poor blind girl could not see those tears of
pity, she knew, by the tones of her voice as they trembled
upon her ears, and the tender pressure of her soft hand, that
she had found a friend—that Ella Shelton was a high-born,
but a kind-hearted lady.

"What is your name, my poor girl?" said Ella, with a
tremulous voice, whose tones evinced the tenderest sympathies.

"Fetie," was the simple and natural reply.

"Fetie! what a sweet little name!" exclaimed Ella, with
delight.   .

"Do you think so? and what is your name, if I may be
so bold?" asked Fetie, in return.

"Ella; Ella Shelton."

"Ella! how sweet that name sounds to my ear! Do let
me feel your face with my hand; I will not hurt you, ma'am?"
said Fetie, reaching forth a very small and plump, but sun-
browned hand.

"Certainly, my dear," said Ella, with a musical laugh;
for she smiled within at the thought of being hurt or injured
in any way by that little hand.

Slowly and carefully did Fetie pass her hand over the face
and features of Ella Shelton. She touched her forehead
with her fingers, and then she touched her glossy hair, which
she could not see glistening in the sun. She was not only
satisfied with her examination, but delighted, for she exclaimed, with rapture:

"O, how very beautiful you are! you are even more
beautiful than my little pet lamb, who died this winter."

"I am not half so beautiful as you are, my dear; nor

half so sweet and good as you must be, with that sweet little
name, Fetie. Surely one who answers to that name must
be good, and lovely, and kind," Ella Shelton replied, in
sincere, heartfelt admiration. "How far do you live from
here?" she then asked, turning her eyes upon the little boy,
who replied:

"About a mile, miss; and about a mile and a half from
Colonel Shelton's."

"Indeed! so near?" said Ella, delighted that she had
come across one to whom she could be useful, and who might
prove an interesting companion in her solitude. "Well,
good-by, Fetie," and she kissed the ruddy lips of the
peasant girl, and then said, in earnest, affectionate tones:
"Be sure, now, that you come to see me; I shall look for
you very soon, and shall think that you can't love me if you
do not come."

"O, I shall be so glad to come," said Fetie, and she
sought Ella's hand again, which she attempted to kiss, but
Ella said:

"Nay, nay!" with a merry laugh, "you shall not kiss
my hand, dear, you shall kiss my lips. There, now; good-
by, and come very soon."

Such was the first accidental interview between the high-
born and accomplished Ella Shelton and the humble blind
girl. The acquaintance thus began was destined to ripen
into an intimacy and an attachment which would prove as
deathless as their own immortal spirits.

Fetie did not wait for another invitation, for the very next
day she came, accompanied by her little brother, who went
everywhere with her, holding his poor blind sister by the
hand.

"I am so glad you have come," said Ella, joyously, who
was then in her flower-garden, with a garden-hoe in her
hand, and which she had been employing vigorously, until
her cheeks grew red and fairly tinged with the hot blood
which rushed to her face and made her look so lovely, like

a fairy princess training her flowers. Poor Fetie could not see her new friend's face, but her heart leaped with joy at the sound of her musical voice. Ella took her by the hand and led her into the parlor, and, after sitting a few moments, asked her if she would like to hear the piano.

"O, yes! so much!" replied Fetie, "I have never heard anything in all my life but the fiddle very harshly played."

Ella sat down to the piano and played several very pretty tunes upon that instrument, to which Fetie listened with delight. But when Ella went from the piano to the harp, and touched lightly at first, and then, with a gradual swell, causing the strings of that harp, which seemed to feel and understand her touch, to fill the room and the very air with sweet sounds, dying away in the distance, and then coming back again like music approaching from afar, Fetie rose up from her seat with a countenance and a look as if completely entranced, and making a few steps forward, held out her hands as to grasp some invisible and heavenly spirit flying toward her through the air. It was the most eloquent tribute which had ever been paid to the skill, seldom equaled, but never surpassed, of Ella Shelton. She felt and appreciated the compliment, because it was one which had been paid by nature herself. She was grateful that she had been able to make a poor blind girl happy; and in her heart she blessed her father and mother, who had so often urged and encouraged her to persevere, when, in her earlier attempts, she was almost ready to abandon in despair her efforts to become proficient and skillful in the use of the harp.

"You love, then, the sound of this, to me, sweetest of all instruments," said Ella, rather as an affirmation of a truth than as an inquiry.

"O, yes!" said Fetie, almost in a whisper, as if afraid lest her own voice should interrupt the sweet sounds which were still lingering in her memory. Then she walked across the room, and went to where Ella was standing by the side

of her beautifully carved and gilded harp. Ella held forth
her hand and led her gently toward the instrument, as she
would a little child who is just beginning to walk. She
guided Fetic's hand to the strings of the harp, and bade her
touch them with her fingers. The blind girl started at the
sound of the strings as her hand touched them, and she
trembled as though she had heard a mysterious voice spoken
suddenly in her ear. But it was not with fear. It was rather
a thrill of delight; the tingling sensation which one experiences when he first becomes conscious of and compre-
hends the poetry of music. It was innate genius, which had
lain dormant, till then undeveloped, and was just beginning
to burst from its chrysalis shell.

Fetic touched the harp-strings again and again, and every
time with increased pleasure, and, as if by intuition, sweet
sounds were produced all in harmonious accord, until they
assumed a regular form, and became, in reality, a sweet accompaniment to a song.

"Bravo!" cried Ella Shelton, clapping her hands with
unfeigned delight. "You have a wonderful talent for music,
for, without knowing it, you have improvised a beautiful little
accompaniment. What a pity we couldn't find words
apropos to the air, for I am sure you must have a sweet
voice."

The tears were in Fetic's eyes, and she did not seem to
hear or understand what Ella had been saying. Her face
was turned upward, and the veins upon her temples became
bluer, and swelled larger and larger, as the poetic fires of
her nature became kindled within her soul. She seemed
utterly lost to surrounding objects, and in so rapt a state
as to forget that she had a listener; and, in a sweet, plaintive
voice, she sang these impromptu words:

> I love the flowers—the lovely flowers;
> How dear they are to me!
> But though their odors are so sweet,
> The flowers I can not see!

For though they have a thousand hues—
    So bright, so rich, and free,
Their varied hues I can not tell—
    I'm blind from infancy!

And there's the sun! the glorious sun!
    The silv'ry stars and moon!
I'm told they are resplendent orbs—
    To man, God's mightiest boon;
But though so bright and beautiful
    To you they seem to be,
To me their brightness is but gloom;
    O! dark they are to me!

And there's the pine! the tall old pine!
    How grand it must appear!
With lofty head, reared high above,
    To drink in heaven's sweet air!
I hear the tree-top's plaintive moans;
    They sound so sad to me!
Like an imprison'd giant's groans,
    Who's struggling to be free.

I've heard old ocean's angry roar,
    As on the beach I've stood,
But though its waves are white with foam,
    They're dark to me as blood!
And there's the bright and silv'ry stream
    That glides on to the sea;
Though like a glass to you it seem,
    O! dark it is to me!

But there's a clime—a glorious clime!
    Its ether's clear and bright!
Far brighter suns and stars are there,
    And there I'll have my sight!
O! happy time! O! joyous day!
    So happy shall I be!
The dumb shall speak where Jesus reigns!
    The blind—*the blind shall see!*

When Fetic had ended her song, which was the impromptu
outpouring of her pure spirit, she leaned her head against
the harp and wept most passionately. Ella, whose heart
was full, and from whose eyes ran a continuous stream of
tears, went up to where poor Fetic stood weeping, and placing her arm around her neck, she fondly drew her head
upon her bosom and pillowed it there, as a kind mother
would her almost orphan child, who is weeping for its dead

father. She spoke not a word, but her action, so simply performed, was eloquence itself. It was understood by poor Fetie, who, from that moment, knew that in her new friend she had not only found a benefactress, but a sister also. She leaned her head heavily against Ella's bosom, and listened long and breathlessly to the steady throbbings of her heart, as though she wished to learn the language of its beatings. When she looked up in Ella's face, she smiled a sweet, happy smile, and seemed to feel that she had learned its dialect—at least, had mastered its alphabet; and she felt assured that every character written upon the pure tablets of that heart was love, all love; not an unkind thought or desire toward man, or woman, or child. No other spirit than the purest and most unalloyed feeling of philanthropy beat in that virgin heart of innocence and love.

Ella looked down into Fetie's eyes and smiled, and Fetie smiled also. There must have been something like mesmerism—a magnetic power in the voiceless smile of Ella Shelton; for Fetie could not see nor hear a smile; for Ella Shelton looked intently into the blind girl's eyes, and as far down as she looked, she could see no light there. All was darkness and night in those windows of the soul, which seemed to have been closed up in early infancy by the hand of a beneficent God, that her pure spirit might remain pure and unshocked by looking upon the deformities of earth. But if she saw neither the beauties of nature, nor the scars and cicatrices with which all nature has been disfigured by sin, there were other senses through which she both saw and felt, perhaps in modified, perhaps in a grander degree, the grandeur of the universe, and the infinite glory of God. She was stone-blind, it is true, but she could both see and feel what the atheist, with all his senses unimpaired, and with all his boastful ignorance, could not discover—that there is a God everywhere, and that his name is Love.

CHAPTER VIII.

THUS passed the months of March and April, and when May came it was still the same with Fetie and Ella, for they were nearly every day together, seated in the parlor, or walking with their arms around each other's waist, as a couple of twin sisters. Fetie, poor blind Fetie, had become quite a proficient upon the harp, which she played very sweetly, although, of course, altogether by air; and she could accompany Ella while she played several of those sweet airs, such as "Blue-Eyed Mary" and "Annie Laurie," which were then so popular throughout the country, and deservedly so, for they are sweet airs still; but sweetest of all the airs they sung was that sweetest of sweet songs—

> "Rock of ages, cleft for me,
> Let me hide myself in thee."

But often was it the case that Fetie became in a moment filled with rhapsody while seated at the harp, and forgetting that there was any one within hearing of her voice, she would pour out her soul's deep inspirations in poetry and song; improvising as sweetly as Corinne used to do before her friends and admirers at Rome.

It was at such a time that she sung and played a very plaintive little air, so soft and low that it drew tears from Ella's eyes, and made even Mrs. Shelton and the old Colonel himself come softly to the door to listen and to shed tears in silent sympathy.   The tune was plaintive, as all her music was, and well adapted to the following words:

> My sister dear is dead!
>   And her sweet face I 'll ne'er behold!
> Nor shall I touch again that head
>   Where clustered curls of brightest gold ;
> Nor e'er again that noble brow
> That 's cold and hard as marble now !
>
> My sister dear is dead !
>   And ere she died, a dream she dreamed —
> That angels hovered round her bed,
>   And beautiful and fair they seemed ;
> Whose white wings fanned and cooled her brow ;
> Whose voices whispered music low.
>
> My sister dear is dead !
>   But though on ivory and in gold
> I see her still, her spirit 's fled !
>   Her smile 's not there ! her lips are cold !
> And though her eyes look kind on me,
> I hear no voice ! no smile for me !
>
> My sister dear is dead !
>   How fair and beautiful was she !
> And though from earth her spirit 's fled,
>   Her memory still is dear to me.
> In heaven, O ! let me meet thee there
> In heaven I 'll see thee, sister dear !

When she had finished her song she pulled out from her bosom a small piece of ivory about two inches square, around whose edges was a narrow rim of gold.   She passed the ends of her fingers over its surface, and then pressed it affectionately to her lips.   Ella went up and looked upon it with admiration.   It was a portrait, most admirably painted, of a beautiful child about five or six years old.   There was a bright, black eye beneath a snow-white forehead of peculiar shape and beauty, and upon her temples, and down her shoulders, hung sweet little curls of purest golden hue, while her cheeks were roseate with health and young life.   Her eye seemed to flash with intelligence, and her lips to move with a smile, as the light played upon the polished surface of the ivory when its position was changed by any motion of the hand which held it. It was, indeed, a transcendently lovely image, and never had a goddess or an infant Madonna been painted with a more lovely countenance, or in more fascinating colors. It had been the work of a poor, dissipated, but once celebrated artist, who had been knocked about from pillar to post, and was sometimes even compelled to beg his daily bread. Driven from the city by the pangs of hunger and the terrors of a sheriff armed with a writ against him, he had taken refuge in the country, and had stopped one night at the house where lived the parents of Fetie and her little sister. Although very poor, and utterly destitute of money, he had an independent spirit, and, when he was able, returned a favor with all the generosity and liberality of a prince.

Although little Annie's portrait would much more than pay for a week's, or even a month's lodging, he determined, with the consent of her mother, to take her likeness. In doing this, he succeeded most admirably, and to the wonder and delight of the family, not excepting even poor, blind Fetie, who passed her fingers—which were her only substitute for sight—over the portrait of her little sister, and then again over her sister Annie's face, just as we would do when looking first upon the likeness and then upon the original to compare them, until she became thoroughly satisfied that it was, indeed, a very representative of her dearly best-beloved little sister, Annie. But, O, how she loved that picture, and held it ever pressed close to her heart after little Annie died; for she sickened a little while afterward, and died that very summer; and her ignorant and conceited father said a great many harsh things about the man who had painted the picture, and declared that if he could only get hold of the villain, he would break every bone in his body, for he believed, in his heart, that the rascal had "cast the evil eye" upon his child. But little Annie's mother and Fetie also knew that it was God who had taken her home, for he wanted another angel in heaven, and had prepared a little stool upon which she could sit and sing, and listen to the seraphim and cherubim playing upon their golden harps and silver lutes, all set with priceless, glittering jewels.

"Your little sister must have been a lovely creature, indeed," said Ella, as she returned the ivory portrait; and wishing to distract Fetic's thoughts from the melancholy channel into which they had turned, she said, gayly : "But wait here, Fetic, till I return ; I have something to show you which will both please and surprise you very much."

She ran into Lucy's house and brought her little baby, which was then just a month old, carefully wrapped up in a shawl. It was with much persuasion that Ella could induce Lucy to let her bring the little baby into the open air ; for, as all young mothers, she was very precious of her little charge, and disliked to see it out of her sight for a single moment. However, to oblige " dear, good Miss Ella, whom she could scarcely refuse anything in this world"—the little thing, who, by Ella's own request, and the secret desire of both the mother and father, was named Ella, "little Ella" after " Miss Ella"—was now borne away very carefully indeed, and very tenderly, in the arms of its mistress. She held up the little infant before Fetic, and bade her guess whose child it was.

"Can you tell what kind of features it has, and what is the color of its skin ? "

Fetic passed her hand slowly and very gently over the child's face, touching every part of it with the tips of her fingers, until she seemed satisfied with her examination, and then she exclaimed, with rapture :

"O, how beautiful! I have never seen a more beautiful, never half so beautiful a mulatto as this!"

Fetic always spoke of her *seeing* an object as though she possessed in reality the sense of sight in all its perfection. But she *saw*, nevertheless, with her fingers, which were the only eyes the blind girl had.

" You say but the truth, Fetic ; it is, indeed, a little angel,"

and the beautiful and accomplished Ella Shelton pressed hei
coral lips to the soft cheek of little Ella, who was her slave.

Nor was she at all ashamed of her act, for she held it up
to Fetie, who kissed it also; and then they chirped to the
little babe, and snapped their fingers until it smiled and
cooed in return for the playful notice which had been taken
of it.

One who has not been reared at the South can hardly
understand a scene like this; and a very refined and elegant
lady in the aristocratic city of Boston will, perhaps, toss her
head, and say that "Miss Ella Shelton was no better than
she should be!" But not so fast, my good lady, you, who
are, perhaps, a zealous member of an Abolition society, a
worshiper at the shrine of the antislavery god. Miss Ella
Shelton was just such a beautiful and accomplished young
lady as any; the proudest matron in the aristocratic city of
Boston would have felt proud to acknowledge as a daughter,
or a bride for her worthiest and noblest son. For, however
convenient it may be sometimes to seek an alliance whose
only object is money, there is a talismanic influence and an
"open sesame" power in an ancient and honorable name,
which destroys our prejudices and unlocks the heart at the
welcome approach of one who has moved in the same sphere
and felt the same influences as ourselves. While the snob
may be repulsed, however heavy his purse, or arrogant his
bearing, the man or woman of true refinement can not fail
to meet with a sincere and hearty reception from the truly
refined and intelligent.

Ella Shelton was just such a young lady as would have
felt at home, and been welcomed with cordiality and affection among the most ancient and honorable of the nobility
of England or France. She was a "bright, particular star,"
whose effulgence would be conspicuous in sunshine and
splendor, as well as in darkness and gloom. She was a lovely
flower, whose fragrance would have filled with sweetness the
gay halls and gilded saloons of fashion, as well as the humble

home, or even the " desert air." Let not then the lordly, or the purse-proud turn away with contempt, and refuse to look upon her portrait, because it is drawn too faithfully, and in colors too fast and true; for her likeness may be found in more places than one in our Southern States, and, perhaps, also, in the homes of the truly benevolent, and intelligent, and refined of the North and of England.

The summer of 1825 was spent by Ella Shelton chiefly in the company and companionship of the blind girl, Fetie, whose attachment grew stronger and stronger for her new friend, who took peculiar pride and pleasure in dressing her up in clothes of the finest texture, such as she wore herself, and which she cut and made chiefly with her own hands, often rejecting the proffered aid of Fanny. Often it was the case that Fetie remained at the house of Colonel Shelton, not only all night, but even for whole weeks at a time, in the constant companionship and society of the kind-hearted Ella, who urged her to remain. They passed their time not only at the harp and the piano, but in many other ways interesting to young ladies only. But, perhaps their greatest pleasure consisted in playing with Lucy's little baby, who had grown and fattened until its cheeks had become dimpled, and its eyes sparkled, and its infant laugh grew louder and more laughter-provoking. Then, how merry grew Ella Shelton, and how she clapped her hands with glee when she witnessed the happiness of Fetie, and saw her *feeling* for the smile which played around the dimpled mouth and cheeks of little Ella; for the eyes of the blind girl seemed to be in her fingers.

But the summer passed on, and the autumn came, and then little Ella began to sicken, and to fade slowly away; and Ella began to be very sorrowful, and to upbraid herself, and to imagine that in some way or other she herself may have been the unintentional and innocent cause of the child's sickness. If the father grew anxious, and the mother seemed grieved, Ella Shelton seemed yet more distressed at the gloomy prospect of losing her little pet, and seeing it laid away in the cold grave. A skillful physician was called in, but although he visited the little sufferer day after day, it was not with hope, for it was "only to oblige that dear young lady, the daughter of old Colonel Shelton."

In vain were his remedies, for the little patient was born with incipient tubercles in its lungs, and consumption had laid its withering hand upon its victim from the very cradle, or, perhaps, when, in embryo, it lay in its mother's womb. O! how Ella Shelton clasped her hands in agony, and how the tears streamed down her cheeks, when she looked upon the wan face of the little sufferer lying in its cradle, and saw that its wanness was every day increasing. And when the babe opened its eyes—those bright eyes of crystalline brightness—and held out its little hands toward its mistress, how tenderly she lifted it in her arms, as if afraid lest she might extinguish the little light which seemed to be flickering in its socket.

When little Ella seemed vigorous and hearty, and before the deceitful worm, which had lain still for a few months only, had begun to eat out the heart's core and consume the young life of its helpless victim, then Ella Shelton used to jerk out the babe from its cradle, and romp so with it that Lucy, its mother, and Old Rinah, its grandmother, would not only be frightened, but would scold away at their young mistress, and sometimes, in their apprehension, take it from her arms, lest the child might be injured by too much romping.

But now Ella Shelton would raise her little namesake as tenderly as one would handle a piece of frost-work in glass, or a tiny vase of the most delicate wax-flowers. October came, and as *teething*—which is often itself alone fatal to the young life of the infant—began to add its weakening influence to the consuming power of consumption, little Ella, instead of growing stronger, grew weaker and weaker every day. And, O! how Ella Shelton wished now that she had embraced the opportunity and improved the time she once had of becoming not only a landscape, but a portrait painter also. Had she done this, she might have been able to transfer upon canvas the features of the little sufferer, who became dearer and dearer to her as it every day approached nearer and nearer the brink of the grave, just as the little child hugs closer to its breast the little pet lamb that is now dead, and will open its eyes never more.

There were no daguerreotypes those days, nor was ambrotyping yet discovered. Painting in water or oil colors, upon canvas or ivory, with the pencil or the brush, were the only means employed—or, at least, in general use—for preserving the images of those whose features we wished to retain after the dear original was dead and gone to its long home.

The idea of having a likeness taken of "little Ella" so filled the mind and heart of Ella Shelton, that she could think of nothing else. The one thought pervaded her entire being, and kept her often awake for many long hours. She took up her pencil and brush, and, spreading a piece of canvas upon a little easel, sat down to her self-imposed task of transferring, upon oil-cloth, as faithful a transcript of little Ella's features as her unpracticed hand could execute. But, although it was a labor of love, and although the outlines and even expression of the little dusky face would have satisfied one less fastidious or less a connoisseur, she tore up the canvas in disgust, and flung the strips into the fire; nor could she be convinced that any but an acknowledged master, or professed artist, could do justice to that bright, transparent eye of the little spirit who had already begun to rustle and flutter its wings, as if trying the strength of its pinions before it should take its heavenward flight—its long journey to the spirit-land.

Persisting in the declaration, although her mother thought otherwise, that all her efforts to paint the portrait of little Ella amounted to nothing more than "*a mere daub*," she

began to think of the possibility of inducing an artist to
undertake the journey from Charleston or Savannah, for
the purpose of accomplishing a work which she herself had
abandoned in despair. She spoke to her mother upon the
subject; timidly at first, and then with urgent entreaty that
her wish should be gratified. Mrs. Shelton smoothed back
her daughter's hair upon her lofty, snow-white forehead,
and sighed when she said :

"Willingly, my child, would I gratify your very natural
desire to preserve the image of our little Ella, who seems
to have been loaned us for a little while only, to teach us
another lesson of humility and resignation to His mysterious
will. But, my dear child, we are unable to do this thing.
Had your father still the means that he once had to
gratify his beloved daughter, he would send anywhere—
to Europe if necessary—sooner than your slightest wish
should remain ungratified. But your father is no longer
wealthy "——

"My dear mother, you misunderstand me altogether. I
am well aware that my father is poor now, and I would not,
for the world, give my poor, broken-hearted father pain by
causing him in any way to remember his former wealth,
which he so lately had and used so worthily, nor recall to
mind his present poverty. No, no; it is not to you or my
father that I would apply in this matter. I only desire that
you would permit Old Daddy Toney, or his son George, to
go down to Charleston or Savannah, with the carriage or the
gig, and bring, as fast as he can, an artist who could paint
little Ella well, and who would be satisfied with the sum
of fifty dollars for the time and labor necessary to be employed in taking the likeness of Lucy's little infant. Do
you think, mother, it would be done for fifty dollars—just
a small portrait?"

"Yes, my child, I have no doubt that some poor, or rather,
I should have said, some kind artist would undertake the
journey, if he could be assured of his pay," replied Mrs.

Shelton, with a smile of wonder, as she still smoothed back her daughter's glossy ringlets.

"Well, then, mother," said Ella Shelton, joyously, "it is a *fait accomplis!* for I have still fifty dollars left of my last year's allowance, and can find no better use for it than this. Do, mother, speak to father about it, and get him to send to Charleston, and, O! I shall be so glad and so thankful!"

Mrs. Shelton could not resist the entreaties of her daughter any more than Colonel Shelton, had she gone to him in the first instance; but, although Ella would have preferred sending to Charleston for an artist, that Old Toney might be enabled to tell her, on his return, that he had seen Herbert, with his own eyes, and, perhaps, be the bearer of a letter from her lover, yet it was determined, in family conclave, to send down to Savannah, and request Mr. Hartwell to procure the services of an artist who would be willing to encounter the fatigues of a journey of nearly a hundred miles for the sum of fifty dollars. Colonel Shelton himself wrote the letter to his friend, Mr. Hartwell, in his usual plain, straightforward way; but Ella wrote another, which she slipped into her father's package. It was a very small note, written in a very delicate Italian hand, and sealed with sealing-wax upon which was stamped a very pretty device; for this was the almost universal style in those days, before envelopes were bought and sold, and, as now, sealed with paste or gum arabic. This little note was slyly slipped into Colonel Shelton's large, man-like, soldier-looking letter, which resembled somewhat, in size and shape, the dispatches he used to send the commander-in-chief, or those which he sometimes received from the war-office.

Ella Shelton's note contained but few lines, but they expressed sufficiently strong her anxiety to that benevolent-hearted gentleman of the old school, Mr. Hartwell, who, although he had seen her but a few times since her childhood, regarded her with most affectionate interest. And was not his interest hightened by the dark mystery which

6

still hung about the fate of poor Langdon, whose body had never been recovered, if, indeed, he had been murdered at all? "Poor Langdon," he often thought; "what has become of him? If he has indeed been murdered, as I verily believe he has, who is his murderer? and where has he concealed his body!"

Mr. Hartwell sighed when he read Colonel Shelton's letter; and then he sighed again when he read Miss Ella's note. For, a little while ago, he knew that Colonel Shelton would have prescribed no limits to his commands, and would have simply given an emphatic order for the transportation of the most celebrated artist in the city, with as little delay as if he were a bale of merchandise. With him *once*, the price, the *cost*, would never have been considered a single moment. But when Mr. Hartwell read these simple lines, and comprehended their child-like earnestness—"Do, Mr. Hartwell, make the dear, good man, whoever he may be, come immediately, before little Ella dies ; and if he won't come for fifty dollars, I have jewelry and diamonds which I do not wear now, but keep shut up in a private drawer ; tell him that I will give him all these sooner than he shouldn't come"—when Mr. Hartwell read these lines, and appreciated the deep and abiding affection of the young lady for her little slave pining away and dying fast, the good old man not only sighed again more deeply, but the tears rolled down his wrinkled cheeks and fell upon the page; and he exclaimed aloud, "God bless the noble-minded girl ! At any cost to me, her wishes shall be obeyed, but not a ring of hers shall be sacrificed."

There was an artist in the city of Savannah, in the year 1824, who was then, as afterward, justly celebrated as a portrait painter. But the time was coming when daguerreotypes and ambrotypes would usurp the place of portrait painting, and tin-plates and window-glass would supersede the ancient and time-honored canvas upon which a Raphael or an Angelo had spoken with the brush of genius. *Then* none but an *artist*, who felt at least some of the fires of genius in his soul, could make the canvas breathe, and look, and almost speak, as the living soul. *Now*, any clod-hopper or wood-cutter can lay down his axe, or give up the plow, and become, in a month's practice, " *a first-rate artist;*" who will boast, as he rubs on a little red vermilion, or white lead, or lamp-black, "that he knows all about painting in all sorts of colors, from white-washing down to the Grecian, or even Oriental, painting."

When daguerreotypes came into use, poor L—— had to give up portrait painting or starve; for who would give fifty or a hundred dollars for a portrait when he could have a daguerreotype for five or ten dollars? And although he had to resort to the new art in self-defense, the time came afterward when the little Frenchman had to lay away his brushes altogether; and folding up his canvas, to be painted on no more, he was laid away himself in the grave.

Old Toney had not been the messenger selected by Colonel Shelton to take the gig down to Savannah for the portrait painter, Mr. L——; for the Colonel well knew the repugnance which the old man would have to going upon such a journey to a city which had disgraced and degraded him by an unjust imprisonment in its jail. The kind master and friend was unwilling to awake sad reminiscences in the mind of his slave. George, therefore, was the individual to whom was intrusted the execution of the mission; and to him Miss Shelton appealed, that if he loved her at all, he would make all possible haste in returning with the artist from Savannah.

Up to this time, and for a good while afterward, George had been a faithful and a trustworthy boy; and the least wish of his young mistress, or her parents, expressed or implied, would impel him to unusual energy and activity for the accomplishment of their designs, or the fulfillment of their desires. He made no delay, therefore—no dilly-dallying upon the road; but went and came with the haste and anxiety of the man who goes for the doctor, and is afraid that the messenger of death may arrive before the physician reaches the patient.

Mr. L—— was a kind-hearted little Frenchman, and, as most little men, and especially little Frenchmen, usually are, he was nervous and fidgety, and believed in going to work at once and without delay, whenever he had anything to do. No sooner had the case been stated to him by Mr. Hartwell, than he immediately laid aside his brush and the work upon which he was engaged, and packing everything necessary into a small trunk, he crossed the Savannah river that very day at Union Ferry, and, entering the gig *sans cere-monie*, ordered George to drive on.

"Allez, mon garçon ; allez avec dépêche et avec vitesse. Mademoiselle Shelton is anxious vere mooch for un' petite portrait of von petite négresse."

No sooner had little Monsieur L—— arrived at the house of Colonel Shelton, and had been made to feel comfortable and at home by a good, substantial dinner, which he had washed down with a few tumblers of pure old claret, than he turned toward Miss Shelton, and bowing as only a little Frenchman can bow, and rubbing his hands as only a little Frenchman can, he said, in his usual style of half French, half English :

"Mademoiselle Shelton, veuillez à donner moi l'opportunité to see la petite négresse ?   Je me flatte mongself dat I will finish de portrait in one leetle while, and dat you shall receive satisfaction complete et parfaite."

"I have no doubt of your ability, monsieur," replied Ella, with a courtesy; "and as regards your dispatch, I can assure you that all of it is necessary.   Make ready, sir, all your necessary preparations in my father's library, which he has offered me for the purpose, and I will have the little sufferer brought in from my chamber ; for she sleeps there now, where we can all better nurse it and attend to its wants."

"Je n'ai pas objection to do de work anywhere. Je n'ai pas

honte, mademoiselle, to paint la petite négresse in your room ou in dis library. Je suis, I am parfaitement agreeable to work anywhere Mademoiselle Shelton may t'ink proper to direct."

Ella was already out of hearing of Mr. L——'s innocent, but offensive remark; and in a few moments afterward had the child brought, in its little mahogany cradle, which was carefully, and, by Ella Shelton's directions, very gently set down in the middle of the library. It was an ancient but richly-carved piece of furniture, which had been kept as an heir-loom in the family. In it Colonel Shelton's own wife had been rocked, in the stormy days of the Revolution, by Ella's maternal grandmother, and Mrs. Shelton had cradled her children in it also. But now that she needed it no more, and had become herself a venerable matron, it was appropriated to the use of little Ella.

When Mr. L—— saw the little patient, he was in perfect ecstasy; and the more attentively he examined her features, and looked into those peculiarly bright, metallic, lustrous eyes, which had now opened, and were looking steadily into his, the more ecstatic he became; and when a Frenchman becomes surcharged with ecstasy, he is a very ecstatic individual indeed.

"Eh, mon Dieu!" exclaimed Mr. L——, clasping his hands together, and raising his eyes upward; "dis petite négresse will make one ver' grand portrait. La beauté! L'esprit céleste! Quels yeux! (what eyes!) De eyes! de eyes! how can I paint les yeux angelique! Dey are de beauty-spot, Mademoiselle Shelton."

Ella assured him that it was chiefly for this that she had sent for him; for while she had herself succeeded in painting a very good representation of little Ella's features, she utterly failed to represent anything like the expression and peculiar brightness of those brightest of all eyes that she had ever looked upon, and which seemed to grow brighter, and become more crystalline or metallic every day.

"It is the eye, monsieur, as well as the features which

I wish you so particularly to represent upon canvas; for, to me it seems not only the brightest, but the most intelligent eye that I ever saw in an infant's head."

"Ver' true, mademoiselle. Les yeux sont intelligentes. Dey are très, ver' luminous. Les yeux sont brilliant as de diamond. 'De même que le soleil brille sur la terre, de même la petite ange brillera dans les cieux.'"

"I thank you kindly, monsieur," said Ella, while tears sprung to her eyes and rolled down her cheeks. "I thank you kindly for that timely quotation, I believe from Fénélon, which, when translated into plain English, would be, 'As the sun shines upon the earth, so also will the little angel shine in heaven.'"

"Vous comprenez parfaitement my meaning, mademoiselle. I t'ank you très beaucoup, mademoiselle, for translate de words à l'anglais. But mademoiselle make one leetle mistake. Dey are not de words of Fénélon, but l'Académie."

Poor L—— labored hard and faithfully to transfer to the canvas those brilliant orbs, whose light seemed already beginning to go out, and grow dimmer and paler every moment, as the light of the glow-worm pales before the rising sun. In vain did the artist strive to do a work which no human skill could execute. God's infinite skill alone had drawn those features and painted those eyes, and there was no paint on earth which could rival the tints of the Eternal Artist; no brush fine enough to portray those eyes through which the intelligent soul of the infant seemed looking out upon God's earth, for a little while only, before it should gaze forever upon the glories of heaven. And even now, as the artist dipped his brush into his paint, and brushed away rapidly upon the canvas, the infant spirit was unfolding its wings for its heavenward flight.

Ella had stepped to the window, and was looking out into the flower-garden, when Mr. L—— turned his eyes again upon the child, and, thinking that he perceived a new and singular expression in little Ella's features, exclaimed, hurriedly:

"Eh, mon Dieu! Mademoiselle Shelton! voilà la petite ange!"*

Ella ran to the cradle, and kneeling down, she took the hand of her little namesake very gently in hers. The babe smiled as it looked, for the last time, into the eyes of its mistress, and then, rolling upward those bright orbs which the artist would never more have an opportunity to paint while the soul—the immortal soul—was looking out of them, she turned her head from side to side for a few moments, and several times flung upward her little hands, as if bidding adieu to her mistress and the world, or impatient to be gone.

Ella raised her head and looked up at Mr. L——. The little man's eyes were full of tears, and his cheeks were wet with weeping. She felt not only grateful to him for his tenderness and sympathy, but thankful to God that he had made the heart of man so tender and kind. She spoke to him in a low voice, and bade him go call the child's mother and the rest of the family; for, at such a moment, she did not think it proper to stand upon ceremonies, or confine herself to the rules of etiquette. Indeed, how could she herself leave her pet when in the very agonies of death? For these signs, as gentle as they were—that tossing of the head from side to side, and those upliftings of the little hands—were none other than those agonies which all human nature must endure, when the spirit is about to leave the body, and the clayey tenement is tumbling in. If little Ella had been a strong adult, or had her constitution never been undermined by disease, she would have been convulsed, perhaps, by hard spasms, whose excruciating tortures would have wrung from her lips suppressed shrieks and agonizing cries of pain. But, as it was, she only tossed her hands into the air a few times, and turned her head from side to side upon the pillow, and then she was still. The spirit had flashed from those bright eyes and left them dull and dark

* See the little angel.

and glazed in death. When the child was dead, Mons. L——, with a sad smile, quoted from. Delille those beautiful words,

> "Voyez ce papillon échappé du tombeau ;
> Sa mort fut un sommeil, et sa tombe un berceau."
> "See that butterfly escaped from the tomb!
> Its death was slumber, and its tomb a cradle."

"So appropriate, Mademoiselle," said Mons. L——; "*Its tomb was a cradle.*"

And the kind-hearted little Frenchman would have been still more ecstatic if he had subsequently seen the little slave arranged for burial, lying in its little coffin, in a bed of flowers, like a little cupid who had gone to sleep upon a bed of roses, and had been treacherously slain in his slumber by the revengeful hand of one of his victims, or had become narcotised by some noxious flower, whose captivating appearance, and delicious, but deceitful fragrance had lulled not only to slumber, but had cheated and oppressed with the sleep of death.

The Cupid sleeping upon a bed of roses, poisoned by some narcotic flower! So looked "*little Ella*"—"*not dead*, however, *but asleep in Jesus!*"

When Mr. L—— returned with Lucy and Mr. Shelton, and before the household could assemble in the library, little Ella was in heaven, with her head pillowed upon the great Shepherd of souls. He who had said, "Suffer little children to come unto me and forbid them not, for of such is the kingdom of heaven," had called the poor, bleating little lamb by its name, and had taken it up in his arms to carry it in his bosom.

Mr. L—— wiped his brushes carefully, and, with a sigh, placed them away. He would need them no more, at least to paint the eyes of little Ella, who was already cold and stiffening. He returned to his home the next day; but, although he had not executed the work he had come to do, and had failed to paint those eyes, even as he had predicted from the first, when he had, with lofty expression and solemn tones, said, as he pointed upward with his hand, "De même que le soleil brille sur la terre, de même la petite ange brillera dans les cieux," still Ella Shelton *would* thrust into his hand the fifty dollar bill, just the same as if he had completed his work to her entire satisfaction.

"Non, mademoiselle! Je ne suis pas one rascaile! non, non. Je n'ai pas—I have not—no artist *could* paint les yeux de la petite ange. I can not—did not earn de l'argent." But notwithstanding the reluctance of Mons. L—— to receive the proffered fee of Ella Shelton, he consented, at length, to accept, as a gift, "one leetle petit memento," a sum of money which he could not claim as a reward for his fruitless and ineffectual labors. And as the little man shook Colonel Shelton by the hand, and bade adieu to the mourning family, his own eyes filled again with tears, when, last of all, he said farewell to Ella Shelton, and, with a tremulous voice, as he looked into her own glorious, brilliant orbs, as if apostrophising them, exclaimed, with rapture : "Quels yeux! quels yeux! (what eyes! what eyes!) Mon Dieu, mademoiselle! I am très sorrowful dat I could not paint les yeux de l'ange."

"Good-by, Mr. L——," said Ella, tearfully. "I am very sorry to have troubled you with a long and tedious journey for nothing."

"No pas apology, mademoiselle. Je suis très bien—ver' well paid for my trouble, for I have seen les yeux de la petite ange."

"Yes, monsieur, and those eyes of that little angel, as you remarked yesterday, will shine forever in heaven."

6*

CHAPTER IX.

THE day after little Ella's death the coffin was made, by a country carpenter hired for the purpose. It was a very neat little coffin, but perfectly plain, without any paint or cloth upon it. This did not suit either the taste of Ella Shelton or her mother. George was therefore sent to the store with an order for some fine white cambric or muslin. When the cambric arrived, the carpenter covered the little coffin very neatly—as neatly as though he had been born and bred an undertaker. It was lined inside and out with the white stuff, and when a little frilled pillow was placed in it, the coffin seemed more like a cradle than a gloomy, narrow cell for the dead. And to add still more to its cheerfulness, and yet to give it an appearance of half mourning, Ella Shelton dressed it very tastefully with black ribbon, which was tied in knots and bows, in a way which can only be adjusted by a woman of ingenuity and elegant taste.

Little Ella was now placed in her death's bed, and when her head lay so still upon the pillow, she seemed as if asleep, with a smile playing around her lips, which seemed to be moving every now and then, as the light and shade fell upon them, as if in her dreams she heard the whisper of angels.

Ella was kneeling down by the side of the coffin, looking, with clasped hands, at the placid features of this dead child, when Fetie entered, silently and as noiselessly as a spirit, the chamber of death. The blind girl, ever fond of flowers, had come with an armful of beautiful roses, and tulips, and jessamines. Ella had been praying when she entered, and it was not until she smelled the delightful odor and combined fragrance of the sweetest of all flowers, that she became conscious that Fetic was in the room. Ella rose from her knees and kissed Fetic upon her cheek, but her heart was too full to speak. Fetic understood the eloquence of that kiss, and the tears streamed continuously down the cheeks of the blind girl. It was the eloquence of grief and the kiss of sorrow.

Fetic had not been to Colonel Shelton's for two or three days past, and had just heard that morning of the death of little Ella. As soon as she was apprised of this sad event —sad to her also—she started off from home, with her little brother to guide her on the way, and gathered flowers as she went. When she brought them into the room, which so soon became filled with their fragrance, Ella Shelton conjectured rightly in a moment for what purpose the blind girl, who loved flowers so, had brought them. She took them from Fetic's hand, and said, "Yes, darling, we will weave a chaplet for the little angel ; at least we will decorate the house in which the angel lived, but which it has left dark and desolate." So they wove a beautiful garland of wild, and of tame flowers also, which they placed as a coronet around the brow of the dead infant ; and then they strewed flowers all around her in the coffin, and placed a white tuberose, plucked from the flower-garden—a single tuberose—in little Ella's hand. Her hands were not clasped upon the breast, as the hands of an adult, who needs to pray all his life, and whose very corpse should exhibit that same attitude of helplessness, and resignation, and dependence upon God. But little Ella herself had never committed sin, and there was no need that her hands should be clasped upon her breast. They were left unchanged, just as she died and had lain in the cradle—one hand upon the pillow, close to her cheek, and the other by her side, as it fell when she waved her adieu, for the last time, to her dear mistress and the world she was leaving. It was in that hand that Ella placed the tuberose, so white and fragrant. Little Ella seemed not dead, nor lying in a coffin, but sleeping sweetly in a bed of flowers. Surely death loses half his terrors when a corpse is thus arrayed for burial; and a graveyard is an attractive and a pleasant spot, when planted in flowers and adorned with tasteful shrubbery.

Little Ella was buried the next day behind the vegetable garden, which was back of the dwelling-house; and thither Ella Shelton repaired every day, to kneel down at the side of the little grave, and pray as she had knelt by the side of the coffin. And she planted flowers, and shrubs, and trees, and watered them with her tears. And around the grave there grew a hedge of the wild orange, which she carefully kept trimmed, as an evergreen wall around the grave, impenetrable almost to man or beast. In this evergreen wall, and at the side facing the east, she had placed a little wicker-gate, woven like a basket, with the long, supple switches of the basket-willow, and the door was fastened with a latch. Within the inclosure, and at the head of the grave, she had caused to be planted, with much care, a weeping-willow, which grew without any difficulty, and put forth, the next spring, fresh leaves; and at the foot of the grave grew a little dwarf cedar. It was a beautiful and a holy spot. Who could have imagined that one year afterward that sacred retreat would be invaded by a ruthless villain, and that Nature's sanctuary should be polluted by the unhallowed footsteps of an inhuman wretch?

But there was a new cause of distress coming upon the family of the Sheltons, which, from its magnitude, was likely to swallow up and obliterate the memory of all other subjects for sorrow and repining. Afflictions seldom come singly, but one by one, as do the merciful favors of a beneficent God. But, as in Nature the lightning's flash is seen

before the thunder's peal is heard, so also God gives us warning of his coming. And although he may seem very angry
now, yet his anger will, by-and-by, pass away, and his sun
shall smile upon the face of the cloud. " God tempers the
wind to the shorn lamb ;" and when the little shorn lamb,
stripped of all its fleece, and left in its nakedness of innocence and truth, is so pelted by the hail-stones that it lies
down upon the rugged heath, bleating for its heavenly Father, and longing to be at rest, then God comes and lifts
the dead lamb in his arms, and breathes back into its nostrils its lost life, and warms, with his infinite love, its frozen
heart, and carries it gently and forever in his bosom. Blessed
Father, O! take the shorn lambs, who are pelted by the
storms of life, and are so bruised, and battered, and broken
that they feel now that earth is no longer their home, and
that their only haven of rest is in heaven ; and the only
pillow whereon they can pillow their aching heads, and feel
so happy, because the head aches no more, and the heart
is cramped no longer with anguish, is the everlasting pillow of the gentle Jesus's breast, who says, " Come unto me,
all ye that labor, and are weary and heavy laden, and I
will give you rest."   O! " temper the winds "—those cold
and cutting winds of adversity—to the shorn lamb.   And
when the winds are too fierce to be tempered, and last too
long for this life, and the shorn lamb is forced to lie down
upon some bleak and flinty rock, where the cold rain can
pelt it, and the hard sleet drive against it most pitilessly—
where the cold is above it, and a frozen rock beneath it—
where all around is nothing but ice and snow, and the winds
are howling in rage, or whistling in derision, the dying or
the dead lamb's dirge, then, even then, O! take the dead
lamb in thy loving arms, and bear it still upon thy bosom.
The warmth of a Savior's infinite love shall thaw the frozen
limbs, and cause the dead life to live again, even as the green
bay-tree, when it is cut down, sends up its young shoots and
tender branches.

The new affliction and subject for grief which was coming upon this already deeply-afflicted family was the failing health—every day failing health—of Colonel Shelton. In less than one short year, the old soldier seemed to have grown at least ten years older. His tread was no longer firm, nor his look commanding ; for his back was bent, and his shoulders stooped, his head bowed, and his eyes were ever bent upon the ground, as though he was looking for the grave of his lost son, where he might lie down by his side and be at rest. Once he had leaned upon his sword only, with the dignity of a soldier " at rest,". and with the imperial look of a conqueror, whose hand had become wearied by his conquests ; but now he leaned heavily upon his staff, a gold-headed cane, which seemed too heavy for him, for he lifted it slowly, and dragged his feet one after the other, as if they could hardly carry him much further—not even to his own grave, which he was looking for, that he might make one last, weary step over its brink, and sink down heavily to his rest.

Poor old man ! there was a weight upon his heart as heavy as many, many pounds of lead, which was dragging him down, and sinking him under the earth as surely as a huge rock which has been tied to a dead carcass to sink it to the bottom of the channel. Once, when he was young, and his spirit was buoyant and strong as his heart was brave, he might have resisted the leaden weight, and flounced, and floundered, and floated at last upon life's current as still as a buoy which has been anchored in the channel to indicate to the life-mariner where the deep water lay. But, alas ! either the channel had washed deeper, or the cable had contracted, and its links kinked upward—that the cable had become too short, and the anchor too heavy, or the buoy too light, longer to remain floating upon the surface, and anchored to the same spot. The old man was sinking, sinking, sinking, as surely as a cork which is too light for the sinker.

Mrs. Shelton and her daughter were deeply pained at

heart, and filled with dismay, as they saw the beloved old man's knees trembling more and more every day, and his gait becoming more irregular and unsteady, as he traveled so rapidly the downward hill of life. How hard it is to move a heavy stone which stands ever almost balanced as on a pivot upon the brow of a hill or brink of a precipice. But once moved from its bed, and it has started upon its downward progress, who so rash or foolish as to stand in its way, or hope to stop it? For as it rolls downward, it gathers velocity as it rolls, with increasing ratio, until it reaches the vale below, and then it is still. So, too, with the old who have started upon the downward journey of life. No medicine can arrest their progress, which sometimes is as rapid as the flight of a bird ; or, like the stone, no one can stop their rolling until they have reached the "valley and shadow of death," and then they lie still— "as still as a stone."

What observer has watched the rapid decay of the old and venerable man, so lately seeming erect in his manly pride and vigor, without a feeling of regret that the old and the venerable are passing away. Sad thought! and doubly sad because we shall become old, also, if we die not young ; and then we shall lie at the foot of the hill where Death has hurled us with his strong hand.

But Colonel Shelton was not dying from old age, although " Time had silvered o'er " his once raven locks. He was dying daily from that fatal marasmus, not only of the muscular system, but of the heart and the brain also, which is induced by a grief which can not be subdued, a sorrow which can not be suppressed.

There is a heart-breaking which is sudden, and a heart-breaking which is slow. In either event, however, death is certain, as the heart is broken.

In vain did they seek to distract the Colonel's attention from the consideration of his secret sorrows. In vain did Mrs. Shelton strive to be cheerful, and Ella to be gay, in

order, if possible, to change the current of his thoughts, and
make him forget, even for a moment only, his dear, darling
boy, who had disappeared so mysteriously, and whose young
life had ceased so suddenly, like a gallant bark, with strong
timbers, and fresh canvas, and wide-spread sails, which has
been, all at once, swallowed up by a maëlstrom, or has toppled
over some ocean cataract. In vain were all their attempts
to make the old soldier smile as he used to do; for his
smile now was only the sad smile which for a moment
plays around the lips, but does not light up the eye of the
broken-hearted.

There was a time, however—it was in the first cold days
of December—when Colonel Shelton seemed to possess the
strength of the lion when he makes his last death-spring
upon the enemy whose arrow is quivering in his heart.

There was a man residing not very far off—but a couple
of miles from the house of Colonel Shelton—whose name
was Timothy Pollywog. He was a little man, but a great
pest to the community; for he was one of those intolerable
mischief-makers and scandal-mongers with which almost
every community is infested, in some shape or other, whether
in the form of a man, a woman; or a child. Yes, every
community has a pollywog who is ever wriggling and ever
twisting the truth into a lie. Pity it is so. But often it
is the case that there is not only one, but a great many pollywogs; and they can always be known by their tale, (tail?)
which is, "They say." As surely as you can say, "*That*
is an embryo frog, although *it has now a tail;* it is a pollywog, it is true, but it is none the less a frog." So, also, that
man or woman is a slanderer at heart, a liar and a calumniator, who invariably preface their calumnious expressions
with "They say." As the pollywog is forced to drop its
tail and become a cold and repulsive animal, pity that all
the human pollywogs could not relapse into as harmless and
quiescent a state of existence as that of the toad, or leap
into the more dignified condition of the bullfrog. Better

that their tongues should never wag, if only to engender strife and produce heart-burnings.

Mr. Pollywog was just one of those men who envies the riches or the talents and superior attainments of another, which he can never possess. Too indolent to work, his whole time was spent in going from house to house making mischief and retailing scandal. It is astonishing that one whose character was so well known should have been received so freely into their houses. But is it not true that the majority of persons love to listen to slander, although they may despise the slanderer? Indeed, when we come to examine into the subject more closely, we conclude that, as a general rule, and in most communities, the society of the tale-bearer and teller is usually courted and sought after from two separate reasons : the first, as a means of self-defense, indulging the vain hope that you yourself will be spared, or let off more easily, and your character not so badly riddled as your neighbor's by the invidious tongue of the slanderer ; and then, again, that you may be gratified a little —just a little—to hear, from the lips of the human pollywog, how very badly riddled your poor neighbor's character has been. It is only the noble and the high-minded who spurn them with contempt, and shrink from their touch as from the approach of a worm, or toad, or hideous reptile.

Now, it is natural to suppose, that for such a man as Timothy Pollywog Colonel Shelton could have no fancy, but rather a decided repugnance. While, therefore, he would receive him politely, and with his old urbanity, as even he would an unbidden guest, in his heart of hearts he despised him as a tattler and busybody in other men's affairs. Whenever Timothy Pollywog dropped in, as he sometimes did, notwithstanding the reserve with which he was treated, Colonel Shelton as often invited him to be seated, but never joined in nor participated in the conversation further than to reply in monosyllables. This, of course, invariably nettled such a narrow-minded fellow as Timothy Pollywog, who, in his heart, felt that the Colonel despised him, while he, in proportion as that contempt became more apparent, or was made more manifest by still greater silence, envied the superior dignity and learning to which he could never hope to attain.

"Good-morning, Colonel Shelton," said Timothy Pollywog, as he took the seat which the old gentleman indicated with his hand, but without attempting to rise from his seat to welcome the intruder. "Still grieving, Colonel, about your son?"

Not a muscle of the Colonel's face moved now, although at other times he would have exhibited, at least to a shrewd observer, some signs of distress.

"No, sir!" he replied, "my grief is ended, for I feel that it will not be long before I meet my boy in the spirit-land, *for I well know that my days are numbered.*"

He dropped his voice almost to a whisper when he uttered the last words, as if afraid that his wife or daughter might catch his words, and be distressed by their import. Mr. Pollywog understood him perfectly; but such was his innate love of causing pain in others, however feeble or distressed, that he drew his chair closer to the Colonel's, and placed his hand confidingly upon the arm-chair in which the old soldier was seated.

"Don't talk so, Colonel! I wouldn't think of dying, if I was you, about that young scapegrace, as *they call* him!"

"Who calls my son by such a foul title?" said Colonel Shelton, drawing himself back and looking Timothy Pollywog full in the face.

Now Mr. Pollywog was by no means a downright coward; at least, he was not afraid of an old man trembling upon the brink of the grave. But it is exceedingly improbable that he ever would have said as much on the present occasion, and with so little apprehension of the consequences, had he understood the strong character with whom he had

now to deal. Without any fear, and not feeling the scorn
with which Colonel Shelton regarded him, he coolly replied:
  "O ! *they say* "——
  " And what, sir, do *they say?*" was the question asked by
Colonel Shelton, in low, suppressed tones, while his teeth
were set hard together, giving the angle of his lower jaw
the appearance as if he were biting upon a nail, or other
hard substance, until the muscles of his face became prominent and rigid, and his eyes began to burn with their
old ferocity when kindled by the flash and smoke of
battle. "What do they say, Mr. Pollywog?" he repeated
sternly.

  "O, sir, don't be so excited! But they do say a great
deal," was the reply of Timothy Pollywog, who paused for
a while, as if waiting for Colonel Shelton to ask him what
"they" did say. `But as the old Colonel sat motionless,
without repeating his question, he made bold to add: " *They
say*, Colonel Shelton, that 't ain't at all likely that your son
was ever murdered; that it do n't look reasonable-like! For
if he had been murdered, ain't it probable that the corpse
of the young man would have turned up by this time?
Now, you see, *they say* that the buzzards have sharp eyes
and a keen scent, and they had ought to know where to
find the dead body of your son before this."

  " Well, sir, what then?"

  " Why, you see now, Colonel, the fact of the business is,
that under such circumstances, if I was *you*, and it was *my*
son what had gone off so suddenly, I would n't grieve for
him a bit; you ought n't to take on so ; for they say, that ten
chances to one, that your son has run away with the money,
and has gone to make his fortune in the West, where he
will get to be a very rich man after a while, and come back
like a good boy when he has sowed all his wild oats, and,
perhaps, at last, make his old father and mother very rich
and comfortable again in their old days. They say that he
ought to do it; and, for my part, I have no doubt in the

world, if he is a good son, that he will do it.   So just wait,
Colonel, and have patience; do n't fret so."

Old men are apt to receive impressions slowly. A thought
does not flash upon them with the vividness or suddenness
of youth; but once the impression is produced and the idea
becomes daguerreotyped upon the brain, they feel as strongly, and suffer as acutely, as do the young, whose impressions
are only quicker, though not a whit more powerful. The
young man avenges an insult the moment it is given; the
old man feels the insult slowly, gradually, and his muscles
are all the while tightening as he begins to comprehend
the nature of the indignity, or feels the smart of the blow
which has struck him.

Thus only can it be explained by any principle of physi-
ology that Colonel Shelton did not strike Timothy Pollywog to the floor, or strangle him to death in a moment of
indignation, before the contemptible fellow had half finished
the long paragraph which we have written down. For if
the old Colonel had been as he once was, young and vigorous,
and prompt in action, or even if the same words had been
addressed to him just one year before, Mr. Timothy Pollywog
would never, perhaps, have been able to have finished those
sentences, so infamous and so cruel in their insinuations. In
all probability Colonel Shelton would have knocked his
teeth down his throat, so that he would have been as much
choked in swallowing them as he ought to have been in
giving utterance to his vile slanders. But, as we remarked
before, Colonel Shelton was an old man, and he *perceived*
the insult slowly.   But as the red-hot iron hisses and smokes
until it heats the coldest water, and will create sufficient
steam to burst a boiler, however strong, or propel a locomo-
tive, however heavy, so, also, were those seething words
gradually producing their legitimate effect; and when Timothy Pollywog had finished his string of calumnies, the old
man's indignation had risen to its hight, and he became
strong as the wounded lion, who gathers up his limbs and

concentrates all his strength in one last death-spring upon
his murderous foe. His eyes opened wider and wider, until
they blazed like two fire-balls, or rather with that fixed,
electric light, which never flares nor flickers, but grows
larger and brighter. His firm and still undecayed teeth
were pressed hard against each other, as if immovably locked
by tetanus or lock-jaw, and his temporal muscles became
swollen and as rigid as stone. His face grew pale at first,
and then gradually assumed the livid hue of death. It was
only then that the muscles of his hands began to twitch,
and his fingers to move convulsively. He reached forth
his right hand and moved it slowly toward the throat of
the slanderer, and Timothy Pollywog sat motionless in front
of the Colonel, for he seemed to be spell-bound, and could
not move from his seat, upon which he sat still, as if chained
down by a strong and heavy chain.

Colonel Shelton seized the slanderer by the throat, and
clutched his wind-pipe with a vice-like grasp; his fingers
never clutched any tighter, nor did they relax their grasp
a single instant after he had placed his hand upon the
throat of his victim, whose tongue lolled out far between
his decayed tusks, and his face became red, and then blue,
while his eyes seemed ready to start from their sockets, and
to leap, in very spite, into the face of the avenger of poor
Langdon's honor—his lost son, Langdon! dishonored now
by a foul calumny!

Whether it was that Colonel Shelton became filled with
disgust at the aspect of Timothy Pollywog's face thus hid-
eously distorted, or that the name of Pollywog suggested
the cold and repulsive nature of the frog, we can not say.
The effect, however, was all the same upon the old man's
mind, whose mood had changed from hatred and revenge
into contempt and utter loathing. He withdrew his hand
as suddenly from the throat of Timothy Pollywog as a child
or a very nervous young lady would from the accidental
contact of a cold-blooded frog, or some hideous reptile.

Colonel Shelton had risen from his chair to his feet, and
as his entire being became pervaded by the intensity of his
passion, his form became erect and his mien commanding;
and as he rose up higher and straightened his curved back
straighter, Timothy Pollywog was compelled to rise up also,
until he stood on tip-toe, not by his own consent, but as
if pulled slowly and steadily upward upon a gallows. It
was when Colonel Shelton had assumed his old commanding
hight, and looked himself again, that he withdrew his hand
from Timothy's throat so suddenly and with such loathing;
and then it was that Timothy Pollywog fell heavily to the
floor, like a stone or piece of furniture thrown down from the
wall. The old Colonel did not stop to look for a single
moment upon the apparently lifeless mass, lying like a
corpse upon the floor, but mechanically took up his hat and
went forth from the room, without a stick in his hand, and
with his head erect, and his old soldier-like tread. The
power of passion, which dies away so soon in some persons of weak temperament, in his strong and resolute nature
lasted a long while, and would give him strength for some
time to come. It was like the actual cautery or red-hot
iron applied to the comatose and dying patient, which makes
him sometimes leap from the bed and stand upon his feet
even in the agonies of death.

When Timothy Pollywog fell to the floor with that dull,
heavy sound, as of a dead man who has been held up for
a while and then let go, Ella Shelton, who heard the noise
while seated in her chamber engaged in some sort of em-
broidery, started to her feet in alarm, and then stood trembling for several instants, powerless to move. The first thought
which flashed across her mind was, that her old father had
fainted and fallen from his arm-chair, and she waited with
breathless attention for a few seconds, to hear Mr. Pollywog
call for assistance. But as no words were spoken, and she
heard the firm tread of a man going out of the door—a
tread so much like her father's in the olden time—she

recovered from her terror, and ran toward the late scene of rencounter. What was her surprise, therefore, to see her father going down the steps of the front piazza without a stick in his hand, or even without holding on to the banisters! But greater still was her surprise and dismay when she reached the door of the Colonel's library, to discover Timothy Pollywog stretched at full length, with his neck swollen, and his face livid, and his tongue still protruding from his mouth. She did not shriek, nor scream out, nor faint, as some young ladies, for she was herself a heroine, and the daughter of a brave old hero. She ran to the closet and got a vial of hartshorn, and from her bureau snatched up a little square bottle of eau-de-cologne, and in doing so she called to her mother, who was then walking in the vegetable garden, to come in quickly. Mrs. Shelton knew, from the tone of her voice, that something serious and very alarming had occurred, and love imparted to her limbs unusual strength and activity, for she feared that something serious had happened to her husband. "Perhaps," she thought, as she ran into the house, "he has had a fit of apoplexy, or, perhaps, he is "—— She could not finish the sentence even mentally, but repelled the thought with a shudder. As she entered the room she inquired, in alarm:

"What is the matter with my husband?"

Ella was kneeling down by the side of the prostrate man, bathing his face with cologne, holding hartshorn to his nostrils, and alternately chafing his hands and his temples. Her movements were all very rapid, but very collected and systematic. Although intently engaged in her endeavors to resuscitate Timothy Pollywog, she was not so much absorbed as not to hear her mother's inquiry. She replied, therefore, very promptly:

"Be calm, dearest mother; there is nothing the matter with my father, for I saw him leave the house a few moments ago, seeming stronger than usual; but there is a great deal the matter with Mr. Pollywog. I imagine he must have insulted my father very grossly, for here are the prints of his fingers as they clutched his throat, and I fear that they pressed so hard as to strangle him beyond all hope of recovery. Do, mother, get a little brandy and water and a spoon. Make haste, mother, or it will be too late—if," she added, with a sigh, "he is not dead already."

Mrs. Shelton did not wait for her daughter's request to be repeated, for her sympathies were all aroused now for the unfortunate man, and her old-time propensities came back strong upon her. She ran to the closet, which was usually left open, and seldom, if ever, locked, at least in the day time, and brought from it a glass, a spoon, and a decanter of pure old Cognac brandy, such as was used in those days even in this country, but which sells in Paris now for twenty and thirty dollars per gallon, and very scarce at that price even.

When she returned to the library, Mr. Pollywog had sighed a deep and heavy sigh, produced by the friction and warmth of Ella's hand and the pungent odor of the harts-horn, which she held continually to his nose.

"Thank God," exclaimed Ella, fervently, "he is not dead. Pray God that he may recover altogether, for, O! horrible would it be if the miserable wretch should die by my father's hand, and in my father's house!"

Mrs. Shelton had by this time recovered all her self-command, and, as a skillful and efficient nurse, applied herself to the task of resuscitating the already partially resuscitated Mr. Pollywog. She poured into the tumbler a good deal of brandy, and then added about one-third water—just enough to prevent strangling; to which she added a few drops of hartshorn. A teaspoonful of this mixture she poured down the throat of the patient, and then moistened his tongue with a wet rag, applied constantly to it. A full hour elapsed before Timothy Pollywog, under this judicious treatment, was enabled to close his swollen eyes voluntarily, and then open them again; and when Mrs. Shelton discov-

ered that the swollen condition of his tongue was relieved,
and that he could draw it back into his mouth, she took
away the wet rag which she had applied to it.

And now, for the first time, Mrs. Shelton remembered
that Colonel Shelton kept a lancet in his secretary, and she
rightly conjectured that the man ought to be bled. The
secretary was left open, and the keys were hanging from the
door; for the old Colonel, even in his days of wealth and
prosperity, was never suspicious of robbery, and had but
few places constantly under lock and key. From a little
drawer Mrs. Shelton drew out a sharp lancet, and although
she had never in her life bled any one before, her heart
was nerved up to the duty by the necessity and urgency of
the case, and the absence of any one capable of performing
the act of venesection. It is true, she might have sent for
Old Toney, but she knew that he was some distance from
the house, assisting his children in gathering in their little
cotton crop; and she was afraid to run the risk of a moment's delay. With her white cambric handkerchief, therefore, she tied the arm of Mr. Pollywog above the elbow, and,
very cautiously, but firmly, as she had seen the old family
physician do, she made a full and free incision into the
median vein. The operation was performed *secundum artem*,
and the blood spun out in a bold stream, black as tar itself,
into a basin held by her daughter Ella. There were no
servants called in as yet, and the work was done silently and
effectually. For, as the blood flowed slowly, at first in black,
thick drops, and then more rapidly, until the drops became
a continuous stream, Timothy Pollywog's strength grew
stronger and stronger, and, by the time the bleeding was
completed, he was able to rise up in a sitting posture upon
the floor. Mrs. Shelton then wiped the blood from his arm,
and secured the orifice with a piece of cloth and a bandage,
and gave him the remainder of the brandy and hartshorn
which was in the tumbler. Pollywog smacked his lips, and
thought he had never drank better brandy in his life, nor

7

even half so good; for it was *fourth proof*, and still further strengthened by the addition of the aqua ammonia.

"Much obliged to you, ma'am, for your kindness, but I do n't deserve it at all, at all. The old Colonel sarved me right, ma'am; but he come mighty nigh onto fixin' my flint. I remember it all now. I can see it before me as plain as a vision. It 's all been sent on me as a judgment. I shall take it as a warning, and 'go and sin no more.'"

Mr. Pollywog recovered completely his strength, and in a little while afterward was enabled to leave the house. He kept his word faithfully, and never more wagged his tongue in slanderous tales and lying insinuations. The hard choking which Colonel Shelton gave him did him great good; for it cured him of a very sinful and annoying habit. Like the pollywog, which suddenly drops its tail and leaps from the water a veritable frog, so, also, Mr. Timothy Pollywog was suddenly transformed from being a lying rascal and a mischief-maker, into a truthful and a true man. His regeneration was sudden and alarming, for it was like one being born from the dead; but the signs of his new birth and truly wonderful conversion were ever afterward apparent. Henceforth, therefore, should he ever be called upon the stage, we shall drop his surname, and call him no more Pollywog, nor even Timothy Pollywog, but simply Timothy—plain, honest Timothy—who, like a whipped spaniel, will revere, to his dying day, the memory of Colonel Shelton, and love and honor his wife and his daughter, through whose instrumentality he was brought to life again, and of whose constant and unremitting efforts he could say, with a grateful heart, "Whereas I was dead, I am alive again, and whereas I was only a Pollywog, I am now an honest and a truthful man—no longer a mischief-maker, nor a busy-body in other men's affairs. Thank God, I am no longer a 'Pollywog,' but honest Timothy. And, O! how happy! what a new feeling of delight I experience in my soul, in making others happy instead of making them miserable, and uncomfortable, and wretched, as I used to do! Verily, my con-

version has been as sudden, and almost as miraculous, as
that of the apostle Paul."

Reader, do you not, in your heart, wish that in these very
different days—these "evil times upon which we have fallen"
—there was a brave old Colonel Shelton, with the strong
hand of the soldier, to choke out the life of the pollywogs
who are wriggling upon the surface of society, and making
black and offensive the clear, cool waters of life? to trans-
form them, not from pollywogs into a yet more loathsome
reptile—the toad; but into honest, truthful Timothies. Pray
God that the *Almighty Hand* may do it; for the Christian
reader would rather that the grace of God should do it than
the constraining hand of a mortal. Then, how calm and
peaceful shall become your little community, now disfigured
by scars, and made unhappy by heart-burnings, all the result
of tale-bearing and slander, and downright, willful lying.
Pity, we say, that *all our* Pollywogs couldn't become transformed into honest, truthful, neighbor-like Timothies, such
as Timothy afterward became, *for he slandered never more.*
He was as effectually cured by the choking which Colonel
Shelton gave him as was the wicked blacksmith who gave
up his atheism, burned all of his books on infidelity, and
acknowledged that "the Methodist parson had mauled and
hammered the grace of God into his unprincipled soul."
He was a powerful man, that infidel blacksmith, who wielded
the ponderous fist of a Vulcan. He was the terror of the
community, and no one dared to dispute his word, or gain-
say his authority—a petty tyrant, who held his weaker
neighbors in the most abject bondage. For a long time he
had driven off every Methodist preacher who had attempted
to ride that circuit. There was a church not very far off
from his shop, upon which he kept his diabolical eye, like
Cerberus guarding the entrance to the cave which led down
to Tartarus ; and, like those wicked worshipers of the false
idols, he had vowed to whip and to beat, if not to put to
death, any divine who should possess the temerity, in de-

fiance of his objections, to enter the sacred portals of the
temple to offer up sacrifice and kneel to the "God of
Daniel and the holy prophets."

The result was, that for several years past this little church
became defunct, and was suffered to go to decay, for the
manifest reason that there was no preacher in the conference who was bold enough, or who felt himself physically
capable "to stand fight" with the bully ; for he must first
fight "a regular fist fight," and succeed in whipping "Old
Vulcan" before that would-be worthy would give him permission to enter the pulpit.

At last, however, there was one man found at the General
Conference who volunteered to go upon that particular
circuit, and to preach in that particular church—feeling
that it was his peculiar mission to humble this "Goliah"
who thus persistently "defied the armies of Israel." Like
David, with his "little sling" and "a smooth pebble," this
man of God rode upon the circuit; and as he approached
the blacksmith-shop, he came leisurely on, singing one of
those good old Methodist songs which he so much delighted
to sing. He was about to pass the shop, when Old Vulcan
came forth, cursing and swearing at a furious rate ; for he
was already very indignant that the preacher should, as it
seemed to him, blow his trumpet notes of defiance in his
ear, instead of skulking by in silence and alarm at the ringing of his anvil. His shirt sleeves were rolled up above
his elbows ; and his grim-looking face, and huge, sledge-
hammer fists were covered with the soot and dust of the
forge and the anvil. The preacher was ordered to dismount
and take a thrashing, or give up his determination of preaching upon that circuit.

"It is a hard case, my friend," said the preacher ; "but
I must obey God rather than the devil."

So he deliberately tied his horse to the nearest tree, and
went on singing the hymn,

"How firm a foundation, ye saints of the Lord ;"

and as he sung he poured in his blows "so thick and fast"
into the bully's face that he had no time to return a single
one of them, and was soon utterly discomfited. At last the
preacher knocked down "Old Vulcan," and got upon him,
never once ceasing his song throughout the fight. Vulcan
cried out, "Enough! hold, enough!" but the preacher replied, "I do not think you have got enough," and went
on singing as before.

"Stop!" cried the blacksmith; "you will beat me to death."

"I shall not beat thee to death, my friend," said the parson; "but it is my desire to beat the grace of God into
thy unprincipled soul. And for this glorious purpose I
shall proceed in the order of the Christian work, and the
three great cardinal principles of Methodism, in which I
do most firmly believe, and to which it is necessary, for your
salvation, that you do most cordially assent—I mean Conviction, Conversion, and Sanctification. This shall be the
general division—the *heads* of a discourse which I design,
God willing, to preach on next Sabbath two weeks, at this
church, and which I intend that you shall hear. But, for
the present, I shall proceed only with the *application* of
my sermon, thus reversing the usual order of pulpit dis-
courses: *Firstly*, then, you must promise to abstain from
swearing and all other wicked and immoral practices."

To the very first proposition the blacksmith indignantly
objected, swearing, with a dreadful oath, that "he was a
free man—that he lived in a free country, and he would
therefore curse as much as he pleased."

The parson made no other reply than to resume his singing, and to continue the thrashing—letting fall his hard
blows upon the already bruised and battered face of the
prostrate bully as mercilessly as the blacksmith was accustomed to strike, with his sledge-hammer, the face of his
iron anvil.

"I will do it! I will do it!" cried Vulcan. "I will
promise you never to swear again as long as I live."

"Very well, my friend," said the parson, with a happy and benignant smile, "*that is conviction.* Now, to take the second step, and proceed from one degree of grace to another, you must promise to burn up all your infidel books, of which, I have been informed, you have a goodly number, and henceforth to read the Bible, a copy of which I shall give you."

To consent to this surprising, and, to the mind of the partially-humbled infidel, tyrannical condition, seemed an utter impossibility. What would men say, who had heard him argue so acutely, and reason so learnedly, *against* the Bible, and in defense of his atheistic sentiments? O! no. The parson must really excuse him. He would promise anything else in the world. He was willing to burn up his infidel books, but to read the Bible—never!

In vain did the preacher urge and persuade, in the most earnest tones, while seated astraddle of his prostrate enemy, that it was his solemn duty to read God's Holy Word; and now, *that he was under conviction,* that he should not stop there, but "go on from one degree of perfection to another" —to "get religion" by the next important step, which was *to read the Bible.*"

"Can't do it," said the blacksmith.

"But you *must* do it," said the parson.

"But I won't do it," replied the blacksmith, in an angry tone.

"But you *shall* do it," said the parson.

"But I'll be d——d if I will do"——

Down came the blows, harder and faster than ever before, and the strains of the hymn rose louder and floated higher through the still air. So loud was the holy songster's voice, and so near stifling was the blacksmith, from the streams of blood which flowed from his wounds, and nearly strangled him, as he lay upon his back, that his before stentorian voice, grown feeble from exhaustion, as grew Cæsar's in the act of drowning, that it could scarcely be heard this time crying for help, and saying:

"Enough! enough! I will do it! Anything! everything! only don't sing that song any more; it will kill me outright!"

"My friend, I sincerely rejoice in your conversion, and that the words of that sacred song have had so overpowering an effect upon your hitherto hard and stony heart," was the condoling reply of the preacher, as he leaned over the now thoroughly cowed and humbled bully, whose face was literally beat to a jelly. "But in order that you may reach the topmost round of the ladder, and proceed to sanctification, you must promise that as soon as your wounds have healed, which will be in about two weeks' time, you will come out to hear me preach upon the subjects of Conviction, Conversion, and Sanctification. Will you promise to come out?"

"Yes, yes," said the humbled blacksmith, who was true to his word.

There had been no witnesses to the rencounter, and the secret was never told by either the preacher or the blacksmith until after the conversion of the latter; when, upon relating his experience to the church, he told all the particulars of the fight. The parson was present at the blacksmith's recital of his Christian experience, and the manner in which it was first brought about, by which he was first induced to burn up his infidel books, and then to read the Holy Bible. Rising up in the assembly with his usual sedate but earnest countenance, and with a smile of happiness lighting up his eye, he said:

"Yes, my brethren; the brother has related all the particulars of the case just as it happened. The Lord helped me, and I did it alone through his help. *I mauled the grace of God into his unprincipled soul!*"

Akin to the conversion of the infidel blacksmith was that of Mr. Timothy Pollywog, the *reformed slanderer.*

CHAPTER X.

WHEN Colonel Shelton left the house, the reader will recollect that he went away without a stick in his hand, and with his head erect, as in former times. The stimulus of his rencounter with Timothy had imparted to his nervous and muscular system an energy and a power which did not desert him for some considerable time. He opened the little garden gate and walked leisurely up the road. He had been gone more than an hour; and when all the circumstances related in the latter part of the last chapter had transpired, and still he did not come, Mrs. Shelton and her daughter became uneasy concerning his protracted absence from the house. Ella put on her sun-bonnet and walked anxiously up the road; and as she walked on, her anxiety became greater the further she went. She began to be very anxious, indeed, and had walked more than a half-mile, when she heard a deep groan proceeding from the bushes on the left hand side of the public-road. She immediately turned in that direction, and saw her father lying in the shade of a large tree, with his head leaning against the trunk of an old oak, and in a very prostrate and exhausted condition. If his passion had made him strong for a while, the subsidence of his violent feelings had left him very weak. He had walked more than a mile from the house, and was returning homeward, when his strength gave way, and he had crawled to the shade of the tree. He had been thinking of his son

Langdon, and the foul slander which had been hurled at his memory, when he gave utterance to that groan which had called his daughter to his side.

"My father!" said Ella, anxiously, as she approached Colonel Shelton.

"My daughter!" was the reply of her father, as he slowly rose into a sitting posture, and leaned his back against the tree.

Ella dropped down by his side, and seated herself upon the grass also.

"I have been very anxious about you, my father. I am so glad I have found you at last."

Colonel Shelton drew her head toward him and kissed her lips affectionately.

"Father," said Ella, placing her hand upon the old man's cheek as she used to do when a very little child; "you did wrong, father, to walk so far, and weary yourself so much."

"I was only trying my old limbs, my child, to see if they would hold out in a very long journey I am soon to take."

"Whither are you going, my father?" asked Ella, in almost childish surprise.

"I am soon—very soon—to travel toward 'that bourne whence no traveler returns.'"

"O, father! do n't talk so. It will kill your Ella!" and she leaned her head upon his shoulder, and wept long and bitterly.

The old man did not speak, nor attempt to interrupt her weeping, but let her weep on. He had respect for her sorrow, and, in his heart, pitied the loneliness which he felt would soon come upon his wife and his daughter. The spectacle of Ella's grief had no little influence upon Colonel Shelton, in nerving up his exhausted energies.

"Come, my daughter," said he, "let us return home. With the aid of this stick, rough and uncouth as it is, I hope to be able to reach the house, and then "—— but he did not finish the sentence.

7*

Ella entreated her father to lean heavily upon her arm; but the old man smiled sadly and said, "No," that the weight of his arm would crush down one so fragile as his daughter; that as well might the oak lean heavily against the ivy for support, as for him to lean heavily upon her.

"No, no, my child! If I have not strength to walk, you have not the power to hold me up, and both the oak and the ivy would fall together. But do not be uneasy; for I trust that I shall reach the house in safety, at least by resting a few times on the way; and then "—— he checked himself again, and left the sentence unfinished a second time.

By resting at regular intervals of every four or five minutes, Colonel Shelton at length succeeded in reaching the steps of the piazza, where he sunk down at last completely exhausted, and utterly unable to go any further. Indeed, it was necessary to call in the aid of Old Toney and his two sons to lift the old gentleman to a couch, where he lay for a very long time like one in a trance. For even after he had recovered from the partial syncope into which he had fallen, from his unwonted exertion and excitement, he did not sufficiently recover his strength to speak, or even to raise his hand, or move a single muscle.

That night Colonel Shelton slept in his bed very quietly until a few hours before day, when he became restless; but when Mrs. Shelton, in a kind voice, inquired if he was in any pain, he replied, "No," and then she knew that his mind was disturbed by anxiety or some other feeling. As soon as the day had dawned, Colonel Shelton sent for Old Toney to take a note which he requested Mrs. Shelton to write at his dictation. She sat down to her little escritoir and did as her husband desired; but the tears were falling fast upon the paper as she wrote. The letter was directed to the nearest relative of Colonel Shelton, Mr. Thomas Shelton, who has been already casually alluded to. It conveyed a simple request that he should come speedily himself, and bring with him Mr. Green an old lawyer who had pretty

much given up the practice of the law, but who would come
gladly, at Colonel Shelton's bidding, to draw up properly
the will of an old friend.

. Early in the afternoon Mr. Thomas Shelton arrived, in
company with Mr. Green. When the two gentlemen entered
the room, with Old Toney following in the rear, with a very
mournful expression upon his countenance, the brave old
Colonel raised himself upon his elbow, and resting it upon
the pillow, thus supported his head upon his hand. It was
a posture he had often assumed upon the eve of battle, when
in the hummocks and swamps of Florida he used to lie down
thus, listening to the war-cries of the Indian savages, and
meditating upon the chances and the horrors of war; and
arranging his plans of attack or defense against the foe.
And now he must encounter a sterner, grimmer foe, whom
he could see in the distance galloping rapidly toward him,
seated upon his pale horse, with his drawn sword in his
hand. The brave old Colonel had never quailed before an
enemy; he did not quail now. Death had no terrors for
him. He had silently made his preparations to meet his
grim enemy, careering and vaulting toward him, crowned
with the dark cloud upon his brow. Without ostentation,
and all unknown to others, he had been "putting his house
in order," and had put on his secret armor, as a coat-of-mail
to blunt the arrows of the foe, who would not find him
unprepared. He knew that he was soon to fight his last
battle on earth, but he would die with his colors in his hand.

Reader, the colors to which the brave old Colonel now
clung, was a snow-white banner upon which was painted, in
bold relief, a red cross, the cross of Christ; and just above
the cross were inscribed the letters, " I. H. S "—" Jesus
Salvator Hominum," or, " Jesus the Savior of Men." Christ
was now his last hope and refuge—his *forlorn hope;* and
through him he would conquer the grim enemy Death. In
Him only did he trust, now that his old walls were so battered
and broken, and the fortress was tumbling down. In Christ

only did he hope to become immortal, and though covered with the dust of ages, and with the sweat and the mold of death, to rise up from the contest at last, a conqueror over death and the grave.

It brings sad reflections, when we hear that an old man has made his will, for we are apt to think that he feels death creeping upon him as his bones become drier and drier, and his old hinges become more rusty, and his joints are stiffening with age and its infirmities. We are apt to be startled amid our daily avocations, and with the busy hum of life around us, just as we are startled when we hear the cracking of a gnarled old oak, whose trunk is decayed, and whose lofty and venerable boughs have been blown too rudely and bent too low by the blast of a tornado. We look with regret to see the tree fall whose cracking has arrested our attention; and we look with greater regret still, and more painful anticipation, to see the old man die.

When the will was drawn up, and the signature had been affixed, with as firm and as steady a hand as he had ever signed a document, the old Colonel sunk back upon his bed, and said, in a low, murmuring voice, "Now, Langdon, my son, we shall soon embrace each other in the spirit-land! May God give me strength for the journey."

Not long afterward, the family were all called together, by the request of the dying man; for, although the usual signs of death were absent, the old man said that he was not only ready to depart, but that, in reality, he would soon be with Christ, "to see him as he is." One by one they came in; the whites and the blacks also. To each and every one he gave his hand and his blessing. Even little Fetie, the blind girl, was there; and, although she could not see, she could feel his hand laid gently upon her head; and through her sobs she heard him say:

"I have listened to your little songs, my child, when you knew it not. I not only *like*, but I *love* that little song of yours which talks of the flowers, and the sun and moon, and stars also, because it is the voice not only of the harp but of the heart also—

> " 'Where Jesus reigns the blind—the blind shall see.'

" Yes, my child, in heaven you shall be blind no longer."

During this scene, Old Toney had been standing in front of the fire-place, with his hand resting against the mantle-piece. Involuntarily a heavy groan escaped him, and just then he heard his name called in distinct tones by his old master; and Old Toney was by the bedside in a moment.

"Old Toney," said the Colonel, as he grasped the hand of his faithful slave, and pressed it, for the last time, affectionately in his, "we are going to part company, old man, for a while. One of us 'is taken, and the other left.' We have fought side by side in many a hard-won contest, but in this, my last battle, I must meet the shock single-handed and alone; and the day will come, old man, when you must do likewise. I hope and trust that you are a Christian warrior, and that death will not find you sleeping upon your post. Farewell, old friend; I leave my wife and children in your care. Be a friend of my wife, as you have been a friend and faithful servant to me. Watch over my child, and be her constant guardian, as you have watched over me often when sleeping unguarded by any other sentinel upon the tented field."

Old Toney's only response was a single, deep, sepulchral groan, which sounded as if it came way down from the very lowest, most unfathomable depths of his soul. Save this one groan, his grief seemed dumb, or was too great for words. He would have left the room and fled into the woods, but he could not move, and seemed as if chained down to the spot. He felt that his arm was powerless now to strike down the tomahawk of death, and he must see his master die without being able to arrest the hand which laid him low. Just then, O! how gladly he would have laid down his own life, to prolong the days of him he loved so well!

But, alas, the Conqueror's hour had come; for there is a time appointed for every man to die. And even to those who are left behind, the "days are few and full of trouble."

Mrs. Shelton and her daughter were standing on either side of the beloved patient, who now held out to them both his hands in silence, to bid them a simultaneous and last adieu. He had already given an affectionate farewell and a blessing to each and every of his servants, and now that his voice had failed him—left him as he spoke his last words and gave his last charge to Old Toney—all that he could do was to place his hands in the hands of those he loved best and last on earth. He looked upon his wife, and then upon his daughter, and then again, for the last time, upon the dear partner of his bosom. It was his last earthward look; for a few moments afterward he looked upward and turned his steady gaze heavenward. Heaven now seemed to contain the most powerful magnet over his disenthralled spirit. The Mohammedan turns his eyes toward Mecca, and the Jew toward Jerusalem; but the Christian looks heavenward, and puts his trust in Christ alone. This seemed now to be the veteran soldier's trust, for there was a radiant smile upon his lips, and his eyes never blenched at the prospect of death, which came stealing slowly over him, benumbing first his lower extremities, and creeping upward, with stealthy movement, to paralyze, last of all, his slowly-throbbing heart.

But though his heart beat slow, its pulsations were all full and strong. The family physician had arrived but a few moments before. He had been sent for at an early period by Mrs. Shelton; and, although he came too late to do any good to the patient, he was still a great comfort to the distressed family. The fingers of his left hand were now upon the dying man's wrist, and in his right he held an old-fashioned gold watch. He was counting to himself the slow and regular pulsations of the radial artery, and wondering, in his own mind, at their singular slowness and regularity, so unusual in other persons when they are dying.

"The heart has ceased to beat," said the physician, but he did not remove his fingers from the Colonel's wrist.

Just then, when the heart had ceased to beat its last death-stroke, and when the intelligent physician declared that never another pulsation would be given, the old Colonel closed his eyes by a voluntary effort, and in one deep expiration his life seemed to have gone out in a moment. So deep and singular was this *expiration*, that his chest seemed drawn down and his abdomen flattened by the sudden contraction of the pectoral and abdominal muscles; and the air rushed from his throat with a fluttering, rustling noise, as though *the spirit had passed out that way.*

Up to this time, his eyes and his mouth were open, as is usually the case with the dying. But when this most singular event happened, instead of remaining open, as is common with the dead, his eyes closed and his mouth became shut, as if by a voluntary and conscious effort.

"He is dead," said the physician a second time, but he still kept his fingers upon the wrist of Colonel Shelton's corpse.

When Mrs. Shelton heard these words, which, though spoken in a whisper, sounded to her as the loudest knell ever pealed in the ears of a mortal—for, in thunder tones, those dreadful words had told her how forlorn and disconsolate a widow she was—then Mrs. Shelton could restrain herself no longer, and, uttering a single loud and piercing shriek, she threw herself upon the dead body of her husband and fainted away. Then it was, that the strangest thing in nature occurred; for when has anything happened like it before?

The physician declared—and we know that his testimony is true—that the heart had ceased to beat and the lungs to act for at least a minute or more, and *that they never afterward resumed their lost functions.* Colonel Shelton was, therefore, no longer a living soul, but, to all intents and purposes, a lifeless corpse. But, strange to say, after all the

phenomena of life were no longer apparent, and just as Mrs.
Shelton had uttered that piercing shriek, and flung herself
in her despair upon the dead body of her husband, Colonel
Shelton opened his eyes again and looked upon his wife,
then smiled mournfully a smile of pitying love, and closed
his eyes again. The smile did not fade away, but rested
upon his lips still, and lighted up his countenance, thus
robbing death of its grim and terrible aspect.

Just here let me ask the psychologist—let me inquire of
the most learned physiologist—Can the precise moment be
ascertained when the soul leaves the body ? Does the spirit
quit its clay tenement immediately, or does it wait until
there are unmistakable signs of decay ? In Colonel Shelton's case, had the spirit indeed left the body, and did it
return for a single moment only to look with its old eyes
of affection upon his wife, and wave, with a smile, its last
adieu to the loved one whom it left behind overwhelmed
with sorrow ?

We are ourselves unable to solve the mystery; but we
know that he did smile upon his wife as she lay inanimate
upon his cold and motionless form, after the physician
exclaimed "He is dead." The by-standers certainly considered him dead, for there was never a sigh uttered, nor the
twitching of a single muscle, nor the throb of an artery.
He was dead! dead so far as physical, if not psychological
life, was concerned.

It is a case interesting alike to the psychologist and
physiologist, and one which shows how far the deathless
spirit may exert an influence over inanimate matter. It
proves, at least, that the soul does not quit the body as
soon as some theorists have supposed. A Romanist would
say—and in truth a Romanist *did* say—that had Colonel
Shelton died in the faith of the Catholic Church, he would
have *been canonized and enrolled among their saints;* that it
was a miracle which he himself had wrought upon his own
body after death.

When Colonel Shelton breathed his last, or rather when the family physician said "He is dead," the clock struck twelve—twelve o'clock at night—that cold night of the 10th of December. He had been dying, indeed, for several days, even while moving about upon his feet, but no one knew it, nor even suspected so sad a casualty; dying from the slow but certain power of marasmus, or paralysis of the heart, or, perhaps, both combined. But he did not begin to die visibly, and, to the perceptions of others, there were no manifest symptoms of death until he had signed his signature, with a fair hand, and had set his seal to his last will and testament. When this, his last work, was accomplished, it was five o'clock in the afternoon, and the sun had set, or was just setting in the West. It was when the last rays of the sun glanced backward upon our hemisphere, as if in regret to leave in darkness a world it had shone upon, that Colonel Shelton's sun also began to decline, and his life to die out, so that others could see his sun was beginning to set also.

Mr. Thomas Shelton went to the center-table and wrote in the old family Bible, just under the place where Colonel Shelton himself had recorded the first death in his immediate family: "Departed this life, at twelve o'clock, on the night of the 10th of December, 1825, Colonel James Shelton, in the sixty-third year of his age. He was a gallant soldier, a faithful friend, a loving and a devoted husband and father, a kind and indulgent master, a forgiving and a noble enemy, and an humble Christian; he fought life's battles well, and he sleeps calmly after its storms and tempests are over."

Just above his own obituary, Colonel Shelton had written: "My poor boy! Would to God that I could find his corpse, that I might first give it decent burial, and then lie down by the side of my murdered son, poor Langdon! He left his home flushed with health, and full of manly hopes and promises. Mr. McPherson writes me that he was never taken so much with a young man before, and that when he left his house that afternoon, his prayers went after him that he might one day become not only the pride of his State, but the glory of his country. But he has been cut down in his prime, and has fallen a victim to the bandit's lust for gold! Who is the murderer? God only knows; and God shall one day bring him to judgment for his crime."

Mr. Thomas Shelton turned over the leaves of the old family Bible, and he read upon the margin many shrewd comments which even able theologians would have acknowledged as the clearest expositions *then* known of certain supposed mysterious passages of Scripture. But that which attracted the reader's attention most, and affected him deeply, was the writing he saw opposite the eighty-third Psalm. It was dated the "10th of November, 1824," and had, therefore, been written late at night, after all his guests had retired to bed on the night of that memorable day—the day of the hunt—and after he had made arrangements by which he effected the speedy sale of all his large property. Stripped of everything, he could, like Job of olden time, exclaim, "Though he slay me, yet will I trust in him," for just here the words in print were reiterated in the Colonel's own handwriting: "The Lord is *my* shepherd; I shall not want. No! never." Mr. Shelton was not a Christian, but he closed the book reverently, and with his elbows upon the table, rested his head upon his hands.

"Brave old man!" said he aloud. "This then was his trust; it was this that made him brave in battle, but braver still under the heavy pressure which he must have felt, and which must have galled his sensitive spirit—the galling yoke of poverty! Who, but a Christian, can come down from the hights of honor and of wealth, whether by his own misstep or the misconduct of another, to tread the gloomy vale of poverty, and under all his trials and tribulations, and losses and crosses, say, with a cheerful heart, even write it in a book, 'The Lord is my shepherd; I shall not want!' Brave old man! He has italicised the possessive adjective pronoun '*my*,' to show that he had appropriated the good Lord to himself, and made him become *his* shepherd. With such sentiments as my honored relative entertained, it is a wonder he did not attach himself to some Christian society. But when I come to reflect upon his case, I do not wonder either. He was an Episcopalian by birth, and there was no church of that persuasion nearer than twenty-five miles. The churches nearest him were either hard-shells or ranting Methodists. Colonel Shelton stood alone in sublime grandeur in advance of the times and the community in which he lived. He was, it is true, out of the pale of the visible Church; but he died none the less a Christian, and a member of the Church in heaven. Would God that I may die as he has died! *Requiescat in pace.*"

Perhaps, had the Colonel lived in the present day in that same community, which has advanced in knowledge and refinement, and where there are now no hardshells or ranting Methodists, but intelligent, missionary Baptists and pious Methodists, he might have been one or the other. We know not; but judging from the manner of his death, we believe that he was an humble Christian, as he was a brave warrior.

CHAPTER XI.

IT was not until the third day after his death that the burial of Colonel Shelton took place; for Mrs. Shelton not only wished to give his old servants and numerous friends an opportunity of attending the funeral of one who had been so widely known and universally beloved, but she also earnestly desired that the same clergyman who had performed their marriage ceremony should now officiate upon this mournful occasion. It was necessary, therefore, to send a messenger, post-haste, with a letter to the city, where lived the godly man, who could read the service for the burial of the dead as few men then or now could read it.

All this while the corpse of the distinguished man lay in state in its black coffin, covered with black velvet, and resting upon two chairs in the library; and thither repaired the numerous friends of the deceased, who gathered from every quarter to look for the last time upon the remains of the departed hero. And even strangers were there, to do honor to one so universally beloved and respected. Herbert himself had opportunely arrived, although he had been unapprized of the sad event before his departure from the city of Charleston. His presence was a great comfort to the family, and especially to Ella; for upon his manly bosom she could confidingly pillow her sorrows, and receive strength from his sympathy and love.

There was lamentation and mourning in that now desolate

house, and there was need of all the sympathy and all the love to stay the sinking spirits of the bereaved ones, whose very hearts were hung with mourning. The outward aspect of things indicated the sorrows and the woes within. Kind hands and considerate hearts had hung the very walls with black drapery, and covered the antique furniture with crape. The curtains were looped with black crape, and the very harp itself was dressed in mourning.

Herbert and Ella were seated upon the sofa opposite the harp. They sat motionless, with clasped hands and mourning hearts, when Fetie came into the room. She knew not that the lovers were in the parlor, and closed the parlor door after her entrance into the chamber. Ella saw by the expression of her countenance and the peculiar luster of her eye, through which her soul seemed to be shining, that the spirit of poetry was upon her, and that her genius, so to speak, had relighted its torch at the funeral pile of the veteran warrior. Fetie's was a genius of native growth, and, consequently, was governed by no conventional rules. A prim old maid, or the devoted slave of fashion, would have been horrified at the sound of music in the house of mourning and death. But Ella Shelton and Edgar Herbert were just in that frame of mind when something soft and low—something like "the wailing of the harp," or, rather, like "the sighing of the harp"—would relieve their spirits, overburdened with sorrow. They sat still, therefore, and, with breathless expectation, watched all the motions of the blind girl. Fetie went up to the harp, and started and trembled when she touched the stiff crape with which the gilt frame was wound. She stood a moment in silence, and turned her eyes downward, as if looking upon the crape which she could not see, but whose touch so forcibly recalled the memory of the dead warrior, whose cold but friendly hand seemed still pressing upon her head, that she fancied she could feel its pressure still. The tears rolled down her cheeks; and, with a tremulous voice, she breathed

rather than sung the following tribute of love to the veteran
who was lying stiffened in death in the adjoining room :

> Another veteran warrior 's dead,
>   Another captain's race is run
> Another spirit 's upward fled,
>   And set another glorious sun.
> Like that good patriarch of old—
>   Like Jacob, propped up in his bed—
> So also he his end foretold,
>   Then soon was numbered with the dead.
>
> His race was bravely, nobly run ;
>   He fought life's battles long and well ;
> With harness buckled firmly on—
>   With sword in hand, he bravely fell.
> Then saw his friends, who gathered round
>   As death, so grim and stark, drew nigh ;
> They saw *his* smile, but heard no groan—
>   No keen regrets, nor painful sigh.
>
> He met the foe with smiling eye,
>   But no bravado spirit there ;
> Through faith his hopes were all on high—
>   In Christ, his trust, without a fear.
> Now let God's Holy Word be read,
>   Let one prayer more—the last—be given,
> Make haste ! Nay, nay ! Too late ! he 's dead !
>   He 's ta'en his upward flight for heaven.
>
> Farewell, brave warrior ! though dead
>   The pressure of thy hand I feel
> Distinct and plain upon my head,
>   Still warm as life, though cold as steel.
> Go, try the glories of that world
>   Where war's alarums never come
> Where hostile banners all are furled,
>   And never 's heard the beat of drum.
>
> Up, soldier ! up ! and higher rise !
>   Away from bloody contests run ;
> The spirit-land beyond the skies
>   Has other victories to be won.
> There, a crown of glory shall be thine,
>   A star-wreath placed upon thy brow ;
> And there you 'll drink the heaven-made wine,
>   And weep no more as we are weeping now.

She ceased her song, and stood weeping for some moments, when she heard Ella's sighs re-echoed by the sighs

of her lover ; she seemed very much confused, and sought
to leave the room ; but Herbert went up to her, and, taking
her kindly by the hand, led her to the sofa, upon which
he had left Ella weeping the silent tears of gratitude and
love.   Herbert seated her very gently and carefully upon
the sofa, as he would a little child, and then sat down between her and Ella.   He passed his arms around the waist of
both, and felt very happy.   Neither Ella nor Fetie moved
nor shrunk from this liberty, as they would have done, perhaps, at another time.   The one leaned upon him now, in
her loneliness and distress, as her only manly support ; the
other loved him as the friend of her best friend, who had
first awoke the fires of genius within her, which otherwise
might have lain dormant forever, or become extinguished
by the cold embers of indifference, or the want of recipro-
cal feelings.

Thus Ella Shelton, the affianced bride of Edgar Herbert,
sat by the side of her lover, whose left arm was around
her, while his right encircled the waist of the blind girl.
But the heart of Ella Shelton was pained by no pangs of
jealousy.   If her love was almost idolatrous, it was not
groveling and low.   A high-born maiden, her love was high-
born also ; and her soul as lofty as the source from which
she had sprung.

But Herbert, himself a gentleman, and used to all the
refinements of life, although possessing an affectionate disposition, would not, perhaps, have taken this liberty with
the confiding maidens if placed under any other than the
present painful circumstances.   But death is a grand leveler
of forms and ceremonies ; and the stormy winds of adversity will scathe the frost-work, and break to pieces the ice-
bergs of etiquette and conventional stiffness.   There was
death and sorrow in the house ; and there was true love and
manly honor in the heart of Mr. Herbert.

While this affectionate trio of youthful persons were thus
seated in close and friendly proximity, a sudden noise, as

of a dead weight falling upon the floor of the library, caused
them all to start to their feet in consternation and alarm.
It was early in the morning of the third day, and no one
had yet come from a distance to attend the funeral of Colonel Shelton, and Herbert conjectured that the corpse might
have been tumbled to the floor by the old Colonel's dog,
who was, perhaps, seeking to win a last smile and a last
friendly recognition from his master. Supposing this to be,
in reality, the case, he urged Ella to remain where she was,
that he might himself go and see what had happened. To
this Ella readily consented ; for, thinking as Herbert did,
she was trembling from head to foot, and ultimately had to
sit down upon the sofa—trembling from that kind of shocked
feeling which we all have when the corpse of one we love
has been handled too rudely—as if a corpse had any more
feeling. But such is our nature, that we shrink and tremble
even when we hear the clods fall too hard upon the coffin.
But if the corpse itself be handled never so lightly, we are
afraid lest the jar should be too great, and give pain to the
dead. But, O ! to strike that corpse a blow ! to maltreat
it ! to tumble it upon the floor ! Horrible ! No wonder
that Ella was compelled to sit down upon the sofa, overcome by her agitation.

Herbert left the room in haste, and in passing through
the entry and then out into the portico which led to the
wing, he met Mrs. Shelton at the door of the library. They
both seemed surprised that they did not find the door open
or ajar ; but, without exchanging a word, they entered
simultaneously, and discovered poor Old Toney lying upon
the floor in strong convulsions. His jaws were locked, and
he was foaming at the mouth. His eyes were rolled back,
and his features very much distorted ; and there was a
choking sound in his throat, as if he was strangling from a
bone, or other hard substance, pressing against the larynx.

Mrs. Shelton ran to the medicine chest—for every planter
has his medicine chest, and frequently is his own doctor—

and procured a vial of nitrous ether. She poured a good deal of it upon her handkerchief and applied it to his nose. In a little while, the convulsions became weaker, and, at length, the old man lay quite still. A deep sigh came from his chest, and then he groaned aloud. He opened his eyes and looked around him, and seemed to understand what had happened; for he pressed first the hand of his mistress, and then the hand of Mr. Herbert, as they still held his to prevent his arms from jerking upward, as they had done while the fit was upon him. Old Toney closed his eyes again, and seemed to be asleep; but he heard Mr. Herbert ask Mrs. Shelton if he had ever been subject before to convulsions of any kind.

"O, no," said Mrs. Shelton, in reply, "it is only the result of strong emotions which have been unable to find vent in any other way. He could weep and find relief in tears when his young master perished so mysteriously, but now his sorrow is too big for tears. Poor old man! For his and for Ella's sake I must try to bear my own burden, and help them bear theirs also. May God give me strength to stand up under these heavy afflictions."

The poor, grief-stricken widow could say no more. All the fountains of her soul were opened, and she wept copious tears, the first which she had shed since the death of her husband.

Although a woman's tears are always refreshing to her own spirit, and seem to relieve her soul, which has been parched and withered by sorrow's blighting touch, yet those same tears are ever distressing to the man whose heart is tender and kind. Herbert felt deeply moved, and his voice trembled when he said:

"Do not weep, madam! The God of the widow has promised to be your friend, and he will raise up friends on earth also, to protect and love you."

Old Toney had heard the words of Mr. Herbert, and was conscious of the weeping of his mistress; and these, com-

8

bined, effected a complete restoration, so that he rose from
his recumbent position and sat upright upon the floor.   A
few tears trickled down his sable cheeks, but they were the
irrepressible tears of sympathy and love.   From that moment the old man resolved to master his own sorrow, and
assume the important responsibility of being, in the absence
and loss of a master, the friend and protector of the widow,
the guardian of her child—the father—servant—all—and to
stand by them to the last in all their troubles, as he had
stood faithful in their times of prosperity, and happiness,
and peace.   It was the assumption of an important responsibility, or, rather, one which had been delegated by his
old master in his dying moments; and the old slave resolved
in his soul that, come weal or woe, he would not only support his mistress and her daughter by the labor of his own
hands, if need be, but shield them from harm, and, with
his broad breast to screen them from every storm, lest the
blast should blow too hard and rough upon their delicate
woman frames.   May God help you, old man! for darker
days are coming, not only upon them, but upon your own
household also.

It was not until one o'clock in the afternoon that all the
friends and relatives of the deceased had assembled at the
house of Mrs. Shelton, to follow the corpse of the departed
old hero to its last resting-place.   The procession was an
unusually long one for the country, but at the grave they
were met by many hundreds more, the most of whom were
the black people of the surrounding neighborhoods, who,
in company with the former slaves of Colonel Shelton, had
come to commingle their tears at the grave of the departed
hero.

When the procession reached the avenue of cedar trees,
which led up from the public road to the family burying-
ground of the Sheltons, the coffin was lifted from the wagon
and borne upon a litter by six pall-bearers, who were the
friends of Colonel Shelton.   As the procession moved on

foot up the avenue, the minister began to read the beautiful and most impressive burial service of the Episcopal
Church; and the sweet but distinct tones of his melodious
voice floated mournfully upon the air, and thrilled many a
heart. With his hat in one hand and his Book of Common
Prayer in the other; with his flowing black silk gown and
his solemn tread, as he marched in front of the procession;
with his sweet voice and his heaven-beaming blue eyes,
which shone as bright stars of hope and faith upon a world
of sin and sorrow, who could look upon that godly man,
and hear him say: "I am the resurrection and the life,
saith the Lord; he that believeth in me, though he were
dead, yet shall he live: And whosoever liveth and dwelleth
in me shall never die," without feeling his heart melt within
him, and experiencing a sense of gratitude to God that he
had created us with an immortal soul? And that feeling
was still further increased, and the audience, most of whom
were blacks, all alike felt their gratitude to God grow
stronger, and their faith mount higher, as they came nearer
the grave and heard the melodious voice of the preacher,
clear and distinct as the trump of an archangel flying
toward the earth with his message of "glad tidings" and
"good news" to fallen men, exclaiming, "I know that my
Redeemer liveth, and that he shall stand at the latter day
upon the earth: And though after my skin, worms destroy
this body, yet in my flesh shall I see God: whom I shall see
for myself, and mine eyes shall behold, and not another."

Then, when he had reached the grave, he added, "We
brought nothing into the world, and it is certain we can
carry nothing out. The Lord gave, and the Lord hath
taken away: blessed be the name of the Lord."

Then could be heard a murmuring as of many voices; and
if a stranger, unaccustomed to such scenes, had been present, he would have looked up and around to discover the
meaning of that confused murmur of many voices, so unusual at ordinary funerals; and he would have found out

that those sounds proceeded from the blacks, who, in their usual manner, were assenting to the words of the divine, whom they now regarded with an admiration akin to that with which they would have looked upon an angel from heaven. As they bowed their heads toward the minister, in token of their hearty acquiescence in the words he had spoken, and as they waved their bodies to and fro until the whole multitude seemed to be controlled and swayed by one impulse, and waved together in regular wavings of the body—*like an army "marking time" to the roll of the drum* —one might have heard, from numerous lips, the assent of the pious Africans, whose responses were : " Bless de Lord ;" " Tank de good Lord ;" " De Lord's name be praised."

Foremost among these sable mourners stood Old Toney, who could not be induced to remain at home, notwithstanding all the earnest solicitations of Herbert and of Mrs. Shelton, who insisted that he had been too ill, and had too recently recovered, to bear the ride of several miles, or withstand any further excitement. His reply had been:

" I have been de body-sarbent ob my dear old masser all my life long; let me be his body-sarbent to de last! I know dat if I had died fust, my masser would hab follow me to de grabe, and see me at rest! Let me follow my old masser, and let me see him put away wid my own eye! Let me do dis, missis, and I satisfy."

His earnest and very natural request could not be denied, and the faithful old man-servant now stood at the foot of the grave in mournful silence, partaking in no other way in the ceremonies than watching, with the closest scrutiny and interest, everything which was said and done, with the eager curiosity of a monitor who watches over the conduct of his fellow-students in the absence of the teacher. Upon his black fur hat had been placed, *by his own request*, a long piece of crape, which waved like a black streamer in the breeze, and as he stood at the foot of the grave he seemed to be the chief mourner there.

And as the minister stooped down, and lifting a handful of earth, flung a portion of it upon the coffin after it had been lowered into the grave, saying at the same time, "Dust to dust,"—and as he threw on the remainder—"ashes to ashes," Old Toney groaned so loud that the minister himself looked up at him for a moment, and felt his sympathetic heart ache with pity for the sufferer. It was, therefore, with double interest in the ceremony, and with an emphasis intended particularly for the old man, as well as those connected by the closer ties of consanguinity, that he said : "I heard a voice from heaven saying unto me, Write, From henceforth blessed are the dead who die in the Lord ; even so saith the Spirit, for they rest from their labors."

Blessed rest for the war-worn, heart-broken old soldier ! He rests now from his labors ! The minister had said so, and his voice sounded as the voice of an angel, never to be forgotten. He has borne fatigues and encountered hardships, and in his old age suffered afflictions which had even wrung a soldier's heart, however brave and strong, but he rested now from his labors. Hear it, Old Toney ! hear it, poor lonely widow and grief-smitten orphan ! your loved one rests now from his labors ! There peacefully and quietly let him rest, "with his martial cloak around him," until the judgment morn, and bow to the will of God, heartily and without a murmur, even as ye bowed your heads when the preacher, with eyes upturned and hands uplifted toward heaven, concluded the solemn and interesting funeral service with the words : "The grace of our Lord Jesus Christ, and the love of God, and the fellowship of the Holy Ghost, be with you all, evermore. Amen."

Who has ever heard the funeral service of the Episcopal Church without a feeling of solemnity? Who does not remember, with sacred pleasure, the hallowed tones of some eminent and lovely man of God, as he walked in front of the hearse by the sexton's side, to bury the form of the dead one whom he loved? O, the days of boyhood, departed never more to return! But, as dear as their memory, there is a pleasure sweetest of all, though so mournful, in hearing still the echoes of a holy voice now hushed in death— echoes through long years, which I heard when a boy, and which I shall continue to hear even when I shall become an old man. Dear, departed, universally beloved, holy man of God; thy voice shall be heard no more on earth, like sweetest music, saying: "I am the resurrection and the life!" And that old sexton, too, who used to walk beside thee, and whose head shook with palsy from side to side, as if he were silently, but continually making his protests against death's doings; he, too, has gone to his rest, and himself in turn needed a sexton to conduct him to his long home.

Yes, the preacher and the sexton shall no more walk together to the grave; but we feel assured that they shall clasp hands in heaven. But, O! that man of God! and, O! the music of that voice! that voice, who can forget?

But although there was just such a voice heard at the burial of Colonel Shelton, and although the funeral service was read in the minister's most impressive style, yet, in Old Toney's estimation, there was something lacking; and he still stood at the foot of the grave, and now and then looked around him, as if expecting more to be done. His mistress and her daughter had already returned homeward, accompanied by the minister and Mr. Green, the lawyer, and several other of her most devoted friends. But still Old Toney stirred not from the spot; but with folded arms looked down into the grave, which they were now filling with earth, shovelful by shovelful. And as the old man looked down at the grave-digger's work, he could not help wishing in his heart that his old master had been buried also with all the funeral honors due to the valiant soldier. There was no beat of muffled drum, no dead march played upon the fife, no solemn bugle-blast, no military salute fired over the grave of the dead hero. The old man had been

used to all this, and he had often been melted to tears by
the mournful tap of the muffled drum, as it heralded to the
grave a dead warrior slain in battle by the bullets of the
conquered and retreating foe—a conqueror slain when flushed
with victory!

Old Toney, we say, looked for something like this; but
he would look in vain for its counterpart, although a substitute might be offered. And as he looked into the grave
and heard the dull sound of the clods falling heavily, painfully upon the coffin, his keen ears caught the tramping
sound of men's feet, which seemed to him as the regular
tramp of soldiers, who were coming to surprise their dead
comrade with military honors. Old Toney looked over the
heads of the crowd which began to give way and part in
the center, and then he saw what he had seen but once or
twice before, a band of Freemasons, who had just arrived
from a distant lodge, to attend the burial of their brother
Mason, and some-time Worshipful Master.

We are no apologists for the ancient and honorable Fraternity of Freemasons. But we must be permitted to say
that the very name of "Freemasonry" is invested with a
charm, and excites an interest which but few persons can
resist, belie their feelings as they may, or, however much
they may be influenced by prejudice. Indeed, its very
antiquity should command respect, if nothing else in its past
history is worthy of admiration. Claiming an origin which
dates back to the remotest ages of civilization and refinement, older than the "Society of Jesus," older than the
Knights Templars, and professing to be older than the religion of Jesus Christ, and coeval with the building of
Solomon's Temple; having disciples in every part of the
habitable globe, and invested with the secret signs, and
grips, and passwords by which they can make themselves
known to each other, whether in the dark or broad light
of day, on land or sea, when near or at a distance, in times
of peril and distress, in war as in peace, in public or in

private; bound by the most stringent rules, and free, as their name indicates; possessing Grand and Subordinate Lodges, and yet each Lodge independent; having a Head, and yet acknowledging no masters, and bound only by their oaths to assist each other in times of trouble and distress, to befriend the widow and the fatherless, to love their country and promote the best interests of society at large; taking care, however, that in dispensing their charities they do not depart from the golden precept of *"not* letting their left hand know what their right hand doeth," thus causing light to shine in darkness, and bringing back smiles to the heart which was overburdened with sorrow—surely an institution like this, whose movements, though mysterious, produce no dread, and whose secret acts of benevolence are so antagonistic to the boastful spirit of the Pharisee, who proclaims his charitable deeds not only from the housetops and in the market-places, but, in these modern times, through the newspapers and by the telegraphic wires; surely, we say, such an institution is calculated to excite the admiration of the intelligent, rather than his opposition and abuse.

But if the antiquity, the mystery, the benevolence, the freedom, the brotherly love of Freemasonry are subjects worthy of thought, and well calculated to command the world's respect, there is something in their outward parade, the simplicity yet grandeur of their regalia, which never fails to command the admiration of the illiterate and ignorant. And such was the case now with Old Toney. It would have been enough for him to know that his own dear master had been a Mason, and that once, in years gone by, he had sat in the honorable chair of the Worshipful Master of the Lodge, and had been recognized as their chief. But now that they came in double file, as a band of soldiers marching with trailed arms to the grave of their dead comrade—and when he saw them all in uniform, with their white aprons of spotless lambskin, and not, as now, of white linen, and around the necks of some the silver

trinkets which they wore as emblems of their office, then
Old Toney felt better satisfied; and he said, in his heart,
while he nodded his head several times, "Berry good! berry
good, indeed! All masser's sojers, disband, and scatter ober
de whole face ob de cart'—from Sout' Ca'lina clean to de big
Norred! Who gwine find 'um again? Masser been a good
Mason, which I forgot. Let de Mason bury him den. I
berry tankful dere is a substitute found for de sojers. Pity
do' dey do n't hab guns and cartridge box."

Old Toney's thoughts were interrupted now by the proceedings at the grave, watching all their movements, to see
if the "*substitute*" would answer or at all approach his idea
of what a great man's burial should be; for as yet *his* master
had been only *half-way* buried; buried only as an ordinary
man; he had not been interred, nor, under the circumstances,
could he possibly be interred with all the honors which *Old
Toney's* master deserved; for the President of the United
States might die, or a king might fall dead from his throne,
but what were they to Old Toney? and in what comparison
could they stand in his estimation with Colonel Shelton?

When Old Toney saw the Freemasons join hands in token
of the eternal and unbroken link which bound them together
as a band of brothers; and when he saw them going round
and round the grave, and each one, at a certain point of the
circuit, dropping in a sprig of green myrtle or fresh cedar,
which, in the absence of the Oriental acacia, served to remind
the spectators of their abiding faith in the immortality of the
soul; when he heard the solemn but hopeful words of the
chaplain, "If a tree be cut down its young and tender branches
shall spring up again," words so like, "I am the resurrection
and the life," which were still ringing in the old man's ears;
and when the ancient form of assent, "So mote it be," sounding
so much like Hebrew to him, was uttered by numerous voices;
and their hands uplifted were brought down simultaneously
with a slap upon the thigh, so loud and sonorous that it
awoke the echoes of the neighboring forest; and when their
8*

wails of distress rose in murmurs, but floated high over the
heads of the multitude, causing the nerves to thrill and the
heart to stand still with awe; and when the music of their
voices, in admirable unison, was added to all these mysterious
ceremonies, and that grand old Masonic dirge had been sung,
then Old Toney could no longer suppress his admiration,
and he laughed to himself the "Holy Laugh," as it is called
by the Methodists, and bowed his head many times in ap-
proval. In truth, such was the old man's enthusiasm, that
he could not resist the impulse, at the close of the Masonic
burial, of going up to the Worshipful Master and thanking
him and his fraternity for burying his master so well, when
he had supposed that there was no chance of his being
buried at all! that is, either by the military or a "substitute."

And besides, Old Toney felt that, as the oldest representative and present *head* of the family, it was his right, his duty,
to return his heartfelt thanks, and the thanks of Colonel
Shelton's family, to these singular men, who had come so
far to do honor to the remains, and shed an honest tear to
the memory, of their illustrious brother.

"I berry t'ankful to you, Masser Mason," said Old Toney,
addressing the Chaplain of the Lodge. "You do my heart
berry much good, and tek a great weight off my mind. Aldo
you ain't sojers, and did n't bring any gun wid you to fire
de big *platoon*, you mek de big slap wid all your hands
togedder! Dat mek me tink ob sojerin'. My masser was
a brave sojer, masser, and I berry glad you bring de big
slap as a substitute for de big platoon! When we can't get
gun we must tankful for pistol."

"Yes, old man," said the Chaplain, with a smile, "your
master was more—much more—than a brave warrior! He
was a good man; a true man; God's noblest work—an
honest man!"

"God bless you, Masser Mason!" (Old Toney did not
know the name of the Chaplain, nor do we.) "God bless

you, Masser Mason, for dat word!   God bless you, masser!
God bless you!   God bless "——

The old negro knew not what else to say, nor could he
say more, for his heart was too full.   He had been touched
in a very tender spot, and upon a very delicate chord.   For
what faithful old slave does not feel proud to hear the praises
of his master, even when alive and flushed with health?   But
to hear the praises of his dead master! and of such a master
as Old Toney's master!   It was like the captive listening to
the pæan, which he hears with rapture, but which his heart
is too full to sing.

Methinks every man should be a good and kind master,
husband, father, friend, and citizen ; that when he comes to
die he may be followed to his grave by such friends, and
mourned by such hearts as lamented the death of Colonel
Shelton.   He had been plucked as a paving-stone from the
domestic hearth, and the other hearth-stones may all tumble in and leave a wrecked and ruined fireside, but he will
never know it.   *Requiescat in pace!*   Rest, old warrior!   Lie
still in your grave, and let not your spirit be troubled about
the future of time or eternity!   For an ocean of tears shall
be shed, and upon its briny bosom your spirit-vessel shall
be wafted heavenward, where the captive's sighing shall
cease, and all tears shall be wiped from his eyes.   Rest in
peace, brave, good old man, and think not that other mourners will not come to your grave to-day.   Look at the crowd
that still linger behind!   There is a perfect sea of heads,
though its waves are black!   But they are not angry waves.
No, no!   *The sea has only dressed itself in mourning!*

As the last of the Freemasons and all the relatives of the
deceased disappeared from the throng of mourning blacks,
the white foam disappeared also, and there was no more a
crested wave.   They were all black waves, but harmless as
the waves of the Dead Sea, upon which, if a man be wrecked,
he will float and never sink.   The white man's grief is terrible, but the grief of the African, as a general rule, becomes

a positive luxury. He can mourn all day, and find pleasure in his mourning. His lamentations become songs which he loves to sing; which make him laugh, while they make others weep.

There are more than five hundred of these dark sons and daughters of Ethiopia who have come to attend the funeral of Colonel Shelton. With some of them—a very few—it is a gala day; but most of them are sincere, hearty mourners. And chief among the latter is Old Toney, and, in some respects, his counterpart, Old Sampson. Old Sampson is a negro preacher, and he has come on horseback full twenty miles, to attend the funeral of Colonel Shelton. Sampson had loved the old Colonel; and well he might, for had not Colonel Shelton often, and over and over, given him a five or a ten, and even a twenty dollar bill, for preaching occasionally to his black people? Old Sampson is a gray-headed old Christian. He is a much older man than Old Toney, but his head is not so white, for he has not endured the hardships of the camp; nor has he been scorched by pestilential fevers. His hands, too, have been clear of blood, and his heart is as pure and as simple as the child's. He has learned none of the vices of civilization, while his soul has been elevated by the meek and lowly doctrines of Christ. He is a sincere Christian and an humble slave. A man of great power and influence among the blacks, he is universally beloved and respected by the whites, who greet him kindly wherever they meet him, shaking him by the hand as an equal, while many believed in their hearts that the illiterate old African was superior to them all in godliness, and many a lordly planter had begged him to pray for them in secret. Yes, the planter and the slave, the Southern man and the African preacher, have gone out together in the thicket and knelt there together at the throne of Grace.

Old Sampson, standing at the head of the grave, waved his hand, as a magician's sable wand over the multitude, and in a moment the crowd stood still.

"My dear belubbed bredren," said the old African preacher,
in his broken English, "we is all met upon a berry solemn
occasion. De corpse of a great man is lying here in dis
grave, but his sperit is now in yonder world. In my mind's
eye I see him now in ole Farer Abraham's bosom, lying
dere at rest like a child nestling on its mudder's breast.
He is a great way off from us, but he can see us mourners
still, and his lips are moving now as if he wanted to say a
word to dis large assembly. Bredren, listen! hearken to
de old Colonel's voice!"

The old preacher stopped and held his hand to his ear
in the attitude of a listener. The murmurs of approbation
ceased in a moment, and every one looked upward, or cocked
their ears to catch the faintest whisper stealing through the
air from the lips of a glorified spirit. The silence was
unbroken for several moments, and naught was heard save
the waving of the tree-tops, blown gently by the frosty air.
During all these moments of silence the sable orator stood
perfectly still, with his hand to his ear, as if expecting to
hear a sound from heaven. At length his arm dropped
slowly to his side, and he spoke again :

"Did n't you hear 'um?" said he, looking around upon
the large audience, who had imitated his action, and were
looking, with strained eyes and open mouths, toward him.

"No, Brudder Sampson," said an old man in the crowd;
"I did n't hear 'um. But I 's gettin' too old fur yerry
good."

"You did n't hear 'um, enty! My bredren, dat's because
you hab no faith. I hear 'um! Me! plain as you hear de
preacher. And de voice dat come to my mind is dis, dat
Colonel Shelton say : 'I hab fought de good fight; I hab
finished my course on earth, and henceforth dere is reserved
for me a crown ob righteousness and glory; I am here safe
and at rest in ole Farer Abraham's bosom; and I now know
de truth ob de sayin' : I am de resurrection and de life.
If any man believe on de Lord Jesus Christ, he shall live,

though he were dead. But if any man believe not on de Lord Jesus Christ, let him be anathema maranatha.' Dat's what I hear, my bredren. And do you know what it is to be anathema maranatha? It's a big word, and I suppose you dunno what it means. Well, I will tell you. It means dis in plain English : Dem dat *won't* believe on de Lord Jesus Christ, and, in dis Gospel land, laugh at his religion, and despise his cross, and say, wid de wicked Jews, 'Crucify him! crucify him! away wid him! not dis man but Barabbas, a tief and a robber!' let such a one be accursed forever! Let him be cursed in his lying down and in his rising up; in his bones and his sinews; in his head and his stony heart; eberywhere and all ober, inside and out; let him be cursed!—cursed in time, and cursed in eternity!—cursed on earth and cursed in hell-fire foreber and eber!—one mighty and eternal curse ob de Eternal, Almighty, sin-offended God! And in de name, and by de authority ob my Lord and Master, I say, dis day, to you around dis grave : Cursed is ebery one who loves not de Lord Jesus Christ!"

As solemn and awe-inspiring as was the occasion, the attitude, the voice, the commanding aspect, and the eloquence of the old African, all combined, were well calculated to arouse the interest and enchain the attention of the audience of even well-educated persons. But now these sable sons and daughters of Ethiopia were perfectly wild with excitement. Some groaned aloud in deprecation of their own conscious sinfulness or short-comings; others shrieked in alarm or despair, as if in expectation of the dreaded curse which was about to pounce upon them in some terrible bodily shape. Some shouted "Amen!" in one part of the crowd, and were answered with an "Amen!" from the remotest part of the excited throng. Some tossed their arms in the air, like drowning men who, giving up all hope when, buffeting the waves in vain, they see the last huge billow rolling toward them, with its mountain of briny

waters, like the curse of the anathema maranatha, so awful
in its consequences to them.   There was shouting and wild,
maniacal laughter; there were shrieks, and there were
groans.   It was just such a scene as we may imagine of a
Church of bedlamites with a bedlamite for a preacher.   It
was time, therefore, to still the tumult; for Old Sampson
was no bedlamite, and could not endure to see disorder.
He was simply a great, though uneducated orator, and sometimes his power was irresistible upon the white man as well
as upon the unlettered negro.   And when such instances
occurred, as they frequently did, he usually paused in the
midst of the excitement, and exclaimed, in a stentorian
voice of rebuke, in mournful, earnest tones : " The Lord is
in *his* holy temple! let all keep silence before him!"   And
those words usually had the desired effect in stilling the
tumult which his own eloquence had raised.

But now he stopped and stood still a moment; then he
raised his hands upward, and lifted his eyes, streaming with
tears, toward heaven, and with a voice which trembled and
seemed almost choked with the intensity of his feelings, the
old man said, " My beloved bredren, let us all pray."   And
the old man knelt upon the fresh, damp earth at the head
of the grave, and Old Toney knelt at the foot.   Immediately
there was a great calm.   Every man, woman, and child of
that vast and excited throng knelt down upon their knees
—bowing upon the cold ground as their priest knelt, in
Nature's temple, to offer up the incense of his prayer to a
sin-offended God.   For where is the negro whose wildest
and most unnatural excitement will not grow less—whose
irreverence will not subside—whose awe will not increase—
whose knee will not bend, at the voice of prayer?   The
white man's knee may be locked by bars of steel, that it
can not bend at a throne of mercy, and he can only sit or
stand stiff and rigid as the unquarried stone or the sculp-
tured marble ; but the negro is emphatically a religious
being, and feels like pulling off his shoes when he is tread-

ing upon holy ground. It was thus that the very attitude and the voice of prayer could hush, in a moment, the tumult which had prevailed.

The old preacher's prayer was short and simple, but fervent and full of faith. It was not a long-winded prayer, such as you hear from the pulpits of your fashionable divines or studied theologians, or pharisaical preachers, who weary their audience to death by a long, dry, and uninteresting oration, which has been previously written and committed to memory in their study—an oration of twenty or thirty minutes, praying *at* the people and not *to* their God; who use prayer—public prayer—as a rod of chastisement, and not a vehicle of mercy. No! Old Sampson's prayer was short and simple, as the prayer of a little child who begs imploringly its mother for bread. But little longer than the Lord's Prayer, it occupied but two or three minutes. Our Lord's Prayer did not occupy him sixty seconds. Old Sampson condensed his desires, although so earnest, so fervent, into a few brief paragraphs, which occupied him but three or four minutes. He tried to imitate his Lord even in the brevity of his prayers; and certainly they were as fervent as a mortal could utter.

The old man ceased when he had said "Amen," and rose slowly from his knees; then waving his hand—his long, bony arm—upward, he commenced to sing, and was assisted by more than five hundred voices, all in unison—voices of melody and sweetness which had never been strained nor cracked by over-exertion or unnatural efforts to pervert the true language of the vocal chord. The song which they sung was a familiar one, which most of my readers have, perhaps, often heard and sung, as it was then sung in the wild woods, by an immense assembly of blacks, standing by a new-made grave. It possessed peculiar power and interest:

"O! there shall be mourning, mourning, mourning,
  O! there shall be mourning at the judgment-seat of Christ!

.Masters and servants there shall part,
Masters and servants there shall part,
Masters and servants there shall part,
Shall part to meet no more."

There were other verses, alluding to the separation of
parents and children, husbands and wives, friends and neighbors, etc.; and the sounds of these words seemed like the
wail of the disconsolate, who were without hope or joy in
the world.

But the spirit of the song changed, and the effect was like
electricity upon the crowd; for although the tune was the
same, yet it seemed very different, for it sounded no more
like a requiem, but like a chorus of happy voices joining in
a song of rejoicing. It was now a shout rather than a low
wailing. The last verse which was sung was so appropriate,
and so soul-subduing, that the preacher himself shed tears
of joy, and many wept through pure gladness of spirit :

"O! there shall be shouting, shouting, shouting,
O! there shall be shouting at the judgment-seat of Christ!
Masters and servants there shall meet,
Masters and servants there shall meet,
Masters and servants there shall meet,
Shall meet to part no more."

While they were singing this song the old preacher, who
seemed a head taller than the rest, stood upon a little mound
of fresh clay, at the head of the grave—thus elevating him
still higher above the heads of the crowd ; and as they sung,
the old man beat time with his right hand, like the leader
of a grand orchestra. And never was there a leader who
beat time better, and never an orchestra who sung more in
unison, and never a grander temple, whose walls were the
green trees of the forest, and whose vaulted ceiling was the
blue canopy of heaven.

But the song of the judgment ceased ; and as night was
nigh at hand, they returned to their homes, singing, as they
went, other songs, which spoke of death, and heaven, and
eternal felicity.

Before Old Toney mounted again his coal-black steed, and ere the preacher had left the grave to return to his home also, he took Old Sampson by the hand; while big tears of gratitude streamed down his old furrowed cheeks.

"I berry t'ankful to you, my brudder Sampson," said he. "You do my heart great good. White buckra's preach berry good, and Freemason burial berry good too ; but, my dear brudder, what you say is better dan dem all. I don't say 'um to fool you, or to mek you wain, my brudder; for it is from my heart, which was berry full, because dere was no *big platoon fired ober my old masser's grave.* But, my dear brudder, I t'ank you berry much ; and I do t'ink dat *all t'ree put togedder*—de buckra preacher, de Freemason, and your preachment—all t'ree on 'em put togedder, is most as good as one big platoon. God bless you, my brudder ! God bless you ! "

" God bless you too, my brudder Toney," said Old Sampson. " I 'se berry sorry for you, and I know how to feel for one like you ; for I too met wid de same heavy loss about ten year ago, when I loss my masser. But God has help me to take care of my missis and her poor little orphan chilluns. I 've tried hard to be a farer to dem; and de little money I could mek by preachin' has help me to send some on 'em to school. I hope de biggest one will yet be a preacher, to tell sinners de way of salvation. But you, Old Toney, hab no missis to educate, and no nyung masser "——

That last unfortunate word was like ripping open a wound still unhealed, and the old man winced and groaned as if in pain.

" Yes, you say true, my brudder Sampson. *I hab no masser* now. My house is lef' unto me desolate, and even my poor nyung missis has hung her harp on de weepin' willow ! "

"I beg your pardon, my brudder Toney," said Old Sampson, with much feeling, while he took Old Toney affectionately by the hand; "I did not mean to reproach

you because you had no masser. No, no! It is a berry
sad t'ing to hab no masser; a berry great affliction to be
widout a masser. God help you, my brudder. I is better
off dan you, for I is hab a nyung masser growing up to be
a man. But nebber mind, Old Toney. Nebber mind—as
my poor dead masser in heben used to say—nebber mind, for
some day or anudder, your nyung missis will get married,
and *den* you will hab a masser."

"T'ank you, my brudder Sampson, for dat word " said
Old Toney, grasping the old preacher's hand and shaking
it warmly and for a long while. "Like a minister of comfort you spoke dat word in my ear when my heart was sad
and my mind a wanderin'. For just den I had forgot!—
Yes! I hope de blessed day ain't berry far off when Mass'
Edgar—I mean Mister Herbert—dat fine-lookin', tall,
splendid man wot you see here to-day wid Miss Ella lean-
in' on his arm—I hope de good time ain't berry far off
when Mass' Edgar will marry Miss Ella, and den I shall
hab a good, and a kind, and a berry noble masser—a rale
Charleston gentleman for a masser—a spic-span new masser,
right from de city."

"I gib you joy, my brudder Toney Shelton. You can,
indeed, mourn, but not as dose widout hope. But it is time
to go now. If not first, we are last at de grave of him of
whom it can be truly said: 'A good man has fallen in
Israel.' Good-by, Brudder Toney, and may God bless and
comfort you. Our roads part just here at de grave, but we
must meet at de grave again, my brudder—you and I. May
we be ready when de Lord Jesus shall call us to lie down
here and rest from our labors."

"Good-by, my dear brudder Sampson," replied Old Toney,
reverently; and he bowed his head over the hand of Old
Sampson to conceal the tear in his eye. But the tear dropped upon the preacher's sable hand, and Old Toney could
could only say:

"May de blessing ob de good Lord be wid you also."

Thus the two sincere old men parted and went away from the grave of Colonel Shelton; and, mounting their horses, rode in different directions, with sad countenances and heavy hearts, to their respective places of abode.

CHAPTER XII.

AS we have before stated, there were several of the
friends and relatives of Mrs. Shelton who returned
with her to her humble and widowed home. They
were sincere, true-hearted friends, who could appreciate true worth, and did not measure one's value by
the length of the purse. There are little souls in the world
who are not men, but who were intended by nature for tail-
ors, who, like the tailor, or the cloth-dealer, with his yard-
stick in hand, looks upon a tall man with more pleasure than
a short one, because his greater hight suggests the additional
yards of cloth necessary to make him a suit of clothes; or
the shoemaker, whose mouth almost waters at the sight of
a large foot, which he hopes to cover with a bigger piece
of leather, at a much bigger price than ordinary. There
are persons, we say, whose souls are no bigger than a cob-
bler's, or a tailor's, are said to be; although, for our own
part, we see no reason why their souls should n't be as big
and as grand as the souls of those for whom they labor.
Indeed, it is our firm belief that there are many persons
whose souls are not half so good as the soles they wear as
a protection to their feet; and it is such as these who value
their friends by "the length of their purse," or the "big-
ness of their pile." The Sheltons, doubtless, may have had
many such friends. If so, it is very certain that not one of
them came to the dwelling of the poor widow in her time
of trouble and distress; for such persons as these are not

of that class who think "it is better to go to the house of
mourning than the house of feasting."

There were none but true friends with Mrs. Shelton now;
and for the honor of humanity and that of the South, be it said,
that her house was as full as it could hold. For there were
mattresses and feather-beds spread all over the floor, and the
small house—every room in it—was filled to overflowing, even
as the great mansion used often to be filled in the time of
Colonel Shelton's riches and prosperity. For these kind
friends well knew that although Mrs. Shelton was comparatively poor—very poor to what she had been—yet she was
independent, and, with a small family and a rigid system of
economy, she could live free from the cold charities and
pitiful contempt of the world. It is true that they all resolved in their hearts that they would never see her want
for anything; this they would nobly and generously see to
in the future; and in doing so, they would take care not to
wound her pride, or remind her of her poverty.

But Mrs. Shelton did not need pecuniary aid at this or
any other time. Old Toney had made a fine crop, and had
gathered in an abundant harvest of corn, and peas, and
sweet potatoes, and rice, and cotton. There was plenty of
provisions to feed many more horses than were used upon
the place; and surely there would be no stint in entertaining the guests and their horses with abundant entertainment. The store-room was filled almost already with fresh
pork—or, rather, pork already salted and almost ready to
be hung up for the smoke; while there was no scarcity of
fowls, and turkeys, and ducks, and other poultry, in the
yard; and there were mattresses, and feather-beds, and a
plenty of warm covering, for all the guests who had returned home with the widow. In short, there was nothing
lacking to add to the physical comfort of the guests; and,
humble as was her home, Mrs. Shelton, so far from murmuring, was contented with the lot which Providence, so
inscrutable in his ways, had assigned her so late in life; for

she was a Christian, and believed firmly in the Christian's doctrine, "The Lord is *my* Shepherd, I shall not want." She had never once thought or felt like murmuring or repining at her lot; and if God should decree that she should wade through fire and blood, she felt that she should wade through them all with a song in her mouth. God help you, poor woman! for your faith shall be tried in a way you wot not of.

No, no; it was only love, sympathy, that she wanted—needed so much now, and her kind and considerate friends well knew this; and, by their coming unasked, they made her poor heart glad to see her house—that small house—filled with so many of her old friends. But it must be confessed that she was in not a little trouble—and her trouble did her good; for, in the kindness of her woman's heart, she was not a little distressed that so many of the gentlemen had to sleep upon the floor, all except the minister. He, dear good man, objected to being made an exception to the rule; for he did not like, he said, exceptions to general rules, which were "good enough for him without the exceptions." But Mrs. Shelton could, on no account, consent that the man of God should sleep so hard—as hard as the rest—after coming so far to bury her dead.

"Their lot, like their Master's, is hard enough, God knows," said she. "For if they are true disciples of Christ, like him they are "men of sorrows, and acquainted with grief."

So the minister slept in the room in which Colonel Shelton died, and thought of the time when he too must enter the "valley and the shadow of death." And in pleading with his God, in the dead hour of the night, when he thought all were asleep, his voice was heard pleading in behalf of the widow and the orphan girl—praying also for himself, that the Savior of sinners would stand by him in the hour and article of death.

There are many who remember him well—that man of

God, with sweet, melodious voice, and cerulean, angel-looking eyes, although he is at rest now, and for many years past he has been sleeping in the graveyard as peacefully—more quietly than he slept in his bed that night—as peacefully as the gallant warrior who has fought many bloody battles, and won many dear-bought victories. But although he is dead and gone upon his long journey home, is there a man now, who was a boy then, who can forget that holy man, with those heavenly, beautiful blue eyes, through which shone a bright, burning, spiritual light, which seemed like the shining of his heavenly soul through those splendid orbs, which reminded one of the eyes of Jesus; who, however, must have looked as no other man ever looked, even as " he spake as never man spake?"

But if he looked not like Jesus, he certainly spoke like him when he used to say, in those peculiarly sweet, melodious tones—melodious and sweet as the sweetest-toned harp: "Come unto me, all ye that labor and are heavy laden, and I will give you rest." And you remember, perhaps, that other text of his, upon which he used to dwell with such rapture and fervid eloquence: " Ho! every one that thirsteth. Come, buy wine and milk, without money and without price."

With these and many other passages yet more appropriate, had he sought to comfort Mrs. Shelton; and when he went away the next day, he did not fail, to the last, to impress the truth upon the minds of the widow and her daughter, that come what may, whether weal or woe, they had a Friend in heaven " who sticketh even closer than a brother."

The minister left, after breakfast, with some others, who were compelled to return to their domestic duties. But Mr. Green, the attorney, with Mr. Thomas Shelton, remained, for the purpose of reading the will in the presence of several witnesses.

Breakfast being now over, and after the gentlemen had smoked their cigars of old Cuban manufacture, which Mrs.

Shelton had nodded Fanny to hand upon a silver tray; for she still kept the old family plate to which she had been so long accustomed. When the gentlemen had finished smoking their cigars in the library, they all repaired to the parlor, for the purpose of breaking the seal and reading the last will and testament of Colonel Shelton. For this purpose the company, both ladies and gentlemen, were assembled in mournful silence; and in the entry were all the servants— Old Toney and Old Rinah, with all their children, from the oldest to the youngest, all anxious to hear the last words of their old master now lying in the grave—words whose purport were known to Mrs. Shelton, but of which even she herself had never read or placed her eyes upon.

There is an interest attached to the reading of the most ordinary and common-place will; and yet we can not call that common-place which bequeathes the body to the earth from which it sprung, and the soul to God who gave it. The last will and testament of a dying man now dead, are solemn words—words of warning to the living—words which seem to come from the grave and recall the form, and the attitude, and the very voice of the deceased. But far greater was the interest felt in the reading of this particular will; not that there was any doubt as to its propriety—its wisdom, but simply because it was the will of Colonel Shelton. He had but little—comparatively little—left to will away; but the few persons most deeply interested loved to hear the echo of his words, although written upon parchment and read by an attorney.

And most interested of all, perhaps, was Old Toney. The old man, with crape upon his arm, leaned against the doorsill, with his head bent and his eyes upon the carpet. By his side, with her hands under her check-apron, stood his wife; in the rear were all his children, from "Young Toney" down to "little Patty," not more than seven or eight years old. With pious care had they been gathered; and, dressed in the clean garments which they wore the day before, they

9

had been assembled, by the direction of their venerable old parent, to hear the last words of their old master—words spoken to them and of them in the last will—the only will he had ever executed. Verily, if an angel from heaven had come down and given notice that he was about to speak to them, they could not have listened with more eager interest, nor regarded him with more attention, than they now listened to the voice of Mr. Green, and looked upon that piece of parchment.

After the usual preliminaries were over, and the seal was broken, Mr. Green commenced the reading of the will in his usual slow and distinct tones. Every word was uttered with distinctness, and prolonged to such length that the hearers might both hear plainly, and understand fully, the purport and intentions of the division.

The disposition and purport of the will, in its first part, was to the effect that the bulk of the property should be given in trust to Mr. Thomas Shelton, for the sole use and behoof of Mrs. Shelton and her daughter; to revert to Ella Shelton and the issue of her body should she ever marry. But if, after the death of Mrs. Shelton, Ella should die also, unmarried, and without heirs, then they should all be free forever; the land to be sold for their benefit, and, with the proceeds of the sale, they were to be removed to Africa.

Such was the substance of the first part of the will. It was unfortunate; but Colonel Shelton did not then know the natural repugnance which his negroes would have for such a removal. But it was null and void *ab incipio;* for nothing ever occurred to render their removal necessary for the fulfillment of the Colonel's wishes. But, in the close, it was worded thus:

"But unto Old Toney, and his wife Rinah also, for and in consideration of their many valuable services to me and to mine rendered, I give their freedom entire and untrammeled, to take effect immediately at the opening and reading of this will: *Provided*"——

Old Toncy heard no more—waited to hear no more; for, before Mr. Green could continue his reading, he was interrupted by the voice of the old man, who left the door-sill, against which he had been leaning, and walked into the middle of the floor greatly excited.

"I can't stand dat. Mass' Green! I can't stand to hear dat!"

"You can't stand what, old man?" asked Mr. Green, who pulled off his spectacles and looked at Old Toncy with surprise.

"My freedom! masser! You must 'a read dat t'ing wrong! *My* masser lub me too much to do dat t'ing. He could n't do it without axin' my leave! You read dat t'ing wrong, Mass' Green!"

"Why, old man, you amaze me! Don't you want your freedom, which you so richly deserve, and have so nobly earned, and which the whole country would acknowledge to be a simple act of justice?"

"No, Mass' Green! I tell you no! My old masser in his lifetime would nebber dare to make me dat offer, 'case he know dat it would break my heart. And Colonel Shelton was too good a man to break de heart of his old sarbent, who lubbed de berry ground on which he walked. No! masser, no! I is an old man now, as old as my old masser 'fore he died. We was born 'bout de same time, we played togedder as boys, and I wanted dat we should die togedder at de same time; but de good Lord's will be done! I am lef' here now, and I must stay wid my missis and her darter, Miss Ella. I hab lib' to be an old and a respectable slave, t'ank de good Lord! I is been wid my masser eberywhere, eben to de big Norred, and far out to de Massissip; and at New Orleans I help to lick de British. And now, Mass' Green, after all dat, *to be made a free nigger!* O, masser! I could n't stand dat disgrace, for it would kill me outright! I could n't hold up my head any more 'mong white folks, and I am too proud to go wid free niggers! Why, masser, just look at de free niggers all

round you! Dey is even 'shamed demselves to be called
free niggers! Dey rudder you call dem Egyptians or Gipseys; and dat's what dey say dey is! Gipseys, not free niggers! Dere's seberal hundred on 'em here, and only two
or t'ree who is honest enough to work! De rest all tief;
dey is all lazy and mean and good for nottin'! Dey is such
a by-word and such a disgrace dat eben der berry dogs look
mean and tief-like demselves! You can tell a free nigger
dog as soon as you can tell a free nigger hisself, and bofe
on 'em will steal sheep!* Masser!" said the old man, with
dignity, drawing himself up to his full hight, and folding
his brawny arms upon his broad chest, "I am an honest
man now; let me be an honest man till I die! De good
Lord lef' us a prayer, and de words of dat prayer is, 'Lead
us not into temptation, but delibber us from ebil!' Masser,
I nebber stole a sebben-pence in my life, for I always hab
a plenty ob money, and got now more dan fifty dollars in
my chest; I got now sebberal gould guineas in my chest
dat I hab for dese fifteen years! I keep 'em for old age
and hard times. But de hard times nebber has come for
me to brek 'um, and I trust in de Lord dat dey nebber will,
and dat de money will stand den for my chillums, when I
dead. But put me in de way ob temptation, mek me a free
nigger, and mebbe I will tief and get as poor and as mean
as any free nigger or sheep-stealin' dog. No, no, I can't be
free nigger, masser! Read 'um ober and read 'um right!
My masser was too sick to write, and you mek mistake,
Mass' Green! And if de berry words is all down dere as
you read 'um, den scratch 'um out, masser! scratch 'um out!"

---

* It must be borne in mind that Old Toney speaks in reference to the free negroes
in the interior of the State, and not of those residing in Charleston, with whom he
was not at this time acquainted. There are many free persons of color in Charleston,
who are good citizens, very well educated, and, to a certain degree, refined, who are
industrious, and some of them may be considered wealthy. Old Toney does not,
therefore, speak of this class, of whom he knows nothing. He only expresses the
general sentiment of the plantation negro in regard to those free negroes with whom
he is best acquainted.

"But, old man," said Mr. Green, with a smile, as he looked
with admiration upon the old man, whose melancholy countenance and earnest tones interested him deeply; and whose
words, all broken and Anglo-African as they were, commanded respect; "but, old man, I can not alter the words
of a will! It would be a penal offense to scratch out a
single line, or even a word of what is written here!"

"Can't help dat, masser! scratch 'um out! scratch 'um
out! or if you is afraid, just gib me de pen and I will take
de 'sponsibility, and scratch 'um out myself! I take de 'sponsibility, masser, 'cause, you know, my masser could n't gone
and done dat t'ing in his right mind, widout fust axin' me;
and as Colonel Shelton did n't ax me about it, den dere is
somet'ing wrong. I know full well dat my masser would n't
hut my feelin' so if he was strong and hearty as he used
to be."

Old Toney had too great a reverence for his master to
say openly, and in distinct terms, that Colonel Shelton's
mind had grown weak, or that he had lost it altogether in
his sickness. As Mr. Green shook his head and smiled at
the old man's words, and sat, for a few moments, almost in a
state of abstraction, Old Rinah—who, before this time had
advanced to the side of her husband, and had been for
some time standing with him on the floor, manifesting her
distress also, by painful sighs, and wiping her eyes streaming with tears with the corner of her check-apron—Old
Rinah dropped upon her knees, and with all the fervor of an
earnest supplicant, implored and entreated the attorney that
the words which accorded them their freedom might be
scratched out, even as Old Toney desired.

"O, sir!" said Old Rinah, "I have tried hard to be a
faithful servant all my life, and I love my mistress! What
have I done to be turned off now in my old age, and be
degraded to a free nigger?"

Old Rinah always used good English, and could express
herself better than her husband; but she felt none the less

keenly her distress, and her heart seemed as if it would
break. What man can withstand the tears of a woman,
whether white or black, bond or free, when he knows there
is just cause for grief? Stern or phlegmatic as usually
seemed the really kind-hearted Mr. Green, he could not be
indifferent to those tears, those heart-breaking sobs, for he
was compelled to draw out his handkerchief in order to
wipe his moistened eyes, and he added hastily and consol-
ingly as he readjusted his spectacles :

"Don't cry, old woman ; it shall be just as you and Old
Toney desire ! Colonel Shelton was a wise man, and I perceive that he understood your case thoroughly. Listen
now to the remainder of the clause, the reading of which
was interrupted by your husband. The will says you can
have your freedom, *provided*—you recollect that was the
place where I left off?"

" Yes, masser," said Old Toney, " dat de berry word ! I
mark 'um, 'prowided.' Well, what dat mean?"

"Provided *you wish it!* but he advises you to remain
with your mistress ; and whether you accept your freedom
now or reject it, *entreats* you to be kind to Mrs. Shelton and
her daughter ; and to guard and defend them as long as you
shall live, or their present defenseless situation requires your
guardianship and protection."

" Bless de Lord ! " exclaimed Old Toney, who now dropped
upon his knees by the side of his wife, seemingly overpowered
by his gratitude.

" Bless de Lord ! " said Old Rinah, weeping now with joy,
with her hands clasped, and her eyes turned up toward
heaven.

" Bless de Lord ! " said Old Toney, clasping his hands
also, as if in prayer. " T'ank de Lord for his goodness ! I
t'ank you, masser, for dat word. It's bad enough to be
widout a dear, good masser ; but to be widout a dear, good
missis, too ! O ! de good Lord would n't afflict a poor nigger
so ! I knew my old masser lub me, and dat he could n't

gib me my freedom agin my will! T'ank de Lord! t'ank
de Lord!"

"Listen now, old man, to what follows; for Colonel Shelton
was not the man to do a thing but half-way. 'And as a
tribute of my gratitude and my love for Old Toney, I give
and bequeath unto said Toney, my gold watch, with the
chain and trinkets attached; together with the sum of one
hundred and fifty dollars; the watch and chain to be given
to him immediately upon the opening and reading of this
will; and the money to be paid to him by my executor,
Mr. Thomas Shelton, out of the proceeds of the present crop,
or as much of it as can be spared, at the present time, from
the expenses of the family.'"

Old Toney seemed not half so glad to hear about the gift
of a watch and one hundred and fifty dollars, as he was to
hear that he was *not* to have his freedom, and *not* to be
converted from a respectable slave into a free negro. But
it must be confessed that when Mr. Thomas Shelton placed
the watch, with the massive fob-chain and trinkets attached,
in his sable hand, and told him that they were now his, and
his alone, and when Old Toney looked upon the shining
metal, glittering and glistening in his ebony palm like a
bright jewel set in a black stone, and when he looked upon
the little second hand going round and round so rapidly,
four times in a minute, and the hour hand and the minute
hand, of pure gold, resting upon a snow-white face, why,
then, it must be confessed that Old Toney's lips began to
part a little, and a little wider, until they parted into a broad
grin of pleasure, and his single eye sparkled with delight.
Then he turned round and touched Old Rinah upon the
shoulder with the end of his index finger, and said, while
he tried to suppress the smile, and to look as grave and
dignified as possible:

"Mek haste, ole 'oman! Go cut hole in all my breeches!
and mek de pocket—de fob! Mek 'um big, so he can come
out easy. I berry t'ankful to you, masser, and to my poor

ole masser for de watch; and to you, Mass' Green, too,
'cause you read de will right. I will hab need ob dis watch;
I stand berry much in need ob 'um to mek dese niggers
work. De corn nebber grow right, masser, unless you know
de time ob de day when you plant 'um. Some people b'liebe
in de moon, and dey plants by de moon, and kill hog by de
moon, and do eberyt'ing by de moon! but for my part I
b'liebe in plantin' and doin' eberyt'ing by de watch. T'ank
you berry kindly, masser, for de watch at dis time."

Old Toney went away very much delighted, bowing and
smiling; and Old Rinah went away also, with low courtesies,
to do her husband's bidding—to "cut big hole" in all his
breeches. And after these two old people followed all their
children; the older ones with a smile, the younger ones
giggling with delight that the old age of their venerable
father and their mother was not to be dishonored. And
those who were left in the parlor—their mistress and her
friends—smiled at their simplicity when they heard some
of them saying to the others as they left the passage and
returned to the yard:

"Ain't you glad Mass' Green did n't mek pappy and
mammy free niggers? Ky! free nigger! We would loss
'um den! Dey would n't be our pappy and our mammy!
Better for 'um to be dead at once dan turn to free nigger!"

That afternoon Mr. Green and Mr. Shelton left the house
of Mrs. Shelton; and the next morning an early breakfast
was ordered for Mr. Herbert, whose intention was to return
without any further delay to Charleston. But although the
breakfast was over and his horse brought to the door at a
very early hour, yet the lover, as all lovers, still lingered as
if undetermined whether to go or to stay. There had been
no time appointed for his marriage; and although he was
exceedingly anxious that it should take place as soon as
possible, yet his innate sense of delicacy and respect for the
sorrows of the family held him back from making any proposition upon the subject of his marriage with Ella Shelton

In truth, he was laboring under a doubt in his own mind, whether, under the circumstances, it would be proper to allude in any way to the period when they should be united in matrimony, since the family had been so recently and so severely afflicted; for it might seem contrary to the strictest rules of propriety to speak of marrying when in the house of mourning, and when they had but just returned from burying the dead father of his future bride.

And yet, on the other hand, he thought their very loneliness and want of protection would seem not only to justify an allusion to the subject, but even to demand some change in their present mode of living. At least, how much better would it be that the marriage should take place at least early in the spring, and then he could be the rightful protector both of Ella and her widowed mother. The varied scenes of the city, too, its refined and elegant society, the kind and friendly reception which they would not fail to meet, and which even the veriest stranger never fails to meet in that most hospitable of all hospitable cities, the city of Charleston; these circumstances, when weighed against the loneliness of their present situation, ought surely to induce Mrs. Shelton at least to waive all etiquette or conventionalism, if, indeed, such considerations could still have any influence upon her mind.

But when Herbert, with great embarrassment, and after several hours of conversation had elapsed—conversation almost entirely in reference to the virtues and many noble traits of character which had been the property, in so signal a degree, of their dear, lost ones—the husband and father, the brother and the son—Colonel Shelton and Langdon—when Herbert said, in one of the intervals which will sometimes occur, even when we are speaking upon a deeply interesting topic:

"My dear madam, I hope you will not consider me rude or heartless to change a little the topic of conversation—one which, although deeply interesting to us all, is mourn

9*

ful in the extreme. For how can we feel otherwise than sad when we recall so forcibly to mind how much we have lost? Excuse me, Mrs. Shelton, for venturing to propose, in some faint degree, to relieve the mournfulness, or, rather I should say, the loneliness of your situation, by "——

Herbert stammered and blushed, and finally added, " by paying a visit to Charleston in the spring."

But finding that Mrs. Shelton had not understood what he wished to communicate, he added, very abruptly, and without further ceremony :

"In short, Mrs. Shelton, my dear madam, I mean to submit to your kind consideration, whether it would not be best, under the circumstances, that my dear Ella and myself should be united in the holy bonds of matrimony as soon as possible. Would it not meet your approbation that the ceremony should take place, say early in the spring?"

"Not yet, my dear Herbert," said Mrs. Shelton, in kind but anxious tones ; " not yet."

"Surely, my dear madam, you are a woman of too much good sense to be influenced by the opinions of the world, or to be controlled by the fashions of the day," said Herbert, rather hurriedly, and in a tone which sounded a little like mortification.

"No, Edgar, you do not understand me. It is not for the world that I care, but for my poor negroes. How could I leave them so lonely, with not a white soul upon the place? Their master dead, and their mistress gone, the poor creatures would feel utterly wretched and forsaken. Accustomed, from their youth up, to the society and daily companionship of white persons, they could never feel happy, but would pine away if they saw the house shut up and the windows closed, and would think that all that they loved on earth had deserted them, or were all dead. They could neither work nor play, if they did not see and know for themselves, with their own eyes, that the dear objects of their love were at their place in their own homestead.

Once or twice in my life, I have had the painful trial of only a brief separation, to spend a summer at Saratoga for the benefit of my health. And if it was painful to me then —very painful to them—O! how could I wring their hearts at a time like this, by telling them that early in the spring, which is close at hand, they must lose their young mistress for life, perhaps, and their old mistress, too? for I can not separate from my daughter, Herbert. I have lost all else, and I must cling to her as my last earthly hope, until the grave shall close over my old head."

"Nor would I have you, by any means, to forsake or give up your daughter, madam," said Herbert, with much feeling, touched by the mournful sound and tremulousness of Mrs. Shelton's voice. "In marrying Ella, I hope to gain, also, a dear mother, who shall counsel us by her superior wisdom, and guide us through life's pathway until we shall gain experience and wisdom for ourselves."

"I thank you, dear Edgar. I knew that you had a kind heart, or I would never have given my consent to your union with my dear Ella. But just now it is impossible for both of us, at least, to leave home; and it is absolutely necessary that, for the year 1826, I should remain with my poor, grief-smitten slaves. Were I to consult my own feelings, I should gladly leave this place at once, where everything I see will recall so painfully the form of my dear husband. But wait a little while, dear Edgar—just one one year—the next fall, say. At that time, I will give my full and hearty consent to your union with my daughter; and I pray God that nothing may occur to prevent it."

Herbert started and turned pale, he knew not why, as if the prayer of Mrs. Shelton had been an imprecation, or an augury of coming evil.

"What *could* prevent it, my dear madam," he asked, eagerly, and in an excited manner.

"Many things now hidden from us could prevent it, my dear Herbert, if God, in his mysterious Providence, should

so determine. 'God's ways are not as the ways of a man;'
and even the French, all atheistic as they are considered,
have a maxim which says: ' *L' homme propose et Dieu dis-
pose.*' This maxim is, in reality, the doctrine of the Bible;
for who can contend against Jehovah?"

"But, my dear madam, how is it possible to suppose that
God himself would object to or in any way hinder a union
which would be hallowed by the affection of two loving
hearts, and which has received the sanction of the parents
of both the bride and the bridegroom?"

"I know not, my dear Herbert," said Mrs. Shelton, with
a sigh. "A woman often entertains fears indefinable for
the future, without being able to give her reasons. I hope
that mine are only sickly vagaries, which do not proceed
from my instincts, and are not prophetic of evil. In truth,
my dear Edgar "——

She hesitated, as if afraid that she had, almost unconsciously, said too much, and added, hastily:

"Excuse me, my dear Edgar. My mind has been fearfully wrought upon of late; I fear me that it will be a hard
struggle to make others cheerful and happy, as has been
my constant aim and desire all through my life. May God
give me strength, that I may be resigned to his holy will
under every dispensation that comes from his holy hand."

"I trust, my dear madam," said Herbert, with much feeling, "that your dark days are ended, and that the rest of
your life will be spent without a cloud to overshadow its
evening."

"I hope so, my dear Edgar. But if afflictions should
come, let us all strive to submit to the will of God. For,
be assured, that the afflictions we are called to endure in
this life, are mercies sent in disguise, since they work for
us, in the life to come, 'a far more exceeding and eternal
weight of glory.' Behind a cloud, black and portentous of
evil, is often hid the smiling face of a beneficent Deity.
Better far, that we should be afflicted and purified in this

life, rather than live in seeming prosperity, careless of eternity, careless of our soul's prosperity, and, after death, to merit the eternal wrath of a neglected, and insulted, and justly indignant God. The man unblessed by a single affliction—the man who has been *cursed* with never-failing prosperity and invariable success—the man who can boast that everything prospers in his hands, and not anything he attempts comes to naught, and whose every wish is gratified —who can say, I have had no losses nor crosses, and know nothing of what is called the displeasure of God—who has never felt the rod of his chastisement laid, however lightly, in love, upon his shoulders, such a man is like one standing upon a mighty mountain-glacier, which will, one day, become an avalanche, to slide, with awful velocity and fearful destruction, his immortal soul into hell. My dear children, let me entreat you both, in your coming life, never to murmur at the chastisements of your heavenly Father; but ever to remember, under every trial and every affliction, however appalling, that 'Whom the Lord loveth he chasteneth, and scourgeth every son whom he receiveth.' "

This sounded, to the ears of the Charlestonian, like very strange philosophy ; but he remained silent, and pondered upon the words of the Christian woman, amazed that she could speak thus when her own heart had been so hardly wrung by such severe mental anguish.

But the time came when Herbert felt that it was necessary that he should depart ; and, rising from the sofa upon which he was seated, he took Mrs. Shelton's hands in his and attempted to say farewell in words, but his lips quivered, and his tongue trembled so that he could not articulate a syllable, for his heart was full, and just then a passing cloud threw its shadow between them, and rested upon the pale forehead of the widow. Herbert was not usually superstitious, or given to gloomy forebodings, but he shuddered then as though a bird of evil omen had flitted between them ; and a painful presentiment kept crowding and pressing itself into his mind, that that noble woman, so brave under trials beneath which stern and manly hearts would quail— that there were darker days in store for her, and that when they met again it would not be in joy, but in great sorrow, and tribulation, and anguish. And he almost said aloud, " What is it? where is it?" but he smiled at himself, and thought he was foolish to anticipate troubles which might never come. Then he bowed his head low over Mrs. Shelton's hand, and kissed it. She felt deeply, and appreciated his kind intention; and before he raised his head again she had pressed a mother's kiss upon his forehead. When he lifted his eyes to hers, and saw that they were full of tears, he bowed his head again and tried to smile a smile of hope; but his lips knew not how to mock his heart, so full of sorrow and foreboding.

Little Fetic was still with the family, as she was nearly all the while; and Herbert, when he took her by the hand, stooped low and affectionately kissed the blind girl upon her cheek. His actions were all very graceful and noble, because so simple, and unaffected, and natural. When he came to Ella and took her, last of all, by the hand also, his knees trembled until they smote together several times, and it required all the strength of resistance of which his strong nature was capable, to control the agitation which had well-nigh completely unmanned him. And the sight of his agitation, which, for a moment, was so powerful and so apparent to others, overcame the young and loving maiden so, that even the presence of her dignified old mother could not restrain her actions. The spectacle of her lover's sorrow, the sight of tears upon his manly cheeks, overcame her so that she threw herself with passionate weeping upon his breast. And as she clung fondly with her arms around his neck, and seemed to feel that this was their last meeting on earth, Herbert felt that he would be willing that they should die thus in each other's embrace; for then the evil days would never come, or, coming, they would reck them not.

Mrs. Shelton did not do as some prudish or stately mothers would have done under precisely similar circumstances. She did not charge her daughter with indelicacy, nor reprove her for a want of maidenly reserve. But she did as a sensible mother would have done, she let her daughter weep, for several minutes, upon the breast of her noble lover, that her surcharged soul might find relief; for she well knew that her heart-strings had been made so tense from suffering of late, that those tender cords must snap asunder if not relaxed by weeping. She let her weep, therefore, just when she was in the arms of her lover, that her agony might, in a measure, be overcome by the flowing of her tears in copious showers, and her heart be made strong by feeling the strong and man-like throbbings of Herbert's noble heart beating in sympathy and love. And her heart caught the tone of his, and the hearts of the two lovers beat in unison.

By-and-by Ella's sobs were hushed, and her chest heaved no more, and she became as still as an infant that has sobbed itself to sleep upon its mother's breast. She raised her head, and looking up into Herbert's eyes as he looked down upon her with eyes beaming with affection, while his hand rested upon her beautiful head rather as the hand of a fond husband about to leave his home for some distant land, and blessing thus his faithful wife, than of the lover only, who vows in his heart to love and to cherish his affianced bride, Ella smiled hopefully and said :

" After a storm, Herbert, comes a calm. Let us hope in God. All that's well shall end well."

Herbert tried to speak, but his lips only murmured inarticulate words, and Mrs. Shelton took her daughter by the hand and led her back to the sofa.

" Go now, my dear Edgar, and may God be with you," she said. " In a little less than one year's time I hope Ella shall be yours in name as she is yours in spirit ; and may the good Lord bless you both, is the prayer of your widowed mother."

Herbert felt that he could stay no longer, and that their hearts would only be wrung afresh by the torture of another leave-taking. He turned away sadly and with a heavy heart, and went out of the room, closing the door after him as softly as though he was leaving a sick-chamber; then, with hurried footsteps, he reached the little gate of the flower-garden, and, vaulting into the saddle, he put spurs to his already-anxious and mettlesome horse, and sped as an arrow from the sight of her whom he loved best on earth. As loth as he had been to leave the beloved object of his heart's affections, now that their adieus had been told, in actions if not in words, in proportion was he anxious to dash forward at the mad rate of the whirlwind's march. There were no railroads in those days; and if there had been even a stage, it would have lumbered on too slowly for the excited state of his feelings. The horse, under whip and spur, was the best agency, then as now, which could be employed to calm down the overwrought feelings of a man's overwrought heart.

If we could follow on after him we should see, that after a reasonable time, the man of prudence and forethought has recovered his outward equanimity; and that, reining in his horse, he allows him to take the usual pace of an animal which has a long and wearisome journey to perform.

While, therefore, Mr. Herbert is performing this journey toward Charleston at a much more leisurely pace than when he left the house of Mrs. Shelton, let us also—the reader and the author—take a journey toward the North; for there lie scenes which we must look at, and there are other persons with whom we must become acquainted, before we can know the *dénouement* of our story.

BOOK II.

CHAPTER I.

A FEW years prior to the commencement of our narrative there was an ill-assorted match in the city of New York. Anna Moultrie was the only daughter of very wealthy and refined parents, who died a short time before their idolized child had attained the age of womanhood. Gay, fashionable, and highly accomplished, she drew a long train of admirers after her, and foremost among them was the Hon. George Williston, member of Congress. He was a man of fair but not extraordinary talents; but possessing considerable money himself, and being, withal, a successful politician, he was thought at that time to be just such a man as the refined and the wealthy Anna Moultrie should marry. But he was not the refined and generous spirit which she needed in the loneliness of her orphanage to make her happy. It was, therefore, only by the persuasion—much persuasion of mutual friends— that she consented to become his wife; and in doing so, there was a half-cheerful assent, for her heart was as yet intact; she had never met the man whom she could say she loved with all her heart.

In marrying Mr. Williston, there was no attempt made to

deceive him on the part of Anna Moultrie, who really thought
that in consenting to become his bride, she would honor
him with the pure love of a virtuous wife. But, alas! how
sadly deceived are sometimes the purest in heart, and how
much woe is the result of indiscretion! An ill-assorted
match! a marriage union without love! Ah! the heart
aches; the mental anguish, the hopeless cries of the unsat-
isfied heart.

When Mr. and Mrs. Williston went to Washington, they
soon became objects of attention, and crowds of admirers
flocked to their *soirées*, which were said to be the most
entertaining of any in that most agreeable and fascinating
city. The *élite* of the country were there. Lords, and
counts, and noble embassadors of every land sought with
pleasure the halls of fashion and elegance where the beautiful and elegant Mrs. Williston ruled as queen beyond
dispute, and where there was not a rival to challenge her
imperial sway. The second winter came and went, and then
the third, and still the parties given by the Willistons of
New York, were all the rage at Washington; while the
young married woman, although a few years older, and
although she had given birth to a son—a beautiful little
boy—instead of having lost any of her attractions, had
become more lovely, more fascinating in her manners and
conversation. If the old and experienced statesman sought
an opportunity to linger a few moments by her side, and
if the old, weather-beaten, war-wrinkled heart of the veteran
soldier was made to expand and smooth out some of its old
wrinkles, whenever the musical laugh of Mrs. Williston was
heard floating through the crowded saloon, surely the young
and the single-hearted may be excused from bowing down
as devotees at the shrine of her matchless elegance and
beauty. But to all such as these her conduct was circum-
spect; and although her manner was not repulsive to those
sincere admirers who would have given their all, perhaps,
for a single smile of love in return for their devotion, yet

she held them at a respectable distance, compelling them
to worship her afar off, as a goddess whose radiant glory
they could look upon, but whose drapery they could not
touch.

There was one young man, however, a member of Congress, Hon. Julius Sanford, of Boston, who gradually approached nearer the shrine behind which shone the radiant
glory which had dazzled his eyes and bewildered his imagination. Mr. Sanford was a young man of about thirty, possessing brilliant talents, consummate skill in oratory, and
by some he was called "the lion of the House;" for upon
him all eyes would be turned wherever he went, and never
did he attempt to speak without enchaining the attention
of his audience. He was an honest and a sincere man in
all the relations of life. Sincere even in his politics, he
could not be otherwise than sincere in his friendships. He
reckoned his friends not by hundreds, but by thousands;
not among Northern members only, but among the warm-
hearted sons of the sunny South. But although a scholar,
and an orator, and a statesman, he was but a mere mortal
at last, and could love as only a sincere-hearted man can
love. His heart, hitherto intact, had never been touched
with the fire of love until he beheld the beautiful Mrs.
Williston; and when he discovered the fact, alas! too late
for his own or her happiness, he sought to tear himself
away from the society of a beloved being whom he could
no more approach and be innocent. In his conception, and
with his lofty ideas of honor, the marriage wall could not
be scaled, for it reached upward to heaven, and God himself stood upon its parapet, with his flaming sword, to smite
down the bold intruder who should attempt to blight the
happiness and mar the peace of the slumberers within the
hymenial circle.

"No, no," said the youthful statesman, with a deep-drawn
sigh, as he sat, one winter night, at his writing-desk, with
his massive head buried in his hands, thinking of her upon

whom he began to reflect that it was sinful and dangerous
to think or to look upon any more. "I must not see her
again; I had better write! But how can I resist her appeal?
Let me read her note once more!"

He took up the little gilt-edged note, sealed with a pink-
ish sealing wax, upon which had been stamped the coat-of-
arms and the initials of Anna Williston. He had been
careful not to injure the stamp, and had cut the paper around
it with his pen-knife. He looked upon it with a sparkling
eye, and, turning the letter over, gazed with rapture upon
its face wherever his own name was inscribed by the hand
of her whom he adored, but into whose presence he could
come only as a goddess whose glory was impanneled and
protected by the cold and forbidden bars of the marriage
relation. Her husband, it was true, did not appreciate the
prize he had so easily won. He had married her for her
gold, and had never sought to win her love; but he was
her husband! and "husband," he thought, is a holy name!
But then the reflection came to his mind, and he said aloud,
with his teeth hard set against each other, while his brilliant
eyes dilated and flashed with indignation:

"Yes, if he were indeed a husband! But with what cruel
neglect does he treat a lovely woman, who sighs in secret,
all unconscious of the fact, for a mate who can appreciate
her loveliness and her worth! The cold-hearted villain!
He does not even attend to his duties in the House, but
vacates his seat continually, to visit the gambling-saloons
and bar-rooms of the city, and thus dishonors not only his
state and his country, but his adorable wife! Wife! She
is none of his! God could never have sanctioned such a
union, which could only have been consummated by the vile
intrigues of Mammon's slaves! Accursed be they who bind
the virgin heart of innocence and purity to the hellish car
of lust, or fetter the free spirit with chains of gold and silver! They may cause a splendid alliance, but they introduce into society splendid misery, and wrap, with a gilded

shroud, a dead heart with withered hope. Sad it is to see the infant corpse whose brow is decked with a garland of green leaves and fresh roses, because the leaves and the flowers, by their very freshness, remind us more forcibly of the fact that the loved one lying in the coffin is withering and perishing away even faster than the rose which has been plucked from its stem. But sadder still to see the young and lovely bride, all bedecked and spangled with golden stars and gilded marriage-wreaths, when her young heart has been unpledged to a monster who claims all the right of the husband, but acknowledges none in return to the wife. Williston is a scoundrel; for he not only drinks and gambles—not only neglects the society of his wife, and leaves her to the care of others, but even seeks that of strange women! And were it not for the beauty and intelligence of Anna—— Ah! bless the angel woman! she loves me, though she herself knows it not! No! She intended these lines simply as a sisterly rebuke—to chide my absence and withdrawal from her society! nothing more. She says only:

"'How can you be so cruel, my dear Sanford, as to tear yourself away from my presence these three whole days, without coming, for even a single moment, to say "Good-evening," or to wish me pleasant dreams for the night? Ah! if you knew how very agreeable you are, and how happy you make me whenever you are near, and how utterly wretched and lonely I feel when you are absent, you would not stay away so long. You know, my dear Julius, that I have never had a brother or sister to love, and you have taught me to love you as an adopted brother. Can you not come to your sister now? I feel very sad and lonely, for Mr. Williston is seldom at home, and I have no one to talk to. Come.

"'Yours, ever truly,

"'ANNA W ——.'

"Yes," said Mr. Sanford, with energy, striking his hand upon the table, ".I will go, if only to tell her that I love her more than life itself, and then to leave her forever, to

wander in unknown lands, where none can have the right
to pry into the grief of the stranger."

He took his hat and cane and walked out into the cool
air, and as he drew nearer the residence of the Willistons,
his heart beat quicker, so quick and hard that its throbs
became painful, and he stopped still to reflect upon his
situation.

"Let me consider," said he to himself; "mine is a hopeless situation; for I love, and I fear that I am loved in
return, by a married woman—a wife! O, God! mine is a
hard case! I could brave it better if my love were unrequited; for then, in secret, I would nurse the wound in my
heart, and no human eye should ever look upon its festering.
But Anna! poor, wounded dove! she is like a mourning
turtle mated to a kite; and to tear her from his cruel tal-
ons would only cause misery and death. Better to let her
die under the grasp of the tyrant, than to see her all mangled
and torn by any attempt to rescue her from her forlorn situation. No, no! cruel and unmanly would be the wretch
who should tempt her to fly with him from a husband,
however hateful; for then the holy name of wife, which
she bears so nobly, like a martyr now, would be sacred no
longer, and her lover would become dishonored as her
paramour. O, God! forbid it! Stamp the wretch with
eternal infamy who would sully the fair fame and dishonor
the woman whom he loves, because she trusts to his love
and his honor!"

Sanford's heart beat slower now. He raised himself to
his full hight as he felt within him the lofty thoughts of
the high-born soul. He felt conscious that he was an honorable gentlemen, and that the villain's brand could never be
stamped upon his forehead. He passed his hand over his
brow, slowly and deliberately, as if feeling for the villain's
brand. He felt conscious that God had never stamped it
there; and he was resolved that his conduct should never
merit the villain's or the traitor's doom. He loved an-

other's wife, it is true; but he would die to defend her honor as soon as he would her person. He would never deflour the dear object of his heart's idolatry; and he felt his arm grow strong to strike down her betrayer—his heart nerved with a brother's love. He moved forward slowly and with solemn tread, rather like a man marching to a funeral than a lover hastening to his trysting-place. He reached the door of Mr. Williston's residence and raised the brass knocker, but he gave no rap; for the door stood ajar, and was pulled back by the hand of the dear being whom he loved only too well. She had been looking for him with an eagerness which she knew not how to account for to herself. She had not stopped to inquire into or analyze 'her feelings. She only knew that Sanford was very dear to her, and that she was happy only in his presence.

"I am so glad you have come, my dear Sanford," said she. "I was looking for you, and felt sure that you could not resist my appeal, nor treat me longer with such cruel neglect."

Sanford made no reply to her salutation, but took her hand in his and pressed it tenderly. Her hand was very cold, and he felt like warming it in his, with something of that feeling of the parent-bird when she covers, with her wing, the young fledgeling that has strayed from her side and returned to its mother's nest benumbed with cold. He led her gently from the dim passage into the brighter light of the parlor, and drew her to the sofa; seating her by his side as a brother who feels very sad and mournful because he is about to leave a beloved sister, and travel far away into untrod and savage land. There was a deep melancholy upon his brow, which sat there as the shadow of the cloud upon his heart. So mournful was the expression of his countenance, that Mrs. Williston felt her heart throbbing with painful sympathy for the man she loved, but did not know it. She placed her left hand upon his shoulder, and looked into his sad eyes with an earnest appeal for his confidence and trust in her.

"Tell your sister," said she, with a tremulous voice, "tell your sister what is the matter."

Sanford could not make any response to this appeal, for there was a mighty struggle going on within him. His strong and manly frame became almost convulsed for a moment; but, with a mighty effort, he subdued the emotions of his soul, so that she felt only the tremulous movements of . his hand, which became steadier as he grasped hers with a tighter, steadier grasp. His silence and evident emotion excited still more the sympathy of the beautiful young woman, whose head moved unconsciously still closer, until her fragrant breath fanned his fevered cheek, as a zephyr, loaded with the sweet fragrace of odoriferous shrubs and flowers, wafted from fairy gardens. He felt then like clasping her to his bosom, and kissing, with rapture, those ruby lips, which, gently parting, revealed the pearly whiteness of her beautifully-formed teeth. As those beautiful black orbs of hers were turned upward, and gazed so tenderly into his; as her soft, delicate hand rested confidingly upon his shoulder, and her sweet breath blew upon his cheek, it required all the moral and mental control of a strong-minded and upright man to command the feelings by which he was almost overmastered. But he succeeded sufficiently to sit still and motionless as a statue, but with the mournful look of the lifelike portrait whose eyes only seem to move and whose chest to heave, as if with the suppressed emotions of a brave but suffering heart.

"Do not look upon me so," said Mrs. Williston, as her voice trembled still more, and her eyes filled with tears; "you make me feel very sad, and as I never felt before. Speak, dear Sanford, and tell me what is the matter."

"Dear Anna," said he, sorrowfully, "I am very sorry you have asked again the fatal question. I would have sat thus in mournful silence, as when we gaze upon the face of the dead, for the last time, before the coffin's black lid hides forever from our sight the dear object we have loved too well. I would have looked thus in mournful silence without uttering a word of complaint, and then turned away, with a bleeding heart, to leave you forever."

"To leave me!" cried she, in alarm, as she started back and looked upon him with anguish depicted in her countenance.

"Yes, Anna," said he, in a choking voice, which told how deeply smitten with grief he was, "yes, I must leave you now and forever; and "——

"But why should you leave me? what have I done? what has happened?" she asked, in eager tones. "Have I done anything to offend you, Sanford, my brother?" she sobbed.

"Offend me? No, no, dearest Anna! You could do nothing to offend me. It is because I love you, and you are the wife of another. It is because I love you as man never loved a woman, and because my love is hopeless."

The queenly head of Mrs. Williston drooped now as it never drooped before. She spoke not a word in reply for some considerable time. So long did she remain silent and motionless, that Sanford began to feel alarmed lest he had deeply offended her by a declaration which his own heart already began to condemn as unmanly and ignoble. He was relieved from his suspense by feeling the clutch of her woman's hand upon his, as she raised it upward with a steady but convulsive energy. Upon his dear hand she bowed her beautiful alabaster forehead, and held it there so hard that the head of the one seemed glued or nailed to the hand of the other. Then the words which proceeded from her lips were rather the sobs of a heart suddenly crushed and broken by the unlooked-for intelligence that all its brightest hopes had been wrecked in a gulf of woe and misery.

"O Sanford!" she sobbed; and then pressed his hand to her bosom, as if with the hope that his friendly hand

10

and manlike power might still the wild, and tumultuous, and painful throbbings of his anguished heart. "O Sanford! would to God that we had never met, or had met sooner! for you are dear to me also."

She could say no more, for her tears were running fast, and her chest was heaving upward, as the sea mourning for the wreck and ruin which it has itself caused, and which now lie buried in its bosom. So, too, the human breast must heave minutely, hourly, daily—ever heave with slow and solemn movement over the agonized heart, wherein lie buried, from the world's heartless scrutiny, wrecked and ruined hopes, dead loves, and withered affections. Alas! the human heart is but a sepulcher to conceal our dead loves or our sinful thoughts. Poor wounded hearts! love-smitten, but without hope. The marriage altar stands between you and your love, call it by as holy a name as ye may. Incense is burning upon that altar ; and God's angel, with his flaming sword, guards the shrine, which ye can not touch with impunity. You may look, and kneel, and worship together, but you may not touch that altar, or hope to overleap it, lest ye die ; for the incense burning upon it is lighted by the hymeneal torch, and its flames rise high, forming a wall of fire, which will consume you with certainty if you attempt to penetrate the wall which God has raised between the married woman and her quasi-lover. O! tell me not that such a thing as Platonic love ever existed, or can exist, between a mortal man and a loving woman, however honorable or virtuous. The stoic, whose heart is made of stone, or has become petrified, by habitual indifference to the emotions and sufferings of actual life ; or the miser, who is so wedded to his gold that his heart has dwindled and shrunk into dross—hearts like these, not human, may look with indifference upon a weeping woman, whose sobs came upward from a broken spirit, like the dying notes of the organ, played upon by aërial hands, or touched plaintively by the fingers of the wind.

Julius Sanford, all statesman, and orator, and scholar as
he was, was but a man—a mere man—with a noble heart,
it is true, but with all the strong impulses and passionate
energies of a man who could feel deeply, and love with the
deathless devotion of a martyr. When he looked upon the
weeping form by his side, and heard her sobs, and listened
to her low and plaintive wails, he forgot himself, and abandoned all his high resolves ; for, in a moment, his love was
clasped in his arms, and pressed to his bosom with the feeling that she was his own and not another's, and that he, and
he alone, had the right to protect and defend her against all
the world.   It was but a moment—a single moment—that
Mrs. Williston was clasped in the arms of Mr. Sanford—
that her head rested upon his palpitating heart ; for she
drew herself away with wounded dignity, hurt not so much
with Sanford as with herself. But she had not withdrawn
herself from Sanford's embrace in time to prevent her husband seeing her in a false position.

Mr. Williston had just returned from the gaming-table,
greatly irritated by his bad luck ; for, as it subsequently
appeared, he had lost his all. His last stake that night had
been the finishing stroke to his jeopardized possessions, which,
with prudent care and management, might have assumed
princely proportions—all hazarded upon the throw of the
die, or lost upon the turn of a card. His desperation was
increased when informed by one of his wicked companions
that he had better now return to his home and guard a
neglected treasure there, lest his jewel should be stolen in
his absence.

This hint was sufficient to arouse the demon of jealousy,
now rendered doubly furious by his want of success at play,
and the excitement of ardent spirits. Imagine, therefore,
his rage when he saw his wife lying passively upon the
breast of Hon. Julius Sanford, whose head was bent so low
that he saw not the form of the enraged husband, as he
stepped into the room, armed with a stick, which he had

snatched up from the corner.   It was Mr. Sanford's own
walking-cane, which was wielded by the enraged husband, who
showered blows upon the defenseless head of his victim, with
the determination to dash out the brains of the supposed
libertine, and hurl them into the face of the wife who had
betrayed him.   Fortunately, however, the stick was a light
one, and did but little injury, except to cut the skin in two
or three places, causing the red blood to stream down upon
his cheeks, and redden his white shirt-bosom like crimson.

Mrs. Williston screamed aloud when she saw the blood,
and raised her arms imploringly toward her furious husband,
deprecating his wrath, and imploring his mercy in behalf
of his victim.   The only answer of the brutal man was to
strike down her uplighted arm, and, with a horrid execra-
tion, to call his virtuous wife an abandoned wanton.

This was too much for the spirit of Sanford, who felt now
that it was his duty as a man to stand up in defense of an
injured woman, whether wife or maiden.   He could submit
to insult, and, under the circumstances, even blows from a
cane; but he could not endure to see the woman he loved
treated with indignity and loaded with opprobrium.

"Stop, sir!" he cried in tones of indignation.   "Another
word of insult to that pure woman—another term of reproach
to her whom you call your wife—another finger raised to
touch too harshly her delicate person—and, by the God who
made us both, I will shoot you dead where you stand!"

His hand was upon the trigger of a small brass pistol,
and its muzzle was pressed hard against the temple of Mr.
Williston, from whose hand the stick fell to the floor, while
his arms fell motionless to his side.   *The bully was effectually
cowed.*   The pressure of the brazen muzzle upon his temple
had suddenly cooled his excited passions, and driven away
the enraged demon which was urging him on to deeds of
violence and bloodshed.   He was afraid to move, lest Sanford might, indeed, shoot him down in his tracks; so he
stood still and trembled like a crane.   Sanford still held

the pistol to his head, while in slow and deliberate tones he said :

" You have wronged, sir, an innocent woman and a true wife ; one who has been truer to you than you deserve. What you saw when you entered the room was enough, perhaps, to excite your suspicions against her honor, and arouse your indignation against my supposed villany. I can, however, solemnly assure you, as a man of untainted honor, that it has not been the result of any deep-laid schemes or plans matured in secret. It was the accidental response of two hearts for the first time discovering the fact that they were mutually beloved. But it was also the farewell! the last and sad adieus of two hearts devoted to each other, but separated by the intervening obstacle of a human monster called husband!' She is as pure and as holy now as ever she was, and may God keep her so always ! Hear me, Williston, at your peril ! for should any evil betide her from this affair, either in person or character, it were better for you a thousand times that you were hurled from the hights of Mount Athos into the depths of the ocean, with Mount Athos itself tied around your neck ! Farewell, dearest Anna !" he added, mournfully, as he stooped to kiss her marble brow, for she had fainted away and had fallen upon the sofa, lying there pale and lifeless as a corpse. As he leaned over the woman so dear to his heart, some drops of blood trickled from his wounds and fell upon her forehead, as·if to baptize her with his love. He did not attempt to wipe away those crimson stains, but left them there as the grief-drops of his weeping heart. As he rose erect again, he turned toward Mr. Williston with the authoritative air and tones of a potentate who would be obeyed :

" Your wife, sir, needs attention. I leave her now in your hands. If I have done you or her any wrong, whether unintentionally or with design, I am heartily sorry for it. At all events, I stand ready to render you any satisfaction which you may feel called upon to require at my hands."

He bowed low as he spoke, and left the apartment in possession of its rightful occupants. He returned to his hotel by a private entrance, and at a late hour of the night summoned a physician to dress the trivial wounds he had received, that they might heal the more rapidly. The physician kept his secret, and but for the subsequent indiscretion, the baffled rage, the unalloyed jealousy, and drunken, diabolical whims of Mr. Williston, the world would never have known that a serious difficulty had occurred between the member from New York and the honorable member from Boston.

CHAPTER II.

A FEW days after the occurrences recorded in the last chapter, Hon. Julius Sanford was well enough to resume his accustomed seat in Congress. A subject of considerable interest commanded the attention of the House, which was crowded with anxious auditors; for it was expected that eloquent men would take the floor, and that among them Mr. Sanford would appear conspicuous. This gentleman rose from his seat with the calm dignity of a man who felt the importance of his mission. There was no excitement, no bluster in his manner; nor did he attempt any oratorical flights upon that occasion. His speech was rather a statement of facts from which others might draw their inferences and their arguments; but his every word was listened to with profoundest attention and interest.

It was while making a statement which he said he would vouch for himself upon his own personal knowledge, that the House was thrown into confusion by the outrageous conduct of the member from New York, Mr. Williston, who, rising from his seat, half drunk, cried out, "That's a lie! Sanford is a d——d liar!"

This gross insult and brutal interruption would have unnerved and so confused most men, that they would either have been unable to proceed, or would have left their place immediately, resolved upon instant personal satisfaction. As it was, Mr. Sanford turned red and pale by turns; and discovering the situation of his enemy, and conscious of his

own superiority, he smiled and bowed to Mr. Williston, and
then went on coolly with his statement of facts, feeling
satisfied that he had the confidence of the Speaker and
House of Representatives.

Mr. Sanford was not a duelist; but he had admitted there
were times and occasions when he would fight; that although
he might bear much personal abuse, and submit to much
personal indignity, yet that sometimes forbearance ceases to
be a virtue, and that of one thing he felt certain, that he
would not suffer the honor of his native State to be assailed;
but as David fought in the duello with Goliah, so, also, he
would fight the enemies of his State and country, be they
few or many! This was an error of the head, however, and
not of his heart.

The reader has seen that Mr. Sanford was not a coward,
but a brave and noble spirit, who verified, upon this occasion,
the truth that " Greater is he that governeth his spirit, than
he that taketh a city." But the world knew none of these
circumstances, and they could make no allowances for the
man who could tamely, and with a smile upon his lips,
submit to such an indignity as the member from New York
had cast upon the member from Massachusetts. The world
does not know always the motives which influence a brave
man's civil or political actions. The world does not know
that it often requires a braver heart and a more courageous
spirit to bear an insult than to avenge it; to withhold the
hand rather than to strike the death-blow at one's enemy.
In Mr. Sanford's case, while many men would have rejoiced
at an opportunity so favorable of getting rid of a hated rival,
and, by a hostile meeting, hope to remove an otherwise in-
surmountable obstacle to the gratification of his desires, he
felt that, as an honorable man and a philanthropist, he ought
to endure, to the last degree of provocation, everything which
Mr. Williston might heap upon him in the shape of opprobrious epithets. He had felt his blows—blows struck with
his own cane—and had not returned them. Why now should

he notice his insane abuse? It is true he smarted under the insult thus publicly given in the People's Hall, and in the face of the whole country. But it was a personal insult, and he alone could know how hard is was to be borne without in any way attempting to resent it. Had the slander been hurled at his own native State he would have felt it his duty to demand redress for her wrongs, or scathed with his sarcasm, and blasted with his withering scorn, the bold blasphemer of his country's honor. But, under the circumstances, he felt that the indignity was intended for his own person; for himself and not for the State he represented.

Hence it was that Mr. Sanford resolved to submit in silence to the insults of a man whom he felt, in his own conscience, that he had wronged, in fact though not in intention. For, however innocently he had gone to the house of Mr. Williston on that fatal night, his own conscience upbraided him for having allowed his judgment to be controlled by his passions.

"Why did you allow yourself," his inward monitor often asked him, "to throw yourself so frequently and unreservedly into the society of a lovely young woman who is the wife of another? Did you not know that the experiment was, at least, a dangerous one, and that, to say the least, you were throwing yourself into the way of temptation? And on that memorable evening, why did you not stay away as you had at first determined? And when first you felt your heart draw toward the lovely, the fascinating, the artless, the glorious creature, why did you not stay away altogether? why did you not cease your visits at once, before the injury, now irremediable, was done? before she had learned to love you, and you had loved her to madness? O, Sanford! Sanford! see now the woe, the untold misery which your imprudent conduct has brought upon her and upon yourself also! May God help you both to bear it!"

Such were his thoughts, and such the motives which restrained the hand of Hon. Julius Sanford, the youthful
10*

orator and statesman from Massachusetts. But when Mr.
Williston saw that he bore so patiently the insult which he
had so publicly offered him, and when he had waited for
several days in vain for a challenge, he resolved to insult
his now hated rival still more grossly, for Williston began
to writhe under the contemptuous silence of his adversary,
even more than he had done from any other treatment or
injury which he felt that he had received at the hands of
Mr. Sanford.

But now he was still more urged on by his false friends
and advisers, who made him believe that he was not only
a very courageous man himself, but that Sanford was so
arrant a coward that it was extremely doubtful whether he
could be made to fight under any circumstances, however
provoking. It was when laboring under this opinion, so
erroneous, and while his feelings were greatly excited by
the influence of liquor, that he met Mr. Sanford, in company with several of his friends, in front of his hotel. Williston had his friends, or rather backers, with him also; the
most of whom were professional gamblers and genteel blacklegs. Without any ceremony, Mr. Williston stepped forward and said:

"Julius Sanford, I called you a liar in the House of
Representatives, and you gulped it down like a d—d
coward! Now I say that you are not only a liar, but a
scoundrel!"

He waited for a reply, but there was no answer; and
seeing Mr. Sanford remain perfectly still and erect, as a
king pelted by a mob, he added:

"And if that does not affect you, take that!"

There was a quid of tobacco in his mouth at the time.
He took it from his mouth, and held it for a moment between his thumb and forefinger, then threw it full into the
face of Mr. Sanford, squirting some of the tobacco juice into
his face also.

"There! d—n you! swallow that!" cried Williston, in

a rage; "all the waters of the the Potomac can not wipe
that off! Nothing but *my* blood can wipe that stain
away!"

Mr. Sanford took out his pocket-handkerchief and wiped
away the foul stain of the tobacco juice from his face. To
others, he seemed to be perfectly cool, until they saw his
lip tremble and his face turn deadly pale. He placed his
hand upon his heart to still the violence of its throbbings,
and bowing to Mr. Williston, said, in low tones—so low that
they sounded rather like a hoarse whisper:

"I will do it!" said he, with a lip which now curled
upward until it became stiff and rigid with contemptuous
hatred. "I will do it! I will wipe out the insult with your
heart's blood, as you desire it!"

He turned away with a lofty step, and entered his
hotel. He was followed by his most intimate friends, whose
feelings shared with his in their indignation at the outrage, which had been so wantonly perpetrated upon his
person.

The preliminaries were soon arranged for a hostile meeting, to take place the next morning before sunrise. As the
challenged party, Mr. Williston had the choice of weapons,
and being a fine shot himself with the rifle at sixty yards,
he imagined that it would be an easy matter to wing his
adversary at the first fire, and escape himself without injury.
But, unfortunately for his calculations, Mr. Sanford himself was a dead shot with the rifle at almost any reasonable
distance; for he not only possessed a keen eye and a steady
nerve, but he had often practiced for amusement at a target,
contending that a good citizen ought to prepare himself
for war, when his country might require his services against
the common enemy. In all these attempts at target shoot-
ing, however, he had never once supposed that circumstances
might arise when he would .be called upon to turn that
rifle with deadly aim upon the body of one of his fellow-
countrymen, as a duelist in the hateful arena of the duello.

He had hoped to reserve his practiced aim for the time when war's alarums should summon the sons of liberty to the defense of their altars and their firesides, and, as freemen, to repel the invaders of their country.

When Sanford thought of his novel situation, as he lay that night upon his bed—when he remembered the impotence of his adversary, and felt his own superiority towering above him in conscious intellectual strength, as the tall giant rises above the insolence of the pigmy, or the lion listening with cool scorn to the barks of the cur, he said to himself: "I have changed my mind; I shall give him a wound which he shall remember to his dying day. Perhaps, it will do the fellow good, and he, himself, shall say I have shed enough of his blood to wipe away all the insults he has heaped upon me!"

Having satisfied his conscience with this reflection, the young statesman turned over upon his side and fell into a quiet and refreshing slumber, which lasted until an hour before daylight. Not so, however, with Mr. Williston, who was up all night with his companions, drinking, and smoking, and chewing ; so that when the morning dawned, instead of being calm and collected, he was nervous and fidgety ; in short, in any other way than the proper plight to stand up at sixty paces and be shot at with a rifle. And besides his physical derangement, consequent upon a night of debauchery, his courage began to flag in proportion as the time of hostile rencounter drew near. For not only did he begin to have misgivings himself, but his companions had wickedly played upon his fears, by supposing imaginary issues, and conjecturing probabilities which *might* arise, and casualties which *might* prove fatal to. himself. And some went so far as to say that it was a great pity he had chosen the rifle, at sixty yards, for it was currently reported and believed that "Sanford was the deadest shot in all Massachusetts, and perhaps in the Union."

It may readily be supposed, therefore, that, under such

opposite circumstances as these, while Sanford appeared upon the ground as calm and as cool as if he had come out to enjoy a little target-shooting, his antagonist, Mr. Williston's, manner was agitated and greatly disordered, insomuch that it was necessary for him to take frequent drinks of brandy.

It was a clear, frosty morning, and the sun was just rising in the east; but it had not yet reached more than half way to the tree-tops which were in Mr. Williston's rear. The parties had been placed east and west, with design on the part of Williston's friends, but with no suspicion of foul play on the part of Sanford's, who were less experienced in matters of dueling.

"For," said they in whispers, "let Sanford face the east, and let us make excuses, and incur delay until the rising sun glances over the tree-tops, and glistens upon the sight of his rifle, and then his eye will become so dazzled by the reflection, that he can not see you at ten paces, much less sixty yards. *Then* you can shoot him down at your leisure, as you would a wild turkey, or a bullock tied to a stake."

They had made their calculations well, but the battle is not always to the strong, nor the race to the swift. Delays had been occasioned; full five minutes had elapsed; the sun was just glancing over the tree-tops in the east; the propitious time had arrived; the parties were placed in position. As Sanford took his place, he said to his second:

"I am a dead shot, but I will not kill him. That murderous right arm of his, however, I mean to shiver up to the elbow. *That* will cure the gentleman's mania for fighting, and convert a cowardly bully into a peaceable citizen. In this, my first, and, I hope, my last duel, I trust that I shall render the country a great and signal service."

"Are you ready, gentlemen?" cried the second of Mr. Williston, who had won the toss of the half dollar.

"Ready," was the response.

"Aim! fire! One! two!"——

The word "*three*" was drowned by the sharp crack of both rifles, simultaneously fired. Sanford remained unharmed, with his rifle brought down to a rest; but he dropped it in a moment, pale and trembling with agitation, as he saw Williston reel backward a few paces, and fall heavily to the earth.

"Great God!" cried he, almost gasping for breath, " I am afraid I have killed him, without intending to do so. The sun glanced and glistened so upon the barrel that my eyes became dazzled, and I could not see. I fired at random."

"Don't fret about it, Sanford," said his second, soothingly; "if the coward had stood his ground, your ball would have gone where you sent it. But the fool stepped out of his tracks a little too much to the right, in order to dodge your ball, and I imagine he has got it where you did not wish it to go, right through his heart. It was no fault of yours, however; he ought to have stood his ground like a man, or not come at all upon a field of deadly risks."

This reasoning did not quiet the conscience of Mr. Sanford, who began to say to himself:

"I ought not have accepted his challenge. I ought to have treated his insults with silent contempt. Surely all the opprobrious epithets he could have showered upon me could never make me a dishonorable man or a coward, if I were not so at heart. And what matters it if men call us ill names, if we do not deserve them, and have the consciousness of rectitude within us? And if I were a villain, could all his heart's blood wash me clean? No, no," he mused and groaned in spirit, "I ought not to have come upon the ground; and in doing so—in challenging Williston to mortal combat—I am a murderer before God and the country. The brand of Cain is upon me, and whosoever of his blood-avengers finds me, ought, of right, to slay me."

As these reflections passed through his mind, he had traversed the sixty yards which separated him from his fallen enemy. ' Williston's friends were kneeling upon the ground, examining the wound in his left breast, as Mr. Sanford and his party came up; but they rose immediately and saluted them with courtesy.

"He is dead, gentlemen! shot through the heart! A nice shot, an elegant shot, Mr. Sanford," said Williston's second, with a very obsequious bow, feeling greater admiration for the successful combatant than he had ever felt for the orator or the statesman.

Sanford's only reply was a deep groan, rolling upward from the lowest depths of his heart, hard, and hoarse, and hollow, like the moaning echo of the vocal sphynx. He sunk down upon a bank of earth hard by, and buried his face in his hands. Conscience, with its scorpion lash, was flaying his naked soul, as the scalpel which lays bare the heart. Conviction of guilt was gnawing, like a fierce cancer, at his very heart-strings. His ideas were in a whirl, and his feelings all in an uproar; and in the midst of the mental whirlwind and the spirit-storm, the " still, small voice of God" was calling upon him to repent, and Jesus Christ himself whispered kindly in his ear: " Though you have done this, and have sinned so much and so greatly, come unto me and be saved; for I will have mercy upon whom I will have mercy."

The conversion of the duelist is exceedingly rare. Their consciences may be often pricked by guilt, but they seldom repent of their sins. The conversion and final salvation of Mr. Sanford was as remarkable as that of the thief on the cross. Let it encourage others not to despair, nor rush into yet more bloody scenes, and commit yet darker crimes, until their hearts shall have become seared and stultified; but let them come to the Cross, their only refuge, where the blood of Christ can alone wash white and clean the guilty hands which they have dyed crimson in their brother's blood; for the subsequent career of the Hon. Julius Sanford proves that the mercy of God is wonderful indeed, since the duelist and successful combatant became an humble and a contrite spirit, a meek and lowly follower of "the Lamb slain for sinners."

It was a strange time and a strange place for the conversion of a soul; but God's ways are not as our ways. For right there, on the field of battle, and in the presence of his slain enemy, the Hon. Julius Sanford pledged himself to serve his God with all his heart, and flee the devil, who had caused him to commit this great and heinous sin. When he raised his head again, all his friends remarked how awful and how awe-inspiring was his countenance; reminding them, in its expression, of the poet Dante's, of whom it is said that, when writing "*L'Inferno,*" on going into the streets fresh from his poetical labors, he used to be followed by the little Italian boys, who spoke in whispers: "*He looks like a man who has been to hell, and has just come back* from L'Inferno."

Somewhat of this feeling or superstition flashed across the minds of Sanford's friends, when they witnessed, but, in reality, knew not of his conviction; but they made no remarks, and in mournful silence they all returned to the city of Washington.

No very great sensation was occasioned by the death of Mr. Williston in social or political circles, for he had withdrawn himself so completely from them during the last few months of his life, that his place would never be missed. But great was the sympathy felt for Mr. Sanford, upon whom all knew that the difficulty had been forced against his will, and greatly to his regret, and contrary to his avowed intentions had been the result of the rencounter, so fatal to his antagonist. But as deep as was their sympathy, as sincere was their regrets, openly expressed, not only in the streets, but in the national councils, when, a short time after the duel, Mr. Sanford rose in his place, and declared it to be his solemn determination to resign his seat in Congress at the close of the session, and that he took this opportunity of announcing to the Speaker and House of Representatives, that he had already informed his constituents at home that he could not be a candidate for re-election. No persuasion nor entreaty could induce him to abandon a resolution thus deliberately formed, and he retired from his seat in Congress with the heartfelt regrets of the whole country, who thought that it was a pity that more men like him could not be found—conservative in principle, and patriots at heart—to stand by the Constitution and defend the rights of the people when invaded.

Pity, says the reader, perhaps, that Sanford did not remain in Congress to battle side by side with such men as Clay, and Calhoun, and Webster, in after years; we know not; the future shall tell whether it was even a pity that he gave up his seat in Congress. Perhaps, he had other views more congenial with his natural tastes ; perhaps he wished to resume the practice of the law, or pursue the ministry, or take up with literary pursuits, in which he was so well calculated to distinguish himself; and perhaps his resolution was induced by another cause, which the reader will think more probable.

When Mr. Williston's estate was wound up, or rather when his debts were all paid, it was ascertained that there was not a dime left, either of his own or his wife's property.   Mrs. Williston was left, therefore, a young widow with an only child, almost helpless, it is true, but in her own mind resolved not to be dependent.   Her friends in New York urged her to live among them free of charge, but her spirit was too independent for this, and she had already resolved in her own mind to seek a home elsewhere, when her movements were hastened by the sudden arrival in the city of New York of "Hon. Julius Sanford, from Washington," announced in one of the morning papers. Mrs. Williston immediately sat down to her little portable escritoir, and penned the following lines :

"MY DEAR SANFORD:

"If you love me, do not seek me here or elsewhere; we must part forever! May God give us grace and strength to bear the ordeal which must be for this life! We can meet no more on earth! O! may we meet in heaven!

"Yours, in suffering as in love,

"ANNA."

Nor could he or any of her friends discover the course she had taken, or whether she had left New York at all. Henceforth the beautiful and accomplished Anna Williston would be dead to the world and lost to her lover. In New York she could hide herself from society and the world, as surely as in the grave. For what, at last, is the great "Empire City," but a huge mausoleum to hide the living and the dead?

CHAPTER III.

HE city of Boston is a famous city, and the State of Massachusetts has been, from its earliest settlement, a famous State. "The Old Bay State" is a name which has been well appropriated, because it represents her as a grand commercial harbor and emporium of trade; while from her soil have sprung brave warriors, and great statesmen, and learned jurists, and eloquent orators, and many talented men. From her prolific womb have sprung men of genius and sterling worth, such as Franklin, and Adams, and Webster, who have dazzled the world by the splendor of their genius and the grandeur of their intellect. But Massachusetts, and Boston in particular, has been famous, also, for many wonderful things which have been recorded in history; some of which she may point to with exultant pride, while others she must remember with shame and mortification. For while she still exults in the heroism and consummate daring of the men who flung into Boston harbor the cargo of British imported teas, she must remember, with abhorrence, the foul murders which were committed, "*in the name and by the grace of God*," upon innocent persons unrighteously accused of the sin of witchcraft; when many of her most godly men and loveliest maidens were led to the stake, or swung from the gibbet— the victims of the hatred, and malice, and vile calumnies of the malevolent and the invidious.

But, for our present purposes, Massachusetts was famous,

or rather notorious, in nothing more than as the birth-
place of Alfred Orton—Rev. Alfred Orton, the rabid Abolitionist—who did not die a hero or a martyr, because his
life, justly forfeited, was given him by a generous and noble-
hearted Christian slave.

Had Rev. Alfred Orton lived in the days of witchcraft,
he would have been foremost in denouncing the wickedness
of those who got "possessed," and in exorcising the imaginary devil, with fiery tail, and sharp horns, and cloven
hoofs, while he would have fancied an imaginary diabolical
tail sticking out from every person, however innocent, who
might cross his pathway or interfere with his plans. Had
he lived at the present day, he would have been found in the
camp of the outlaw John Brown, saying his hypocritical
prayers and singing his psalm-tunes to the Goddess of
Liberty; denouncing slavery as it exists at the South, and
urging all, both white and black, to rebellion, and recom-
mending that they be shot as traitors if they refused to
rally to the standard of the outlaw. But if he had lived
till that time, and had been present at Harper's Ferry, he
would have been the first man to slip through a loop-hole
when the tramp of the "marines" was heard, and the cry
of the "Old Dominion" "To arms! to arms!" broke upon
the morning air. Then, it is very likely, that had he been
caught and brought back as a fugitive from justice, and
charged with high treason against the laws of Virginia and
the United States as the infamous chaplain of a rebel band,
he would have flung away his psalm-book and denounced
the Bible as a book of lies, and by his oaths and blasphe-
mies proven to his captors that a great mistake had been
made—that they had captured not a servant of the Lord,
but a servant of the devil!

Mr. Orton's hatred of the slaveholder sprung from his
college associations with wild, frolicksome young fellows
from the South, who, accustomed to being waited on and have
their boots blacked when at home, liked to be waited on

and have their boots blacked when abroad; always willing, of course, to pay well for the service, provided they could enjoy the privilege of flinging said boots at the head of said boot-black, whenever they felt disposed to enjoy the liberty of an American citizen; *i. e.*, to do anything they pleased, provided *they paid well for it!*

Mr. Orton was the college boot-black both for the Northern and Southern students; and, in mentioning this fact, we do not mean to insinuate that it was any disgrace to him. Far from it; for we think it was the only thing commendable in his character; that of striving for an education by the labor of his own hands, even though he had to do so by performing menial offices. But he was essentially a menial and a sycophant. The Northern students at Yale College despised him, and the Southern boys—the wildest and most imperious of them—used to fling their boots at his head and call him "boot-black," ordering him, at the same time, to "go and clean their boots better."

At such treatment he never murmured, provided he was well paid for the privilege of being kicked and cuffed, although, in his heart, he hated the South, and Southern students in particular, because many of them had the money to buy his silence, and make him submit to their whims. But the noblest of the students, both North and South, hated him because they had the best proof possible that he was a mean spy upon their actions—*a hired one!*—paid by some of the professors to report the misdemeanors of his fellow-students. Thus it was, that by blacking boots and shoes, and serving the Faculty in the capacity of a secret monitor, Alfred Orton paid his way through college, and ultimately received his diploma.

But he was a good scholar, an excellent linguist and mathematician; for he could "calculate like all wrath!" Indeed, where is there a Yankee from New England who does not know how to "calculate?" For while the South has furnished statesmen and orators, the North, or New

England, has produced mathematicians, theologians, and metaphysicians. While the climate of one section is better adapted to poetry and sentiment—while from the genial womb of the South leaps, full grown, the poetical genius and ardent orator, (for must not an orator be a poet also ?) from the cold and frozen soil of New England rises slowly up the cool logician, or the metaphysical giant.

But Mr. Orton was not repulsive in his physical aspect, if he was in his private or personal character. He was a man of excellent exterior, and obsequious manners ; capable, at all times, of insinuating himself into the good graces of the stranger, who would generally believe that he was a capital fellow until he was found out ; but he generally managed to keep from being found out, by having but little to do with any one man. With the women he usually succeeded well ; for he had a handsome face, and he well knew it ; for he was frequently caught gazing with rapture at himself in the looking-glass ; and such was his vanity, that he would have been very much astonished to hear it asserted that there was a woman North or South who could resist his personal attractions. And, to reduce the thing to a *reductio ad absurdum*, Mr. Alfred Orton, A. B., went off immediately and married the prettiest girl in Salem ; and, in order to support her, he took up preaching for a livelihood.

Rev. Alfred Orton remained, however, but a few years at Salem. This hot-bed of Witchcraft and Abolitionism would, in the course of time, have got even too hot for him. For, in consequence of certain secret propensities, he was advised by his father-in-law, one of the good deacons of the Church, to leave Salem forthwith, lest a certain affair should become too generally known, and his standing as a minister of the Gospel, and especially as *the deacon's son-in-law*, should become seriously injured, and his *usefulness* greatly impaired.

Acting under this advice, Rev. Alfred Orton repaired to the huge city of Boston, where his vices could become swallowed up and his virtues shine more conspicuously ; where his father-in-law's influence secured him a position as a pastor of a very respectable Church; where he might sin and repent at leisure; where his next door neighbor would never hear his praying and psalm-singing, unless he wished him especially to note the fact by singing and praying, at times, in an unusually loud tone, to let said neighbor know that said Rev. Alfred Orton was, just at that particular time, engaged in very devotional exercises, prior to going out into the streets and by-lanes to engage in very great rascalities.

Mrs. Orton had not as yet discovered, nor had she ever been informed of her husband's secret villanies. A circumstance which had recently occurred, however, had led her to suspect that there was something wrong—something monstrous in the conduct of her husband. Cute as the fox is, he is sometimes caught in the snare. As patient as a woman is, she can lose her patience, and become irrascible and unkind. As confiding as a true wife may be, she can lose her confidence in her husband; lose her woman's faith and love, and be filled only with jealousy, and hatred, and revenge. Great must be her wrongs, however, when she discards from her bosom the husband of her children, and lifts the hand of vengeance against his heart. Look to it well, Rev. Alfred Orton! Mrs. Orton may be your Diana now! she may one day become your Nemesis!

CHAPTER IV.

N one of the loneliest and least frequented streets of the city of Boston, and in one of the smallest and cheapest of low-stooped houses, lived a poor widow woman, with an only child—a little boy—a beautiful, curly-headed, black-eyed, intelligent little fellow, of about five years old. The widow herself was a lovely young woman, apparently not more than twenty-five or six; or, at least, so said some of her neighbors, who had occasionally got a glimpse of her features by accident, when the wind blew up her vail once or twice, and exposed to their astonished view a loveliness almost unrivaled. No one knew her name or her history; but there was such an air of refinement about her, such a queenly tread and imperial bearing, that those who saw her come and go thought that she was a woman who had seen better days, and had once moved in the highest walks of life. The few attempts at intimacy which had been made by some of the prying women of the neighborhood had been met with such courtesy, but repelled with such stately dignity, that they had begun to regard her either with hatred and envy, or with admiration, as an unapproachable queen, shut up in her dark cell, barred and bolted from the world's prying curiosity by the cold, black bars of poverty and misfortune. In her isolation, though surrounded by hundreds of the poor, who are ever curious, and prying into the secrets and misfortunes of others, she resembled the unfortunate Marie Antoinette when in the loneliness of the *Conciergerie*—her husband butchered already upon the guillotine, her children torn from her loving embrace, her darling boy daily sinking into idiocy from a systematic course of brutality—bereft of all, yet dignified and noble still—striving to hide from others her great grief, and refusing to answer the inquiries and gratify the impertinent curiosity of her heartless jailers.

Noble is the sight of a woman stemming alone, in her widowhood and poverty, the tide of adversity, which bears her further and further from the shores of life, every wave beating her back and back, ever backward and nearer to the maëlstrom of death from which she struggles to escape! Poor, lonely, wrecked female on the sea of life! Poor, lonely widow, with your orphan child bound to your back! You strive hard to swim with your infant burden, but your arm is weak and your strength is feeble! God help you to breast the storm! God send a strong hand to lift you, with your burden, from the bitter, briny waves of woe and misery, before the last huge billow shall roll over your soul, and your tiny woman's hand shall be seen no more lifted above the foaming waters, beckoning for help!

The very next door, in a similarly constructed house, lived another woman, two or three years older, but of a very different character and appearance. She had an only son, also, of about seven or eight years; but her boy was not born in wedlock, nor was her face ever vailed when she went into the streets. It was to this house that Rev. Alfred Orton, often in disguise, and very stealthily, came. She was a gentleman's daughter whom he had basely ruined in Salem, and had brought away and supported in Boston; not by his own free will, but by compulsion; for not only did her father insist upon it, but she herself demanded her support at his hands. But she had grown tired of him of late, and he of her, so that his visits were not so frequent now—less a matter of pleasure to himself than of profit to her; for he never came without being fleeced of his money. She felt that in

11

giving birth to an illegitimate child her character was gone
forever, and she resolved to replace the loss of character
and friends by winning gold in any way she could. From
Orton's purse she took all she could lay her hands upon;
and now she had begun to launch out in other directions,
and take the gold of other men's purses. If one man had
ruined her, she was resolved to ruin many men, body and
soul, in return.

But, to succeed well in her infamous calling, she discovered, rather late, it is true, that it was necessary to have no
incumbrances. She must neither have a constant lover, unless he could pay well for the privilege, nor must she have
a child dangling at her apron-strings and calling her mother.
She resolved, therefore, that Rev. Alfred Orton should take
his son to his own home. He was the boy's father, and
she felt that it was his duty to maintain him. No persuasion of his, no entreaty, could induce her to alter her determination. "He must take his son to his own house; she
could be bothered with him no longer; and henceforth she
would occupy new quarters, and launch out into a new field
of operations." Now, to do this thing, which was so peremp-
torily required of him, required no little ingenuity and a
deal of downright lying on the part of Rev. Alfred Orton.
It was necessary to tell his wife—or, at least, he thought it
necessary—that little Johnny was the son of a poor widow
woman, who was weak and nervous, and dying every day,
whose health was so impaired that her physician had declared that she ought not to be bothered with the cares of a
child, nor disturbed by the noise of a rude boy. He had
determined, therefore, to adopt little Johnny; or, what would
be the same thing, to take him into his service as a servant,
a *bona fide* slave!—*white*, it is true, but as complete a slave
as any little negro upon a Southern plantation.

To this arrangement Mrs. Orton gave her reluctant consent. She knew not, it is true, that the mother of the child
had been for some years the concubine of her husband; but

she felt a very natural dislike "to be mixing up her own
with other people's children," her own being small and of
tender age. But when her husband brought little Johnny
home, Mrs. Orton felt an instinctive and sudden dislike
spring up in her heart toward the child. She knew not why
it should be so, but there was a strange, a peculiar likeness
between the bastard and her own children; and what mother
likes to have her child look like another's? As months
passed on, the dislike which Mrs. Orton first felt for little
Johnny increased in intensity until it amounted to positive
hatred. She had been unusually cross to him one day, and
had boxed his ears upon more than one occasion. Johnny
had been, for some weeks past, sick with intermittent chills
and fevers. She ordered him to go up stairs and lie upon
his coarse mattress on the ground. But it was very cold and
cheerless up there, and Johnny came down, contrary to positive orders, and lay down in the kitchen by the cooking-
stove. The Irish girl, Margaret, was a kind-hearted young
woman, and she let him lie there to warm himself, and
recover from his ague. When Mrs. Orton unexpectedly
entered the kitchen and found that her positive commands
had been disobeyed so soon after they were given, she flew
into a violent passion, and seizing the broom, belabored the
poor boy severely over the head and upon his bare feet,
causing several unsightly contusions. The sympathies of
the Irish girl became greatly aroused in behalf of the poor
boy, and she could restrain herself no longer, but losing all
respect for her mistress, and jerking the broom from her
hand, she cried out, in indignation :

"Would ye be after murderin' the spalpeen? Would ye
kill your own flesh and blood?"

"My own flesh and blood!" said Mrs. Orton, in amazement. "What do you mean by such impertinence?"

"I mean just what I say, Misthress Orton," replied Margaret, taking up the boy and washing away the blood which
trickled down his cheeks. "Johnny is bone of your bone,

and flesh of your flesh! for if he is n't your own darlint, he is at least Misther Orton's by anither wife; or, rayther, by anither woman. Shure, ma'am, an' I tell you the thruth, if it is disagrayable. I found it out myself by accident, but I would n't grave your leddyship for the world by tillin' ye, but for now."

Poor Mrs. Orton! She never said a word in reply to Margaret's astonishing revelation, but sunk into the nearest chair, as if crushed by the dreadful intelligence. The mist had all at once faded from her vision, and the clouds of uncertainty had rolled away, and she could see more clearly than ever the resemblance between the bastard boy and her own children. She understood now why her antipathy had been so strong and unconquerable. In her heart there was an instinctive admission of the truth of Margaret's words; and, though they cut like cold steel to her heart of hearts, instead of gainsaying or denying them, she felt rather like pushing them in deeper and deeper, like so many sharp stillettoes.

Poor, deceived woman! How we pity the wife who is mated to a villain, who deceives her with a kiss or an apparently warm embrace, and then leaves her alone, that he may go away and pillow, in secret, his head upon another's bosom. Vile traitor! You know not how great a monster you are! Foul debauchee! You know not, that while breaking the heart of your poor, desolate, and forsaken wife, God will bring you into judgment, and, sooner or later, the hand of the avenger shall be upon you!

Mrs. Orton sat for a long time in silence, as if stunned by the blow; but after several minutes—perhaps thirty or more—had elapsed, she began to moan, and to rock herself to and fro, like a maniac mother bemoaning in her cell her dead child which they have carried away for burial; for her hope was dead. It was just then that Mr. Orton came in; and, not understanding how matters stood, he interrogated his wife as to the cause of her distress. The poor woman made no reply, but sat moaning and rocking to and fro as before. There was no intermission in her rocking, nor did she cease for a single moment her moanings.

Perceiving that he could get no satisfaction from her, he turned to Margaret and asked her what it all meant. The Irish girl replied, in her straightforward, honest, Irish way:

"The misthress is waping and moaning because I tould her not to bate the poor boy so; for shure an' he was none ither than her own darlint, since you was his own thrue father! An' I suppose"——

"And who told you such a base falsehood?" asked Mr. Orton, choking with rage.

"An' shure an' it was the boy's own mither that told me"——

Before the girl could say another word, she was knocked sprawling upon the floor, and denounced as a liar.

The result of all this affair was, that Margaret left the employment of Mr. Orton; and though she spoke much against her old employer, she was advised by some to hold her tongue; while there were others who believed her story, and urged her to prosecute the preacher for assault and battery. This she resolved to do; but a few dollars in hard silver, and not a little coaxing, with a great deal of flattery and "soft sawder," which but few Irish girls can resist, induced Margaret to forego her revenge, and "let bygones be bygones." Indeed, to make sure of Margaret's silence concerning the whole difficulty, Mr. Orton even prevailed upon her to return to her former service, at an increase in her wages of from seventy-five cents to one dollar per week. When Mr. Orton had accomplished so adroitly this *coup d'état* in a domestic way, he felt more easy for the future.

But not long after this a more serious difficulty arose— the result of his own passionate nature—from which it was not likely that he could extricate himself so easily, and which, in reality, caused him to abscond very suddenly from the city of Boston. The case was as follows:

Since Johnny had come into his possession—forced upon

him against his will—and there was no safe expedient by
which he could rid himself of the incumbrance, he determined to make the most out of a bad case, which was to
make Johnny useful as a servant. So he was not only sent
on errands by Mr. Orton, but did the *chores* of the household in general; and, among other duties, he was put to
cleaning Mr. Orton's boots. Now this was the preacher's
old trade; and, although he was an adept in the art, or
"*profession*," as the boot-black calls it—dubbing himself
"*Professor*" and "Artist"—yet Mr. Orton, like all other
boot-blacks, was exceedingly glad to resign the "profession" to other and more juvenile hands. It was in vain,
however, that he attempted to teach little Johnny the art in
which he had excelled. The poor little fellow either could
not or would not learn; nor is it likely that he had the
strength to impart that brilliant polish which only a man
or a very skillful and experienced hand can give to leather,
which they make to shine as a mirror, and glisten like polished ebony. Many a time did poor Johnny get a rap upon
the skull, or upon the knuckles, with the hard brush or
boot, when he failed to give even tolerable satisfaction. It
was one Sunday morning, just before service, when the last
bell was tolling, and it was time to go to church, that
Johnny was called into the kitchen by Mr. Orton, and told
sternly to bring in his boots.

I ain't done cleanin' 'em, sir," said Johnny, trembling
from head to foot; for he had been engaged at play with
the children, and had forgotten to attend to his duty.

"Bring them here, in a moment, sir. Be quick; for I
have no time to lose," was the stern reply of Mr. Orton.

Poor Johnny went out, and returned with the boots all
soiled and filthy, as when pulled off the night before. The
moment Rev. Alfred Orton caught sight of the boots, all
soiled and covered with mud, and remembered how late it
was in the day, and heard the last chimes of the church-
bell—chimes which should have brought a mellowness to

his feelings, and awoke holy echoes in his heart, if there had been ever any holiness there—his anger became so great that he seized a steel fork lying upon the shelf, and flung it at the head of his illegitimate son. It is likely that he did not intend to injure him seriously. It is likely that he did not think for a moment of the probable consequences. But it was too late to recall the fatal missive which he had flung, so passionately, and with such force, at the culprit. One of the prongs of the steel fork penetrated the eye-ball of poor little Johnny, and injured its sight forever. ·

Margaret entered the kitchen just at the moment. She had returned from mass, and her feelings were rather inclined toward charity. But her indignation against Mr. Orton knew no bounds ; and she poured out a torrent of invective upon him in so loud a strain that her angry denunciations attracted the attention of several of the neighbors and street passengers, several of whom came into the kitchen to see what was the cause of the uproar.

There were other witnesses, therefore, to a horrid brutality, committed upon a helpless child, and upon the Sabbath day, which was enough to arouse the indignation of the most callous and indifferent heart. It is a wonder that, in that mobocratic city, they did not tear him limb from limb. Doubtless, had the poor boy been a negro slave instead of a white one, they would have built a bonfire to liberty with the slaveholder's mangled body.

But they did right in not hanging him then and there as high as Haman. They cried "shame!" and there was one man who resolved upon immediate prosecution ; and went forthwith to a magistrate, to issue an indictment against Alfred Orton, for maltreating and maiming the poor illegitimate boy, his own son, but who was supposed by the community to be his hired servant or bound apprentice.

That gentleman did right. He acted so promptly from the noble impulses of a humane and benevolent heart. For, remember, O reader ! that there are humane and benevolent

men in Boston as elsewhere. For if Massachusetts produced
an Orton, remember that she produced a Sanford also ; and
a Franklin, and a John Adams, and a giant Webster, and
many other great and good men.

That gentleman, we repeat, acted as any humane man
would have done, anywhere under the sun, where there were
laws to redress the wrongs of the oppressed. He did as
many a Southern man would have done, who was witness
to the fact that a brutal and insane master was trampling,
with brutality, upon the rights of his slave. For, remember, O Northern fanatic and ultraist of New England !—
remember that the slave has rights as well as the master;
and an intelligent community will not only sanction the
law, but even back its officers—ay ! *compel* them to maintain those rights when they have been invaded by tyranny
and oppression. Wherever any other spirit than this—the
spirit of the most refined humanity—exists, there is neither
law nor intelligence ; *it is a community of savages and bar-*
barians. We know not of such a community at the slandered South ; nor do we believe there is one, at the present
day, in New England, although it is greatly to be appre-
hended, that unless the spirit of fanaticism is soon suppressed,
that people will become as insane upon the subject of slavery
as they were in the days of Cotton Mather upon witchcraft.
Would to God that the spirits of her old giants—the spirits
of a Franklin and an Adams might awake from their long
sleep of death ; and that, in their waking, their convulsive
throes might cause a mighty revolution, that shall shake
old Massachusetts to her foundations; and tumbling her old
granite hills from their basis, shall bury, in eternal ruins,
the wild spirit and maniacal fury of abolitionism. Amen,
let every patriot and lover of his country say ; for only then
can the South and the East, the North and the West, hope
to live in peace and harmony in this, our once so glorious,
and happy, and peaceful Union.

We have great faith in the idea that there are good and

true men everywhere, whether at the South or at the North, whether in America or in England. But while we do firmly believe that there is a much greater proportion of good and true men at the South than elsewhere—kind, humane, charitable, hospitable, and godly, men—we honestly attribute the fact not so much to a genial climate and friendly atmosphere, *as to the institution of slavery as it exists at present among us !* This may sound like strange philosophy to the ears of a Northern man or an Englishman. Men like Spurgeon may say—Spurgeon himself may declare—that he would as soon " commune with a horse-thief or a murderer, as to admit to the Lord's Table a slaveholder." Was it malice or ignorance which made him say that ? God. have mercy upon the poor, deluded abolitionist, who professes to be an advocate and lover of God's Bible, and yet challenges God's right to establish society upon just such a basis as he thinks proper ; *for slavery is established upon an eternal basis. The Almighty God himself established it, and gave slaves to his children in the days of the patriarchs.* For the sins of his own " peculiar people " he sent them into captivity for many hundred years—many years longer than the African race have been in bondage in America. For the salvation of the heathen and the benefit of the African race—perhaps of his own elect, out of a besotted and sin-degraded people —he has brought four millions of immortal souls to the knowledge of " the truth as it is in Jesus." Four millions of souls have thus been invested with the power to become " the sons of God," whereas they were doomed before to eternal darkness, and damnation, and death.

But the fanatics of the North and England would send these four millions back to Africa, which is the road back to hell ! For to give them their freedom *en masse* is *to pronounce the doom of expatriation upon them, or to devote them all to a final and a bloody extermination, more sudden, and heartless, and complete than has been the almost extermination of the Aborigines of America !* For is it not true that,

11*

aside from the well-known fact derived from the statistics of each recurring census, that the free negroes of the North-ern States, so far from increasing in a healthy and natural ratio, are daily diminishing in numbers? Is it not true that several of our Northern and Northwestern States are seri-ously agitating the question of a speedy removal beyond their borders of the few free negroes with whom they are pestered?

Poor, degraded, despised, maltreated free negro! Kicked and cuffed hither and thither, without a kind master to de-fend you when wronged, without a friendly soul to sympa-thize with you in your woes and troubles! cheated and fleeced on all sides, with poverty, and cold, and hunger, and starvation staring you in the face, and the gloomy walls of a prison looming up before your terrified imagination!— whither and to whom shall you flee? Cursed by the white man, hated and despised by the slave, and pitied only by the slandered, and abused, and grossly-misrepresented slave-holder, who at last is your best and truest friend, you are destined to be driven into the wilderness and the desert, and forced back into a savage condition worse than the moral death and corpse-like state from which you are only just beginning to awake by the helping hand of the beneficent institution of slavery!

Should that sad day ever come, when slavery shall no more exist at the South *as now it exists*—not European, nor Asiatic, nor African, but *Southern slavery;*—should the arch-fiend of hell succeed in his diabolical designs, and the fanat-ics of the North ultimately triumph over the ruins of their country; and the Constitution become obliterated, or torn into fragments; and the dome of the Capitol has tumbled in; and the Capitol itself should one day lie moldering in ruins; and slavery be swept like a dark wave across the Atlantic, to resume its original forlorn and hopeless degra-dation upon the sandy plains and arid deserts of Africa, again to put on the fetters and to be weighed down by the heavy manacles of Ethiopian bondage, from which they have been rescued by the beneficent hand of Christian American slavery, and elevated from the degradation, and oppression, and manacles of the barbarian, to the comparatively free and happy condition of contented laborers—an *almost free and happy peasantry*—slave in name, but *free peasants in reality ;*—should ever such an exchange be made—so sad for them, so calamitous to the world at large, so disastrous and so suicidal to the Union—then, perhaps, when too late, some misguided but repentant patriot will be seen, like Marius, standing, with grief in his heart, and consternation and horror in his countenance, wringing his hands in despair, and looking with utter agony of soul upon the spectacle of woe and desolation which his own suicidal hand has caused, or helped to consummate, but which a race of giants can not repair through a long future of untold centuries.   *The ruins of Carthage are ruins still!*

CHAPTER V.

AT the commencement of our last chapter, we spoke of an interesting and lovely young widow, with a single child, who preferred to bear her own burdens alone, in her isolation and separate independence of the community in which she lived; preferring to struggle on through the dark vale of poverty by the labor of her own hands, in an honest way, and as an honest woman.

Without any other assistance than her needle, she had managed to support her darling little Willie and herself; that is to say, by dint of hard work, and constant, almost unremitting application to her needle, she had barely managed to pay her house-rent and buy victuals and clothes for herself and her child. She is unable to hire a servant, and has been compelled, full many a time and oft, to wash and to scour, and to perform all the offices of a menial or a slave. Her delicate, fairy-like hands were never made for such work; but what else could the poor, poverty-stricken woman do? She had tried to teach music, to be employed as a teacher; but who would employ an unknown musician, unless she had hailed from Europe—from Germany, or Italy, or France—and could bang upon the piano with the frenzied energy of a maniac or a wild Chimpanzee, and speak not a word of English! She had tried painting, had resumed her brush and her easel, and painted several lovely landscapes, and even portraits, sketches which would have been pronounced most captivating, in her days of sunshine and prosperity, by her friends and ardent admirers; specimens of art worthy the skill of a Raphael of ancient, or a Sir Joshua Reynolds of more modern times. But who would buy the works of an unknown American artist, unless they could be bought at a sacrifice, a trifle, "a mere song?" Wait, poor woman, until those works of art, which seem so beautiful now, in their freshness and rich simplicity, shall have become old and covered with the dust of many years; wait until you have starved to death, and you and your little boy have both become so attenuated by poverty, and cold, and starvation, that you have been at last forced to lie down in the grave a century or so; write your name in the corner, and let the dust cover it up and hide it so effectually that no one can either read or see it; *then*, when you have waited in vain for bread—waited so long that you could wait no longer—and your attenuated, exhausted frame had lost all its little strength, and could hold up your drooping head no more, so that it drooped still lower, and lay forever still upon your breast, as your eyes closed in death from very weariness and exhaustion, and cold and hunger!—wait till then, poor artist! and some one will then wipe away the dust which has been accumulating for many years upon your picture, and exclaim, with rapture, "O, how very beautiful! how exquisitely fine! Where, sir, and who, is the artist?" "Ah, my dear madam, the author of this piece was a lovely young woman, who died from neglect when quite young— from starvation, or cold, or consumption. She was taught in Italy under the best masters, but she was a master herself. I could not sell that piece without getting a very large price for it; not less than five hundred dollars!" And, perhaps, a few pitiful shillings had been all that the merchant, or his father before him, had paid for a beautiful design, whose only objection at the time it was purchased from the unknown artist was, *that it was too green*, and lacked the mellowness of age to make it sell as a *chef-d'-œuvre* of *la grande artiste!*

Poor painter, poet, author, artist! The world seldom
rewards you while living on this side the grave! Cotem-
poraries envy and malign you, and your publishers, as a
general rule, with but few exceptions, receive the profits of
all your hard labor, and application, and diligent research.
But never mind! Toil on! not so much for renown as to
do good, silently and unseen, to others—to make a miserable world as happy and as comfortable as you can. Toil on
for the good of mankind, who dwell in palaces, and sit upon
thrones, and are clothed with fine linen, and silks, and satins,
and are decorated with gilded stars and with softest ermine,
while you are forced to dwell in some lonely cot, and to
wear the humblest apparel. Toil on, I say—not so much
for purposes of self-aggrandizement as to benefit and befriend a world of sinners, and God will reward you in secret,
by bringing happiness and peace to your own soul—the best
of earthly riches—while He shall reward you in the spirit-
world with eternal riches, and a crown of glory which shall
never fall, nor be snatched by others from your head. You
will have food enough then—bread enough and to spare.
Poor widow! you shall not feel hunger nor cold any more,
and God shall wipe away—the Son of God himself, with his
blood-stained scarf, "shall wipe away all tears from your
eyes."

She had been weeping—this poor widow. It was a cold,
a very cold night in January, 1826, a few weeks only after
the death of Colonel Shelton ; and the stove had grown cold,
and there was no more any wood to warm it again. It was
past midnight, and she was still seated by a little work-
table, upon which an oil lamp was burning. The oil was
red, and emitted a thick, disagreeable smoke and offensive
odor which was almost suffocating. She ought to have had
better and purer oil to burn in her midnight lamp, but what
better could she get with the last few coppers she had left
in her purse? And why did she sit there, shivering in the
cold and plying that needle so rapidly, when she should

have been in her bed, hugging her little Willie to her
mother's breast? Listen to the words which she is murmuring in a low but peculiarly sweet and musical voice, spoken
low, lest they should wake her sleeping boy:

"It is cold, O! so very cold to-night! but I have burned
the very last stick of wood in the house, and Willie will
have to lie in bed in the morning, until I can get some
more to warm up again our little stove. Yes! and Willie
will want his breakfast, too, and I will have no money to
buy him bread, unless I finish this work! Mr. Ashmore
told me I must certainly finish it to-night; that it was
wanted very early—at daylight, or, at all events, by sunrise—for a customer who was going off in the morning. I
must, therefore, stitch away, and not disappoint either Mr.
Ashmore or the customer. Poor little Willie! How disappointed will he be when he wakes up in the morning and
finds himself alone, and his dear mamma absent from the
room! gone out to carry home her work, and get money to
buy him bread and milk! Poor little fellow! I think I
shall have to wake him up and coax him to stay alone a
little while, covered up in the bed, like a good boy waiting
until his mother shall return from the tailor's. How sweet
he looks, with his curly head resting upon his fat, cherub-
like form! What a Cupid he would make, if painted
among roses by a skillful artist! O! that I could afford to
lose the time, and how gladly would I attempt to—— No!
no! I would fail, utterly fail! Nor do I believe that the
best artists could succeed in doing full justice to my angel
boy!"

The fond mother could resist no longer a mother's natural impulse to go to her sleeping child. Thus talking to
herself, and looking up every now and then from her needle-
work, she had gazed again and again with fond delight upon
her beautiful and idolized boy. But now she rose from her
seat and leaned gently and softly over him. She kissed his
forehead, and then placed her cheek against his very softly

and tenderly, and the tears ran fast down her cheeks, and
her chest heaved painfully, and her heart brooded sorrowfully over her sleeping child—almost as sorrowfully or with
a feeling akin to that which a young mother has been leaning over and looking sorrowfully upon her still-born child,
which has never breathed, which was still-born in the dead
hour of the night, and which she knows full well will be
carried away in the morning. The thought of leaving her
darling boy, even for a short while in the morning, pained
her mother's heart, so that she could not help shedding
tears, and one of those tears dropped from her long eye-
lashes and fell upon her boy's up-turned face. The child
was immediately wakened by that single tear-drop. He
threw his arms around his mother's neck, and said:

"Willie is cold, mamma! Do come to bed and keep your
Willie warm."

"Yes, my love, your mamma will lie down by your side,
for she is cold also, and little Willie will warm his mother
with the generous warmth of his loving little heart."

"Yes, mamma; do come to bed, and let your *sweet* little
son warm you, for mamma's hands are very cold, and she
is shivering."

The mother, thus urged by her little son, lay down by
his side, and covered herself with the bed-clothes. She
pulled off none of her clothing except her slippers, but got
into the bed dressed, with Willie, who nestled close to his
dear mamma, like a little pet lamb lying by its mother's
side. His curly head was pressed close against his mother's
warm, soft breast, and his ear was listening to the charming
melody of her heart's fond beatings. The throbbings of his
fond mother's heart had been ever a sweet lullaby to soothe
little Willie to slumber, and the child was soon asleep again,
no longer cold; and the warmth of her child's body had
warmed and put new life and vigor into hers also. Her
hands and fingers were no longer cold and stiff, and her
frame was no longer shivering. She rose very cautiously

from her recumbent position and sat upright in the bed. She threw a thick shawl over her shoulders, and reaching over to the little work-stand, took up the lamp and her work at the same time. She adjusted the lamp very carefully upon the bed, and resumed her needle; plying it now a great deal faster as the hours passed on toward morning.

Two o'clock came, and as the huge hammer of the old town-clock rose slowly in the frosty night-air, and fell heavily upon the tower-bell, and as all the other clocks of the city echoed back the response—"two o'clock"—the watchman from the tower cried—"All is well!" And the watchman below, leaning upon his musket or his cudgel, answered, "All is well!" And the other watchmen, in all the wards of the city, answered back like so many hearty cheers, "All is well!" "Three o'clock" struck, and "four," and "five," and "six o'clock," and still the cry was—"All is well!"

Yes! all may be well without, but all is not well within! Many an anxious one is bending with an agonized heart over the dying form of a loved and cherished one. Is it well with him who is racked and tortured by pain, and scorched with fever? Is it well with him whose hollow cough sounds like the voice of the soul shortening its adieus to the world from the cavernous sepulcher of the body? Is "all well" with you, poor widow, half-sitting, half-reclining in your bed, with your sleeping boy by your side, and your fingers bleeding, and almost worked to the bone for a morsel of bread to feed you in your hunger, and for a billet of wood to drive out the cold of to-morrow? Say, ye poor of the North, are ye richer and more independent than one of Napoleon's greatest marshals, who asked, in his old days, as the only reward of his pristine energy and ancient valor, that they would give him bread, simply bread enough to eat the residue of his life, in his old days.

Say, ye poor of the North, who have been pinched by hunger and numbed by cold; who have felt the hard grip

of the cruel old frost-king, and have worn so long and so
hopelessly the heavy chains and galling fetters of poverty—
grinding, crushing poverty, such as was never known nor
experienced in a Southern clime, where flowers bloom
perennially, and fruits grow spontaneously from a genial,
God-blessed soil!—say, ye poor of the North! ye down-
trodden, poverty-smitten ones! have you not often been
willing, in your day of trouble and your hour of agony, to
sell yourselves into bondage for a mess of pottage?—for
wholesome, life-giving, life-sustaining food? and when hunger has pinched you too hard, and there was no hope of
relief from your sufferings, have you not, in your despair,
been willing and eager "to eat the husks which the swine
did eat," that you might be filled? I ask it not by way
of taunt, or reproach, or contempt; God forbid! but with
earnest, sincere pity. Have ye not committed crimes, even,
that you might be cast into prison, that there you may be
provided with a few hard crusts, that ye may eat and not
die? but, alas! only to die the more slowly, to dwindle
away and "die by inches," from the cold and damp of your
prison walls, because you were *starving*, dying beforehand
of hunger; and you committed a theft, a felony, that you
might be cast into a dungeon to be fed at the expense of
the country, preferring a prison, however gloomy, to the
darker dungeon of despair!. Have you not only committed
theft to appease the fierce gnawings of your rabid hunger,
but arson also, that you might thaw your frozen limbs, and
warm your freezing bodies by the conflagration of a city?
Alas! for the poor of Boston, and New York, and London!
those mighty cities, where cold and hunger prevail; those
hell-gates of crime and poverty, where the rich roll in
wealth, and die from the plethora of their riches, while
thousands around them are dying for the want of a few
"crumbs which fall from the rich man's table!"

How is it with you, poor widow? Daylight came, and
she rose very gently from the bed in which she had been

sewing since two o'clock. Her work was just completed as the day began to dawn. She folded it up neatly and put on her bonnet and large worsted shawl. Just then, little Willie, missing his mother from his side, awoke from his slumbers; rubbing his eyes a little while, as all children usually do, then opened them wide, and clear, and bright, and looked anxiously at his mother.

"Mamma!" said he, " I want to get up and go with you, mamma; you are going somewhere now and I want to go too."

" No, my child," said his mother, kindly; "it is very cold in the streets, and the keen, sharp north-wind will cut my little cherub's face in two."

Willie acquiesced, like a good boy, for although an only child, and a widow's son, he had been taught to obey his mother's slightest wish, as a loving subject obeys the commands of his sovereign. During his mother's absence of more than an hour, the little fellow lay awake and covered up in the bed, thinking over the very same thoughts which he will think one day, perhaps, when he becomes a man, for the thoughts of the child are the thoughts of the man in miniature, and Willie's thoughts were of his dear, absent mother, as he would think of her and love her all the same when he became a full-grown man. Willie's mother went out into the street, and with her bundle in one hand, held under her worsted shawl, and her thick vail held down by the other, she walked as rapidly as she could to the tailoring establishment of Mr. Ashmore. She delivered up her work, and was paid in hard silver for her all-night's toil. It was but a small sum, it is true, but sufficient, and more than enough, to buy a loaf of bread and a few sweet cakes at the baker's, and a few billets of wood for her stove, and some hyson tea. She made a single bundle of them all, except the tea and the cakes; the clean, sawed wood and the loaf of bread she wrapped together in a piece of brown paper, tied around with a string; the little paper of tea and the

cakes she placed in her frock-pocket. With her load car
ried under her shawl as she had carried the tailor's work,
she could not walk so fast, nor could she hold down the
vail so carefully. The wind was blowing hard against her,
and she had, at times, to lean forward to resist its power;
and the snow had began to fall in broad flakes. There
were not many people stirring in the streets, or, at least,
in that part of the city where she then was; but there were
several early risers, who had already been to market, and
were returning home with their baskets filled with provisions, and among the latter whom she encountered was the
preacher Alfred Orton. This was several weeks before he
had put out little Johnny's eye with the fork, and he still
stood fair in the community at large, although there were
some who whispered their opinion in their neighbor's ears,
that "he was a wolf in sheep's clothing," and that if his
Church did not look sharp, the wolf would, some day or
other, eat up the little lambs, if not the sheep themselves.

As Mr. Orton approached nearer the widow, whom he had·
never in his life seen before, the wind tore her vail from
her grasp, and sent it flying through the air like a topsail
whipped from the topmast by a sudden squall. Her vail,
thus rudely torn away by the rough hand of the old storm-
king, left her beauty, surpassing all the boasted loveliness
of the *Venus de Medici*, exposed to the gaze of the astonished and lustful Alfred Orton. Never had such transcend-
ent beauty, almost regal in its aspect, burst upon his delighted
vision so suddenly before.

"Ye gods," he said within himself, "I have seen beautiful
women in my time, but I. have never seen such a *houri* as
this. To think, too, of its being covered up with such
somber black, to conceal, with widowed weeds, the loveliness of a Madonna! But hush, my thoughts! lie still, my
heart! nor let my face portray the lustful passions of my
soul."

He smiled, or endeavored to smile, very benignantly upon

the manifest distress and embarrassment of the stranger, then ran after the vail, and took it down from a lamp-post, around which it finally wound itself. When he returned he handed her the truant vail, and assisted her, with his own hand, to readjust it upon her bonnet; and was thanked for his kindness by a sweet smile, which Rev. Alfred Orton thought was the sweetest smile he had ever seen upon the lips of a woman. Perceiving that she carried quite a large and rather weighty bundle under her arm, he very gallantly insisted upon taking it from her, and carrying it himself as far as her door. In vain did she protest against such inconvenience to himself; in vain decline his proposal to accompany her home. Mr. Orton was not to be balked thus in his gallant and apparently benevolent intentions. He assured her that it was his business and his solemn duty to assist the needy and the distressed ; that he was only a poor, despised minister—an humble minister of the Gospel— and how could he perform his duty toward his fellow-creatures better than to assist her with her bundle, and enable her to reach her home as speedily as possible, and find shelter from the increasing snow-storm ?

The mention of his calling—the name of minister—was, to the poor widow, a holy name ; and instead of making any further objections, she rejoiced in her heart that she had found such a friend, who could indeed afford her great assistance, and enable her to reach her home, and see again her darling Willie much sooner than she could otherwise have done. So Mr. Orton walked by her side, and carried his basket of provisions in one hand and her bundle in the other. When she reached the low stoop of her humble dwelling, she thanked him for his kindness with such a sweet smile, and with such grateful sincerity, that he felt his heart almost leap into his mouth. But although he did not then offer to enter the house, he requested permission, indeed, declared his intention, to call again to see her ; and hoped that the acquaintance, thus *providentially* formed in

the street, might grow into intimacy and friendship. And
the widow said yes ; that a minister of the Gospel was most
welcome at her humble house. But, before leaving, Mr.
Orton insisted, and positively refused to take any denial,
that she should receive from his hands a portion of the
market supplies—his piece of veal, and a few Irish potatoes,
and a plate of fresh butter ; for he had an abundance of
everything he wanted ; and if he lacked anything, could he
not easily send out and get more from some one of his
parishioners, if need be ?   And, besides, ought she not to
accept, as a gift, his first offering of friendship? for they
were already no more strangers, but friends.

How could she refuse, when his gifts were thus forced
upon her ? and how could she suspect his villany, when
his handsome face seemed so frank, and his words so loyal?

That very night Mr. Orton knocked at that same door,
which was opened by the unsuspecting young woman; who,
although a little surprised to see him again so soon after
their first meeting, nevertheless answered his salutations
with her usual habitual sweet smile, and welcomed his coming as a friend.   For, had she not a right to look upon him
already as a new-formed and most beneficent friend, whom
God had suddenly raised up for her ?   For, had she not
that very day received a load of nice sawed wood, which
the woodman had brought to her door, and, with his own
hands, put away in the woodhouse adjoining the kitchen ?
And when she insisted that he must have made a mistake,
did he not declare that there was no mistake about it, for
he had been paid to do so by Preacher Orton ?

Surely God had raised up a very kind friend in behalf
of the poor widow !   Nay, nay, not a kind friend ; but God
had made him send, nevertheless, the load of wood and the
provisions.   For God had promised to feed the widow and
the fatherless ; and did then as he has often done before,
and will do again, make the very devil himself feed, and
clothe, and minister to the wants of his poor children.   It

is true that the devil, in doing so, in bestowing alms upon the poor, and distributing his charities with a most lavish hand, never does it without expecting to be well paid for his expense and trouble. If he gives like a prince, of course he expects to receive great favors—a priceless jewel—an immortal soul, in return. But Satan is most wretchedly self-deceived, and becomes the dupe of his own rascality; for, after making himself almost bankrupt by his benefices and his charities, God kindly reaches forth his hand, and saves the victim from his grasp.

Just so with Alfred Orton, who, although a reverend, was the devil in disguise—"the gentleman in black!" He was dressed in a decent suit of black broadcloth, and wore a white cravat, which made him *look*, at least, very much like a clergyman. Why, therefore, should she be afraid? But are there not those who *look like lambs*, while they are only wolves in sheep's clothing, who devour widow's houses? who *look* like the archangel Gabriel, when they are the arch-fiend himself—the devil in disguise or *en masquerade?* While, on the other hand, there are some who look very little like ministers of Jesus Christ, who wear no ostentatious regalia, no white cravats nor black gowns, and seem, in appearance, as other men, "with like passions as ourselves," who are, indeed, the great harbingers of the Gospel and evangelizers of the world!

Mr. Orton seated himself by the stove until he became quite warm, talking upon a variety of topics, and making inquiries, as most *inquisitive Yankees* do, whether born north or south of Mason and Dixon's line. He expressed himself as being deeply interested in the welfare of the young widow; until, drawing his chair close up to hers, he passed his arm around her waist, and attempted to draw her to him! Like a scared fawn which leaps high into the air at the sudden alarm of the rattlesnake, or a young maiden frightened by the cold, slimy touch of some hideous and deadly reptile, she started to her feet, and sprang from the desecrating touch of the libertine. She trembled very violently at first, but in a little while she regained all her womanly control, and, drawing herself up to her full hight, she resembled then, more than ever, the majestic Marie Antoinette, when, standing upon the scaffold before the multitude of her enemies, the executioner drew off from her shoulders the scarf which had concealed her voluptuous breasts, and left her exposed to the obscene gaze of countless thousands! If Marie Antoinette blushed then till she was crimson, and if, with the dignity of a martyred queen and an outraged woman, she bade the executioner do his work quickly, so that he became so awe-struck by her majesty that he could scarcely perform his office ; no less embarrassed, and confused, and awe-struck was the libertine, Alfred Orton, who stood on the floor like a culprit arrayed for condemnation before an awful and indignant empress! With queenly dignity she pointed to the door, and bade him begone from her sight and presence forever! He took up his hat mechanically, and obeyed the order with the look of a slave who has been caught in the act of robbery, or as a " suck-egg cur " who has been robbing the hen-roost, and sees the poultry-raiser coming with a lash or a cudgel in his hand.

When he was gone the widow sat down, or rather sunk into a chair and sobbed as though her heart would break! sobbed so loud that little Willie, who had dropped to sleep upon the settee, awoke, and surprised his mother in her tears and her sobs.

"What is the matter, mamma? Don't cry so," said the little boy, soothingly, while big tears gathered in his eyes at the sight of his mother weeping.

"A great deal—and yet not much either, is the matter, my child," his mother replied, drying up her tears almost in a moment. "A strange man, who gave his name as Orton —whether true or false I know not—whom I took to be a preacher of the Gospel, but I now know to be a villain! whom I took to be a sincere friend in my need, but whom I now

know to be my bitterest enemy—he, my son, has offered
your mother a great indignity, the nature of which you
can not understand. He has insulted your mother grossly!
wronged a defenseless woman deeply!"

"Insulted you, mamma!" said Willie, whose eyes burned
and flashed with indignation. "Never mind, mamma; wait
till your little Willie gets to be a big, high man, and Willie will
lick him! lick him! lick him!"

"Not so, my son;" said Willie's mother, who, during her
widowhood, if she was never before, had become a sincere,
and devoted, and humble Christian—"not so, my son; for
'Vengeance is mine, I will repay, saith the Lord!' God
will bring that man yet into judgment, and that is greater,
and juster, and more terrible punishment than any mortal
man, however vengeful, can inflict! Let him be, my son,
in the hands of the Lord. For although his rope may be
long, and he may foolishly think that it has no end, it will
bring him to at last with a sudden jerk which shall fill him
with amazement and consternation! For the doom of the
libertine is a sudden and a violent death, and an awful and
eternal perdition!"

It was only a few days after this that Mr. Orton was in
the tailoring establishment of Mr. Ashmore, ordering a suit
of clothes. He was about to leave the shop, when our
widow, dressed in the same black frock and black vail,
came out of the back room with a bundle in her hand, a
vest pattern, already cut out, which had been given her by
the foreman to make up soon. Mr. Orton felt his heart
grow spiteful and vindictive, and he determined upon a little
revenge. It was a small act, it is true; very little, and
mean, and contemptible in a manly spirit, but momentous
in its consequences to the poor needle-woman and her little
boy if successful; for it might deprive them of every resource
by which to gain an honest livelihood! deprive them of their
daily bread, and let them starve and freeze to death in the
almost ice-bound walls of their humble dwelling!

12

With a mischievous leer in his eye, and a sardonic smile upon his lips, Mr. Orton went up to Mr. Ashmore, and asked: "Do you know," said he, in a whisper, "what kind of a woman that is whom you are encouraging in a life of sin by thus giving her employment for her needle?"

"What kind of a woman is she, Mr. Orton?" asked Mr. Ashmore, in surprise, for he had been giving her employment for more than a year, and he had not only been pleased with the neatness and dispatch of her work, but had been very much struck with her modest and lady-like deportment. "What kind of a woman is she, Mr. Orton?" he asked again.

"Why, sir, I calculate that she is a very bad woman! a common harlot, sir!"

"I not only doubt your statement, but disbelieve it altogether!" said Mr. Ashmore. "No common woman, no harlot, sir, would come to my establishment for work. That class of women are too idle and dissolute in their habits; and *she* is too beautiful a woman to need employment with her needle if she chose to live the life of a prostitute! Her price would be high, very high! and she could make a fortune at the business in the moral and religious city of Boston! Don't you think so, Mr. Orton?"

Mr. Ashmore said this with a sneer; and, for the first time since his acquaintance with Mr. Orton, he began to analyze and study the features of the *reverend gentleman* in his presence; and he came to the very correct conclusion that he was talking with none other than a cold-hearted villain, "a wolf in sheep's clothing." The result of his scrutiny confused the clerical libertine so much that he added hastily, and with evident embarrassment, and, at the same time, with much apparent earnestness:

"I can assure you, sir, upon the honor of a gentleman and a clergyman, that what I tell you is the truth, the whole truth, and nothing but the truth, so help me God!"

Mr. Ashmore's only reply was to put the forefinger of his right hand upon the right side of his long nose, and smile with that peculiar twinkle of the eyes which only a man can assume who has discovered very suddenly another man's secret, and wishes to let him know, without saying a word, "I have found you out. You can't gull me. Can't come it, old fellow!"

O, Rev. Alfred Orton! you overdid the thing, with all your Yankee ingenuity. There is such a thing as being a little too ingenious. The serpent will let himself be known by his hiss, crawl he never so stealthily, when he is going to strike. It is only poetry, absurd nonsense, to say that the rattlesnake is the noblest of the serpent-kind, because he gives warning with his rattles before he makes his deadly spring. It is not the nobleness of his nature, but the fierce-ness of his anger, which makes him ring so loud his stunning battle-cry. All serpents, before they strike, lick forth the tongue and hiss their deadly hiss, not as a warning, but because of their eternal hatred and antagonism to mankind. And Mr. Orton hissed out his snake-like hiss into Mr. Ashmore's ears because he hated innocence and truth, and had been baffled in his villany by the indignant virtue and insulted honor of a noble-minded, right-hearted woman.

Look sharp, Mr. Orton! The hiss of the serpent, crawl it never so stealthily, foretells its coming, and warns its victim, or some one else outside the bush, that the serpent has drawn back its head to make its death-spring or give its death-blow! and shall give power to the heel of the man, that he may crush and grind in the dust the head of the serpent.

"That man is a villain!" said Mr. Ashmore, between his clinched teeth, as Mr. Orton left the establishment. "He hates that poor widow, for some cause which he would be unwilling to have known. Cease to employ her, indeed! I shall *increase* the price of her work; for God forgive me if, in order to support my family and make money, I have hitherto made her do work too cheaply, and thus robbed the widow and the orphan!"

Thus a second time was Mr. Orton baffled and defeated in his iniquitous designs; and God, in his providence, caused good to come out of evil, and proved himself, in reality, the Friend of the widow and the Father of the fatherless orphan.

CHAPTER VI.

THE Sabbath bells were chiming; those heavenly bells of which the poet has spoken with rapture, and to which the Christian ever listens with joy and holy gratitude. How sweet their music! how prolonged their echoes! The Mohammedan sentry, from the hights of his mosque, cries, "*Allah il Allah!* To prayers! to prayers!" and the worshipers of the false prophet answer, "*Allah il Allah!* There is no God but Allah, and Mohammed is his prophet!" falling prostrate to the earth, or upon their knees, with their faces turned toward the city of Mecca. But the Sabbath bells of a Christian land sing the song of "the Lamb slain for the sins of the world." They, too, cry, although in another tongue, and with a more hopeful voice, "*Allah il Allah!*" but they add, with sweet emphasis, "Jesus Christ is the only begotten Son of God; and whosoever believeth in him shall in no wise perish!" The preacher of salvation, echoing the words of the blessed Savior, cries, "Come unto me, all ye ends of the earth, and be ye saved!" and the Sabbath bells echo back the invitation, "Come! come! come!" It is their never-failing cry, their only voice. They seem never weary of saying, "Come! come! come!" Each returning Sabbath that single word of welcome as of warning is heard pealing all over the city, and all over our Gospel land, crying, "Come! come! come!"

But what different answers are given by different characters of persons. "I am coming," says the humble soul;

"God give me strength to come humbly to a throne of grace!" "I am coming," says the Pharisee, with lofty head and haughty look; "do n't you see that I am coming? Out of my way there, ye publicans and sinners! Do n't you see that *I* am coming?" "I am coming," says the fashionable woman, standing before the mirror; "but let me finish my toilet, will you? A body must take time to dress. I know I shall be a little late, but, after all, I shall only miss the prayers or the 'first lesson;' and anybody can say their prayers or read their Bible at home in a few minutes." "Come! come! come!" says the church-bell. "Just wait a little while, will you? Do n't be so very impatient. If I do miss hearing the text, I shall find out from my neighbor in the next pew, who is always there in time." "Come! come!" says the church-bell, very mournfully now, and with more feeble voice, as the last strokes of the hammer ring upon the metal, like the last notes of the dying swan. "Come," it says, "O come!" "Just one minute more. I know that I am late, and not near dressed yet; but I shall be there in time to hear the preacher say "Amen!" when he has finished his sermon."

"I am coming," says the mercenary business man. "By the way, I shall see Colonel Jones there to-day, and I must not forget to ask him about a certain little business transaction in which I am deeply interested."

"I am coming," said Rev. Alfred Orton, just before he put out little Johnny's eye with the fork. But Rev. Alfred Orton did not come, never came, but went away in a great hurry from the city of Boston. But, although the people of Boston never saw him more, yet we—the reader and the author—as we are traveling to and fro, from North to South—*we* shall see him frequently in our travels.

"Come! come! come!" were the last sweet notes of the Sabbath bell. "I am coming," said the poor widow—*our* widow—in faint tones, and with feeble steps, as she moved slowly on through the now almost deserted streets, holding little Willie by the hand, more to steady her own footsteps than to guide her little boy. She had been sick, and she was doing very wrong to go out so early. Ever since that memorable morning when she had gone to the tailor's to return the work upon which she had been sewing the live-long night, the young widow had not been well. She had contracted a very bad cough, which troubled her so much, and made her so very weak, that she stopped, one day, at the office of a kind-hearted physician, and got him to pre-scribe for her. At that first interview, he became so deeply interested in his lovely patient that he took down her name and address, and the next day called to see her at her own home, where he found her in bed. Like a good Samaritan, he visited her often and nursed her well, not only without hope of reward, but furnished her with many little comforts which he could only procure for her with his private purse. The woodman was sent there with a load of wood; the baker was ordered to furnish her bread every morning, and to carry it himself to the door; and the doctor's boy carried many little luxuries which the doctor himself had abstracted from his wife's closet of conserves and confectioneries with-out her knowledge. Verily, doctors of medicine are char-itable men, who do alms without letting their left hand know what their right hand doeth, or *vice versâ;* and there is no city in the world which possesses more charitable physicians than the ancient city of Boston. But our phy-sician, Dr. Boring, stood a head and shoulders above his brethren in his charitable deeds. He was rather rough, it is true, in his manners, and some thought him unkind. How could they think so? Are words always the symbols of a man's kindness of heart? Do not "actions speak louder than words?"

The good Doctor Boring had urged our widow—nameless so far, and, for a little while longer, she shall be nameless still—to be very careful and not leave the house for some time to come. But she felt a great deal better on that

Sabbath morning, and the sun was shining brightly, and the Sabbath bells were singing, "Come! come! come!" How then could she resist their invitation, so often repeated, their song so sweetly sung? Those bells sounded to her heart like the voice of her Savior, saying from heaven, as he leaned over its battlements, and looked down so affectionately into the widow's cot: "Come! come unto me, poor, lonely, friendless woman, and I will be your husband, and lover, and friend!" And she said, in her heart of hearts: "Yes, Lord! I come quickly, gladly!"

But her strength failed her on the way, and she felt that she was not able to walk so far to the humble church to which she had been in the habit of going for a good while past, to listen to the earnest voice and fatherly tones of a godly and God-fearing old man.

"I will go in here," she said to herself. "It is a grand church, and only very rich people go here. But God is everywhere, and I trust that the wings of his cherubim and seraphim hover over the altar of this tabernacle, built by the rich, but dedicated to the worship of Almighty God; for the rich can serve God with as honest and sincere hearts as the poor. Why not? But, ah me! not all of them—very few! for Christ said: 'It is easier for a camel to go through the eye of a needle, than for a rich man to enter the kingdom of heaven.' Better, then, to be afflicted with poverty; for 'whom the Lord loveth he chasteneth, and scourgeth every son whom he receiveth.' Better, then, to be poor and despised, if we are made to love the Lord Jesus as he loves the poor. But, ah me! I was rich once, and did not love nor serve him then! and now that I am poor, and I know that he loves me, I do not serve him as I ought! O, God! what shall I render to thee for all thy goodness to a poor, weak sinner. Help me, Lord! for in thee alone is my trust!"

There were tears in her eyes, but the sexton did not see them, as he conducted her, with stately step, to a vacant pew—the "stranger's pew." And well for her, too, that her eyes were blinded with tears, that she could not see through them and the thickness of her black vail the sexton's look of contemptuous surprise, and the astonishment of the congregation, many of whom turned round and gazed for a moment, but wondering a good while "what curiosity that was who had come in black" to a church of gay colors, where only the rich and the fashionable attended!

But if any of that vast assembly felt disdainfully proud and arrogant, not so with the preacher, who was just advancing toward the sacred desk for the purpose of reading his text. He looked toward the lady in black with a sweet smile of welcome, such as we may imagine Jesus Christ to have assumed when he said: "Come unto me, ye weary and heavy laden, and I will give you rest." But she did not see the smile upon his beautiful, heaven-breathed lips; for her head was drooping low, and her eyes closed as she sat upon her seat, with her hands clasped beneath her vail in earnest, fervent prayer—praying to the widow's God.

And now, with a solemn look, the preacher cast his eyes down upon the large Bible lying upon the desk before him. Then was heard the sweetness of a voice, clear and distinct, which floated like music over the heads of the congregation, rising upward to the vaulted ceiling, and filling the whole house with melodious accents, but without a single jarring echo, like the music of a heaven-bought harp, in perfect unison with the grandest tones of the organ. Who is that preacher? Never mind his name now, but listen to the words of his text, and hearken to his exposition of it:

"Then came the soldiers, and brake the legs of the first, and of the other which was crucified with him. But when they came to Jesus and saw that he was dead already, they brake not his legs: but one of the soldiers with a spear pierced his side, and forthwith came thereout blood and water."—JOHN XIX: 32-35.

Hark to that voice! The "lady in black" raised her
12*

head suddenly, like one who is startled by the mention of a
name, or the voice of a loved one which has not been heard
for long years. She trembled violently upon her seat, and
had, at one time, to reach forth her hands and lean forward,
holding on for support to the back of the pew in front of
her.

"It is he!" said she; "O, God! it is he! Sanford!
Julius! but older, by ten years, although but three have
passed away since we last met! *Three long, weary years!*
Ah! how they have thinned his temples, and sprinkled with
gray hairs his once raven locks! He seems now like a man
of sorrows, and acquainted with grief!"

And Mrs. Williston—for it was she—held on to the back
of the pew with convulsive energy, like Marie Antoinette
holding on to the rusty bars of the Tower, looking down
upon her husband as he entered the carriage, and following,
with her eyes, the vehicle which bore away her husband and
her king to the scaffold, and gazing after it still with vacant
look, when it was gone from her sight forever; and when she
could see it no more, the poor, persecuted queen of France
staggered back to her arm-chair, and fell into her seat,
without a groan or a single cry of distress that a single
enemy could hear. And so, too, Mrs. Williston fell back
against her pew, and listened, with breathless attention, to
every word which proceeded from the lips of the eloquent
divine, who had abandoned his seat in Congress, and given
up a lucrative practice at the bar, to talk to his dying fel-
low-men about Jesus Christ. She drank in his every word
now, and looked and listened as a loving woman to her
dying husband, who, with his hand in hers, is giving his
last earthly advice, and telling his last adieus. And none
of all that crowd knew how near she had been to fainting.
Not one knew her secret, and not a single one could have
suspected how near and dear had been the relations of the
humble widow and the man of God who was so earnestly
breaking to them the bread of life.

The first argument of Mr. Sanford was to show that Jesus Christ *did not die of the physical sufferings which he endured upon the cross.* "These," he said, "were of the most excruciating character; for he was a perfect man of the finest mental and physical organization; and to such a one, we may reasonably suppose, that the tortures of crucifixion were painful in the extreme. That he suffered those pains is evident, from the thirst which he complained of, and which is always attendant upon severe wounds and agonizing pains of the body. It was common to hear the cry, 'I thirst,' when a malefactor was suspended from the cross. But as the victims of the law were suspended too high in the air for any one below to hand them up a cup of water, vinegar upon a sponge was usually provided to moisten their lips, and quench, for a moment, their raging thirst; not to relieve, but in order to protract their sufferings. But in the case of Jesus Christ, it was in mockery and hatred that they answered his appeal for relief, by mingling the vinegar with gall, which was, doubtless, the suggestion, the refined cruelty, of some one of the wicked Jewish priesthood, who had previously ordered the vinegar—perhaps reserved in a separate vessel for his special use—'vinegar mingled with gall,' or vinegar steeped with wormwood.

"In a physical point of view, therefore," said Mr. Sanford, "our Lord suffered all the agonies which a martyr endures at the stake, or upon the gibbet. But his death was peculiar, and different from any other martyr who has ever perished for his principles. Not only did he die very *suddenly*, but he died *giving utterance to a loud voice*, so that they all heard him cry, 'Eli, Eli, lama sabacthani!' Now it was *not* common for malefactors who were crucified to die in this manner. In others, the voice grew weaker and weaker as they became exhausted by their sufferings, or as the life-blood oozed slowly away from their hands and their feet; and had they been able to cry at all, it would have been but the faintest whisper of a spirit worn out and exhausted by pain, and unable to utter a single dying complaint. But in the case of Jesus Christ it was a *loud and a startling voice;* the voice of a God dying upon Calvary for the sins of the world, and feeling, in that dreadful hour, his peculiar lonesomeness, and calling to his Father to come back to his side, when he felt that his Father had deserted him ; to his great Father—God, who, overcome by his own emotions, had stepped away from the cross, unable to look upon the cruel scene, and witness longer the agonies of his darling Son ; had stepped away from the cross, to say to the assembled hosts of heaven, who sat upon their seats, pale and trembling with horror, ' My Son, my only Son, is dying ! dying the ignominious death of the cross ! dying for the sins of the people, and see how they are daring him ! In his thirst he cried for water, and they mocked him with vinegar, mingled with gall. Well may ye tremble and weep, ye hosts of heaven, which see my Son and your Lord receiving such treatment at the hands of those devils incarnate below.'

"And the great God, it is said, hid the earth with a thick cloud, so that there was darkness over it for the space of three hours ; and there were thunderings and earthquakes, and the dead were let loose from their graves, and came also as witnesses to the cruelty of the Jews. Yes! God, the Almighty God, hid his face, and covered it up with his broad hand, so that, for the space of three long hours, he looked not upon our earth ; for three long hours our sin-accursed world was darkened by the withdrawal of the heavenly beams which radiate from the shining face of Jehovah ; for three long hours angels and men heard his groans as the thunder, and listened with amazement and terror to that infinite grief which convulsed the world, so that it ' reeled to and fro like a drunken man,' and rocked like a stranded vessel which is fast going to pieces at each thump of every returning wave. Great God ! how infinite was thy grief !

"Nor," said Mr. Sanford, "can we suppose, for a moment,

that our Savior died from the effects of any lurking malady, whose intensity may have been aggravated, or whose fatal power may have been increased, by the torture of crucifixion. It is true, that after death, when one of the soldiers pierced his side, 'forthwith came thereout blood and water.' Now, my hearers, this is an important statement, and a very remarkable fact. If it were not a remarkable fact, the evangelist would never have noted it among the other remarkable facts of the crucifixion. *Whence came this blood and water*, or bloody water, as some have rendered it? Would you profane the subject, and disgrace your reason, by assenting to the false assertion of a certain blasphemous infidel, that your Lord and Master was suffering with a diseased body, and laboring under the effects of dropsy? Away with the thought! Does not his whole life prove the falsity of this assertion, and brand it as a calumny? Was he not ever moving upon his feet as an active, industrious man, going 'from place to place doing good?' Does not his whole history prove that, as a man, he was constantly engaged in the most indefatigable labor; and, from the earliest period of his life, at twelve years, said to his parents, who sought him with anxiety, 'Wist ye not that I must be about my Father's business?'

"Yes, my brethren, our Lord's life was one of toil and labor. Work! work! work! He was every day and night unceasingly engaged in his great Father's vineyard, and slept only from sheer exhaustion and weariness of the flesh. For what tempting and luxurious couch had he upon which he could recline at his ease, and rest his wearied frame? for 'the foxes had holes, and the birds of the air had nests, but the Son of Man had not where to lay his head.' It was only in the humble cottage, the hovel, and the bed of the lowly, that he could snatch a moment's respite from toil, and then go on upon his weary pilgrimage. It was only after preaching to five thousand, and feeding the multitude by a miracle, that he could sleep upon the vessel's

hard deck, where the howling winds which were made use
of as a diabolical lash in the hands of the Prince of the Air,
to lash into madness the angry waves, that they might swamp
that vessel, and sink that ship,.which was freighted with
the fortunes and the hopes of a world. It was only amid
the spray of the ocean-lake, and the fierce whirl of waters,
that the Son of God could sleep for a little while, like a
God refreshing himself on the eve of battle, and making
ready for the contest he was soon to wage with devils ' on
the other side of Tiberias ; ' for he had only left the multitude, and was then on his way, with his disciples, ' to cast
out devils on the other side of the sea of Galilee.'

"Away, then, with the absurd idea, which can only be
branded as a monstrous calumny, that Jesus Christ was any
other than a sound, healthy, hearty man, although ' a man
of sorrows, and acquainted with grief.'

"But whence came the ' blood and water ? ' Now, it must
be borne in mind, that the soldier who pierced the side of
Jesus stood "*under the cross*," and hence his thrust was
upward, and from below. The spear, therefore, must have
passed upward and obliquely, from side to side. It could
have entered in no other way; and being, in all probability,
pushed with hatred and contempt for the victim who died
so soon, ' without a bone of him being broken,' when he
had expected to witness a miracle performed in behalf of
himself, even by ' coming down from the cross,' since he
had raised others from the dead. It is likely, I say, that
the spear not only entered, but traversed, the entire cavity
of the chest; and from this ugly wound ' poured thereout
blood and water.'

"Learned pathologists tell us that there *is* such a thing
as a broken heart; that the ventricle can be ruptured, and
has frequently been known to be ruptured, by the intensity
of the feelings and the powerful and overwrought action of
the heart's muscular force. Instances have been frequent
where the ventricle has been lacerated and rent open, as a

sealed envelope, by the fierceness of sudden joy, or the violence of sudden or protracted grief. But the scientific man
and learned pathologist, with the anatomical knife in his
hand, has learned to distinguish, with unerring accuracy,
between the causes which give rise to sudden death. An-
dral, the great French teacher in the School of Medicine,
tells us that it is an invariable rule and a never-failing occurrence to find the blood hard and coagulated in the cavity
of the chest when the heart has been ruptured by excessive
joy, or any other passion *save that of grief;* and that
when *grief* has been the cause of the laceration of the left
ventricle, then the *serum,* or watery portion of the blood,
becomes completely separated from the *crassamentum* or
'fleshy' portion, thus leaving it incapable of coagulation.
In the one case, if a spear or other sharp instrument was
pushed into the breast of one who had died from the effects
of sudden or too great joy, only a few drops of blood would
ooze out of the wound and trickle down the side ; but in
the other, where grief had been the cause of sudden death,
blood and water, or bloody water, would pour forth in a
stream so remarkable, that an observer, at a distance of
several paces, could not fail to perceive it.

" Here, then, my brethren, is the great mystery solved by
the aid of science! The Son of God was dying like a man
upon the cross, but he was dying like a God also! While
his body was tortured by the pains of crucifixion, so that
he cried out, like any other man, ' I thirst,' his immortal
mind was filled with grief at a time when no mortal man,
thus tortured by the acutest sufferings, could have experienced grief or sympathy for the woes of any other but
himself. What mortal man is there, uninfluenced by the
principles of Jesus Christ, and unsustained by his almighty
power, when suspended from a cross by nails driven through
the hands and the feet—hanging by nails which have been
hammered between the bones, and driven through the tender muscles, and lacerating the nerves and the sinews—

what mortal man, thus tortured, could cry, 'Father, forgive them; they know not what they do!'

"O, my brethren, it was grief, God-like grief, which broke the mourning heart of the blessed Son of God!—grief for a sin-smitten, woe-born world of sinners, who were even then crying, with insane fury, 'Crucify him!' What! crucify him 'who spake as never man spake,' and 'who went about doing good!' Crucify 'the Lord of Life and Glory!' Crucify 'the only begotten Son of God!'—the very 'Prince of Peace!' 'Why? What evil hath he done?'

"O! my brethren, look to it that you are not found among the crucifiers of Jesus! Wash your hands of the business cleaner than Pilate washed his. Yea, do more than he did. Help him, like Simon, to bear his cross, 'for it is heavy,' and the Son of God faints beneath the burden. Stand not afar off, as some of his followers did, but like John—that gentle, but fearless 'one whom Jesus loved'—like him, go near to the cross, and leave not your Lord and Master alone in his agonies, and forsaken by all the world in his sufferings. O! stand at the very foot of the cross. Yea, climb up the cross itself; place your hand upon his aching heart, and, like a ministering angel, comfort him with the words, 'Lord, I love thee, and will go with thee into paradise, and be thy companion through the valley and the shadow of death.' O! he needs comfort—this Savior of the world! for but a little while before—in the garden of Gethsemane —he tells us that 'his soul was exceedingly sorrowful, even unto death!'

"My God! what kind of sorrow must have been that! Jesus was not the man to make complaint, or reveal to others the hidden sorrows of his soul; for we are told that he was as 'a lamb led to the slaughter, who is dumb and openeth not its mouth.' But see him now, restless and anxious in spirit, going from one to the other of his disciples and begging even slumbering mortals to watch with him just 'one hour!' O! you think, perhaps, if you had been one of their number, you would have watched and prayed with him all night. But nay, nay; for 'they were weary and their eyes were heavy laden with sleep;' and, though 'the spirit was willing, yet the flesh was weak.' And he had no one to go to—that lonely, lonesome, grief-stricken man! And as he kneeled alone that cold and frosty night, upon the summit of Mount Olivet, thus iso-lated from a slumbering world, and shut in by the garden of Olives from the sympathy of his own friends and follow-ers, the floods of grief which kept on rolling their dark waves, like a mighty deluge, over his mourning soul, seemed as though they would surely overwhelm him in the deep-est, darkest abyss of human woe! It was then that great blood-drops gushed forth from every pore, like a profuse and exhausting sweat, and hung like a crown of crimson coral beads upon his forehead, and rolled like a torrent of woe down the cheeks of the sorrowing Savior of sinners.

"O! let us all cry to-day with hearty repentance : ' My God! my God! why hast thou forsaken us also!'"

There were but few eyes that were dry in that vast con-gregation, and many a sob gushed from the hearts of those who felt, for the first time in all their lives, that they were great sinners in the sight of God, and themselves had helped to drive the nails into the hands and the feet of the blessed Jesus.

But of all that vast throng, which filled nearly all the pews and crowded the galleries of that large building, not one felt more deeply, nor one shook more violently under the influence of the orator's words, than that lonely woman, Mrs. Williston, who, in the loneliness of her widowhood and her self-immolation, felt the more sorrow and sympathy for the lonesomeness and sufferings of Jesus Christ, because, like him, she needed companionship, and there was no one in the world who could understand her heart or interpret her feelings.

The sermon ended, the prayer ceased, the hymn was sung,

and the congregation went out into the streets; many to forget soon, but others to remember long, the solemn discourse which had enchained their attention, ravished their imagination, and touched their hearts, even as the lips of the speaker seemed to have been touched, as by a live coal from the altar of God.

Mr. Sanford passed out of the door with the last of the congregation, and in passing by the sexton, he stopped a few moments to inquire, with evident interest, what stranger —what lady it was who had come that day to his church, who was dressed in black, and seemed to be so deeply affected by his discourse. • He had not seen her face, but as she turned to leave her pew, his eye, involuntarily turned that way, had caught the graceful outlines of her person, and observed her majestic bearing, and there was an instinctive longing to see that face which was hid by the dark vail which concealed its beauty.

Poor Sanford! His heart was lonesome and desolate still, and had never found its mate. It is true that the void of his mourning heart was, in a great measure, filled by the love of Jesus; but our humanity, school it, and fetter it, or free it, as we may, will ever turn with longing, lingering gaze toward the faces, or the recollection of our dear departed, lost ones; and the heart, oppressed by the cares of life, or bound by secret sorrows, will sigh for the joys and "the light of other days."

CHAPTER VII.

LAS, poor woman! whether wife, or widow, or maiden! how she suffers in her heart of hearts!—the inmost receptable of her soul's noblest and truest affections! How, in secret, she broods over her sorrows, and no one ever knows the misery of a heart aching with many painful throbs! ·Disappointment may feed upon her heart and eat away all her virgin or her woman's hopes, like "the worm i' the bud;" and her cheeks may be red, and her lips wreathed with a smile, while her heart's core has been eaten away, and she is ready to lay her head upon the stony couch of her tomb.

The heart of a man bowed down by sorrow, may be likened to a sepulcher which contains the bones of the sacred dead. His sorrows may be so great that he can not tell them to the world; but his head droops low, and his face is sad, and there is no smile upon his lips or laughter in his voice; and the world can see that there is suffering within, and that dead hopes lie buried in his breast. There is no need to write upon a tombstone or a monument erected in a graveyard that some one who has departed this life lies buried here. The tombstone or the monument will indicate the fact, although the inscription may be covered up with mold, or has long since been worn away by the waste of ages. And so, also, there is no need that a sorrowing, heart-broken man should tell to the world that he suffers, and that his heart is breaking. Though his frame may be

stalwart, and his trunk seem never so firm, and hard as the
oak, men can see that his tree is "withering at the top;"
and though he may yet live a long while in the world, he
will only remain as a mournful relic of the past, as a dead
tree standing alone in melancholy decay, with its dead
leaves or its naked branches surrounded by the green boughs
of the forest.

But not so with the heart of a woman, whose spirit has
been crushed by her woes and her disappointments. *Her*
heart is not a sepulcher, but a shrine, whose high-priest is
Love, burning incense and offering up prayers behind a thick
vail, that the multitude can not see what is going on behind
the screen. They may look, and they may look in vain, to
see the chalice which is waved aloft to heaven; and God
alone can see the agony of the soul bowed in constant
prayer, and hear the groans and death-throes of the wounded
spirit. It is only when death's rude and unpitying hand
takes hold of the cord and draws up the curtain, that the
multitude can see the high-priest still kneeling down upon
his knees, with his hands still clasped upon his breast, as
if in prayer, but his head drooped low and resting upon
the altar, before which he shall burn incense nevermore.
For the high-priest is dead! died upon his knees before
the altar, and, like Moses upon Mount Nebo, no one saw
him die but God alone. So, too, the poor, broken-hearted
woman dies, and the world does not know, until she is dead,
or never knows, that she died of a broken heart! Poor,
suffering, but noble, brave-hearted woman!

It was the day after the Sabbath upon which Mrs. Williston had listened, and others, too, had listened with rapt
attention to the discourse of the Rev. Julius Sanford, that
he was walking up one of the most frequented streets of
Boston, thinking of "the woman in black," whose elegant
figure only he had seen, and wondering, in his heart, if her
face was as beautiful as his own dear, lost Anna. While
thoughts like these were in his mind, and he felt most

lonely in a crowd, he saw a beautiful, curly-headed little boy, of about five years, running toward him with flushed cheeks and an anxious look. He was so struck with the beauty and intelligence of the little fellow's countenance, and the neatness of his apparel, that he watched him with eagerness, as, with patting little footsteps and panting breath he traveled slowly, as a wearied child, over the hard pavement. Just before he reached the minister, he stumped his toe and fell at full length upon the hard stone walk, before Mr. Sanford had time to reach forth his hand and save him from a painful fall. Mr. Sanford caught the little boy up in his arms, and tenderly soothed him, as a kind father would his own child, who has been hurt by a hard fall. The tears had gushed to the eyes of the child—who, however, did not cry aloud, nor even whimper, as most children would have done—and as the tears rolled down his cheeks, became thus frozen by the cold; and standing still and frozen there, glittered like icicles upon a rose-bud. Those tears turned into ice, and arrested in their flow so soon, told that he had suffered pain, although he did not cry aloud, for if his frame was delicate, and his years but few, he had a manly little heart. Mr. Sanford brushed away, or rather broke off the frozen tears from his face, and kissed him affectionately upon his cherub lips, and then asked, in the kindest tones imaginable:

"What is your name, my sweet little man?"

"Willie, sir," said the child.

"And whose little man are you, Willie?"

"Mamma's," said Willie.

"And what is mamma's name, Willie?"

"Mrs. Williston," said Willie, evincing the *naïveté* of a child who is astonished that any one should have to ask the name of its mother, whom it knows so well, and thinks all the world ought to know equally well.

"Williston! Williston!" said Mr. Sanford, talking to himself in an under tone, all unconscious that he was heard by the child, who was pressed, it may be, a little closer to his breast, as he still held the little fellow in his arms. "Williston! that dear name! Can her name be Anna? is it she?"

"Yes, sir," said Willie, in an exultant tone, "that's my mamma's name, Anna Williston. Do you know her?"

"Yes—or rather, I knew once a Mrs. Williston, but do not know—indeed, it can not be that your mother is the same Anna Williston I once knew, at Washington; although," he added with a smile, "you are beautiful enough to be her child."

"Yes, sir," said Willie, his eye lighted up and sparkling with pride and pleasure, "it is my mamma, for there is no other Mrs. Anna Williston in the world that I ever heard of, and no sweet lady half so beautiful as my poor mamma, who is very sick now. Please, sir, let me go; I am in a hurry."

"And where are you going, Willie?"

"I am going for the doctor, sir; mamma is sick, and wants to see Doctor Boring again, just for a little while, she said."

"You are not far from Doctor Boring's, Willie," said Mr. Sanford, putting down the little fellow and taking him by the hand. "I will go with you myself to his office, for I have a slight acquaintance with the doctor, and then, if you have no objections, I will accompany you home, for I am a clergyman, Willie, and your mother may not be unwilling to see me."

"O, no! sir, she will be very glad to see you! for ever since she heard you preach yesterday, she has been weeping, and in her dreams, last night, I heard her say how much she loved Mr. Sanford; and when I asked her, this morning, who Mr. Sanford was, she said, he was the preacher whom we heard yesterday."

"The same! the very same!" said Mr. Sanford, in a low, agitated voice. Willie heard him say "the same," but he thought Mr. Sanford had reference to himself, and not to his mother.

"This is Doctor Boring's office," said Mr. Sanford, a little while after, and turning in, he inquired of the "office boy" for Dr. Boring.

"He is not in, sir," said the boy, in reply, and bowing very politely, "he stepped up to the house a few moments since, but said he would be back directly."

Mr. Sanford took out his gold-cased pencil and wrote upon a slip of paper a few lines, and handing it to the boy, said: "Go up quickly to the house and say to the doctor that I have gone on to Mrs. Williston's, and will meet him at her house."

The boy knew Mr. Sanford very well, and did not hesitate, at the request of so eloquent and popular a clergyman, to go immediately in search of his master. As he left the office, Mr. Sanford took Willie by the hand, and walking too rapidly and anxiously, with the little fellow trotting by his side, reminded the street passengers in contrast of size, though in nothing else, of the little pilot-fish clinging to the huge shark, to guide it through the ocean desert of waters. Indeed, Willie became so very tired, that Mr. Sanford, recollecting that a little child could not walk so fast as a man and not be weary, stooped down, with fatherly pity, and took him up in his arms, carrying him the rest of the way, until they reached the cottage of Mrs. Williston.

When Mr. Sanford entered the house, Willie took him by the hand and led him through the short passage into the parlor, or sitting-room, where his mother was lying upon a settee, or sofa, covered up with several thick comforts. She was coughing violently before they entered the room; but her cough ceased almost instantly, from the intensity of her emotions, and the suddenness of her surprise, at seeing Mr. Sanford instead of the physician. Involuntarily she rose up in a sitting posture, and held out her arms to the dear object of her heart's idolatry. A single cry escaped her lips, which stood apart, pale, and bloodless, and tremulous, but revealing, as in the days gone by, the pearly whiteness of her beautiful teeth. The cry which she uttered was not such a cry as we are accustomed to hear. It was a cry of distress and relief; of joy and sorrow; of pleasure and pain commingled. The only word that she uttered was "Sanford!" and the only response which the preacher gave was "Anna!" Then he threw his arms around her, and lifted her from the settee—lifted her from the floor in one long, convulsive embrace; and with her arms around his neck, and her head upon his shoulder, and her eyes closed as if she had dropped asleep, she clung to him then as the poor seaman who has been washed overboard, and has breasted the waves, and buffeted them a long time, until he is tired and almost ready to fling up his hands in despair, when he feels, all at once, a plank drifted under his arms, or reaches a life-buoy toward which he has been struggling; and then, with his wearied arms hugging the buoy, or his elbows upon the plank, his head droops low, and he drops to sleep with his body still surrounded by the foaming waters! So, too, felt Mrs. Williston—safe now—like the "man overboard," who has been almost drowned, but has, at last, reached the plank or the buoy, upon which he goes to sleep.

When Mr. Sanford's arms relaxed their hold, he sat down upon the sofa and drew her head unresistingly upon his breast. In just such a position once before they had sat in her dead husband's home at Washington; and then it was a fatal position, for it brought death, and had caused themselves to be separated three long years—years of mourning, of trials, and of sorrow. It had caused her noble lover to stain his hands, almost in self-defense, in her husband's blood; it had driven her away an exile—a voluntary exile—from the only man whom she had ever loved, for her own sense of propriety, and the stern requisitions of a heartless world, and, most of all, to shield the reputation of the man she loved and worshiped with the love of a saint kneeling ever before the holiest of shrines—these considerations had caused her to flee from the love of one whom she had loved so that her heart was consumed daily with the internal fires of its devotion. She could not marry Sanford, lest the world, ever a base calumniator, should say, as the world would have said then, that he had killed Mr. Williston with design to marry his widow! O! how her soul recoiled at the suspicion! and how she resolved to suffer martyrdom herself rather than have a single vile slander hurled at the god of her heart's adorations, or a single stain polluting the shrine at which she worshiped!

Ah! then she worshiped only at the altar of humanity, and bowed her knee to the blind god of Passion! virtuous and pure it may be, but passion still, because unsanctified by the Holy Spirit, and unsanctioned by the laws of God, or the regulations of society. But now her love was no longer passion; it bore a holier—far holier name. Once her head .had rested upon the noble breast, and she had listened with rapture to the throbbings of the noble heart of that lover upon whom she now leaned for support; and the peering eyes of the suspicious inquisitor, looking through the blinds of her parlor-window at Washington, with a contemptuous smile, or an indignant frown at the married woman, no longer a maiden, but with a virgin heart, might have cried "shame" upon her who could betray her husband, either by a look or a word. But it was no longer treason to her lord, or his memory, to rest her weary head where only it should ever have rested, and where it might have rested from her virginity, with pride and pleasure, through long years of happiness and peace, but for the officiousness of friends, who can never know the wants nor the love of a true woman's heart. O! the sins of foolish, wicked matchmakers, who are the grave-diggers of society, to bury true hearts in the grave of interest; and undertakers to wrap the corpses of those who should be dear to them, in their tissue paper of unrequited or disappointed affections!

13

As she sat thus, with the arm of her lover around her
waist, and her head resting against his breast, her spirit
grew serene and happy; happier than she had ever been in
her life before. And he told his tale of love anew—all
over, from beginning to end, as if she had never heard it,
and knew not that she was beloved. And he pleaded with
her to alter her vows and cast aside her widow's weeds, as
if she had not altered them the moment she had seen his
coming and reached forth her arms of welcome ; and as if
she had not buried her widow's weeds in the grave of her
false husband, and worn them only for him! And as she
listened to the murmuring tones of his dear voice, as his
head bent over hers, with a smile upon his lips but with sorrow upon his brow, as the willow, bending low its head, and
kissing, with its drooping branches, the sweet, cool face of
the waters, she felt, as do the tiny waves, like leaping upward and answering with a kiss the kiss of the weeping-
willow !   .

But her eyes filled with tears, and her chest heaved with
sympathy and with pitying love, as she listened to the
mournful music of his voice, and heard him say how lonely
and how desolate he had been during three long years;
lonely as the turtle-dove sighing for its mate, which returns
not at its cooing, because it has been wounded by the bow
of the archer, and is dead; desolate and inconsolable as
the famished infant weeping upon the breast of its dead
mother, because she will no more awake at its fondest caresses, and because the paps at which it has been tugging
are dry!

"Ah!" said he, "it is a true saying that 'every heart
knows its own bitterness;' for, while I was striving to comfort others, how much did I need comfort myself! I have
often compared myself as a lone beacon built upon a rock
far out in the sea, almost out of sight of land, with nothing
around but the waves dashing against its base. The winds
howl, and the billows roll high, and a night of darkness

shuts in, and the lantern is swung aloft to its binnacle, as
a beacon-light to the distant ship at sea. The tempest-
tossed mariner sees it, and he puts up his helm to alter his
course, for he knows that it is a friendly light to guide him
on his way; and he sails by the beacon, and enters joyously
the port, nor even thinks nor cares how very lonely is the
man who lives in the tower, who swung up that light, and
to whose constant care and unceasing vigilance he has been
saved from shipwreck and ruin, and has entered the haven
in safety. Little have they known, while I have been
preaching patience to others, how impatient was my own
sinful heart! Little have they thought, while I was telling
with so much earnestness, of the grace of our Lord Jesus
Christ, how much I needed that grace shed abroad in my
own sinful soul! Little have my most intimate friends
supposed, when I strove to lighten their sorrows or temper
their joys, that my heart was decked with all the habili-
ments of mourning, and bowed by an oppressive load which
none but your dear hand could remove! But, thank God,
the watchman shall no longer be lonely, for God has sent
him a companion to stand by his side, and help him dress
the lantern and swing it aloft in the binnacle, that the
storm-tossed mariner, bound for eternity, may see that the
beacon is still faithfully kept. Will it not be so, dearest?"

"God helping me, Julius, it shall be so. But, O! pray
for me, that God may give me strength to fulfill all the
duties of a faithful minister's wife."

There was a rap at the door, and Mr. Sanford himself
obeyed the summons. It was Dr. Boring, whom he shook
joyously by the hand, as an old friend whom he had not
seen for long years. So happy was his heart now, that it
made him grasp the hand of a comparative stranger with
the grip of a college-boy who meets upon the highway his
college chum, whom he has not seen for several months or
years. How happy, how kind, and generous, and forgiving

does success in life render a man of noble impulses, even
when that man's heart is unsanctified by the grace of God!
But how much happier, how much kinder, how much more
generous and loving, is the heart of the Christian, who feels
gratitude to God because his prayers have been heard at
last, although the petition has been long deferred, perhaps
in mercy and in love!

Dr. Boring returned the greeting of Mr. Sanford warmly,
but he could not resist a smile and a feeling of inward satisfaction, because he suspected, from the singular warmth
of the clergyman—so good a reader was he of human nature—that Mrs. Williston had found a friend who could be
kinder to her than he had been; one, said he, to himself,
"that sticketh closer than a brother." And as he sat down
by the side of the patient, and experienced the warmth of
the seat which Mr. Sanford had just vacated, and felt the
pulse of Mrs. Williston, and knew, by its pulsations, that
her heart was throbbing steadier, and with more elastic
bounds than he had ever felt it throb before, he raised his
head slowly, and, with a mischievous smile upon his countenance as he winked toward Mr. Sanford, who blushed up
to his temples:

"The parson is a better doctor than I am," said he. "I
think I must resign you into his hands."

Mrs. Williston blushed until she was crimson, and murmured, in reply, something about his being an old friend,
whom she had not seen for several years.

"I am very glad you have found so noble a friend, madam," said the doctor, in his blunt, frank way; "and I hope
you will never be separated again, save by the hand of
death! You need a friend dearer and truer than I can be,
although God knows it would be my delight to see you
happy always and forever. But take this pill, madam. You
are a great deal better than I expected to find you; for
your skin is moist, and although your pulse indicates that
you have been laboring under a high fever, it is rapidly

subsiding. Swallow this pill, and you will experience more benefit than you can imagine. To-morrow morning I will call to see you again. And, by the way, I hope Mr. Sanford will continue to visit my patient every day; for I am satisfied, my dear sir, that your agreeable conversation will do more for the complete restoration of Mrs. Williston's health than all the medicine in Boston. Eh! my little Willie? What do you think about it, sir? How would you like to be a doctor, sir?" said Dr. Boring, as he patted the bright-eyed boy upon his head.

"I would like it very well, sir," said Willie; "but I would like it a great deal better to be a preacher, like Mr. Sanford."

"Ha! ha! ha!" laughed the doctor. "Well then, sir, you will have to remain with Mr. Sanford. He can teach you divinity; I can only teach you to mix up pills and spread blister-plasters. And, to say the least, it is a very dirty business, which no gentleman would, or likes to follow. Don't you think so, my little man?"

"I think *you* are a gentleman, sir, and *you* are a doctor."

"Thank you! thank you! my little fellow. And you are a little gentleman also. One compliment deserves another, I know; but I appreciate your remark very highly, as the highest compliment ever paid me in all my life. Not that I do not feel that I am a gentleman, or that I am not called a gentleman by others, but because I have been called so by a little child of five years. You are a shrewd fellow, Willie, to see so far into a millstone. Good-morning, my dear Mrs. Williston. You have a smart little son, and he deserves a smart daddy. Good-morning, Mr. Sanford. God bless you both, and make you as happy as I am in seeing you all smiling so happily upon me!"

Mr. Sanford rose from his seat and accompanied the doctor to the door. As they stood upon the stoop together, he asked Dr. Boring, in a very anxious manner, if he had any fears whatever for his patient's safety.

"None whatever, my dear sir," replied the doctor. "She has only taken a fresh cold, the result of going out yesterday, which is already giving way, and will soon be removed entirely from her system, with proper care. She only needs a kind husband," he added, with a smile of intelligence, "to keep her from taking cold in future."

As Mr. Sanford returned to the room, he thought within himself, "If that is all, I hope in God that I may be her true and faithful husband, as I know she will be to me a true and faithful wife. May the good Lord unite us in the flesh as we are already united in the spirit!"

When Mr. Sanford re-entered the parlor, Mrs. Williston welcomed his coming with that yearning look and beaming smile of welcome which only a fond woman can assume, who, with a heart throbbing with joy, greets the return of her long-absent lord. And Mr. Sanford, with a smile of happiness, resumed the seat by her side, which he had vacated at the coming of Dr. Boring, and with his arm around her waist, and little Willie upon his knee—who sat there as happy as if he had found a father, far happier than he ever could have been with his own father—thus the happy trio sat, with unalloyed happiness in their hearts and pleasure beaming from each love-lit countenance. Happy, thrice happy were these lovers now, who had been kept apart by a painful separation of long months and years, but so lately united by the providence of God!—who had been separated by the unmeaning customs of life and the cruel edicts of a heartless conventionalism—the conventionalism of a society which has no vail of charity to fling over the faults and foibles of any other but its own—a society which sneers and scoffs at the *appearance of evil*, and who hoots beyond its borders the seeming derelict, while in secret, and sometimes even in the broad light of day, that same harsh arbiter of others' destinies commits the most monstrous crimes and calls them virtues!

But Mrs. Williston and her clerical lover are safe now

from the hand of persecution and the tongue of slander. They have passed through a painful and most excruciating ordeal. They have felt the tortures of the rack. They have walked through the fiery furnace and amid all the flames. Although separated in appearance, they were still united in reality; for there was One who walked between them in the furnace, and his form seemed more than the form of an angel, for it "looked like that of the Son of man," whose breath was as "a cool wind and a moist air" around them, that their frames were not scorched nor their hearts withered by the flames of affliction. And now that' they are united by the hand of God, may the God of the Christian be with them forever!

BOOK III.

—————◆—————

CHAPTER I.

IT is some time since we were at the home of Mrs. Shelton; and when we were there last, Old Toney had rejected his freedom with disdain, or sorrowful indignation, but had accepted, with pride and pleasure, the gold watch and the money which his master had left him as a memorial—a faint estimate, but a heartfelt offering —for his many valuable and inestimable services. There was no master now but Old Toney on the little farm, and he was beginning to prepare for another crop. Young Toney and his brother George were busy with the plow, while the younger children were gathering up trash to be burned. Fanny was about the house, dressed with her usual taste; while Lucy and her mother did the cooking and the washing for the entire family, both white and black. Old Toney himself did as an industrious master of a plantation will do, going from one to the other, giving directions how the work should be done, and assisting the laborers to do it; now picking up trash with the "trash-gang," and throwing sticks, and junks, and branches of trees upon the fire; and then taking hold of the plow and running a furrow or two, either to show how the plow should be governed, or to relieve the

hand and rest the weariness of the plowman. Such, I believe, is a faithful picture, briefly drawn, of the general
habits of an industrious Southern planter.

Old Toney had just let go the plow, which he had handed
back to his son George, and was returning homeward to
attend to certain duties about the yard. The sun was just
setting in the west as he climbed over the fence and sat
upon the top rail, thinking over his agricultural plans and
future farming operations. And as he thought of these, the
memory of his old master came back to him in all its force,
and, for some considerable time, he was compelled to hold
on to the rail with both hands, sobbing with all his might,
and mourning the lost society and companionship of one
whom he should never more see in this world. But the
violence of his grief passed away, and he began to sing, in
a mournful tone, a song which Old Sampson had composed;
and the song seemed to soothe his troubled spirit, because
he felt that, although the old African preacher had composed it for himself, yet it was, in a great degree, appropriate to his own sad case. We can not give the tune, which,
sung by such a songster, sounded like a very sweet and
plaintive Ethiopian melody. But the words were these, as
near as we can remember them, and which we shall call

THE OLD NEGRO'S LAMENT.

I had a kind old masser,
  O! he was very kind;
When poor nigger's griefs were great
  He always said, "O! nebber mind."
When poor nigger's griefs were great
He always said, "O! nebber mind. O! nebber mind."

I had a kind old masser,
  But he is dead and gone;
He died one cold winter night,
  Stiff dead was he before the dawn
    He died, etc.

When dey put him in de ground,
  Poor missis' heart was broke;
When I heard dat hollow sound,
  O dear! I t'ought dat I would choke
    When I heard, etc.

Do' my sorrow is so great,
I'll strive my tears to dry;
But when I see poor missis
I always den am sure to cry.
But when, etc.

And dere's de orphan chilluns,
What can poor nigger do?
I'll be dere fait'ful nigger,
And try to be dere farer too.
I'll be dere, etc.

The public road was quite sandy, and there was a "clump of trees" between it and the fence upon which Old Toney sat, so that he did not hear the tramp of a horse which was approaching, and upon which was seated a traveler, who had reined in his steed to listen, unseen, to the song of the old negro. The traveler had spoken once after the song ceased; but Old Toney was so much absorbed by his feelings, and the contemplation of his own sorrows, that he did not hear the "hello" of the stranger. And is it not true, that when a man's heart is sad, and his soul is exceeding sorrowful, he can listen to scarcely any other sound, and hear scarcely any other voice than his own, however loud that other voice may be, when he is humming some plaintive song, as if it were sweet music, although, in reality, the tones which affect him may be harsh, and possess no melody to the ears of another? Thus the raven listens with rapture to its own harsh croakings; and the night-owl, upon his lonely perch, with its dismal hootings, wakes the stillness of the forest with its unceasing echoes, and thinks the music of his deep, bass voice is grander than the sweet tenor of the whip-poor-will, or the melodious song of the nightingale.

But Old Toney's voice was not so rough that it could not charm the ears of a Southern man of kindly spirit; for it is only one who has been brought up in daily contact and friendly intercourse with the Southern slave who can see virtues in the negro where another could not see them, or discover music in a voice which might seem harsh to the

ears of a Northern man; just as the Frenchman listens with
rapture to the " blood-an-own" cry of the "grenouille," or
large bull-frog, and thinks the music of his voice *so sweet*,
because his flesh makes "*un grand fricassee;*" so that what
might excite the sympathies of the one, would only excite
the disgust or contemptuous laughter of the other.

The listener certainly must have been of this latter class,
and the reader will say that he was an Abolitionist at heart;
and Old Toney himself was as much astonished by the words
of the stranger, as by his "Hello," a second time repeated.
The old negro leaped like a young man from his seat upon
the fence-rail, and, pushing aside the tall underbrush which
had completely concealed from his view the form of the
traveler, walked leisurely toward the public road, where the
stranger awaited his coming.

"Hello! there, you old darkey; what wicked song is that
you have been singing?"

"Wicked song, masser! You extonish me berry much!
I t'ought dat it was a berry good song; for it bring de tears
to my eyes t'inking 'bout my poor old masser," said Old
Toney, with a sigh.

"It *is* a wicked song! a *very* wicked song!" retorted the
stranger; "for the Bible, which is the best of all books,
tells us to call no man master save our master in heaven."

"Yes, masser, dat is true—berry true; but, you see, *my*
masser *is* in heaben; for he went dere ebber since last winter. It's been t'ree munt's since my blessed old masser,
Colonel Shelton, took his journey for his long home;" and
Old Toney brought a deep sigh.

"And he is just where every Southern planter ought to
be, old man; for, I tell you, you want enlightenment on
this subject. Your master never went—could not be admitted into heaven. If he is dead, as you say, he is in hell!
for *no slaveholder can enter the kingdom of heaven!*"

Had Old Toney heard the loudest clap of thunder from
the most serene and cloudless sky, he could not have been

more astonished and amazed. He looked at the stranger for a while, then looked upon the ground; looked up and looked down again; put his hands in his pocket, and pulled them out again. He seemed to be in a quandary what to say or do, or in what manner to treat the man who had uttered what he regarded to be such downright blasphemy. At length he raised his head, to be hung no more in confusion; and aping, in appearance, but feeling, in reality, something of the dignity, the offended dignity, of the Southern planter, with his hands crossed under his coat-tail, and his head thrown far back, and his single eye flashing fire, he looked the stranger in the face with a steady gaze, and with his lips compressed together :

"Look yer, masser, war you come from?" asked the old man, as he seemed to cock one eye, and then squint the other.

"I come from Boston, way up to the North," was the reply.

"I t'ought so ; I t'ought you was a Yankee, come from de big Norrud, as soon as I got de sound ob your voice. Well, look yer, masser, just turn your horse's head turrer way, and go back where you come from. You ain't fittin' to go lib 'mong niggers, nor white folks neader. And I tell you for sartin, if you come talkin' 'bout our Soudern planters dat way, you will get a lickin'. And please God, masser, aldo you is a white buckra, and I is a black nigger, if you talk dat way 'bout *my* masser, my poor, dead masser, I t'inks de law would bear me out in lickin' you myself. But law or no law, I will call my son, nyung Toney here, and mek him lick you for me. I let you know, sir, dat *my* masser nebber larn de road to hell, and could nebber larn 'um if he had lib a t'ousand years, like Mephistoosala. Colonel Shelton now is sittin' on a higher seat in heaben, sir, dan you, or any udder man like you, can ebber hope to sit. You better go back where you come from. Go back, masser, to de big Norrud. You ain't fittin' to lib 'mong niggers."

The stranger from Boston found out that "he had woke
up the wrong customer"—that he had allowed his indiscretion to place him in a trap from which it would require
even more than ordinary Yankee ingenuity to extricate
himself. He tried to persuade Old Toney that it was all a
harmless joke ; that he believed as strongly in slavery as
Old Toney himself, or any other Southern man. In short,
he said a great many things, and used a great deal of flattery, to soothe the angry feelings of the old negro. And it
must be confessed that the obsequious and cringing flatteries of the traveler had considerable influence in mollify-
ing the feelings of the old man—feelings which had been
aroused in consequence of the stranger's harsh remark concerning Colonel Shelton, and the downright falsehood which
had been uttered by the Abolitionist, that "no slaveholder
could enter the kingdom of heaven."

Perceiving that he had partially succeeded in allaying the
wrath of the old man, the traveler inquired, in the meekest,
blandest tones imaginable, if it was possible to be accom-
modated anywhere in that region with a night's lodging—
"entertainment for man and beast"—that he had money,
and could pay for the privilege as well as any other man.
In short, could he or his folk "let him stay until after the
Sabbath, as he never liked to travel on that day, and he
would pay the usual rates."

"Masser," was the reply of Old Toney, "in Colonel Shelton's lifetime it was his rule nebber to turn off a stranger,
and he nebber took money or pay, in any way, from a trab'-
ler in all his life. *Now, I* hab de management, and I wants
to imitate my ole masser as nigh as I can. I can't wear
masser's shoes, 'case my foot is too big ; and I can't step in
masser's track, 'case my foot would out 'um. But I want to
step close by 'um, so I can, ebbry now and den, look down and
see if I goin' straight. So, masser, you can stay at my house
wid my missis, *perwided*, as Masser Green say, when dat word
bodder me so in de will-case—I did n't know de meanin' ob

it den—perwided you behave yourself like a gentleman ought
to behave himself."

"O, certainly," said the stranger, with a cheerful laugh.
" I am a gentleman—nothing but a gentleman. I hope you
don't doubt that, old man."

" Well, masser, I dunno wha' for say. You looks like a
gentleman ; you wear fine broadclot' clo's like a gentleman ;
you hab good hat and good boot on ; and, masser, you got a
berry fine horse. He sound, masser ?"   .

" Perfectly sound—sound as a dollar."

" And ee got a berry fine eye—a berry fine eye indeed ;
ain't old—nyung, enty ?" looking into his mouth and examining his teeth.

" Yes, he is young—only five years old," said the stranger,
with a smile.

" I t'ought so," said Old Toney, triumphantly. " I hold
myself to be a great judge ob a good horse. So he is
nyung, and he is sound, and gentle, too, masser ?"

" Yes, he is very kind indeed. You can make him do
almost anything you want to."

" I 'sure you, gentle, and sound, and nyung, and got a
fine eye—a berry fine eye. Well, masser, I dunno wha'
to say. If I had n't yerry you say wha' you did, I would
t'ink you *was* a gentleman, wid such a horse, and such clo's
on. But now I dunno. I only hab fur take you on trust,
and keep sharp eye on you. You can come 'long, masser.
Follow on straight arter me."

As they went on thus toward the house, Old Toney walking in front and the stranger riding in the rear, the old negro
could not resist the temptation to look back, ever and anon,
at the splendid animal which the traveler rode. He was a
fine, large, and perfectly-formed horse, of a beautiful deep
bay color. Old Toney was a connoisseur in horse-flesh, and
he looked upon the noble steed with the eye of one who
had been trained in a school, or had lived in a stable where
none but the finest horses had ever stamped upon the floor
or trod upon the turf.

"Dat is a berry fine horse ob yours, masser—a berry fine horse; and he hab *a berry fine eye.*"

"Yes, old man," replied the stranger, patting his horse's neck with pride and secret satisfaction, "he is, indeed, a fine animal; but he cost me a very fine price."

"Berry well, I 'sure you. And how much you gib for 'um?"

"I gave three hundred dollars," was the modest reply.

"T'ree hundred dollars; berry well; and he wut ebbry dollar you gib for 'um. T'ree hundred dollar; and he got such a fine eye! Masser, I declare I would n't trade 'um; for if he good as he look, he is well wut ebbry dollar you pay for 'um. *I would nebber trade or sell dat horse as long as he keep dat same eye in ee head.*"

Let me tell the reader something about the history of this horse, and how he came into the possession of Rev. Alfred Orton; for it was he, and no other, who sat astride the splendid animal.

When Mr. Orton reached Savannah, in the fast-sailing schooner "Excel," after a quick passage of seven or eight days, he very wisely concluded that it would not be prudent to remain in a city where he was liable, at any moment, to be recognized by gentlemen hailing from Boston, who would, upon receiving information of his cruelty to little Johnny, either denounce him as a bad man or a downright impostor. So he resolved to strike out for the country, and try his hand at anything in the way of trade, (except his old trade or profession of blacking boots,) from making wooden nutmegs up to coining pewter half dollars; repairing clocks, or putting raw-hide strings into an old banjo or a piano, and calling them "new-fashioned, lately invented, patent catgut;" in short, anything and everything, about which he knew perhaps little or nothing; for such is the usual practice of the "rough-scuff" of Yankeedom who go South to make a fortune in a hurry out of the "poor, ignorant, squash-pated, or leather-headed Southerners," as they call them. After paying his passage "in advance," and his board-bill at the hotel—or, rather, the old "Mansion House," which used to stand at the corner of Broughton and another street, the name of which the author does not now remember—Mr. Orton found that he had but twenty dollars left, and he determined either to buy or hire a horse with this sum, and try his hand a little at horse trading and a good deal at preaching in the country, as a special missionary sent out by the Northern Churches to collect funds for the poor Esquimaux in Greenland.

"Yes, that will do—a bright idea—a capital Yankee invention—that card is trumps," said the Rev. Alfred, chuckling with inward satisfaction, and talking to himself in a low tone, that no one might hear, although no one was within twenty yards of him. "They have all—I mean these ignorant Southerners, who are little better than savages themselves—they have all heard the song, 'From Greenland's icy mountains,' and the greenhorns will think, no doubt, that I am right from Greenland myself. Indeed, I see no reason why I should n't tell them that I am a regular out-and-out Esquimaux, converted to grace, and wanting to convert the rest of my poor, ignorant countrymen. For these ignorant Southerners, I am told, will believe anything, however *outré* or absurd, that a Yankee will tell them. If they will swallow a wooden nutmeg and never once detect the taste of the Northern pine or cedar out of which it is made, and never suspect, by the weight of a grindstone done up in canvas, that it is not a genuine cheese, nor that the chirping of a cricket tied by its hind leg to the cog-wheel of an old wooden clock which has been long since worn out and cast away in Yankee land—bah, what dupes they must be ! Well, here I am, at the upper end of Broughton street, and here is what they call, at the South, a livery stable, is it? A grand livery stable that ! It looks more like an old dilapidated barn, or a large *keow-house* where they winter their *keows* in old Massachusetts."

A bargain was soon struck between Mr. Orton and the horse-dealer, who, having about as keen an eye to his own interests and as elastic a conscience as the Abolitionist, determined that the Yankee should pay for his ride if he killed his horse. The price which he charged for two days' ride into the country, was equivalent to a sale of the horse, being twenty dollars, just ten dollars per day.

"I don't like the looks of that Yankee fellow," said the partner of Mr. Kittles. "Didn't he say that he was a parson, going into the country to preach a little?"

"Yes, that's what he said; can't you see, by his white gills, that he is chuck full of cod-liver oil?"

"Well, if he is a Yankee parson, I doubt very much if you ever see your horse again! These parsons from Yankeedom—most of them, although I must confess there are some very fine fellows among them—but most of 'em, I reckon, are pretty slippery fellows.* Why, I'll tell you what I knew one of 'em to do once; he came out South, he said, for his health, and to rest his throat, which had almost worn out, and had got very sore from reading his sermons in a cold climate. Well, he wanted something to do, and thought he would make a little money by practicing dentistry, or rather, what I call *tooth-carpentering*. So he got an old jaw-bone of a dead horse, and borrowed a gimlet from a carpenter, and an awl and a punch from a shoemaker, and at it he went, learning dentistry. With the gimlet and the awl he bored holes in the jaw-teeth and the front-teeth of the dead horse, and rammed in with the awl and the punch little pieces of lead which he got from an old tea-caddy. In three weeks' time he called himself 'Doctor Amsterdam, Surgeon Dentist, from Vermont,' and went about the country boring holes into people's teeth where there wasn't a sign of decay, and plugging up the cavities with tin-foil. But when any one who didn't mind

---

* The author disclaims this as his own individual sentiment.

the expense insisted upon his using gold-leaf, although he hated, like 'the deuce, to swap gold for silver, he would sometimes do it, or pretend to do so.* Well, sir, would you believe it, how that fellow served an old lady who happened to have a very large hollow in the biggest stump of a jaw-tooth you ever saw—a hollow big enough, almost, for a rabbit to hide in. Well, sir, she had insisted upon gold—nothing but 'gould,' she said, was going into her mouth. 'None of your tin,' she said, ''twill spile the taste of my water; nor none of your lead, that might give me the cramp-colics, and make me take to drinkin' campfire. If you put anything into my mouth, it must be gould! mind now, none of your Yankee manufacture, but genuine gould out of the gould-mines.' When the Yankee preacher heard that, he laughed or smiled outwardly, but he groaned in spirit, for he had but little gold-leaf left. He had started out with but two leaves, and now he had not half enough to fill the remotest corner of that hollow stump. So he thought a while, and then he said, 'Yes, madam, I will do it.' 'Thank you, sir,' said the old lady. She supposed that he had promised to fill the cavity with pure gold-leaf, as she desired. No such thing. When the Rev. Dr. Amsterdam said 'I will do it,' he meant simply to say that he would perform, for her special benefit, a nice little innocent Yankee trick, by which he would do her no very great harm, and benefit himself a good deal. He meant to split the difference between the old lady and his conscience —between the big hollow and the little bit of gold-leaf. How do you think he managed it?"

"Well, I declare I can't imagine," was the reply of Mr. Kittles.

"Well, sir, he filled up that cavity with a piece of cotton, which he said was to clean it out, but he left it there, and then, with a little soft, prepared glue, he stuck on a bit of gold-leaf, as big as your thumb-nail, right upon the top of the cotton; then he called upon several people to look at what a beautiful gold plug he had put into the old lady's hollow tooth. It was a beautiful fit, as nice a looking plug as you ever saw; but the next day cotton, gold-leaf and all came out together; but the reverend dentist was a good ways off—several miles. The old lady lost her five dollars, and the gold-leaf was no manner of account but to sprinkle iced-cake with, and there were no weddings on hand just about then. Take care, Kittles, we do n't lose our horse as the old lady lost her plug."

"O, well," said Kittles, a little petulantly, "it would n't be much if we do lose him, for he is nothing but a wind-broken, wind-sucking beast; and then he is blind in one eye, and, in a month or two, he will be blind in the other."

"Yes, that is true. If he never comes back, you have sold the horse pretty well, although we might have stuck him upon some greenhorn for perhaps twice the money, with a little management."

Mr. Alfred Orton had n't heard all this talk behind his back, but his ears tingled, and his heart leaped with joy as he went further into the interior of the State and saw that he was not pursued. "Ah, Mr, Kittles, you thought you had jockeyed me, did you, when you charged me such a price—such an exorbitant price for only two days' ride! Well, now, I will show you that a Yankee parson is better on a horse-trade than a horse-jockey who thinks himself ever so keen! You thought, *in your heart, that I might not return* with the horse, and that is the reason you charged me only about half price! Well, I won't disappoint your expectations, Mr. Kittles!"

But Mr. Orton felt a little uneasy, as we before intimated, about pursuit, and his guilty conscience made him look back, every now and then, to see if any one was coming after him to take away the horse. So he determined to swap him off as soon as possible, and make tracks for South

Carolina. But he would not have been so very uneasy if he had known that in Georgia any one had a perfect right to steal a horse, provided he managed the thing with dexterity, and was never caught in the act of horse-stealing; and that even then, the horse-thief was sometimes, though not always, rewarded with good board and comfortable lodgings at Milledgeville, the capital of the State, all "free gratis and for nothing," for a term of years. Nor did he know that in some parts of South Carolina even, a man who could cheat his neighbor out of every horse he had, and, for that matter, out of all his lands and negroes—would be considered "a very smart fellow, who deserved even more than a leather medal; deserved a great deal of credit"—credit for "easing his neighbor of a few thousands" which were only "burdens to his neighbor," and helping himself so bountifully to his neighbor's goods, by permission of said neighbor, however, who was fool enough to be gulled by said "smart fellow."

Alfred Orton swapped horses with the very first man he met, and got "*boot*," and then he swapped again, and got boot this time also. Indeed, in his very first swap, he determined to adopt the horse-jockey's rule, "*never to swap unless he got boot.*" Thus he went higher up the country, swapping and getting boot, until, at last, he got a very fine horse from a man who had stolen him in South Carolina, and was running away from the "hanging law," which he did n't like so well as the penitentiary business. Mr. Orton met up with him just in the "nick of time," when the horse-thief was not only scared out of his life, but wanted a little money—"Anything, if it was only ten or fifteen dollars"—to pay his way on. And that was the only time Mr. Orton paid any boot in two or three horse-swaps which he had made in the course of a week. So Mr. Orton crossed the river at Augusta, and found himself safely hid among the pines of the "Old Palmetto State," with a splendid

animal and three hundred dollars clear money in his pocket.
He had just been thinking what a good week's work he had
made of it, when his happy thoughts were interrupted by
the song of the old negro, as he sat upon the fence mourning, and pouring out his lamentations concerning his dead
master.

But now that they are at the little wicker-gate of the
flower-garden, and as Mr. Orton dismounts from his horse,
Old Toney asks him, as he takes hold of the bridle :

"What's your name, masser? You ain't tell me your
name yet?"

"Orton—Rev. Alfred Orton," was the reply.

"You a preacher, massa?" asked Old Toney, in surprise
and agitation.

"Yes; I am a minister of the Gospel, and preach, or try
to do so, sometimes; and I would like to preach for you
before I go away. Would there be any objections? For I
see you have a little church about two miles back, which I
passed on my way hither."

"Objections! bless de Lord, no, masser! We hab a
church dere, it is true; but we do n't hab preachin' in 'um
more dan once in t'ree munts. T'ree whole munts, masser,
is too long. Now, I can feed berry well on sarment once
a munt! Dat will do for my breakwas. But when ee go *t'ree
whole munts*, den poor nigger hab no dinner nor supper,
and he get so hongry dat his fait' get berry weak before
quarterly-meetin'-time come round. And so, masser, you is
a preacher," said Old Toney, lifting his shaggy snow-white
eyebrows in amazement, as he stepped around the stranger
and surveyed him with the admiration of a horse-jockey
who is silently noting, in his own mind, all the fine points
of a full-blooded horse. "A preacher, eh! De good Lord
be praised! How come you, masser, no fur let me know?
I nebber would 'a said such a wicked word to you. Pardon
me, masser. I did n't know you was a preacher. Ain't a

preacher hab '*license?*'   A parson same like a woman, masser; dey is privileged characters, and has de perfect right
to say whatebber dey please."

Mr. Orton assured him, with a bland smile, that he had
his entire forgiveness, and hoped the old man would forgive, or think no more, of his thoughtlessness and unintentional rudeness.

"Go in de house, masser, and God bless you!" said the
old man, cordially.   "You is berry welcome, and your horse
shall be welcome, too; for he shall hab plenty ob corn, and
be 'up to his eyes' in clean oats.   Go in, masser.   Missis
berry glad to see all de preachers, and will mek you berry
welcome."

Mr. Orton went into the house as directed, and introduced
himself as a traveling clergyman from Boston; and Old
Toney carried his horse around to the stable; and as he
went, the old man kept on saying aloud, but in an under tone
of exultation, "A preacher, enty?   Berry well, I 'sure you!
A preacher, for true!"

CHAPTER II.

MRS. SHELTON was very much delighted with Mr. Orton, whom she regarded, upon first acquaintance, as an excellent, godly man. Not so, however, with Ella Shelton, who felt an instinctive aversion for the man who looked so boldly and so frequently at her, with a singular expression in his eyes, which caused her to blush and to lower her head in evident confusion. Rev. Alfred Orton mistook this manifestation of maidenly modesty for love; and the godly saint was very careful to impress upon her the statement, so false, that he was a single man, and, therefore, upon the matrimonial carpet in search of a wife.

Mrs. Shelton had gone out of the room while her daughter was playing upon the harp one of her sweet songs, at the request of the stranger. Ella had just finished her song, and her hand was still resting gracefully upon the instrument, when Alfred Orton suddenly took hold of it, and attempted to press it to his lips. The queenly maiden pulled her hand away, and gave him a look of indignant surprise. With cool scorn she surveyed him from head to foot, and then left him alone in the room without saying a word; leaving the amorous but cowardly Orton trembling with fright lest she had gone to call in Old Toney and his dark sons, for the purpose of chastising his insolence.

When in Boston he had been guilty of gross rudeness and similar evil intentions toward Mrs. Williston, he had been rebuked with the queenly scorn of a virtuous woman, who felt that her waist had been polluted by the desecrating touch of a libertine. If, at that time, Orton had been humbled and abashed by the withering scorn of a Northern empress, he was no less abashed and cowering before the wilting contempt of a Southern queen. He attempted to call her back, to explain his motives, and assure her that his conduct was only the natural impulse of a heart overcome by admiration of her skill as a musician. Ella Shelton did not stop to listen to any explanations from his false lips, but went straight to her room and locked her door. When she was alone, she threw herself upon her bed and wept most passionately. In her heart she knew, by intuition, that the Northern preacher was a villain, and she felt that he had intended to offer her an indignity. So mortified was her proud spirit, that she would have felt greatly humbled if any one, even her mother, should know how deeply wounded had been her honor by the lascivious looks and unmanly action of the stranger.

Thus it is ever the case with the virtuous, and high-born, and sensitive woman when insulted by some base-born hind. She will never let the world know, and will seek to hide it from her dearest friends, that she has been the victim of his persecuting attentions or base machinations. It is only in extreme cases that she seeks redress for her wrongs, and throws herself under the protection of one who shall promise to become her champion and her avenger. Hence, many a rascal has escaped chastisement purely from the self-respect and womanly pride of the wife or the maiden, who feels that she would be exposing her own shame in appearance, though not in reality, by calling in a friend or protector to avenge the insult offered to her chaste spirit.

The Sabbath morning came, and Ella Shelton met Mr. Orton with that distant and contemptuous politeness or hauteur which only an offended woman knows how to assume, and which would henceforth teach him that she was

14

on her guard, and would repel his slightest advances toward intimacy. Mr. Orton looked at Mrs. Shelton, and saw no frown upon her brow, no reserve in her manner, which was the same as last night; and he felt greatly relieved. Just three hours after breakfast, Mrs. Shelton, with her hat and shawl on, said, with a smile and a courtesy:

"The carriage is at the door, Mr. Orton. Ella declines going, but I am ready for church. I have sent two messengers around to the neighbors, to let them all know that there will be preaching to-day, and I have no doubt that a very good congregation has by this time assembled to hear a preacher from Boston."

Mr. Orton preached a very good "*sensation sermon*" that day. Although he knew nothing, had never felt anything, of the grand emotions of the orator, yet he had a good voice, and was well practiced in giving utterance to grandiloquent words and well-rounded sentences. There was but little substance, no argument, no sentiment, in his discourse, but it was, nevertheless, a *telling* sermon, and produced a *feeling* effect upon that particular audience. It is natural to suppose that most of his congregation, who heard preaching so seldom, especially the more ignorant portion, should be highly delighted. Indeed, one old lady in particular seemed so much excited by the discourse that she could not help screaming aloud, and clapping her hands, and shouting "Glory!" She astonished even the reverend impostor himself, for he had never heard anything like it before, not even in that most excitable of little towns, Salem. When the old lady was asked afterward what part of the discourse had affected her so much:

"O!" said she, with upturned eyes and hands clasped in ecstasy, "I was almost bilin' over all the time! and sometimes I had to stop my ears with both hands, to keep from bilin' over in yearnest, so sweet did that saint on earth preach the Word! But when, one time, I opened my ears again, just to ketch a few more sweet crumbs which was a fallin' like pearls from his lips, and hearn him tellin' about them God-blessed men, Paul, and Silas, and Cicero, and Thimblestockings, and the value of Jehosaphat, (valley of Jehosaphat?) I could n't stand it any longer! I had to holler; 'specially when I heard him say 'the value of Jehoshaphat!' And I thought how much I ought to value Jehoshaphat, seeing as how it did my poor dear old grandfather so much good, and kept him from so much sin. For you must know that my poor old grandfather used to cuss a good deal before he jined the Church; but arter the old man got religion, whenever he was tempted that way he always used to say, 'Jehoshaphat!' But sometimes he used to forget himself, and rip out an oath; but, in ginerally, he'd check himself in time. But sometimes the dear, good old man, without meaning any harm, used to say, 'Damn'—and then stop and add, 'Jehoshaphat—Damn—Jehoshaphat!' all in one breath. He used to say, then, that it was hard work 'to split the difference' between his religious and his old habits."

If such was the effect of Mr. Orton's sermon upon some of the white portion of his audience, it produced a still more powerful impression, in appearance, upon the black people, who regarded him as somewhat superior to the ordinary preachers they were accustomed to hear. Old Toney himself was completely carried away with the general excitement, and henceforth he resolved that as long as the preacher chose to stay at the house of his mistress, no other hands but his own should curry and clean the horse of that "God-blessed man, who had given him breakwas', dinner, and supper, all at once! enough to last him long enough for two quarterly meetings, and mebbe for de whole year!"

Thus having gained the ascendency—such popularity in the community, so easily, and by a single *coup de main*, or rather *coup de voix*—Mr. Orton concluded that he could do no better than to remain a little while where he was, and practice upon a people whom he regarded with contempt, as being little better than Esquimaux!

"Hum!" he ejaculated to himself. "It is useless to talk
to these people about Esquimaux, for they are no better than
savages themselves! They have heard, for they sung to-day,
'On Jordan's stormy banks,' but I doubt very much if they
have ever heard 'From Greenland's icy mountains.' I think
I shall stay a while and preach to them until I have given
them a few more evidences of Yankee power!"

A whole month passed off, and Mr. Orton was still at the
house of Mrs. Shelton, preaching on Sundays, and riding
around to the neighbor's houses, delighting them all by his
merry jokes and amusing stories; so that they all thought
him a capital fellow. To Ella Shelton he was ever respectful;
insomuch that she began to upbraid herself for being too
harsh toward him, and for, perhaps, entertaining unfounded
suspicions. But never did Mr. Orton fail to embrace a
private opportunity of chucking Fanny under the chin, or
patting her cheeks, and telling her what a pretty girl she
was—as pretty as her pretty mistress—and if she was only
in a free state, and no longer a slave, she could marry a
white man as good and as sweet as himself, and drive in a
carriage of her own, with her own house and her own nice
furniture, and her own servants—*white servants at that*—to
wait upon her, and call her 'mistress!'"

No wonder that the poor girl's head was turned by the
artful words and sweet flatteries of the wily, oily tongue of
the Rev. Alfred Orton. Fanny soon became no longer the
good and dutiful servant she used to be; but assumed airs,
and used insolent language toward Mrs. Shelton, as she had
never done in her life before. And when, upon one occasion,
Fanny was not only exceedingly impertinent to her mistress,
but grossly insolent to Ella, Mrs. Shelton could stand it no
longer, but was compelled to appeal to Old Toney for protection against the impudence of his daughter, and to threaten
Fanny herself with driving her away from her sight by
putting her into the field as a "hoe-hand."

Old Toney was even more indignant at Fanny's conduct

than had been his mistress ; and he felt it to be his duty to
administer the correction which her willful conduct deserved.
It was the first time Fanny had ever been whipped since
she was a very small child. Mrs. Shelton had never laid
the weight of her hand upon her, nor had Colonel Shelton,
during his lifetime, ever seen cause to punish her. In fact,
the only punishment she had ever received was when in her
infancy her little faults had been corrected by her parents.
To be whipped now by her old father for "Miss Ella," with
whom she had so often played and romped when they were
little children—for "Miss Ella," whom she had ever regarded
as a companion than as a mistress—especially, too, after
having been told by Mr. Orton, that if she would only go
to a free state, and, by flight, rid herself of her bondage,
she would be as grand as any "grand lady, either North or
South "—why, then, in her indignation, Fanny resolved, as
some other girls in her situation would have done, to go
where she could enjoy the luxury of being her own mistress.
That very night she told Alfred Orton that she was ready
to go with him to the end of the world !

Nor was Mr. Orton idle in another direction. He had so
completely dazzled the imagination of George, by holding
up before him bright pictures of wealth and independence,
if he would only go with him to Philadelphia, "where he
would be sure to marry a rich young lady, who would glory
in his ebony skin, and carry him about with her in a splendid
carriage, to exhibit him, with pride and exultation, as an
African prince"—that George grinned from ear to ear, and
scratched his head !

"He! he! he! Mass' Orton! Dat mus' be a great country,
fur true, where black boy can marry white gal! If titter
Fanny go, I gwine wid you, sure an' for sartin !"

So the matter was easily arranged. George intentionally
neglected to do his work that day, or did it so badly that
Old Toney threatened to thrash him if he did not go and
do it over as it ought to be done. Old Toney had often

threatened to thrash his son George, but he had never run away, nor had ever such a thought entered his head. But that day George went off and never returned, and that same night Fanny went off also; meeting her brother a little way from the house, with two bundles of her own and her brother's clothing. Two days afterward Mr. Orton bade adieu to Mrs. Shelton and her daughter, expressing many regrets that he was compelled to leave them, and hoping that it would not be many years or months before he should see them all again in that neighborhood, "where he had spent the most pleasant days of his life!"

As he mounted his horse, he asked Old Toney if he had heard anything of his "wicked children who had run away from so excellent a mistress, and so kind a father?"

"Not a word, masser! not a word!" said Old Toney, with a sigh.

"Bad children! bad children!" said Mr. Orton. "But never mind, old man; they will come back again; you will see them soon, I hope."

"I hope so, masser! I hope de Lord will pinch dem wid honger, so dat dey will be 'bleeged to come home and git something fur eat."

"Well, good-by, Old Toney! good-by!"

"Good-by, masser! good-by! God bless you! and, whereebber you may be, pray fur Old Toney, and his missis, and my chiluns."

"I shall never forget you at a throne of grace!" said Alfred Orton, solemnly, as he turned his eyes upward, with the hypocrisy of the devil himself! Such was the character of the first engineer on the underground railroad!*

---

* In this description of the Yankee preacher who operated as the first engineer on the underground railroad, it is to be hoped that the author is not attacking the clergymen of the North who stay at home and preach God's Word. By no means. For there is no man living who has a higher respect for men like Dr. Wayland, Dr. McClay, Dr. Adams, of Boston, (the latter has written a very interesting little book, in which he acknowledges that his views have undergone great changes by a visit to the South,) and a host of other godly men, too numerous to be mentioned here; for their names

Have the successors of Alfred Orton improved in any respect?

Thus parted Old Toney and Rev. Alfred Orton; but they
were destined to meet again under very different circumstances,
and woe betide the man who falls into the hands of an enraged
negro, whose patience has become exhausted, and whose anger
has become thoroughly aroused! Whether man or beast,
wife or child, he knows no mercy then, if unrestrained; and
revenges himself upon the powerless victim of his infuriated
passion, with as little humanity as the savage, and with all
the blind fury of the enraged beast! He is no longer a mild,
and a peaceable, and a loving spirit, but seems possessed
of such a legion of devils that he would kill himself, perhaps,
if he could not vent his spleen upon the object of his fierce
wrath and fiery indignation. Look to yourself, Mr. Orton!
Look well to yourself, we say!

"are *legion*," and, if published, would themselves fill many volumes. But the Rev.
Alfred Orton is a *bona fide* photograph of several Northern preachers, who were not,
in reality, God's ministers, but were, doubtless, either discredited at home, or whose
true character was hid by the cloak of the hypocrite—the mantle and the surplice—
who disgraced their profession by becoming "kidnappers" themselves, or in some way
aiding and abetting the escape of fugitive slaves from their rightful masters.

CHAPTER III.

N a cellar, not far from Camden Ferry, in the city of
Philadelphia, lived Alfred Orton, whom we will no more
call reverend, because he had been lately excommuni-
cated from the Church in Boston, and his place supplied by another and a better man. In this cellar,
which has since been used as a barber's shop, the once
clergyman, but now blackleg, lived in adultery with Fanny,
the runaway slave of Mrs. Shelton. George was a smart
fellow, and, at heart, a good boy; but he found no rich
heiress in Philadelphia, nor even a " buckra gentleman "
who would condescend to greet him in the streets with even
a friendly shake of the hand. The poor fool soon found
out that he had been sadly deceived; and that the black
man, all slave though he be, is treated with more consideration, and stands upon higher ground at the South than at
the North. He found no friend to help him, and Alfred
Orton left him to shift for himself. This George did right
well, and soon began to lay up money; for he had been
raised about the house, and knew all the duties of an active, experienced waiter. He soon found employment, therefore, in this capacity, at one of the large hotels in the city,
where he rendered great satisfaction by his faithfulness and
diligence to business. Often, however, his heart yearned
for his home in the South, and he longed again to see the
dear familiar faces he had left behind him in a moment of
folly. And whenever any gentleman arrived from the South,

how much more attentive was he to his wants than to any
other! How well he polished his boots, and how tenderly
—almost reverently—he placed them at the door of the
sleeping stranger, fresh from the land of flowers, where
bloom the palmetto and flourish the pine! And when
the traveler gathered up his baggage, and made ready for
his departure to the South, how often it was upon his lips
to entreat the stranger to take him back with him as far
as Savannah or Charleston, that he might again tread upon
the soil, and reclaim the home he had foolishly exchanged
for one which could never be dear to his heart! How often
was he ready to confess all, and throw himself upon the
protection of a stranger, that he might surrender himself
to his mistress as a runaway slave, who was already tired
of his freedom! But the recollection of his sister, whom
he would be forced to leave behind; of Fanny, whom he
knew was deluded and betrayed, and would likely be deserted by her seducer, who would fling her from him with
disgust, after a brief season of sinful indulgence. His sister,
and his sister alone, held his spirit captive, when otherwise
it would have been free.

And poor Fanny, before the cold of November came, was
beginning to awake from her delusion also. Never a carriage
had she rode in since her arrival; and the only parlor she
possessed was the dingy brick cellar, which more and more
seemed to her like a dungeon; and more and more did
Alfred Orton resemble a brutal jailer, who renders more
miserable, by his cruelty, his helpless captive; for often he
returned to the cellar, reeling and staggering from the effects
of ardent spirits, and sometimes he would pull her ears, or
pinch her skin, like an inquisitor executing the *auto-da-fe*,
by applying the torture of the pincers; but more often he
struck her blows, when the cards were unlucky, and his play
had been unsuccessful; for Alfred Orton not only drank
now, but he had learned to gamble also; gambled well and
better than many of the old experienced hands who had
14*

taught him the tricks and deceptions which they had long
practiced. The quondam Yankee preacher had invented
new tricks—could beat everybody at "old sledge," and
"out-general even the Philadelphia blacklegs." If they
had taught him how to win the "odd trick," he had taught
himself to win the *odder*.

It was when in the full tide of success as a gambler, that
a gentleman from Boston, while standing at the Exchange,
saw Alfred Orton passing by in a fit of intoxication, reeling from side to side of that wide stone pavement. He followed him at a distance, and saw him enter the cellar, which,
we believe, is even now used as a barber shop. He made
inquiries into the habits and pursuits of the quondam
preacher, and, on returning to Boston, made known the
result of his inquiries. Mrs. Orton had been mourning
the sudden departure of her husband, from whom she had
not heard nor received a line since that memorable morning when, in a fit of passion, he had put little Johnny's
eye out. Woman-like, her heart still yearned toward the
man who was the father of her children; and, in her
heart, she made many excuses for the irregularities of his
conduct. In proportion as he had been reproached by
others, she had clung to him, in his absence, with all the
tenacity of a true wife; and over his faults, now so widely
known, she had flung the thick vail of a woman's love. The
world might see huge scars and corroding ulcers, but the
faithful wife, if she had indeed caught a glimpse of them
with her own eyes, just for a single moment, with a shudder and with her head turned away, she had flung a cloth
over the scar and the ulcer, and saw them now no more.
Like Shem and Japheth, walking backward with a garment
upon their shoulders, to cover their father's nakedness, and,
with reverential pity, to hide the drunkenness of their
venerable parent from the eyes of another, so now Mrs.
Orton sought to hide the faults and defend the character
of the man who had deserted her, and for whose return

she was ever looking with a sorrowing heart and tearful eyes.

It was while the tears were chasing each other rapidly down her cheeks one day, that Margaret said to her mistress, by way of comforting her in her distress :

"An' shure an' if I was the misthress, I would n't be waping for that bad man, Misther Orton ; for I hear he has a new wife—a mulatto nager, that he shtole from the South, and is kaping her in Philadelfy."

"Who told you such a falsehood concerning my husband, Margaret?" asked Mrs. Orton of the Irish girl, in tones half tremulous with alarm, half filled with indignation.

"An' shure an' I got it from Misther Williams, who seen him dhrunk as a coot in the streets of Philadelfy, and followed him to the dark hole where he hides the yaller birdie which he shtole from her roost in the far South, (bad cess to him!) and kapes her in a dark cellar, like a poor canary in its cage."

"I do n't believe a word of it," said Mrs. Orton.   "It is a malicious lie!"

But her eye did not flash fire, for she knew Mr. Williams well; and she felt that if he had indeed said so, it must be, at least, half true, unless he was mistaken ; for the well-known character of Mr. Williams was proverbial for veracity, and forbade any doubt.   With trembling footsteps, therefore, she went to his house, and, with a light touch, rapped at the door; letting fall the brass knocker ever so lightly, as if she feared lest her summons should be heard too soon, and all her secret fears be confirmed.   Poor, forsaken wife ! Poor—worse than orphan—children, abandoned by your wicked father !

When Mrs. Orton heard from the lips of the benevolent-hearted Mr. Williams, who disliked exceedingly to tell all the truth, but who, when urged to reveal the worst, frankly declared his belief that Alfred Orton was no more worthy to occupy a place in the shrine of a true woman's

heart—when he told her that he was not only a drunkard
now, but a gambler also ; and, worse than all, that he was
indeed living in adultery with a mulatto girl, whom he had
already begun to ill-treat and abuse, then her cup of bitterness was full! But Mrs. Orton turned away with a firmer
tread, and went away with more rapid footsteps than she
came ; with no more a tremor upon her lips, nor anxiety
in her countenance; nor a painful look of suspense and
anxious fear. Before, she had been as the trembling, anxious
Mary, seeking for her Lord, and knowing not where they
had lain him; now, she was the Nemesis of Grecian myth-
ology, the fierce goddess of retribution, and the avenger of
her own wrongs. She returned to her home, and bade Margaret take care of her children, during her absence, for only
a brief season. Then, arming herself with a pistol, she
started for the ancient city of "Brotherly Love," with any
other feeling than love in her heart. For love can become
extinguished by the flames of hatred ; but, in the heart of
a loving wife, the conflagration can only rage in all its fury
when her tears have all dried up, and the fountain of her
love has been licked dry by the flames of revengeful passion.

It was a cold, cloudy day on the tenth of October, that
Mrs. Orton arrived in the city of Philadelphia. Thick, dark
clouds were flying overhead, but the wind was blowing too
strong and it was too cold for rain. But as night approached,
some few flakes of snow fell, and then the cutting sleet began
to drive against the faces of the street passengers like so
many pointless needles, driven with force from an old blun-
derbuss fired from the clouds—blistering but not punctur-
ing the tender skin.

But while others muffled up their faces closer, and hurried
on faster, Mrs. Orton heeded not the storm, nor was chilled
by the sleet; for there was a fiercer storm in her heart—a
fire in her breast, which the frozen rain could not extinguish, and which only her own or her husband's blood could

cool with a kiss, as the last remains of her love would thus be made to seethe out from the heart.

On that cold day, Alfred Orton did not go out, but sat by the stove, perfectly sober, and with all his senses about him. Fanny was seated in his lap, with her arms hugged close around his neck, and her head upon his shoulder, weeping tears of joy at the prospect of returning happiness. Orton was attempting to soothe her by promises of better treatment and more steady habits; for he had began to think that liquor did not agree with him, and interfered much in his success in gambling. It was just then, when the guilty couple were thus engaged in mutual acts of endearment, that the form of a woman darkened the cellar door. She looked upon the revolting spectacle before her for a moment only; then placed her hand upon the pistol lying like a cold block of ice upon her hot bosom; but all its coldness could not cool the flames of her revengeful and insane heart. The pistol was already cocked, and easy upon trigger—too easy, alas! for her; for, as she attempted to draw it from her bosom, it went off with a startling report, so loud that the guilty couple started, almost at the same time, to their feet. Mrs. Orton stood still for a few seconds, then fell backward, with a groan—baffled by her own haste, and thwarted by her own hand of her vengeance.

Alfred Orton fled with terror from his dead wife, like a man suddenly awoke from a trance by the claw of the hyena which has ripped open his grave and torn away his winding sheet, fleeing with the haste of terror, and never once looking back to see the beast which has clawed him from his grave. And Fanny fled also; but whither could she flee? There was no hiding hole in whose covert she could take shelter from the officers, who were, doubtless, already examining the corpse, and forming their conclusions as to who was the murderer. But the pistol clasped in her hand with the rigid grasp of death, foreshadowed a mystery of false vows and wounded affections; and a coroner was called in and a jury summoned, whose verdict was that the "deceased came to her death in some mysterious way unknown to them —perhaps by her own hand—perhaps by the hand of one Alfred Orton."

The cold had increased in severity, and the sleet was rattling like hail against the windows, and sheeting the pavement with ice, which would shine like a mirror when the sun rose on the morrow. But before that sun would rise in the east, or those sleety clouds flee away, how many of the poor may be frozen stiff, and, like an icicle, snapped off from the tree of life by the rough hand of death. And Fanny wandered through the deserted streets, cold and shivering, almost barefooted, without a shoe, and only her stockings upon her feet, and without a shawl upon her shoulders; for, in her terrified haste, she had left them in the cellar where Mrs. Orton lay weltering in her blood. And Fanny grew weary, and felt like lying down to sleep forever. Then she turned into the portico of a church, and lay down to rest beneath its friendly shelter from the pelting of the storm, which still drove the sleet, with pitiless spite, against her. But she could not sleep ; for now there was a fiercer woe to come upon her than the cold and the sleet; for she had begun to feel the pains and the throes of a woman in labor with her first child.

"All night," said the watchmen, "we thought, as each one took his round, that we heard the moans, and sometimes we could hear, through the raging storm, as it lulled for a moment, the faint shrieks of a woman as if in distress. And when we listened again, we heard the wind only whistling under the door-way, and rolling up the broad aisles of the old church ; and when the wind blew louder still, and drowned the moans and the shrieks, we hurried on with superstitious fright, thinking it was the wailing of a ghost from the church-yard, singing her ghost-song in unison with the storm."

When the morning dawned, they found Fanny, frozen to

death, and her still-born child lying doubled up upon the cold, ice-covered pavement of the portico of the temple— doubled up as it had come into the world.

And George heard of the death of his sister, and knowing better than any other all the circumstances of the sad case, resolved to wreak his revenge upon her betrayer, who had kidnapped her by his wicked lies and false pretenses. Look to yourself, Alfred Orton! for the avenger of blood is at your heels, and woe unto you if you shall find no city of refuge!

CHAPTER IV.

UST two weeks after the death of Fanny and of Mrs.
Orton—that ill-fated wife and mother—Alfred Orton
rode up to the door of honest "Timothy," whom the
reader doubtless remembers as Timothy ——, but whose
surname we promised never to mention again. Timothy
received him kindly, glad to entertain, beneath his humble
roof, the "smart preacher from Boston." Alfred Orton
accompanied his host to the stable, and as he put his horse
carefully away, although a very different animal from the
one he had rode upon his previous visit, he requested Timothy not to say anything to the neighbors about his coming,
at least for several days—until he had rested a little, and
then he would take them all by surprise, and play them
such a Yankee trick as would make them weep and laugh
at the same time. Ah, Mr. Orton! your words were likely
to be verified; for while some might laugh, others would
weep tears of blood at your second appearance among them.

It is strange what a hankering a rogue has after the old
spot where he has been most successful in his villainies,
but where his chance for detection is so much greater than
elsewhere. It may be explained only upon the doctrine,
"Be sure your sin will find you out." For, like the poor,
senseless, but miscalled cunning, rabbit, which strives to get
in at the same hole where it has been accustomed to enter
the garden, and gnaws at the rail or scratches in the dirt

until it has been caught in the snare formed by the more cunning gardener, so, too, the thief and the villain whom God would bring into judgment, creeps once too often, like the fox into the hen-roost, and is at last caught in a snare.

When the afternoon came, Alfred Orton strolled away on foot, saying to his host, Timothy, that he would walk into the woods and gather a few roots of wild flowers he had seen bloom in the spring, when last in the settlement, which he wished "to transplant in his hot-house at the North." He took a hoe with him, but he did not go far with it before he hid it away among the bushes. The direction he took was rather obliquely, but he soon veered his course sufficiently to come up to the back part of Mrs. Shelton's residence. On his way thither, and often before, he had said to himself: "Fool that I was, to be so easily scared away, when, by a little ingenuity, I might easily have caught my lady-bird. Perhaps she may not be so easy to be caught in a trap, but there is never a bird sailing aloft in the air, which may not be brought down upon the wing by a good bow and a skillful hand. Ella Shelton, you scorned me once, but see, if once in my power, you will scorn me then."

He seated himself upon a log behind a tree just back of the vegetable garden, not far from the grave of little Ella, where he knew Miss Shelton came every day to kneel down there and pray to her God. It was her sanctuary, and a beautiful and a holy spot it was; and the shrubs and the flowers which she had planted with her own hands, and then watered with her tears, had grown rapidly, so that they formed now a green wall around the grave, and could hide so completely the form of the devoted girl as she knelt in prayer, that none without could see her or know that she was within the sacred inclosure.

The sun had sunk in the west, and twilight was at hand, when Ella Shelton entered the little doorway, which could admit but a single person at a time into the evergreen inclosure formed by a hedge of cedars and wild olive. Alfred Orton cautiously rose from his hiding-place, and taking his long black cloak in his hand, stepped through the doorway, that the kneeling girl did not hear his stealthy, cat-like approach. Without uttering a sound of warning, he threw his cloak over her head, and bore her away in his arms, deep into the dark forest, as though she had been an infant carried in the strong arms of its mother. It was in vain that the poor girl struggled to free her arms, which were held down by his own, as if pinioned to her side. It was in vain that she attempted to scream for help, for her voice was smothered under the thick folds of his cloak, and sounded strange to herself, and hollow as the voice of one far under ground, like the echo of a voice from a tomb! By and by, as they went deeper and deeper into the forest, and farther and farther from the house, she heard and knew at once the voice of Alfred Orton, telling her not to be alarmed, that no harm was intended her, that she was in the arms of one who loved her to madness. That voice! she remembered it well; and the consciousness that she was powerless in the grasp of a libertine, a Yankee scoundrel, whom she had suspected of evil intentions from her very first interview with him! O! how her heart ached, and her brain whirled! How the blood rushed through her veins, until they seemed to be on fire!

When Alfred Orton thought he was safe from interruption in his hellish designs, he put down his precious burden, and drew off the cloak whose folds had enveloped her person. But when the wretch placed her upon her feet, and before he could speak a word of endearment, or utter her name in a soothing voice, as he had at first intended, he felt her finger-nails driven into his flesh, and plowing deep furrows into his face, and knew, by the fierceness of her looks, and the wild screams of frenzy which she uttered, that the beautiful woman, who was fighting like an enraged

tigress, was mad! mad!!* Then Alfred Orton fled with
terror from the maniac, and the poor girl, thus suddenly
bereft of her reason, ran after him, crying, at the top of her
voice, which rang through the dark forest, and sounded in
the distance rather like the screech of the night-hawk, than
a human voice. "Orson! Orson!" she cried after him as
thay ran. "Ha! ha! ha! Orson is whipped by the she-
bear! Orson is afraid of the she-bear's claws!" The poor
girl had read some romance, when a little child, about
"Orson and his bear," and she called, in her insanity, Mr.
Orton "Orson." When Alfred Orton returned to the house
of Timothy, his clothes were all torn by the bushes, and,
in his terror, he had left his cloak behind him; a fatal
proof it would be of his guilt he knew, but he resolved to
flee from that neighborhood by break of day. When asked
by Timothy why his clothes were so disordered, and his
face so scratched, his reply was, that he believed he had
had a battle with a she-bear, and had narrowly escaped with
his life. Timothy believed the "parson," but he thought
she must have been a very merciful or a very weak bear, to
have let him off so easily, and not ripped open his abdomen
once she had placed her claws in anger upon him.

"Either so," thought Timothy, "or the parson is a
smarter man than any one in these parts."

It was late in the night, past midnight, before Ella Shelton was found, a mile or more from the house, lying upon
the frost-covered ground, moaning most piteously, and almost
frozen with the cold. Mrs. Shelton was herself almost
distracted, almost crazy, at the sudden and mysterious disappearance of her daughter. The whole house and yard
had turned out with torches to seek the lost one; and Mrs.
Shelton, holding hard to Old Toney's hand, was led rather
than followed by the faithful old slave. The anxious

---

* This is not, by any means, a fancy sketch, not a creation of the author, but a
melancholy reality, which occurred a few years since in one of our Cotton States.
A horrible fact, but the author hopes that the parties will not be even suspected.

mother, whose eyes were sharpened by her love and anxiety, was the first to discover her daughter, and to hear her piteous moans. She ran forward eagerly, and cried joyously: "O! my child! I am so glad to find you! How could you stray so far into the forest and get lost?"

"I am not lost, mother," replied Ella, "but *it* is lost."

"What have you lost, my child?" said Mrs. Shelton, anxiously, when she observed the strangeness of her daughter's look, and wondered what was the matter.

"My poor cub, mother; I can not find it! Orson and the bear had a great battle! *I am the she-bear;* but Orson fled from me like a base coward!. I scratched up his face terribly, but he has carried off my poor pet cub!" And she resumed her moaning; striving to imitate the moans of a bear whose cubs have been killed by the rifle-ball of the hunter.

Mrs. Shelton looked up at Old Toney with clasped hands and an imploring countenance, and, in a beseeching tone, begged the old negro to tell her what was the matter with her child.

"Gone daft, missis, gone daft from de cold!"

Mrs. Shelton answered not a word, but her head drooped slowly down upon her bosom, and she tried to say, "God's will be done!" but she could not articulate the words, for each syllable that she attempted to utter sounded like a hiccup, which prevented her from giving utterance to the prayer of her lips, *for the Christian finds it hard sometimes to say, "God's will be done!"* Poor, grief-smitten woman, her husband dead, her son's mysterious disappearance, and now to see her daughter thus! Better, far better, she thought, that her "dear Ella had died suddenly, than thus to be bereft of her reason, and bereft in such a way! O, God! *by whom, and how!*"

With his arms folded upon his breast, Old Toney stood by in sorrowful silence, without attempting to utter a word of sympathy, when he knew sympathy would be unavailing.

The old man's heart was too full for words, and he felt that his own soul needed comfort. He seemed like one stunned by a blow which had confused and bewildered his senses. In his great love and pity for his mistress, he felt that he could willingly give up everything, wife and children, and life itself, to restore to her reason that dear young mistress whom he so much loved, and upon whose approaching nuptials he had thought with pride and pleasure. *But to see her thus!* lying upon the cold ground and clawing the dry leaves, imagining that she herself, who had ever been as "timid as the fawn, and gentle as the daffodil," was none other than a wild beast! O! horrid thought! which, as it grew in intensity, seemed to render the reality still more awful; and the old man groaned in spirit, and shivered like an aspen.

As if by design, though, in reality, only by accident, all the rest of Old Toney's family gathered at the same spot, coming in from different directions; and when they looked upon the countenances of Mrs. Shelton and of Old Toney, and saw Miss Ella lying upon the ground, they were not long in coming to a correct conclusion in regard to the true situation of their young mistress. Old Rinah sat down upon the dry leaves a little way off from Mrs. Shelton, and rocked her body to and fro, resembling an old Indian squaw wailing the death of her dead infant. Young Toney came up, last of all, with a torch in one hand, and the cloak which Alfred Orton had dropped in his flight, in the other.

"Here, pappy," said he, "here's what I found in de woods. It's de cloak ob some strange buckra."

Just then, Ella Shelton's quick eye, as it glared round upon them all, like a wild beast glaring upon those who have tracked it to its den—her eye, as it fell upon the cloak, lighted up with frenzied joy, and, leaping to her feet, she clutched the cloak with both her hands, exclaiming, with passionate eagerness, "Give it me! It is my poor lost little cub, which Orson carried with him. Ha! ha!

ha! ha! ha! ha! How scared the fellow was! Ha! ha! ha! ha!—ha! ha! ha!" and she gathered up the cloak into a bundle, and lay down with it by her side, thinking, all the while, that she was a she-bear, and that she had found her cub which had been stolen from her by Orson. Her mother knew that there was a little book in the library, which she herself had never read, about "Orson, or the Wild Man," but she never once suspected that Alfred Orton had anything to do with her daughter's mental derangement. How could she have supposed so, when she knew that he was many hundred miles away, and supposed that he was so pure a man?

We will not weary the reader by narrating the many abortive plans which were tried to coax the poor, crazed girl back to her home, nor tell how they succeeded at last. Suffice it to say, that, after several ineffectual efforts, they induced her to return home; and, when she had been put to bed, and Old Toney felt that she would be safe, during his absence, in the hands of Old Rinah and his daughter Lucy, he said to his son, in a low, but firm tone—a tone of resolution and danger, "Nyung Toney, de man wot had dat cloak mus' find! *Call up Spring and old Towzer!*"

"I tink so, too, pappy. Whoebber dat man be, he hab much to do wid dis ting," was the reply of his son, as he chirped to the dogs, and called them to his side.

They were both fine, well-kept dogs, and had ever been favorites with Colonel Shelton, who valued them as much for their keen scent as for their long-windedness. Spring was a full-blooded blood-hound, while Old Towzer was half cur, half beagle. They were both not only splendid watch-dogs, but great hunters also, and would follow the trail of anything they were put upon, whether hot or cold; ever keeping together, the one leading forward the other by the keenness of his scent, while the other would discover the trail as much by the eye as the sense of smell. They would trail anything, from a rabbit up to a deer; and would follow

the track of a man, whether white or black, from morning
till night, and never seem to tire.

Old Toney and his son saddled two of the horses, and
rode away from the stable, followed by the two dogs, in the
direction where their poor, crazed young mistress had been
found. They did not ride briskly, but like men who were
going to a hunting-ground where there was plenty of game,
and they were sure of the quarry.

"Let's go on to where you find de cloak, my son," said
the old man, as they stopped, for a moment, to look, with
sorrow, upon the spot where they had seen their young
mistress lay; regarding it now with the same sorrowful feeling with which they would have looked upon her grave.

Before the dogs reached the place where Young Toney
had picked up the cloak of Alfred Orton, they were in full
cry on the trail of the Abolitionist. In less than thirty
minutes, they were at the door of Timothy, who was sound
asleep in his bed, but started up in amazement when he
heard the baying and scratching of the dogs at his front
door. Old Toney and his son alighted from their horses,
and hitched them to the nearest trees in the yard, and entered the front piazza just as Timothy opened the door. No
sooner had he done so, than both the dogs rushed by him
and went straight to the door of the room in which Alfred
Orton was sleeping. The Abolitionist started up in alarm,
and sat trembling with terror in his bed, when he heard the
low whining and scratching of the two dogs at his door;
for his own conscience told him that they were Ella Shelton's avengers.

There was no time for explanation, and Timothy asked
no questions of Old Toney or his son. He went with them
to the door of the *ci-devant* preacher, and pulled the latch-
string, which hung outside ; for there was no lock or other
fastening upon Orton's door. In a moment, the blood-
hound sprang into the room, and, leaping upon the bed,
seized the terrified and guilty man upon the shoulder, while

Towzer seized him by the arm. Towzer was easily induced,
by a few kicks and cuffs, to let go his hold, but not so with
the blood-hound, who had driven his teeth deep into the
deltoid muscle, until they fairly met together. He did not
pull nor tug at the flesh, as do other dogs, but remained
perfectly still, with his eyes fixed immovably upon the eyes
of his victim, and his teeth craunched down upon the muscle.
It was in vain that they beat or coaxed the beast to let go
his hold ; he would have suffered them to kill him, sooner
than relax his hold, once he had tasted blood.

At length Timothy's sympathies became so much aroused
in behalf of the helpless victim, that, in a fit of desperation,
he caught hold of the hind-legs of the blood-hound and
jerked him away with all his force. It was a sudden and
a violent jerk, and the result was that the deltoid muscle
was completely torn loose at its insertion, or lower end,
where it tapers down to a narrow point, and hung down in
long shreds. It was a horrid spectacle, and well calculated
to arouse the sympathies of the most obdurate heart. It
did arouse greatly the sympathies of Timothy, who called
his wife to bind up the wound, and pour on a little lauda-
num and spirits of turpentine.

As soon as this kindness was rendered Alfred Orton,
Timothy inquired of Old Toney, in an angry tone, why he
had come out with his dogs, at that time of night, to disturb his repose, and endanger the life of the "parson who
was lodging with him."

"Him no fit to be a parson, Mass' Timoty. *You* know
ole Towzer and Spring well, and *you* know dey nebber lies."

"Yes, old man, I know that very well," replied Timothy,
who recalled to mind the scratched face and disordered apparel of Alfred Orton, and had been previously thinking
that something more had happened than he chose to reveal.

"Well, Mass' Timoty," said Old Toney, "dish yer man,
who call hisself Orton, done a berry bad ting to-night.
Like a tief, he stole up to de back part ob our house, where,

you know, Miss Ella always go, ebbery ebening, to pray at de little grabe ob my little gran'child. What happen dere I do n't know; but we found Miss Ella more 'n a mile from our house, 'way off in de woods, lyin' on de cold ground, a moanin' so pitiful it would 'a made your berry heart cry!"

At this point of his story the old man's voice trembled so that he could scarcely proceed. The tears streamed down the deep furrows of his sable cheeks, and young To-ney also had to wipe his eyes repeatedly with his coat-sleeve.

"We found my nyung missis dere, Mass' Timoty, lyin' upon de ground, callin' ob herself a she-bear! sayin' dat she had a big fight wid a man named Orson, but dat she had scratched up his face so dat he had to run away; and dat Orson—who is Mr. Orton—had stole her little cub! And when my son, Nyung Toney here, bring de cloak he pick off a hawt'orne bush, she snatched it from his hand, and said *dat was her own little cub!* Gone daft, Mass' Tim-oty! gone daft, complete!"

"*Crazy!*" said Timothy, opening his eyes wide.

"*Crazy!*" echoed his wife, with uplifted hands and a hor-rified countenance.

"*Crazy!*" replied Old Toney, solemnly, "*and dis bad man done it!*"

There was no longer a doubt in the mind of any one present that Alfred Orton was, indeed, the guilty wretch whose vile conduct had driven mad the lovely young lady. Where there was love and respect before, there was now nothing but hatred—deep and revengeful hatred. A con-sultation was held as to the disposition of the man, whom they now regarded as an outlaw, who had fallen prisoner into their hands.

"What you say we mus' do wid de Yankee buckra, Mass' Timoty?" said Old Toney, in deference to the white man, although, in the community at large, the old negro was held in much higher respect and esteem than Timothy himself, or even most of his white neighbors in his immediate vicinity.

15

"I say, let us give him a coat of tar and feathers!" replied Timothy.

"Berry good, masser, so far as ee go. What you say, my son, Nyung Toney?"

"I say, let us duck 'um in de hoss-pond out yonder, till ee dead!"

"Berry well!" said the old man, solemnly as a judge passing sentence on a criminal whom he condemns to death. "And *I* say, let's *lick* 'um to de't'! Now, dere being t'ree wotes, all different, I will hab *to split de difference.* Fus and foremus, den, I will try Mass' Timoty's plan ob de tar and fedders, which do berry well as far as ee go, as I said; if Mass' Timoty had den said, arter dat, '*Set 'um on fire!*' Den I will try my son, Nyung Toney's plan, and *duck 'um to de't'* in de horse-pond by de road-side; and if dat do n't *drownded 'um,* he will sartin *friz to de't' wid de cold!* Den, arter we done drownded 'um, I mus' try *my* plan, and *lick 'um to de't' like a dog, as he desarves to be licked!*"*

The reader may think there was little chance for the life of Alfred Orton; and Alfred Orton thought so himself; for he began to shiver with fright, and to beg most piteously for his life. But to all his entreaties they paid no more attention, nor even half as much, as they would have done to the howling of a cur, but sat down in silence by the fire, waiting until the morning dawned, when they could see better to execute their three separate modes of punishment. For three long hours the prisoner sat awaiting his doom, as a trembling felon, who is morally convinced that there is no earthly chance for his escape from the execution of

*The author has been informed that, only one year ago, a peddler, who, while selling his wares to a parcel of negroes on one of the Georgia plantations, attempted to tamper with them on the subject of Abolitionism, and went so far as to make them certain murderous propositions and incendiary appeals, *was actually seized by the slaves themselves, stripped naked, and whipped to death!* If true, it was certainly very cruel in them to push their vindictive punishment to such an extent. But it was just after the Harper's Ferry raid; and slaves, as well as slaveholders, were very much exasperated at the murderous designs of fanatical Abolitionists, who, in that affair, made the first experiment of the doctrine of the "irrepressible conflict."

the sentence, which will be executed upon his person on the morrow.

As soon as the day dawned, and it became light enough for the accomplishment of their designs, Alfred Orton was led out into the yard, and stripped entirely naked. There was a barrel full of tar near the horse-lot, and they led him up to it. Just as they began to apply the tar to the denuded surface of his body, George came up. He had just arrived from Philadelphia, and had tracked the fugitive thus far, with the unerring instinct of a blood-hound. The vessel in which he had sailed for Charleston had arrived at that port just twenty-four hours after the one in which Orton himself had sailed; and George had no arrangements to make—no horse to buy; and, on foot, could travel as far in the day as a man usually travels on horseback.

As soon as George recognized the features of Alfred Orton, he cried out to his old father, even before he reached the group :

"Kill 'um, pappy! kill 'um! for he killed my titter Fanny."

"Killed your titter Fanny!" exclaimed Old Toney, in amazement.

"Yes, pappy! his bad treatment kill' her! for she friz to deat' in Philadelfy, where he carried us all to, pappy! Fooled and betrayed us!"

"You tell de God's trut', George?"

"De God's trut', pappy!"

Then George told the whole story, or as much of it as he knew; and as he proceeded in his thrilling narrative, his own eyes, and the eyes of his old father, opened wider and wider, until they glared like fire-balls, as if he could have eaten Alfred Orton up—like a Siberian wolf making a meal of a single man, and then howling for more! more! ever, *more blood!*

When George ended his story, the old man said, in a lower voice than he had yet spoken, and with a countenance which seemed a shade lighter :

"Yes, my son; we mus' kill de varmint. Mass' Timoty, you mus' 'mend your motion right away 'fore ee too
late. Say, arter we *tar and fedder* 'um, *set fire to* '*um*, den
drownded 'um, den *lick* '*um to det*'; den, if he lib t'roo all
dat, we mus' tek' up wid George *fourf proposition;* den we
mus' kill '*um, and t'row* '*um to de buzzards!*'"

To Old Toney's proposition for an. amendment to his resolution, Timothy readily assented; and the work of "tar-
ing and feathering," which had been interrupted by George's
sudden appearance and exclamation, proceeded more vigorously. When this operation was performed, the torch was
brought by George himself, who ran eagerly to the dwelling-house to procure it. Just then Old Sampson came
riding by on his bob-tailed bay-horse. He was going "to
preach a funeral" several miles below. The venerable old
preacher, seeing what was going on, rode up in evident consternation, and cried out:

"In God's name, my bredren, what are you going to do?
Commit a horrid murder? What has happened?"

Old Toney related all the particulars of the case, and
appealed to the old preacher of the Gospel if it was not
right and proper, under the circumstances, that they should
wreak their revenge upon the criminal as they had all together determined.

"In God's name, I say *no! no!* NO! my dear brudder
Toney. It's a berry bad case, I know; and dis man, whom
you hold a prisoner here, is a berry bad man, I fear. But
remember de word ob de holy God, 'Vengeance is mine;
I will repay, saith the Lord.' Leave de matter in de Lord's
hands, and *he* will bring him into judgment fast enough,
and *sink him deep enough into the lake of fire and brimstone!*"

The old preacher spoke with even more than his usual
solemnity, and with a peculiarly thrilling effect upon his
audience; for he felt the electric thrill pervading his entire
frame, and he seemed as a sable prophet, not only looking

into the future, but, by the authority of Almighty God, pronouncing the doom of the wicked sinner. His voice, his manner, his words, produced, even upon the criminal himself, a startling impression, that they blanched his checks, and made his heart stand still ; *for he knew that he was a hypocrite, and expected the doom of the impostor !*

"Well, brudder Sampson, you knows best. I will gib 'um up to de Lord ; and if *he* punish 'um in de lake of fire and brimstone, dat awful hell, dat's wus' punishment dan all on us put togedder can do to him. You can go wash yourself, and put on your clo's, Mass' Orton, and go clean out ob dis country. You in de hands ob de Lord now. He got you hard and fast ; for we gib you up to him to t'row you in de big lake. Go, Mass' Orton. De Lord got you in his hands now, and *he* will t'row you in de lake! de lake ! "

And the words of the old man rung in the ears of the wicked wretch, and would continue to ring, like an alarm-bell which never ceases until the fire is extinguished. Wherever Alfred Orton shall go in future, the lake of fire and brimstone, already burning in his heart, shall rise up before his imagination like a terrible mirage, ever moving and flitting before him ; or, like an *ignis fatuus*, which shall at last guide him over the precipice which overhangs the lake. In his waking hours, and in his dreams, he will see that fiery lake boiling up as a cauldron ; and, in his ears, shall forever ring, as a never-ceasing, ever-ringing death-bell, the words of the old negro, "Vengeance is mine ; I will repay, saith the Lord."

CHAPTER V.

N two days—indeed, in one day almost—after the sad
.occurrences related in the last chapter, the news, like
all evil tidings, spread like wild-fire over the country,
and Mrs. Shelton's house became crowded from morning till night with anxious friends and relatives, and
many curiously inquisitive persons; for, while some came to
offer their heartfelt sympathy, others were influenced only
by motives of curiosity, to learn, from the fountain-head,
all the particulars of the truly novel and distressing case.
Among the former, came Mr. Thomas Shelton, as the nearest relative and dearest friend, to render any service which
he had a perfect right to offer.

There were many indignant persons who offered to go
after the villain, Alfred Orton, and bring him back, that
he might suffer all the terrors and pains of lynch law, or
be cast into jail until the spring term of court, to answer
to the charge of abduction and attempted violence upon the
person of Miss Shelton. But to all these overtures and
offers of assistance in this way, Mr. Shelton's reply was:

"No! no! let the scamp go! Old Toney has lynched
him already once too often. And as regards any criminal
prosecution, God forbid that my cousin's name should ever
be mentioned in connection with that of so great a rascal
as Alfred Orton, the Yankee Abolitionist!"

Then, after a pause, Mr. Shelton added:

"Indeed, gentlemen, you are all mistaken about this matter; and if you are my friends, and the friends of the dear young lady, you will oblige me, and her mother also, by circulating it as much as possible, that the sudden insanity of my cousin Ella has been brought about by some other cause—any other than the one which has been so currently reported, and which, alas! will be too generally believed, with many false additions and exaggerations. In all probability, her insanity is the result of sudden cold, suppressed perspiration, or some inward disease, the character of which we can know nothing. Indeed, there are various causes, seemingly slight, which may give rise to the most alarming and unexpected cases of mania. Ask the physicians, and they will tell you that what I say is true."

Thus Mr. Shelton attempted to convince others, and even himself, if possible, that Alfred Orton had nothing to do with the matter; for his family pride revolted at the idea of having the name of any of his family coupled with that of such a wretch, as he in his heart regarded the guilty man who had been the sole cause of blasting the intellect of one of the fairest and loveliest of God's creatures. But when one of the simple neighbors, who was unconvinced by the speciousness of the arguments, nor could understand the refined delicacy of Mr. Shelton, replied, in the simplicity of his nature: "But, 'squire, the cloak! the cloak! what will you say about the cloak?" then Mr. Shelton replied: "Well, the cloak is indeed a mystery; but, like other mysteries, it may be a very simple affair, after all."

And Mr. Shelton turned upon his heel and went away; but when alone, he ground his teeth together, and clinched his hands, and said, in a low, suppressed voice, while his breathing became hard, almost painful: "Yes, the cloak is a damning proof of Orton's guilt. Would that it were in the lake of perdition with him also."

This was a very harsh remark for Mr. Thomas Shelton to make; but he was greatly excited. He felt conscience-smitten in a moment, and went out into the yard, where no

one could see him but God alone, and smote upon his breast,
exclaiming: "God be merciful to me, a sinner. Nay, nay,
my God; let me take that back; for, O, God! I would not
pray for the damnation of Orton, but rather his salvation!
Save him, O, my God, from the lake of fire and brimstone,
and the gnawing of the worm that never dies!"

But while speaking of others, we must not forget to mention the dear young friend of Ella Shelton, the poor blind
girl, Fetie, who came over the next morning, and when she
was repulsed and driven away from the room by her who,
before her mental derangement, had ever welcomed her coming with so much gladness, and embraced her with so much
affection; when she saw her dear friend striving to imitate
the actions of a savage she-bear, repelling the approach of
strangers, lest they should take away her cub; O! then
poor Fetie's heart seemed broken and torn into shreds, as
Mrs. Shelton's, and she wandered over the house alone,
wringing her hands in silence, or clasping them with passionate grief upon her aching breast, praying that she might
die, and that her friend might die also, and both be laid
away at rest in some friendly tomb. And once, when, in
passing by Ella's harp, which had been hung with even
deeper mourning than it had ever been before, and vailed
by some friendly hand with a dark shroud, for its voice was
dead, like the song of its mistress, whose soul seemed to
have fled forever from her body, leaving it animated only
by a corporeal and not spiritual existence; once, I say,
when Fetie, in her wanderings over the house, struck her
knee or her foot, by accident, against the harp-strings,
which vibrated and resounded with harsh and confused
echoes from the unconscious blow, the blind girl started
backward in alarm, and stood trembling and as scared as if
she had heard the grumbling of a ghost whose bones had
been disturbed and made to rattle in the grave. For that
harp, if it were struck never so lightly now, would sound
as harshly to her acute sensibilities as it sounded then—as

harshly as would the skeleton of a man hung in chains and blown by the wind when it is thus suspended from a gibbet—when the rattling of those chains and those bones become painfully distinct to the ears of the wife, or the child who has loved the criminal, condemned justly, it may be, but condemned to a most ignominious and revolting death. ·

Ah! that harp has been touched full many a time by the hand of a superior being, and its strings have been breathed upon by the spirit of inspiration, and the impromptu whisperings of the genius of poesy and song; but by the hand of Fetie, at least, that harp shall never more be touched; when she sings again, it will be a new song; and when she plays again, it shall be upon a golden harp, in unison with those other harps and cymbals which accompany " the song of Moses and the Lamb." But as long as she lives upon earth, she will sing of the flowers no more, and weave no more chaplets for her hair. For, as the Israelites " hung their harps upon the willows" in the Babylonish captivity, and, because of their mourning, could no more sing " one of the songs they used to sing," so, also, the harp of Ella Shelton was hung in mourning now, and there was nowhere a joyous hand to awake its thrilling echoes. *The spirit of the harp was dead*, and none but the omnipotence of Jehovah could bring it back to life again.

But if Fetie was greatly overpowered at first, and if her grief seemed almost insupportable, like a little Christian, as she was, she strove to suppress it for Mrs. Shelton's sake, that she might comfort, as much a spossible, the poor, desolate mother, who seemed so suddenly bereft of her only and her darling child. And as Mrs. Shelton talked to Fetie about her poor dear Ella; as she recalled to mind her many excellent qualities of head and heart, and as she pitied poor Herbert, as yet ignorant of the great calamity which would overwhelm his soul with anguish, and tried to pray for him, that he might be held up by the Almighty Hand, and not

15*

be crushed completely by the heart-stunning blow, Fetie's cheeks were wet with a broad stream of bitter tears, for her eyes could weep if they could not see.

But not so with the eyes of Mrs. Shelton; for the fountain of her tears could not flow. For a great stone had been rolled upon it, and its mouth was closed up by the stone, and the stone which closed it was grief. And as Fetie listened to her voice, the grief-stricken mother seemed to be weeping, though her eyes were dry; for her lip quivered and her voice was tremulous; and then it sounded like low wailing; and any one who saw not her face, would have declared that the bereaved Mrs. Shelton was weeping copious tears. But if she wept at all, her tears were all shed inward, and bitter was the taste of them. O! it was a piteous sight to look upon her thus—to see that tremulous lip, and hear that trembling, weeping voice, when there was no answering tear to relieve the intensity of that great grief, which, like an incubus, was resting upon the heart and stifling the existence of that sorrowing mother.

God forbid, dear reader, that you should ever be called to witness such anguish, for it would make your own heart ache and your eyes full of weeping. The author, in all his varied experience and close observation of human suffering, has seen just such a sight but once in his life under similar—somewhat similar circumstances; and he prays that he may never look upon its like again. For, O! who can tell or imagine the anguish of a fond mother's heart, who sees her child, upon whom she doated, and in whom was a mother's pride, thus suddenly bereft of her reason, and rendered, whether by the hand of man or the will of God, a raving maniac. Poor mother! Help her! O, help her to bear her grief! for it lies like a great and a heavy burden upon her soul.

And Fetie rose from her seat, and, guided by the weeping voice of Mrs. Shelton, with her hands stretched out in the air, like one feeling in a dark room for the wall, the blind girl went up to the mourning mother, and flinging her arms around the neck of Mrs. Shelton, as she would around the neck of her own mother, she kissed both cheeks of the grief-smitten woman, thinking, in her heart, that she would kiss those tears away, which she thought were flowing so freely, and with her lips she would drink them dry. But how astonished was Fetie to feel no tears streaming down her cheeks! and she *felt* with her fingers, to *see* if the tears were where they ought to be! And when she knew and wondered that there were no tears there, and that her cheeks were dry—only she heard still that weeping voice with that tearless eye—then Fetie drew back in alarm and with wonder, like one recoiling at the aspect of so much woe and untold suffering.

A few days after this, an incident occurred at the breakfast table, which, though trifling in itself, and often observed before by those who have *always* lived at the South—an incident which I must mention, because it serves as an additional illustration of one of the most prominent features of this work, and because it is so true that every one familiar with the institution of slavery, as it exists in the Southern States, will recognize it as a faithful picture of a kind and indulgent mistress, as the largest proportion of wives of slaveholders are.

For several days Mrs. Shelton had eaten nothing, and Fetie, also, ate but little. Mrs. Shelton was a superior housekeeper, and, like all other lady-matrons, she liked to see everything kept neat, and the cooking done in a proper manner, even though it should remain untouched, and was all sent away again, to be eaten by the servants only. More than once, lately, Lucy, who was the chief and only cook now, had failed so miserably, and seemed so criminally neglectful of her duties, that, but for her sorrows and her failure to participate in any of the meals, Mrs. Shelton would certainly have reproved her for the improper manner in which many of the dishes were brought upon the table.

But on this particular morning to which we have reference, Mrs. Shelton observed that the bread was badly baked, and the biscuits were burnt to a coal. She sent little Josh, who was waiting upon the table, to call Lucy from the kitchen, as she wished to see her immediately. When Lucy entered the eating-room, Mrs. Shelton asked, in her smiling tones:

"How is it, Lucy, that you can not cook your meals right, of late?"

"How, missis?" said Lucy, in feigned astonishment.

"How?" echoed Mrs. Shelton. "Why, your bread is almost as hard as a stone, and your biscuit are burnt until they are charred. And several times, lately, it has been so, although I did not think to tell you of it."

"There ain't a piece of bread nor a biscuit burnt on that table," replied Lucy, in an angry voice. "If you don't want me to *brown* de bread, I can let 'um be raw!"

"Very well, Lucy!" replied Mrs. Shelton, in trembling tones, while a tear started to her eye; for those harsh words, at such a time, jarred painfully upon her ear, and she felt her sorrows all the more keenly, as she thought, if she lost the love of her servants also, in addition to her other great and irreparable losses, how utterly wretched and lonely she would be. "Very well, Lucy! You say you have not burnt the bread; let it be so! I shall speak to you no more on the subject. You know that I need but little, myself; but I thought that by mentioning the circumstance —which, I supposed, was only the result of accident, and not willful neglect—you would be induced to furnish something that poor Ella's little friend here might eat. But, never mind, Lucy! You can go now, and do as you think proper."

Lucy made no reply, and turned away in sorrow rather then in anger. She was punished already; for, when alone in the kitchen, she thought of her wicked conduct, and wept tears of penitence and sorrow. Like a good servant— as she really was, in general—she never again gave her mis-

tress cause for complaint; but, confessing her fault humbly
to her mistress, and entreating her pardon, and, in alluding,
with tears of contrition, to the circumstance afterward, she
said that she knew not why she had acted in this unusual
manner, unless, forsooth, she had been possessed of the
devil, who must have fled from her breast at the rebuke—
the mild rebuke—of her mistress, and at the sight of a
Christian's sorrow.

And what more shall we say, in this chapter, other than
to tell the reader that the old family physician, living a
considerable distance off, had been summoned to consult
with the neighborhood doctor, a young man of considerable
skill and ability, who had been called in at the very earliest
period; and that their united persuasions induced Mrs.
Shelton, very reluctantly, to send away her dear daughter
Ella to the Asylum for the Insane, at Philadelphia, where,
if at any similar institution in the world, her chance for
recovery was greatest, and where her wants would be attended to with the most scrupulous care, and after the highest dictates of humanity.   And now that the gates of the
asylum have closed upon her, and the form of the lovely
girl is hid from the world as completely as in a grave, let
us turn away our eyes, nor hope, with prying looks, to see
through the narrow bars of her cell.   Let us drop a thick
curtain between us and the poor lunatic, that we may not
see her insane acts; and let us turn away our heads, when
we meet her friends at home, that we may seem not to see
their weeping, or know the cause of their distress.   For it
is a painful subject to dwell upon, and an humbling calamity, which touches the pride of the human heart most where
there has been any pride of intellect.   But, as mortifying
and as distressing as this calamity is to us all, let us hope
that that God who " tempers the wind to the shorn lamb,"
and who, even " in wrath, remembers mercy," " will not always chide, nor keep his anger forever ; " but that " like as
a father pitieth his children, so the Lord will pity them

that fear him," "for He knoweth our frame, and He re-
membereth that we are dust;" therefore will He "bring
good out of evil;" for "whom He loveth He chasteneth,
and scourgeth every son whom He receiveth."

"May de good Lord," said Old Toney, "restore my nyung
missis back to us again sane and sound, and no longer daft!
but may de wengeance ob Almighty God obertake Mass'
Orton! Yes, de lake! de lake! he shall perish in de lake!"

CHAPTER VI.

SOME years ago, the author was informed, by one of our oldest and most respectable citizens, that, not very long after he married, he became acquainted with Stevens, the land-pirate, in rather a peculiar way; and now he looks back with a shudder upon that time, when he remembers how easily he could have been robbed and murdered.

"I had landed," said he, "at night, from an old and long since exploded steamer—I believe she was called the "Cotton Plant"—which used to run a little way up the river. I had landed at the ancient and now dilapidated village of Purysburg. This village was built long ago—years, I believe, before the Revolution—was once a place of considerable trade, and its early founders thought it was destined to be the great emporium of commerce for Georgia, and South Carolina also. But the hopes of the wisest builders are often blasted; for Purysburg soon discovered that she had not only a rival in the city of Savannah, but that Georgia's seaport was destined soon to annihilate her very existence. But if Purysburg failed to become a city, which perished in its embryo condition; if its streets, which were blotted on paper, became grown up with grass, or converted into roads, and its houses tumbled into decay, and its inhabitants died before they were born ; its grand old trees still rear their heads as proudly as they did centuries ago. It was upon that Indian mound, reared by the Aborigines

on the Savannah river bank, and beneath that venerable old
oak, that I took shelter from the heavy dew which falls in
that locality; and my only companion was Stevens, who had
landed with me from the little steamer. I remember him
well, as if yesterday I had seen him; for I was struck with
his genteel appearance, which, although not altogether that
of 'a gentleman to the manor born,' was, nevertheless,
much more genteel than is ordinarily seen among our hard-
fisted yeomanry. *He was a decidedly smart fellow,* and had
much to talk about which interested me; for, although he
had not read much—indeed, was a man of too active physical habits and restless disposition for that—yet he had seen
a great deal of life and natural scenery, and had studied
human nature very closely. He was a man of about five
feet ten inches in hight, I should think, with an actively-
made, well-knit frame; his legs a little bowed, from constant
horse-back riding, and *an eye as keen as a hawk's,* and, as
near as I can remember, it resembled a hawk's somewhat
in color as well as expression. In fact, there was a peculiar
and disagreeable expression of his eye, which made me feel
a little uneasy, at times; for *it ever seemed to be upon me,
like that of a captured hawk, confined by a string,* so that it
can not move its body, but which moves its eyes at every
gesture you make. I should think it would have been a
very difficult matter for such a man as Stevens to have been
surprised by the most stealthy foe, while, on the other hand,
he would have been a very dangerous enemy; and I thank
God that he did not think proper to consider me one upon
that occasion!

"Indeed, so far from treating me in any way uncivilly, his
conduct toward me was so kind and considerate, being then,
as now, an invalid, that I felt even grateful to him for his
attentions. But there was one thing which struck me at
the time as singular; and that was, that, although Stevens
dressed so well, and even wore a fine gold watch and chain,
I had never heard of his doing anything for a living in the

way of work. But I dismissed the subject from my mind, concluding that my companion must be a pretty shifty fellow.

"Sometime after daylight my gig arrived, and, as Stevens seemed anxious to get up the country, I offered him a seat, which he gladly accepted. It was an old-fashioned vehicle, which would look very singular in these days of fine buggies and carriages; but it rode very comfortably, only a little too springy, and Stevens and I went on very pleasantly chatting together.

"When we reached my house, Stevens left his saddle-bags in my care, saying that he would not be able to call for them for several days. I put them away very carefully in a closet, and, locking the door, put the key in my pocket; for I knew, by their weight, that there was considerable money in them. When Stevens called for the saddle-bags again, he was riding a very good horse, and seemed to be anxious to get away. Of course, I thought nothing of his hurry then, and would never have thought of it afterward, if I had not since heard that he was a murderer and a highway robber. In all probability he had then just committed some recent act of felony—perhaps murdered the owner of that horse, and wished to get away as fast as possible."

The author, who has a better opportunity of gathering incidents connected with this story than either the reader or his informer, will now continue his narrative in his own style, and tell *why* Stevens called for his saddle-bags so soon.

When Stevens reached his home, from which he had been absent for several months, he found his wife very ill—in a dying condition. When I say his *wife*, I do not mean to speak with *historical* accuracy; for I have not been able to ascertain whether she was his wife, concubine, or mistress. The poor woman had sent for Mrs. Shelton "to come and see her die, *for she had a great secret on her mind*, which she wished to impart to her, and *her* alone." But before Mrs. Shelton arrived, Stevens had reached home. He was, therefore, ahead of her, and it would be a difficult matter, under the circumstances, for the poor woman to relieve herself of the dreadful secret which lay so heavily upon her heart, without the knowledge or consent of her husband; especially, too, when he was so very watchful in his habits and stealthy in his movements.

A short time after the mysterious disappearance of Langdon Shelton at the Jasper Spring, Stevens, who had been absent for more than a week from home, returned to his wife flushed with money, and wearing a fine gold watch and chain. Mrs. Stevens asked him how he had got so much money, and he satisfied her very easily by telling her that he had been playing "seven up," or "old sledge," with a parcel of fellows in the city of Savannah, and had been very lucky. But when, a few days afterward, Mrs. Stevens had noticed some blood-stains upon his coat—the coat was a blue one and the stains had become almost black, except where she had scraped them with a knife—astonished at this discovery, Mrs. Stevens asked her husband, very innocently, how his coat got blooded, and, after a little hesitation and some embarrassment, which she observed at the time, his reply was, that " he had had a fight with a fellow who accused him of cheating, and he supposed that he had washed away all signs of blood."

This answer, although given in a hesitating way, very naturally satisfied Mrs. Stevens, who, as yet, had no suspicion that her husband had been guilty of the crime of murder and highway robbery. But when the country became full of the mysterious murder of Colonel Shelton's son Langdon, she felt some uneasiness lest her husband may have been guilty of some foul play; and her suspicions were strengthened by discovering certain initials upon the gold watch which Stevens had left hung up over the mantel-piece, while he went into the horse-lot just before breakfast. During his absence the woman had taken down the watch, and while she was admiring it as a very pretty piece of workmanship, her eye fell upon the initials "L. S." cut on the inner case with a pen-knife, in very small letters. " L. S." thought the woman—" L. S.—That means Langdon Shelton! Great God! It is then only too true, as I have feared, that my husband has killed him! and *that's* why he is so flush with money !"

When Stevens came into the house, he found his wife still looking at the watch. He took his seat in a leather-bottomed chair by her side, and observed, with forced gayety :

" That is a damned fine watch, Mary."

" Yes," was the reply of Mrs. Stevens, who now looked him steadily in the eye, and, with a sad countenance, said : " But, Stevens, my dear, do n't you think you had better destroy this watch, or change your name to Langdon— Langdon Stevens?"

He started as though an adder had stung him, and trembled at the mention of that name. But, recovering his habitual composure, after a few moments, he said, in as careless a tone as he could well assume :

" Why, Mary?"

" Because I see two letters scratched upon this watch-case; they are L. S., which would make Langdon "—— she paused, and saw him wince and become fidgety, then she added, " *Stevens.*"

He took the watch from her hand in a flurried, *brusque* way, and, drawing out his pocket-knife, scratched out the initials of Langdon Shelton ; then he put away the watch in his watch-fob, and said, in a low, determined voice: .

" If you tell any one what you have seen, by God, I will shoot you dead—anywhere—in the biggest crowd—if I swing for it !"

The woman trembled violently, for she knew that her husband would do what he threatened ; and henceforth fear would make her hold her tongue still. But when she felt that her end was approaching fast, her conscience smote her for retaining so long a terrible secret, lest, by doing so any longer, God would hold her as *particeps criminis*, or, at least, as an accessory after the commission of the murderous deed. It was, therefore, with the intention of imparting to Mrs. Shelton all the knowledge she was in possession of concerning her husband's guilt, which she had no doubt would, in a great measure, relieve the mother's anxiety in regard to the uncertain fate of her son, although she well knew that it would rather aggravate than relieve her sorrow.

Mrs. Stevens had sent a messenger in haste to Mrs. Shelton, requesting her to come without delay, as she felt that her end was rapidly approaching, and she wished to tell to herself alone an important secret, which concerned her deeply. But when she arrived and entered into the sick chamber, the dying woman said, in a feeble voice:

"O! why did n't you come sooner? You have come too late! too late!" For she saw her husband's eye upon her, as he stood in the doorway, not far from the bedside.

"I came as soon as I could—just as soon as I received your message," was the reply of Mrs. Shelton. "Why is it too late? What is it that you wish to tell me?"

"Nothing! O, nothing, now!" said Mrs. Stevens, flinging up her hands despairingly; for she felt that her husband's hawk-like eye was upon her, turn her head whichsoever way she might, and she feared lest he would fulfill his threat and shoot her dead as she lay helpless upon her death-bed, "anywhere—everywhere," as he had threatened.

Stevens never left that room again until his wife died. No person could induce him to lie down to snatch even a moment's repose. For two whole days and nights he watched in that sick chamber, watching every movement, however slight, of Mrs. Shelton and his wife, lest the latter might avail herself of only a few moment's absence to impart the fatal secret to the mother of his victim. Only once, and for a single moment, he nodded in his chair, and seemed to drop into a gentle slumber, for once or twice he began to snore. Mrs. Stevens then made a sign with her thin, wan hand, to

Mrs. Shelton to approach the bedside. That benevolent lady rose from her seat very cautiously, and leaned over the dying woman, whose end was approaching now very rapidly. Mrs. Stevens opened her lips, and was in the very act of speaking, when she saw her husband, who was in his stockings, and trod so lightly upon the floor—so lightly that Mrs. Shelton could not hear him—she saw him standing just behind Mrs. Shelton, with a pistol in his hand, leveled at herself over the shoulder of her visitor! When she looked into the muzzle of that murderous weapon, and fancied that she could see the leaden ball coming slowly out, to bury itself in her brain, she threw up her hands imploringly and shrieked aloud; for the love of life is strong even in death, and it is said that the felon condemned to death counts the hours as days, and the moments as hours which he has to live, and for not even the last moment would he take untold wealth.

When Mrs. Stevens shrieked out that way, and threw her hands up in agony, Mrs. Shelton started back in alarm and struck against the body of Stevens, who stood behind her; but before she could turn round he had put back the pistol into his breast, and remarked, in a voice which she thought agitated :

"Please step to the water-pail, madam, and get her some water, or she will faint!"

Mrs. Shelton did as she was directed, and returned quickly with the water ; but in her absence she heard Stevens say, in low tones, not meant for the ears of another :

"If you say one word to her, I will shoot you before you die! By G—d I will, if"——

The poor woman's face became slightly spasmed, and before Mrs. Shelton could give her the water, she was in strong convulsions. But they lasted for a little while only, and when they were over, she sunk into the sleep from which there is no awakening. She was dead! And Mrs. Shelton went away sorrowful, and never learned the secret

which would only have caused her heart to bleed afresh.
Thus a merciful God, in pity for her great distresses, with-
held from her the secret, kept her from knowing that the
man who seemed so kind to his wife, so watchful and so
attentive to her wants in her dying hour, was a cold-blooded
murderer, who had slain her son, and would not hesitate,
for gold, to take her life also.   But when she heard those
cruel, cruel words, although she knew not their meaning,
yet she felt, from that moment, an invincible repugnance to
the cold-hearted hypocrite who could *seem* to be kind,
when he was at heart a deceitful wretch.

CHAPTER VII.

THE death of Mrs: Stevens occurred about two months after the insanity of Ella Shelton. Mrs. Shelton had adopted Fetie as her daughter, by the consent of her parents, and the blind girl now called her "mother," and whenever she spoke of Ella, which was but seldom, although she was constantly in her thoughts, she called her "her poor dear sister Ella." Thus was Fetie the only companion and solace of the poor widow in her afflictive bereavements.

And what shall we say of Herbert, the disappointed lover, whose heart seemed crushed by his load of sorrow; disappointed only by an affliction sent from heaven! Could such a man linger where he had been accustomed to linger, or go through the routine of business with the same steady hand and unclouded intellect? His love had been too great for that, and now his grief was commensurate with his love. He wandered, therefore, over European lands, and sought to drown his sorrow in the loud roar of human voices in the densely-populated kingdoms of the East. But wherever he went, the maddening thought was with him, that he was a deeply afflicted man, and without hope in the world. And as he walked through the crowded streets of densely-crowded cities, even among so many strangers, he was remarked as a man who was overburdened by a secret sorrow too great for utterance. Although still so young, he seemed to others, and felt himself, as did Dean Swift when he returned to Ireland, disgraced and in disfavor with the English ministry, proscribed by his own folly—that "his tree was withered at the top," and he longed that the trunk should die also. " O, that I could lie down in the friendly grave, and be at rest," he often cried aloud; and were it not that he had been early taught by pious parents, he would have committed suicide, perhaps, to rid himself of his misery. But he knew and acknowledged to himself, that, notwithstanding the teachings of Seneca, the teacher of Nazareth was a greater and a better guide.

But there were times when the thought of his betrothed's insanity had such an effect upon him, that he felt like going mad himself. Restless and uneasy, he wandered everywhere without any definite object. He climbed the scarred and blistered sides of old Vesuvius, and looked down into its crater, and, as he felt the hot steam upon his face, he felt like leaping down into the throat of the old grumbling volcano, to make it cease its grumblings; and then he turned away and went down in haste, fearful lest he might be tempted, in a moment of frenzy, to do the sinful deed.

Then he went to Venice, and stood upon " the Bridge of Sighs," and wished that, as in the olden time, he were a Doge, or a patriot prince, whose only crime was that he loved his country too well, and was about to be sacrificed by a jealous and revengeful senate. And he stood upon the lofty hights of the snow-capped Alps, and the frost and the snow cooled not his fevered brow. And he stood upon a rock leaning over an awful precipice, like Manfred, looking down into the black abyss from the dizzy hight; and he wished that some friendly hand could push him from the rock, or that the rock itself would crumble and fall, and hurl him headlong into the dark chasm below! But there was no cruel hand to push him from the rock, and the rock itself stood firm as it had stood for untold ages. Then looking, with a curl of scorn upon his lips, toward the East, toward the imperial city, and back to the ages that had passed, he said, with bitterness :

"Thou hast lied, O, Seneca! when thou saidst that when a misanthrope, when a man is weary of his life, 'he may find deliverance dangling from every limb which he sees,' and that 'even at the bottom of every well there lies deliverance there!' No! no! not even with our own consent, unless God withdraws his almighty hand—his restraining hand!"

And he turned away with a sigh and with a shudder from the precipice among the Alps; shuddering at himself that he had been so sinful as to be tempted so often with the desire for self-destruction. But he had committed no crime to madden him with the tortures of the "worm that never dies;" and great as was his grief, it was not great enough to so distract his mind as to make him rush with bloody hands, and a mangled, self-immolated body, into the presence of his maker—God! Europe, with its myriad rushing throngs of unsympathizing strangers, was not the place for such as Herbert, nor the desert plain, nor the lonely rock. The cross, and the cross only, was the place where he could find comfort and obtain relief! And to the cross of Christ he was ultimately led, and found relief and comfort there. For never yet did "the weary and heavy laden," under any and all circumstances, amidst trials and temptations, doubts or fears, fail to find relief and hope when bowed humbly at the cross of Christ!

It was on his passage home across the wide Atlantic, when lying in his berth and looking upward, that he found faith in Jesus and hope in the future. He could not see, with his natural eyes, through the thick oak planks of the deck; he could not see the sky, nor the stars shining overhead, but he knew that the sky was there, and that the stars were twinkling all the same, and that they were now, as ever, looking down upon the ship. So he knew, also, that God ruled in heaven, and that the Savior of sinners was

16

sitting still—now, as always, and forever—upon the throne of mercy, or by his Father's side, interceding for lost and ruined man!

It was dark in his berth, but he began to feel that there was a little light, faint at first, like the light of the glow-worm lighting up the darkness, and the light would grow bigger and brighter by and by. So he went out upon the deck, and he was astonished to see how bright the stars seemed to shine, far brighter than he had ever seen them shine before; and how merrily the waves seemed to chase each other in the starlight, much more merrily than he had ever seen them chase each other before. And his heart seemed to be catching the contagion of gladness, and he could have shouted to the waves, and laughed joyously with the twinkling stars.

Then, somehow or other, as he neared the port of Philadelphia, as he sailed up Delaware Bay, and passed by "Breakwater," and then up the river, on and on toward the city, his heart grew calm with faith, and hope, and love.

As soon as Herbert had secured his lodgings at one of the most fashionable hotels in the city, he ordered a carriage and drove round to the Asylum for the Insane. On sending in his card, the kind superintendent himself came out, and shook him warmly by the hand, as an old friend, saying, "I am very glad, indeed, you have come, Mr. Herbert; Miss Shelton has frequently spoken of you—at first with an expression of horror, and sometimes with a scream of terror, but now only with a smile or a tear."

"And how is she, my dear sir?" asked Herbert, with an expression of mournful anxiety.

"A great deal better, sir, thank God! Indeed, I may say she is well!—cured! I have already written to her mother that her daughter may, with perfect propriety, be taken home."

Herbert gasped for breath, and seemed so much overcome by his joy, at the announcement of Ella's recovery, that,

for a little while, he was compelled to steady himself, by
placing his hand upon the shoulder of the superintendent,
who passed his arm kindly around his waist, and led him
thus into the building.   By the time Herbert had reached
the ladies' private parlor, he was perfectly calm, while his
heart was even thanking God for his goodness and loving-
kindness.   He had, indeed, "tempered the wind to the shorn
lamb," and, in the midst of afflictions and seeming great
wrath, he had not forgotten to be merciful.

Miss Shelton soon appeared, at the request of the superintendent.   When she entered the room, her steps were
eager, and she had both hands extended to grasp that of her
lover.   But Herbert did not take her by the hand; for, notwithstanding the presence of the superintendent, he folded
her to his breast, as a husband would his wife after a long
and painful separation, or a return from a weary voyage.

"God bless you, dearest Ella!" said he, as she sobbed
upon his breast.   "My lost treasure is found again."

"Yes, Herbert! saved! saved!" she replied, as he led
her to a sofa.   "And O! how rejoiced and how grateful I
am to see you so well and in such health, and to know that
it was all a horrible dream which I had so long concerning
you."

Then she told him the dream, or vision, which had tormented her for several painful months; and when it had
appeared in strongest colors, it then so overcame her that
she could do nothing but shriek, and scream, and flee from
the horrible apparition.   And the dream!—the idea which
had possessed her mind, for a long while after the first
humiliating one had fled, was, that in one corner of her
room she saw her father's skeleton; while, in the other,
she beheld the form of her lover, standing erect, but with
his throat gashed from ear to ear!—a horrid wound made
by a razor! but the lips of the wound were united together
by thin strips of adhesive plaster! and whenever the wind
blew, or the slightest breath of air stirred, she had fancied

that she could hear the bones of her venerable father rattling and crashing against each other! But if the wind blew fresh and strong, or if a storm raged without, that the windows rattled in their casements, then the long, bony arms of her father whirled and flirted from side to side, striking against his ribs, and producing the most painful noise imaginable, like the noise of a dead drummer, playing, with his skeleton hand, upon his spirit-drum, and beating away, with the frenzied energy of a deathless maniac-spirit, his never-ceasing, ever-resounding *reveille*—reminding her of that poor drummer who was hurled down a precipice among the Alps, at "the passage of the Splugen," by an avalanche, which had swept off thirty of Macdonald's brave troopers, and their horses along with it, in its wild plunge into the gulf below. But the drummer fell, unhurt, to the bottom of the gulf, and, crawling out from the snow which had broken his fall, began to beat his drum for relief. "Deep down, amid the crushed forms of avalanches, the poor fellow stood, and, for a whole hour, beat the rapid strains which had so often summoned his companions to arms. The muffled sound came ringing up the face of the precipice, the most touching appeal that could be made to a soldier's heart. But no hand could reach him there; and the rapid blows grew fainter and fainter, till they ceased altogether, and the poor drummer lay down to die. He had beaten his last *reveille*, and his companions passed mournfully on, leaving the Alpine storm to sing his dirge."*

So, too, poor Ella Shelton had been tormented with the idea that she not only saw the skeleton of her father standing erect in the corner of her chamber, but that his own spirit, without shape, as the wind, had been beating, with her father's skeleton hand, its own dirge upon his bony carcass. And then she used to shriek aloud, and tremble, and never recover from her agitation until the wind died

---

* See Headley's *Napoleon and his Marshals*, vol. i.

away, or she had become exhausted by the intensity of her mental tortures; and then she thought that the spirit had become weary or had lain down, like the poor, wearied, frozen drummer who had beat his last *reveille* on earth at the bottom of the steep precipice at the "*via mala.*"

But the other idea which had tormented her at the same time, and added to the horrors of her existence, was even more distressing, because seemingly more real, and, to her mind, was as painful as a reality. Whenever she turned her eyes away, that she might no longer look upon the skeleton form of Colonel Shelton, nor see his long, bony arms writhing, and twisting, and striking against his bare ribs—when she looked toward the opposite corner, O! how her heart must have ached with anguish, to see the form of her lover there, standing in the corner, with his gashed throat, and the lips of that frightful wound held together only by thin strips of adhesive plaster. But that which tormented her most was the painful idea that whenever any one entered the room, her lover, with his usual politeness, would invariably bow his head to the visitor; and that, in the act of bowing the head, the strips of adhesive plaster would give way, and the wound be ripped open, and the blood would gush out in broad, red streams upon the floor. Then it was that she closed her eyes and covered up her face with both her hands, and shrieked aloud, "My poor Herbert!" and sometimes fainted away at the awful spectacle which she fancied she had seen in reality. And sometimes the physician of the asylum had to be called in to administer relief; and several times she came near dying, and was confined, for a long while, upon a sick bed.*

"But, thank God, the horrible dream is now over!" she added, after finishing the painful recital.

---

* This is a faithful description, almost verbatim, of the two tormenting ideas of an elegant Southern lady, who returned from the asylum cured, and, a little while after her return home, told her feelings when insane, to the author. It is, therefore, no fancy sketch.

"Yes, thank God!" added Herbert, fervently; "and my dream also—a horrible dream!—is over now, thank God; for I, too, have been mad, and others knew it not. But the Savior of sinners—the same blessed Jesus of Nazareth who cured the lunatic who was a giant in his madness, and whom no chains could bind and no bars restrain, but who, with a word, released his enthralled spirit, and then bade him "Go and tell his friends what great things the Lord had done for him, and had compassion on him"—that same Jesus has released my spirit also from the bondage of sin, and has blessed me, and made me happy as never man seemed blessed. And now, after relieving me of a great and intolerable burden, he has given me a great and inestimable treasure—restored a casket—a priceless jewel which, I feared, was lost forever."

Then, somehow or other, Herbert found himself slipping down from the sofa, until he got upon his knees, and Ella Shelton slipped down upon her knees also, in front of him; and his arms were around her neck, and her hands were laid upon his shoulders. Then the kind old superintendent, like a benevolent old father approaching his kneeling children, left the large arm-chair in which he was seated, and knelt down by their side, and encircled them both with his fatherly arms; and, with his venerable head, bald and gray, turned upward, and the deep furrows of his old wrinkled cheeks all filled up, brimfull and running over from the deluge of tears which poured from his benignant eyes—with his arms thus around them both, and his heart full of gratitude to a beneficent God, he poured out his thanks to heaven for the restoration and recovery of those two loving souls, even as a kind father would return thanks to Almighty God when his children have been raised up, almost by a miracle, from a sick bed, which seemed, at one time, a bed of death. And Ella Shelton's head then rested with joy upon the shoulder of her lover, because he was not only sane, but converted to God; and the head of Herbert drooped also, because his

great heart was full, and it rested lightly, tenderly, raptur-
ously upon the Madonna-like head of Ella. O! it was a
delightful spectacle—a picture worth the skill of the most
consummate master.

When they rose from their knees, there was a degree of
peace—a calm and a peace "which the world knows not"—
in the breast of each ; and Herbert felt happy, and Ella felt
happy, and the superintendent seemed as happy as any kind
father could be, whose prodigal son had returned home sane
and sound, that he kills for him the fatted calf.

"A vessel sails to-morrow, my love. Let us return home
and tell our friends—your mother and mine."

The superintendent signified his hearty approbation of the
proposed arrangement, and, the next day, Ella Shelton bade
adieu to the kind man who had treated her as a father
rather than as a jailor ; and, when she left the Asylum, she
expressed even regrets at being compelled to leave him, and
declared that, should she ever visit the North, it would
afford her infinite satisfaction to see him again, and assur-
ing him, at the same time, that should circumstances ever
call him to the sunny South, it would be her pride and
pleasure not only to offer him all the hospitalities of her
Southern home, but to wait upon him herself, as an affectionate daughter would upon an invalid father.

The next day, Ella Shelton, accompanied by her lover,
as her friend and rightful protector, sailed for Charleston,
in the fast-sailing barque Estelle. The voyage was a delightful one ; and no storms, but a few calms, occurred
during the first week of November. So they arrived in
safety at Charleston, and immediately went up to the elegant
residence of Mrs. Herbert, the mother of Edgar. And Mrs.
Herbert welcomed Ella as her own daughter, and looked
upon her with pride and pleasure ; and a delightful little
party assembled that evening, to welcome the return of
Herbert and his affianced bride.

Two days afterward, they started together—Herbert and

Ella—in Mrs. Herbert's coach, for the up-country, for the home of Mrs. Shelton, who was anxiously expecting the arrival of her daughter, with joy in her heart, but with anxiety and sorrow also, for she was in much distress, and needed comfort and consolation. Let us hasten on, in advance of their coming, and see what was the cause of the poor widow's distress; for, O! has she not been afflicted enough already? and shall the waves of sorrow never cease to roll over her soul? and shall her eyes never turn away from beholding trouble and sorrow?

CHAPTER VIII.

S we said, at the commencement of the last chapter, Mrs. Shelton had adopted Fetie as her own child, to supply, in only a partial and incomplete degree, the loss of her children, the last of whom seemed to be as hopelessly lost as the first, and for whose death she sometimes even prayed most fervently. But, as if to rebuke that spirit—which was none other than the spirit of murmuring and complaint, a want of faith and humble submission to the will of heaven; for, so deceitful and desperately wicked is the human heart, that it often murmurs and complains, even in prayer, and when we think we are humblest and lowliest in spirit;—as if God would rebuke that spirit of non-submission to his will, little Fetie, upon whom Mrs. Shelton's heart was now set with unwavering attachment, became suddenly ill with the fever. She had never been sick but once before, and that was in the second year of her infancy, when her brain became so much congested and inflamed that her life was despaired of by her physician as well as her friends. When she recovered from that illness she was stone-blind, from a complete paralysis of the optic nerve, which, though not a common occurrence, is by no means an isolated case of total blindness ensuing from congestion of the brain near the optic thalamia, which gives origin to the optic nerves. It is entirely through the sensibility of these nerves that vision is regulated in the sound and healthy eye; for the retina is nothing more than an

16*

expansion of the optic nerve itself. When light acts upon the retina, in its passage through the cornea, it acts as a powerful stimulus, which causes the iris to contract, thus forming what is called the pupil; and when the light is withdrawn, or it becomes dark, the iris, or pupil, expands, and remains open wide, because it is no longer stimulated by light. Cut the optic nerves in two just then, or paralyze them in any way possible, and the pupil would never contract any more; it would remain open forever, as in the case of poor Fetic. Perhaps, had strychnine been employed, in minute doses, or the galvanic battery, or some other powerful agent, the optic nerves, in the case of our blind girl, might have been restored to healthy action, and the pupil would again have expanded and contracted as before. But none of those agents had been tried, and, perhaps, if they had been, might have proved inefficient remedies to overcome a blindness which death alone could remove.

For fifteen years Fetic had been blind; for fifteen years she had enjoyed uninterrupted health. But she was sick now, and destined never to rise again from her bed. For ten days her fever had been almost unintermitting; and, in her delirium, she said many wild and strange things. Mrs. Shelton had become uneasy about her from the very first symptoms of her fever, and had dispatched George for the physician, and Young Toney for Fetic's parents. As a faithful nurse, as an own mother, Mrs. Shelton had watched over the dying girl, moistening her lips and bathing her face with cool water, and brushing away the flies with a little green bough from a bay-tree. And the tears would silently trickle down her cheeks, and her chest would heave with a sigh, as she thought of her poor insane daughter in the asylum at Philadelphia, and of her adopted child lying before her, like a rose withering away in its pristine beauty, and before half its sweets had gone.

Ten days had Fetic been sick and wild with delirium. She was taken on the very day that Ella Shelton left the

Asylum and went on board the vessel bound for Charleston; and it was on the tenth day of her illness that Mrs. Shelton received the letter of the superintendent conveying the joyful intelligence that her daughter was so near well that it was advisable that she should be taken immediately home. The overjoyed mother, when she read the letter to herself, was so deeply affected by her feelings, that she was compelled to go to her room and fall down upon her knees, with the letter spread out before her, reading it thus in fervent, humble gratitude, and thanking God, who, even in wrath, had remembered mercy; for while there were unmistakable signs that he was about to take away her adopted child, he had, in his great goodness, determined to replace her loss by the restoration of her dear Ella, whom she had long given up as lost to her forever.

"O! God! I thank thee! Thou alone canst know how much! True, O, very true is it, that 'Thou wilt not always chide, neither wilt thou keep thine anger forever!'"

She rose from her knees and returned to her post by the bedside of the patient, if not with a smile upon her lips, at least with a look of mournful resignation to the will of heaven; for if she was about to be greatly afflicted, she was soon to be greatly blessed also. And is it not even so, although we know it not, nor can we see, at the time, the hand of Providence thrust through the dark clouds of affection which conceal his face from our view? The heart of the Christian would wither and die, if, amid countless blessings, there were no afflictions to humble, and chasten, and purify, and render thankful the heart of the one who knows nothing but the joys and pleasures of prosperity, and never experiences the mournful pleasures of affliction! Mrs. Shelton was thinking thus as she resumed her seat by the side of Fetic, who had been asleep, or rather in a slumber, and now opened her eyes, which could not see, and reaching forth her hand to her adopted mother, said:

"Mother! dearest mother! I am going away, but I will

not leave you desolate, for sister Ella is coming! I have seen her, mother! She is even now on her way home!"

Mrs. Shelton was very much surprised at the strange coincidence, but she thought that it was only another of Fetie's delirious fancies; and she asked, in her mild voice:

"Why do you think so, my child?"

"Because I have seen her, mother! She is well now, and she is coming home! O! that God would hasten her coming, that I might grasp her hand and feel her warm embrace once more before I shall go to sleep in the arms of Jesus! Mother, I regret very much to leave you, who have been so kind to the poor blind girl; but my place will be better filled, mother! filled by your own natural daughter; for God only loaned me to you, mother, until sister Ella got well; and now I want to go, mother! I want to go to Jesus, who is calling me every hour, and telling me, in a still, small voice, 'Come to me, Fetie! come, poor blind girl, where there is light!' O! mother! in heaven the blind girl shall see, and be blind no longer! Yes, shall see beautiful flowers and ambrosial fruit, and a sea of glass, and rivers of life, and tall trees with broad branches and ever-green boughs, beneath whose cool shade angels, bright angels, are ever walking and talking with the glorious Savior, in the spirit-land! O, won't it be delightful, mother? And, after a while, I shall see you there, mother, and my sister Ella also, and my own dear mother and my father, I hope; and my little brother and sisters, and old daddy Toney! and every body I hope, walking in green pastures and beneath shady groves, and sitting down by the side of cool waters, and drinking, drinking, ever drinking at the cool fountain which shall never go dry!"

And she talked herself to sleep; and Mrs. Shelton listened and wondered. When Fetie opened her eyes again, she said, joyously:

"They are coming, mother! I have seen them! They

are coming in a carriage; and the carriage is coming nearer and yet nearer! I see them now!"

"Whom do you see, my child?" said Mrs. Shelton, leaning over the blind girl.

"Sister Ella and Mr. Herbert," was the reply of Fetie. "They are coming, mother, in a carriage, and the horses look as though they were fleet horses, and they move fast over the level road!"

In a little while Fetie dropped into an uneasy slumber, as before, muttering words which no one could hear. And Mrs. Shelton wondered if it were indeed true that a clairvoyant spirit is possessed by some persons, to enable them to look into the future, or to see objects far beyond the range of human vision; and wondering, also, if the blind or the dying may not be thus endowed with supernatural power in a far greater degree than other mortals; or, if at last it were not the result of a disordered imagination in unison with unaccountable coincidences.

But before she could end her conjectures, or attempt to analyze and compare the various theories or wild vagaries which have been written upon the subject of somnambulism and clairvoyance, she was startled by the sound of carriage-wheels rolling up the avenue leading from the public road; and Fetie, starting again from her slumbers, exclaimed joyously:

"They are coming, mother; they are nearly here now! O, how happy I shall be to see my dear sister Ella before I die! God has, indeed, heard my prayer!"

And Mrs. Shelton, answering her not a word, dropped the green bay-bush from her hand, and ran out of the sick chamber with tottering footsteps, her whole frame trembling, and her knees almost giving way as she ran toward the carriage which had already stopped at the little garden gate. Then the mother and the daughter were locked in each others' arms, weeping and laughing with joy; and the arms of Herbert were thrown around them both, to sustain them in their weakness, lest they should both fall to the ground, but his man's heart, strong, as he might think it, and steel it against emotion as he would, gave way also, and his head drooped over them, and then shook and trembled as his broad chest heaved as the sea when it is joyous only; and as his eyes witnessed the great and inexpressible joy of that daughter and that mother in whom he was so deeply interested, his cheeks were wet with tears, which fell like . rain-drops upon their heads, and baptized them both with his love.

It was a long time before the grateful and overjoyed mother could recover her strength sufficiently to raise her head from her daughter's shoulder, and when she did so, she said, with her eyes upturned to heaven:

"O, Ella! very true is it, as that wonderful bard hath said, 'God tempers the wind to the shorn lamb;' for, in the midst of death there is life."

"Is any one ill, mother?" asked Ella, anxiously.

"Yes, my child; you must prepare your mind, so lately restored, to bear the sad affliction which, I greatly fear, will soon come upon us. Poor Fetie is very ill, my daughter. She has talked a great deal about you; and, but a little while ago, she declared that you were coming, in a carriage, and that Herbert was with you. Is it not strange? Truly the blind can see more clearly sometimes than those whose sight has never been impaired."

They delayed no longer in the garden, and Ella went with her mother and Herbert, into the house; and as she walked up to the bedside, Fetie fairly screamed with delight, and sat up straight in the bed, and leaned over the bedside, and seemed as if she would have leaped into the arms of her dear friend and adopted sister. She would have fallen from the bed to the floor if Ella had not stepped forward so quickly, and caught her in her arms. Then Fetie, with her arms around the neck of Ella Shelton, fell back upon her pillow, and held her adopted sister clasped to her bosom, while Ella, who had previously pulled off her bonnet, rested her cheek upon the fevered, burning cheek of the dying girl, and shed tears of joy, and of sorrow also. And the tears of Ella Shelton, as they trickled down upon the face of the patient, seemed to cool, like rain, her fever, and she sunk into a gentle slumber, with her arms still about the neck of her dear sister Ella. But, by-and-by, her arms relaxed their hold, and she sunk down more deeply into her pillow in slumber ; and Ella rose up very slowly and cautiously, as a mother who has patted and sung her infant to sleep, and fears to move too rashly, lest it shall be waked by her movements. Thus noiselessly did Ella rise up from that embrace, and sat down in the same arm-chair in which Mrs. Shelton had been seated, for ten days, with the bay-bush in her hand, brushing away the flies as they alighted upon the face of the blind girl, who lay in unrest upon her fevered couch.

Once again Fetie opened her eyes, after sleeping for a half hour or more, but her eyes seemed different, and her countenance wore an expression it had never worn before ; for her countenance seemed radiant with glory, and her eyes shone and sparkled with intelligence, and there was a look of rapturous sight in them. And she held out her hands toward Ella, and exclaimed, joyously, "Am I indeed in heaven? and do I see a beautiful angel—but an angel without wings?"

"No, Fetie," said Ella, with a sweet smile—her old smile of love, "you are not in heaven, and it is only me whom you see."

"O! how beautiful you are ! Could an angel with wings be more beautiful? Sister Ella, I am dying ; and I thought that the poor blind girl would never see until she reached heaven, and saw her Jesus first. But, in his great love, he has permitted me to see you first, and to look, for a little while—just a little while—upon the beauties of earth, lest the glories of heaven should bewilder and dazzle me so that the heaven-born sight would leave me wrapped in eternal mist and darkness. O! sister Ella! I can see! Look! I can see! The blind begins to see before she gets near enough to look upon 'the city of our God,' and to see 'the lamb slain for sinners' seated upon his great white throne!"

Ella Shelton leaned over the dying girl, and looked down into her eyes. The pupils were no longer stretched wide, as they always had been before, and the optic nerve was no more paralyzed. Other patients die differently, with the eyelids parting wider and wider, and the pupils becoming more and more expanded, until the eyes are fixed, and glaring, and glazed. But, in the case of *our* blind girl, the very reverse of this was true; for her eyelids drooped lower and lower, and her pupils became more and more contracted, · by the contracting power of sub-acute inflammation of the brain; just as when a ray of light, of increasing intensity, is slowly and steadily let into the chambers of the eye. And when death was just at hands, the lids became closed, as in sleep, and the pupils became contracted and drawn up tightly, as a bag whose open mouth has been closed by drawing slowly, steadily, upon the string.

When Ella had looked, for several moments, into Fetie's eyes, she exclaimed, joyously—for she thought the restoration—the temporary restoration—of sight, was a favorable symptom—"O mother!" said she; "come here, mother!"

Mrs. Shelton leaned over the bed from the other side; and when she looked into Fetie's eyes, she knew that her darling, adopted child was blind no longer; but she knew, also, that it could be no favorable symptom, for great drops of cold and clammy sweat stood upon her marble brow, like cold dew upon a white rosebud. And her fever was gone, and there was no longer a trace of delirium, but her face was lighted up with intelligence and with love.

Slowly the pupils contracted, tighter and tighter, until the pupil seemed as though it had never been; and the light which had been let into the chambers of those eyes, for a little while, was shut in, never to be let out again from those windows of the soul. It was the only light which had ever entered, or had ever been retained, by those sightless eye-balls, for fifteen years of total blindness. And her soul, as if jealous of that light, and as if needing all its rays to light it on its way from earth to heaven, pulled down the curtain to hide, from the eyes of another, the lantern which God, with unseen hand, had thrust in at the window. Si-lently and noiselessly the spirit of the blind girl, blind now no more, took its flight from that chamber of death. Her pupils opened never more to let in or out any more light; and her eyelids remained closed, that her friends did not have to press them down with their fingers, nor place pieces of money upon them, to prevent her eye-balls from glaring, as a corpse, upon her friends.

And they buried Fetie by the side of Colonel Shelton; and Ella planted roses around her grave, and watered them with her tears, and then went away with her mother to Charles-ton, the bride of Mr. Herbert, who soothed her with kindest caresses, and bade her affectionately and tenderly "not to mourn as those who have no hope."

And Mr. Herbert sold the farm for much more than Colonel Shelton gave; and neither Mrs. Shelton nor Mrs. Herbert desired again to look upon a spot where they had experienced so much sorrow and suffering. And Old Toney and his family were carried to Charleston, where they were as faithful to their young, as they had been to their old, master, although their old affection and reverence for the memory of the brave old hero could never be extinguished, save in death. And although their employments were all different, and varied in their character, and although they were now as happy as mortals could well be, in the queen city of the South—seeing, every day, their "dear, good Masser Herbert," and beholding their old and their young mistress in the elegant home to which Herbert had con-

ducted them—a home of elegance, in which these faithful
servants felt even more pride than did the actual owners;
and notwithstanding their happy lots, and the new comforts
with which they were surrounded, and the fish, and the
oysters, and the many positive luxuries which they enjoyed,
and the new dignity to which they had been elevated, from
"country to city niggers"—still they would sometimes cast
their eyes, with longing, lingering gaze, toward the "up-
country;" and, as the cow lowing for its old range, they
would sigh for the dear, old homestead where Colonel Shelton used to live in the days of his wealth and glory, and
wish that they could live over those happy days again; for,
"as the deer pants after the rivers, and the hart after the
water-brooks," so the negro longs to look upon the scenes
to which he has been accustomed—*unless he has been de-
naturalized*—although the spot of his nativity has become
a desert or a barren wilderness, and although the palace,
upon whose outward show they gazed with pride, may have
tottered from its foundations and fallen in ruins, and the
cabin in which they dwelt themselves has become a miserable hovel, or tumbled into decay.

CHAPTER IX.

BUT the reader, perhaps, would like to know something of the after history of those who have figured so largely, or acted such important parts, in this drama; and to gratify their very natural curiosity, we will tell them all that we know in these two last chapters—reserving the last for Old Toncy and others in whose welfare we feel most interested.

And first, then, in reference to Alfred Orton and his children : When Margaret, the Irish girl, had waited full three weeks for the return of her mistress, and knew that she would return never more, and not until she had heard that her mistress was dead, did she consent to give up the children of Mrs. Orton, and turn them over to their rightful guardians, their grandparents in Salem. But little Johnny, who was a bastard, had no grandfather or grandmother, since, in law, he was not recognized as the son of Alfred Orton—little Johnny, who had no one to look to for protection and support, was turned over to that most humane of all human institutions, the Orphan Asylum in Boston.

And his poor mother, that once fair and virtuous girl, but now abandoned woman, perished in the hospital, dying that lingering and horrid death which all women of her lost and abandoned character die, unless they have been destroyed by the hand of violence.

And Alfred Orton—what became of him, and whither did he flee? Ah, yes! whither! whither could he flee?

Not to Boston, for he feared that even the "Emporium of Literature" would be too hot a place for him, and that there was no corner there, or in New England, where he could hold up his head. Not to Philadelphia, for he had read an advertisement in the newspapers describing his person, and offering a reward for his capture, as the supposed murderer of Mrs. Orton. And everywhere he went, conscience, wide awake and dressed in all her horrors, with her scorpion-lash in hand, was lashing his soul into madness, and urging him deeper and deeper into the desert and the wilderness, where he hoped the foot of a white man would never tread. And as he went further and further, the echoes of that pistol still reverberated in his ears, and he fancied that his own hand had indeed pulled the trigger which had sent the ball through the broken heart of his poor, abused, cheated, and neglected wife.

And then he heard the dying moans of poor Fanny, dying in the portico of the temple from the bitter cold and the throes of premature labor; for he had read the account of her death in the papers, and his own guilty heart told him how deeply implicated he was in the death of the once happy and virtuous slave.

But as he went further, and fled faster, he heard the deep-baying of the hounds pursuing his trail, and their scratching at his door, and their eager whining for his blood, and, in disordered imagination, he sprang forward, with terror, to elude the leap of the blood-hound, which, he fancied, was close upon his heels, and felt the teeth of old Towzer sink deep into his arm, and heard again the craunching of the blood-hound upon his shoulder. And then he trembled all over, like a man shaking with the palsy, as he remembered the voice of Old Sampson, and his solemn words, echoed by Old Toney, saying, "Vengeance is mine; I will repay, saith the Lord;" and "Go Mass' Orton; you are in de hand ob de Lord now; you will fall in de lake! de lake!"

But if he was affected so deeply by all these voices of the

guilty past, which terrified him as the ghost of Banquo and the other murdered spirits terrified the guilty monarch who sat upon Scotland's blood-stained throne, Alfred Orton positively shrieked aloud, as he fancied that he heard still the screams of the poor maniac girl ringing through the frosty night air, and waking the deep silence of the forest in the old Palmetto State, calling, as a trumpet, her sons to arms, and urging even good and peaceful men to revenge the outrage and attack—though baffled—upon the honor of one of Carolina's fairest and loveliest daughters.

But, although terrible as the reality to a guilty conscience, it was but a fancied reality. It was the beginning of the worm's gnawings in Alfred Orton's heart. " The worm which never dies " had burst forth from its chrysalis shell, and was now tumbling and tumbling, over and over, in his black heart; and as the hideous worm rolled from side to side, how his guilty heart began to bleed, and to fester, and to ache! " The worm that never dies " was just born in him, and was only trying its infant teeth; taking hold here and there, and letting go its hold again; and then, as its young life grew more vigorous, driving its growing, sharpening, dreadful teeth deeper and deeper in that heart which, though it seemed like stone, could feel as a guilty heart of the flesh! By and by, " the worm that never dies," which has been born, and which will grow to a monster worm, until it fills up full all the dark, dismal, foul and loathsome cavity of Alfred Orton's heart, by and by, it shall take fresh hold—an eternal hold—upon a core which, like the worm, " never dies! "

And Alfred Orton went on and on, pursued thus by his own guilty conscience, which followed him as a hell-hound wherever he went, until, at last, he stood upon the shore of Lake Michigan. It was in the latter part of October, or the first week in November, and only a thin crust of ice was yet upon the surface of the lake. But as Alfred Orton walked by the shore, and as he remembered the solemn tones of Old Sampson, saying to Old Toney, "Let him go, for God hath said, 'Vengeance is mine; I will repay, saith the Lord,'" then he himself echoed, in reply, the words of Old Toney, "De lake! de lake ob fire and brimstone!"

And he looked upon the frozen lake, and wished that he was buried deep, deep under its cold surface, where he hoped the fires of hell could never reach him, unless they licked up first the waters of Lake Michigan! but he was afraid to take the leap, for the hot flames of hell had not come near enough as yet, although he was beginning to feel their hot breath, and to hear the crackling of the flames rolling, as a prairie on fire, down upon him! So he took from his overcoat a flask half-filled with brandy, and from his vest pocket a little vial containing a white powder. The powder he poured into the flask, which he shook violently, until he supposed that the poison was dissolved. Then he put the flask to his lips, and drank down, at a few gulps, all the brandy, which was made bitter—very bitter with strychnine. He went down to the edge of the lake, and, with the flask, attempted to break a hole in the ice, that he might relieve his taste of the bitterness of the strychnine; but the flask broke upon the ice as soon as the ice was broken, and the fragments of the flask sunk noiselessly to the bottom of the lake. He took in his hand several pieces of the frozen water, and ground them, with frenzied energy, between his teeth, and commenced pacing rapidly up and down by the level shore, like a man in great mental anguish. When several minutes had elapsed, and he had eaten up all the ice which he carried in his hand, he went to the same spot where he had broken the flask and got more ice, which he craunched with yet more energy, and tried, in vain, to get rid of the bitterness of the strychnine; but the bitter taste of the terrible poison seemed to have gone deep into his tongue, and to have steeped his palate as in gall and wormwood, and he began to feel the pains and the cramps, the dreadful contortions and terrific death-throes of strychnine, bowing his body backward, and drawing his head and heels together, in spite of his resistance, like a strong cord binding down, in spite of its toughness, the full-grown and sturdy sapling. Then Alfred Orton felt that the fires of hell were beginning to smoke and to crackle, to blaze and to roar, as a mighty conflagration within him. And in his agony he cried out, "The lake! the lake!" even as Old Toney had done, who meant, however, "the lake of fire and brimstone," and not the Lake Michigan.

It was when he felt the contortions and the spasms of strychnine strongest upon him, that Alfred Orton, the Abolitionist, leaped into the frozen lake, which was broken through by the weight of his body, which sunk down through the hole in the ice to the bottom of Lake Michigan; but his soul—the immortal soul of the suicide, all stained with crime, and tormented, before its time, with the flames and the pains of perdition, sunk down, down, down, and yet deeper down, into the lowest depths of the bottomless pit, with an infinite ocean of fire, whose waves, hot and burning, would ever roll, and surge, and hiss, and roar, above his guilty head and his damned-forever spirit!

When the spring came, and the ice had broken up, the body of Alfred Orton floated to the surface, fresh, or uninjured, to any great degree, by decomposition; and his head and his heels were still drawn together, even as he had fallen into the lake. There were some who charitably supposed that he had been accidentally drowned, or, perhaps, murdered; but a physician of intelligence, who arrived upon the spot, said: "Gentlemen, that man has come to his end by strychnine, and in no other way." Then they searched his pockets, and there was a little vial found in one of them, upon which was labelled "strychnia;" so they all felt satisfied that Alfred Orton had died by his own hand, and that he had committed the shameful act, the monstrous crime of suicide!

Many years after the death of Alfred Orton, Stephen Stevens died the death of a felon upon the gallows. But

he did not die by the verdict of a regularly constituted
judge and jury, for he suffered the terrors of what is com-
monly called "lynch law." So notorious had he become as
a highway robber, and as the bold leader of a cohort of
that apparently disbanded, but not, in reality, disorganized
corps of banditti, known as the "Murrel Band," or "Murrel Gang;" and so repeated had been his depredations
amid a peaceful and prosperous community of one of our
most peaceful and inoffensive Southern States, that the indignant citizens determined, at a regular meeting, to take
the law into their own hands, and punish Stevens and his
companions whenever they could lay hands upon them within
the limits of their jurisdiction.

It was useless, they thought, to cast those robbers into
jail to await in prison their trial at a regular term of the
court; for there was no jail which could hold them, since
they had friends enough outside, who would always, as they
had repeatedly done, effect their liberation or escape, either
by force, or by craft and cunning.

The citizens of an outraged community, therefore, advertised a reward of one thousand dollars for the capture and
delivery into their hands of Stevens, the notorious robber-
chieftain of a robber-band. Stevens saw that advertisement,
and read it in the papers of another State, and yet still
lingered near, instead of fleeing in time, and hiding himself
in the gorges of the loftiest mountain, or losing himself in
some distant valley. Fool that he was; he had better have
fled to the wilds of Texas, and dwelt among the savage
Camanches, than to risk his head when a reward of a thousand dollars was upon it! But though the rope may be
never so long, and the villain's range never so wide, when
God's strong hand is laid upon the cord, and when He begins
to pull in, hand over hand, the victim as a sacrifice to just-
tice, there is no chance for his escape. The fisherman
may never once pull upon his line, and may let out his
reel until the salmon is tired, and can swim no longer; but

by and by, the reel is slowly and steadily wound up by the expert hand of the fisherman, and the salmon is pulled to the shore with scarcely any resistance, and often not a single flounder. So, too, does God suffer the felon to be caught in a snare, or become fastened to a hook, and then he is pulled to the gallows, or he rushes thither himself.

There were two men who had noticed the advertisement, and who resolved together upon the capture of Stevens, that they might claim the reward. They knew that he was then stopping at a house not many miles away. So they started at night, with well-trained hounds, and arrived, after midnight, at the house where Stevens then was. No sooner did he hear the barking of the dogs and the steps of men approaching the house, than his guilty conscience told him they had come for him, and in his terror he leaped from the window and fled in his night-clothes. But he might as well hope to escape the bite of the cobra da capello, once it has coiled thrice around his arm, as hope to escape now the avengers of blood. In an instant the dogs were in full cry after the fugitive, and Stevens was compelled to climb a tree to escape being torn to pieces by the sharp teeth of the blood-hounds. "The coon was treed," and the fox was caught at last in his hole.

But Stevens was not yet without hope. At the very first town through which he was carried by his captors, he succeeded in inducing a lawyer to undertake his release. The humane attorney, actuated, perhaps, as much by that spirit of chivalry and generous sympathy which, it is said, actuates the high-minded of the legal profession, or that blind submission to the "*Lex scripta*," rather than to the spirit and intention of both written and unwritten law, whose legitimate object is to punish the guilty, and aid the innocent to escape, thus affording a double protection to society, and with the lawyer's very laudable hatred of everything which looks like, or which tends to strengthen the mobocratic spirit, which is the greatest tyranny and most intolerable

17

oppression which can afflict any people; actuated, perhaps,
by such motives as these, rather than the liberal fee which
Stevens could afford so easily to pay, out of his ill-gotten
gains, the humane attorney was induced to undertake the
case of the highwayman, and actually had him set at liberty
under a writ of *habeas corpus*.   But although the act of
habeas corpus is, rightly considered, the great bulwark of a
freeman when his liberty is unjustly invaded, and with this
act in his hand, and his home for his castle, he may defy
"the sheriff and his *posse comitatus*," not so with the outlaw, who has no right to demand a *habeas corpus*, and no
home which he can call his castle, and no domestic altar
where he may throw himself, and even where, with his hand
upon the very "horns of the altar," he may justly be slain;
with such men as were his captors, stern and inflexible, and
themselves invincible in their determination and their might,
no castle was strong enough to hold him, and all the acts
for relief in the world would be set aside as idle forms and
mocking ceremonies.

No sooner, therefore, was the back of the attorney turned,
and he had pocketed his fat fee with an inward chuckle of
delight and satisfaction, and no sooner had the judge who
had granted the *habeas corpus* returned to his home, or was
at a safe distance, than Stevens, who thought himself safe
from further molestation, was again "nabbed," or "grabbed,"
or "kidnapped," and hurried on a captive between two
resolute and determined men, from whose grasp he felt certain now that he could not hope to escape, unless by some
unforeseen accident, or the performance of a miracle ; and he
felt that a miracle was not likely to be performed in his
behalf, nor could he imagine any accident which could
happen.   Once across "the line," and once in the hands
of "the avengers," Stevens gave up all hope, and resigned
himself passively to his fate ; he did not blame his captors for
doing as he would have done himself, under similar circumstances, and acknowledged the justice of the sentence which

condemned him to death. On the gallows, which had been erected for his especial benefit or execution, just "upon the line" where two states meet, he confessed to the murder at the "Jasper Spring," and to many other horrid crimes. But he had not time to mention all his diabolical acts, for the avengers were in a hurry, as they knew not how soon a determined effort might be attempted for his rescue, nor how many secret banditti stood with concealed weapons in the crowd.

Numerous and bitter were the attacks made upon the men who were most prominent, and who felt it to be their duty to become self-constituted judges, and jurors, and executioners, all combined. They were denounced in some of the leading journals, and by high functionaries, as murderers and outlaws, who deserved a halter themselves. And because two of the men who cast their votes for the execution were ministers of the Gospel, and, as godly men, offered the consolations of religion to the felon while standing on the scaffold; and because one of them offered a most solemn public prayer, while kneeling upon the platform of the gallows, they were denounced, these men of God were denounced, by hot-headed or wrong-hearted men, as hypocrites and vile pretenders to religion.

We know nothing of the character or motives of the men who offered up prayer at the execution of Stevens, but we do believe that it was the act of Christian men. We are no advocates for mobocracy, whose spirit we loathe and detest as unmanly, ignoble, and tyrannical. But was it a mob who condemned Stevens to die upon the scaffold? A *mob*, we understand, to be a promiscuous crowd of greatly excited persons, acting contrary to law, or without regard to the law when it was within their reach, and they had the power to wield it. But, in this case, the law had been repeatedly tried without effect upon Stevens himself, or some one of his companions. There was no jury which could be formed, upon which they could not get at least one or two of their number. There was no jail which could not be entered either by a bribe or by force of arms. The law, in short, was either dead or bankrupt, and could build no scaffold high enough, nor provide a rope strong enough, to punish these bold invaders of the rights and property of the people.

Stevens and his band were, emphatically, outlaws; and when could an outlaw claim the protection of the laws which he had repeatedly and daringly set at defiance? Such men are not only fugitives and vagabonds, but savages, whose hand is against every man, and against whom every man's hand should be turned, to protect a peaceful community from their aggressions; just as much so as against the warlike and blood-thirsty Indian, with his hand upon his "tomahawk," which he has "dug up," and his deadly arrow drawn to the very barb.

In the case of Stevens, therefore, we contend that it was not a mob who condemned him to die, but. a body of calm, collected, dignified men, who felt pained and grieved at the step which they felt that a stern and unavoidable necessity compelled them to take in their own self-defense, and the protection of their property. Does it look like bluster, or cruelty? No! There have been judicial murders at which the law must hang her head with shame, and blush with confusion at the wanton cruelty of those who were her appointed ministers; and if those ministers themselves have a conscience whose voice has not lost its power, they must be startled sometimes from their slumbers, with its thunder tones, or terrified upon the bench, and at the bar, or in the busy throng, with the startling charge of judicial murders and the legal homicides they have committed. Let such men hold their peace and be silent.

No, no! it was not a heartless and excited, nor a blood-thirsty mob which condemned Stevens, the Land-Pirate, to the ignominious death of the gallows! It was the voice of a free people, who had a right to make their own laws, and to execute them, if need be, themselves, without the inter-vention of officers regularly elected and duly appointed by that same people.   And if the maxim of law is correct—"*Vox populi, vox Dei*"—then the voice of the people was the voice of God.

Thus, in the case of Stevens, the truth of Scripture was verified, and Old Toney's prophecy fulfilled—"Vengeance is mine; I will repay, saith the Lord," and "De judgment ob Almighty God will obertake de murderer, and bring de guilty wretch to de gallows."

CONCLUSION

EVERAL years after the marriage of Mr. and Mrs. Sanford, "little Willie," who had grown up to be a man, came to the city of Charleston, on part business, part pleasure. He was now a fine-looking, handsome young man, with the same bright, black eye and intelligent countenance, and looked as innocent in manhood, almost, as he had looked when a boy. Mr. Herbert's eldest daughter was just "sweet seventeen," and looked so pretty and so sweet that young Williston felt like eating her up, as a sweet stick of candy, at his very first visit to the house of the Herberts. The Sanfords, of Boston, and the Herberts, of Charleston, were old friends, and in some way distantly related. It was not a very hard matter, therefore, for a handsome young man, with fine talents, thus situated, to persuade a lovely young maiden of seventeen to form a matrimonial alliance. Would that there was nothing to disturb the harmony of our country, or that the union of the States could be held together as pleasantly, and that their relations were as happy as those which ever existed, and still exist, between the families of the Herberts and the Sanfords. "For behold how good and how pleasant it is for brethren to dwell together in unity."

Mr. and Mrs. Herbert have never felt a jarring note of discord between them, and have raised several children to usefulness and honor.

Old Toney's family have increased in number from ten to upward of forty souls, all contented and happy.

Old Sampson never laid aside his armor as a Christian warrior, but died in his battered harness in his death-struggle with the grim warrior who sits upon the pale horse.

"Young Toney" was called Young Toney until after his father's death, although he was himself upward of sixty when the venerable old hero paid the debt to nature which we must all pay.

For twenty years, Old Toney's only employment, or rather amusement, consisted in paddling up and down the Ashley and Cooper rivers, fishing in a little canoe for whiting, and sheep-head, and mullet. The old man usually went alone, but sometimes his master, Mr. Herbert, or George, or some other of the family, asked permission to go with him. Old Toney had grown very mild and Christian-like, and was seldom known to get into a passion, except when any obstinate youngster would persist in saying "Alligator." It was then his invariable rule "to pull up anchor" and go straight home, never mind how well the fish were biting, or what the promise of success. But if Mr. Herbert or any grown man happened to be with him in his little boat when an alligator came swimming slowly toward them, or seemed motionless as a log upon the water, then the old man said, in a low voice, as if afraid that the beast might hear his words, and understand them: "Turn your head turrer way, masser. Don't look at 'um. Mek b'l'ebe you don't see 'um. For it 's berry bad luck to talk 'bout dat t'ing, and mebbe," he added, in a still lower tone, "to t'ink 'bout 'um, too."

Poor old man! He was in his dotage now, and was dreaming of the sad time when he leaned against the prison wall, or looked through the rusty bars of his cell, and thought of the foreman Cæsar—"It is berry bad luck for true to call de name ob dat t'ing."

At length the time came when Old Toney laid aside his

"fishing tackle," and tied up his canoe ; for he was about to start upon a very long journey, "to see his dear old Masser Shelton." He thought of the battles he had fought by his master's side, and imagined that the brave old Colonel was fighting still, and needed his services very much. He must make haste to go, for the Indians, or the British, might kill his master before he could arrive upon the field of battle, to shield with his person the gallant old soldier from the shafts of the enemy.

Lying upon his death-bed in the kitchen, he saw, in imagination, the swarthy, dusky forms of Seminoles and Cherokees around him, and heard their terrific war whoops, which, instead of making him tremble, so aroused his indignation that he strove hard to get out of the bed and chase away the cowardly savages with his single right arm. His children, assembled around his cot, were compelled to hold him down, and Old Rinah had to coax him to "lie still and let the Indians and the British alone." At the mention of that, to him, hateful name—the British—the old man's eye lighted up with its last brightest fires. Like Napoleon, dying on the lone, sea-girt rock of St. Helena, a martyr to British fear, and cowardice, and cruelty, and cupidity—a captive, but unconquered hero—like Napoleon, uttering in death his last battle-cry, "Tête d' Armie," and then was dead—so, too, Old Toney rose upon his elbow and shouted, "De British! de British! dey run! dey run! dey take to de water!" and then, falling backward upon his pillow, the old hero was dead.

There was a long procession of both whites and blacks commingled, which followed Old Toney's corpse to the burying-ground. Not only was the carriage of Mr. Herbert there, but numerous others, also, of Mr. Herbert's and Mrs. Shelton's friends, who desired to swell the cortège which accompanied the old hero, as a sable prince, to the tomb. But, most remarkable of all, because so unusual, several military companies preceded the hearse, to point out the spot where the old soldier, who had fought in the War of 1812, should rest his old patriarch bones. And when the minister had said, "Dust to dust, ashes to ashes," and when the prayer had been uttered, and the benediction given, then these volunteer corps formed a line in front, and fired several platoons over the grave of Old Toney. The old hero could not hear "de big platoon," fired over his own grave, nor the music of the drum and the fife as they played the martial quick-step, and returned quickly and with such lively tread to their homes, but let us hope that the brave old man is hearing now, and singing with his master, close by that master's side, the song of Moses and the Lamb.

Reader—kind, gentle reader—may you and I sing, one day, as Colonel Shelton, and Old Toney, and Old Sampson, and Fetic, we hope, and Mr. Sanford, and that "poor widow" whom he married, and all other of God's dear children, who have been "saved by grace" and not by their "might," nor "strength," nor any of their "good works," which, at last, is, as their "righteousness," but "filthy rags"—all saved, because they were sinners, and felt the need of that Savior who died for them. O! may we also sing, one day and for-ever, "the song of Moses and the Lamb slain for sinners." Then shall the reader and the author shake hands joyously, and feel that, although *in life* they had never beheld each other's faces, yet *in spirit* they were acquainted, and knew each other through mutual friends, but knew each other best through "the Friend of sinners," who is the "Go-between" and "Bond of Alliance" to reconcile differences, and unite Christian hearts, whether they throb under the burning sun of the Equator, or stagnate under the cold of the Arctic Circle.

THE END.

17*

MISCELLANEOUS WORKS.

The Old Pine Farm; or, The Southern Side.

By a SOUTH CAROLINA MINISTER. Illustrated, and bound in cloth. 75 cents.

This is one of those delightful tales that every Southerner will read with pleasure. Since its appearance it has received hundreds of flattering notices from the Southern Press.

[*From the Baltimore True Union.*]

This is a very interesting and entertaining volume, exhibiting Southern country life. The sketches of a minister's experience are graphic and life-like. The book will be read with interest both by the youthful and the aged. We commend it to all our readers.

[*From the Religious Herald.*]

This volume is also issued by the South-Western Publishing House. It is a sprightly and interesting sketch of some of the features of Southern ministerial life among country churches. The incidents are skilfully narrated, and it is well worthy a perusal.

Old Toney and His Master;

Or, The Abolitionist and the Land Pirate. Founded on Facts. A Tale of 1824-27. By "DESMONS." $1.

This is from the pen of one of South Carolina's gifted sons—a work of *thrilling interest*.

The Science of Life.

By Rev. W. C. BUCK. In cloth. 75 cents.

Prof. Watson, of the Nashville Medical College, and J. W. King, of Murfreesboro, Tenn., have each written an Introduction to this work. Scientific men will appreciate it.

Blackwell's Acrostics.

Acrostics on the Names of every President of the United States, with their Portraits; also on all the States, with their Seals. Population, white and black, in 1860; on the Names of Persons and Things: enriched with Moral Lessons and Choice Fables. Richly illustrated. 8vo. $1.

Napoleon Dynasty.

By THE BERKELEY MEN. 1 vol. 8vo, in cloth. $2 50.

This is a *new edition* of the History of the Bonaparte Family, brought down to the present time.

Josephine, Hortense, Maria Louisa, Joseph Beauharnais, Murat, and indeed all the race, figure in these pages; and each has a portrait said to be, and with great probability, accurate likenesses.

Young Men of America.

By SAMUEL BATCHELDER, JUN. 1 vol. 12mo, in cloth, 40 cents.

His essay is well written and practical; free from visionary ideas or sentimentality, but with an earnest purpose in view. Its tone is healthy, its style clear and chaste, and it can be read both with pleasure and profit.

MISCELLANEOUS WORKS.

Life-Pictures from a Pastor's Note-Book.
By ROBERT TURNBULL, D.D. 1 vol. 12mo, in cloth. $1.

Peterson's Familiar Science. 60 cents.

Esop's Fables. 50 cents.

The Pastor's Handbook.
Comprising Selections of Scripture, Arranged for various Occasions of Official Duty; Select Formulas for the Marriage Ceremony, etc.; Rules of Order for Churches, Ecclesiastical and other Deliberative Assemblies, and Tables for Statistical Record. 50 cents.

Dr. Resin Thompson on Fevers.
Large 12mo, in sheep. $1 50.

A work for every physician and every family. In this work is presented a new, simple, and certain treatment of Fevers, Typhoid especially. It is approved by the medical profession generally. The "Journal of Rational Medicine" thus speaks of it:

Dr. Resin Thompson, of Nashville, Tenn., after an experience of over thirty years in the practice of medicine, gave his opinions in regard to the nature and treatment of Fever in the form of Lectures and Essays; which he afterwards embodied in a small volume, the third edition, under the title of "A Treatise on Fever," he has sent to the "Journal of Rational Medicine."

Without endorsing all the views of Dr. Thompson, either as to the cause or treatment of fever, I feel privileged to express the opinion that the teachings of this book are decidedly in advance of the profession, and that the author has proved himself to be a deep thinker, and an earnest, honest man. His book can be read with great benefit.

Liddell and Scott's Greek Lexicon. Indispensable. $5.

Greek Concordance.
Englishman's. Very valuable. $4.

Greek Prepositions and Cases of Nouns. $3 50.

Latin Lexicon. Crook and Schem. $3 50.

Webster's English Dictionary.
4to. Unabridged Pictorial. $6 50.

TRANSLATIONS OF THE CLASSICS.

Cicero's Orations—Interlinear, (Clark.) $1 75.

Sallust—Interlinear, (Clark.) $1 75.

Cæsar's Commentaries—Interlinear, (Clark.) $1 75.

Virgil—Interlinear, (Hart & Osborn.) $1 75.

Dictionary of Classical Quotations. $1 75.

Let all those who have not had the opportunity to study them at school, read these admirable translations of them.

JUVENILE PUBLICATIONS.

PLEASANT PAGES.
By S. P. NEWCOMBE.   1 vol. 16mo.   In cloth, 75 cents.

A book of Home Education and Entertainment, containing a great variety of subjects presented, consisting of Moral Lessons, Natural History, History, Travels, Physical Geography, Object Lessons, Drawing and Perspective, Music, Poetry, etc., and, withal, so skilfully treated as to make truth simple and attractive, renders it an admirable family book for winter evenings and summer days.

LITTLE COMMODORE. 75 cents.
PLEASURE BOOKS, (on Linen, in Oil Colors,) each 20 cents.
RICHARD THE LION-HEARTED. Gilt, $1; cloth, 75 cents.
PICTURE PLAY BOOK. By Peter Parley. 75 cents.
YOUNG AMERICANS ABROAD. 75 cents.
HOW TO BE A LADY. By Newcomb. 50 cents.
HOW TO BE A MAN.   "   50 cents.
ANECDOTES FOR BOYS.   "   42 cents.
ANECDOTES FOR GIRLS.   "   42 cents.
KIND WORDS FOR CHILDREN. By Newcomb. 42 cents.
AGNES HOPETOUN'S SCHOOLS AND HOLIDAYS. 63 cents.

AUNT MARY'S STORIES. (In Boxes.)
12 vols. 16mo.   In paper, $1 50; in cloth, $3.

The Series comprise:

The A B C Book.....2	Nursery Rhymes....2	Annie's Speller 2
The Rose..............1	The Violet 1	The Daisy..............1
The Lily 1	The Tulip 1	The Jessamine........1

COTTAGE LIBRARY. (In Boxes.)
By PETER PARLEY. 10 vols. 18mo.   Fancy muslin, gilt, each 37½ cents.

This Library contains:

Make the Best of it.	A Home in the Sea.
Right is Might.	Wit Bought.
Persevere and Prosper.	The Truth Finder.
Tales of the Sea and Land.	A Tale of the Revolution.
What to Do, and How to Do it.	Dick Boldhero.

BRIGHTHOPE SERIES. (In Boxes.)
By J. T. TROWBRIDGE. 5 vols. 18mo.   Gilt back, uniform, $2 50.

The Series comprise:

The Old Battle-Ground.	Iron Thorpe.
Father Brighthope.	Burr Cliff.
Hearts and Faces.	

JUVENILE PUBLICATIONS.

SUNNY SIDE SERIES. (In Boxes.)
> By Mrs. STUART and CORA BELMONT. 4 vols. 18mo, uniform. Price of each 50 cents.

The Series comprise:

Peep at No. 5.	Tell-Tale.
Last Leaf from Sunny Side.	City Side.

THE ROLLO BOOKS. (In Boxes.)
> By JACOB ABBOTT. 14 vols. Illustrated. 16mo. Per set, $7. 14 vols. Uniform 18mo, $5 25.

The Series comprise:

Rollo Learning to Talk.	Rollo's Museum.
Rollo Learning to Read.	Rollo's Travels.
Rollo at Work.	Rollo's Correspondence.
Rollo at Play.	Rollo's Philosophy, Water.
Rollo at School.	Rollo's Philosophy, Air.
Rollo's Vacation.	Rollo's Philosophy, Fire.
Rollo's Experiments.	Rollo's Philosophy, Sky.

ROLLO STORY BOOKS. (In Boxes.)
> By JACOB ABBOTT. 12 vols. 18mo. Illustrated. Price per set, $3.

The Series comprise:

Trouble on the Mountain	Georgie.
Causey Building.	· Rollo in the Woods.
Apple-Gathering.	Rollo's Garden.
The Two Wheelbarrows.	The Steel Trap.
Blueberrying.	Labor Lost.
The Freshet.	Lucy's Visit.

THE FLORENCE STORIES.
> By JACOB ABBOTT. 3 vols. 18mo. Illustrated. Price, each, 60 cents.

The Series comprise:

Florence and John.	Grimkie.

The Orkney Islands (in press.)

THE AIMWELL STORIES.
> By WALTER AIMWELL. 6 vols. 16mo, gilt. Price, each, 63 cents. 6 vols., uniform, with box, $3 75.

The Series comprise:

> Oscar; or, The Boy who had his Own Way.
> Clinton; A Book for Boys.
> Ella; or, Turning Over a New Leaf.
> Whistler; or, The Manly Boy.
> Marcus; or The Boy Tamer.
> Jessie; or, Trying to be Somebody.

JUVENILE PUBLICATIONS.

TREASURY OF PLEASURE BOOKS.

Illustrated by Colored Plates. 1 vol. 8vo, muslin antique, gilt, $1 50.

CONTENTS.—The Boys' and Girls' Illuminated Primer; Tom, the Piper's Son; Simple Simon; The Bear and the Children; Courtship and Wedding of the Little Man and the Little Maid; Hans in Luck; Little Bo-peep; Henny Penny; The Fox and the Geese; Maja's Alphabet; The House that Jack Built; The Ugly Little Duck; The Life and Death of Jenny Wren; The Charmed Fawn.

THE A. L. O. E. BOOKS.

18 vols., uniform in cloth.

The Series comprise:

The Claremont Tales	50	The Roby Family. A Sequel to the Above	30
The Adopted Son, and other Tales	50	Wings and Stings	25
The Young Pilgrim	50	Walter Binning	25
The Giant-Killer and Sequel	50	True Heroism	25
Flora, and other Tales	50	Rambles of a Rat	30
The Needle and the Rat	50	The Story of a Needle	25
Eddie Ellerslie and the Mine	50	The Two Paths	25
Precepts in Practice	50	Old Friends with New Faces	30
The Giant-Killer. Alone	30	The Mine	40

We would rather be "A. L. O. E." than Thackeray or Dickens. We have not the least idea who or what the author is, represented by those four letters; but one thing is certain, he (or she, perhaps) is exerting a power far more to be desired than the reputation of the mere novelist, however dazzling that may be. Who shall undertake even to guess how many young minds on both sides of the Atlantic have received permanent impulses in the paths of virtue and piety through the influence of the charming books which have appeared under this authorship?—*Christian Times.*

ATTRACTIVE HISTORIES FOR YOUTH.

I. National Series, by Banvard.

Plymouth and the Pilgrims;

Or, Incidents and Adventure in the History of the First Settlers. With Illustrations. 16mo, cloth. 60 cents.

Novelties of the New World.

An Account of the Adventures and Discoveries of the Explorers of North America. With numerous Illustrations. 16mo, cloth. 60 cents.

Romance of American History;

Or, an Account of the Early Settlement of North Carolina and Virginia; embracing Incidents connected with the Spanish Settlements, the French Colonies, and the English Plantations, etc. With Illustrations. 16mo, cloth. 60 cents.

Tragic Scenes in the History of Maryland and the Old French War.

With an account of various interesting Contemporaneous Events which occurred in the Early Settlement of America. With numerous elegant Illustrations. 16mo, cloth. 60 cents.

☞ Each volume is complete in itself, and yet, together, they form a regular Series of American Histories.

II. By Jacob Abbott.

1. ABORIGINAL AMERICA. (Now ready.)
2. DISCOVERY OF AMERICA. (Now ready.)
3. THE SOUTHERN COLONIES.
4. THE NORTHERN COLONIES.
5. THE MIDDLE COLONIES.
6. REVOLT OF THE COLONIES.
7. BOSTON IN SEVENTY-FIVE.
8. NEW YORK IN SEVENTY-SIX.
9. THE CAROLINAS IN SEVENTY-NINE.
10. CAMPAIGN IN THE JERSEYS.
11. BURGOYNE AND CORNWALLIS.
12. THE FEDERAL CONSTITUTION.

PERIODICAL PUBLICATIONS.

I. Weekly.

THE TENNESSEE BAPTIST.

EDITORS:

RELIGIOUS.

J. R. GRAVES.
J. M. PENDLETON.

CORRESPONDING.

C. R. HENDRICKSON, Cal.
G. H. ORCHARD, Eng.

SABBATH-SCHOOL DEPARTMENT.

A. C. DAYTON.

SECULAR.

J. TOVELL.

THIS Paper entered upon its SEVENTEENTH VOLUME the first of September, 1860. It is designed to be the exponent of true Baptist faith and consistent Baptist practice, and to reflect the leading aspects of the present times, and to meet and discuss fairly and fearlessly the great issues of the day. It has also already reached a circulation *larger than any weekly religious paper in the world.*

One paper for universal circulation in the South and Southwest, for purposes of intercommunication, is greatly needed. The Tennessee Baptist is becoming that paper.

TERMS, $2. The name of no new subscriber entered without payment in advance. Old subscribers delaying payment to the end of the year, $3.

☞ Any preacher of any denomination, not a subscriber, can have the paper the first year for $1.

☞ When the circulation reaches 15,000, all ministers can have the paper for $1 per annum. Try it one year, and see whether its friends or its enemies tell the truth about it.

☞ Every new subscriber at $2, or any friend sending one, and $2, shall be entitled to any one dollar book of our publication.

II. Monthly.

YOUTH'S MAGAZINE.

A Monthly Serial—Beautifully Illustrated.

Only One Dollar per Year!

A MONTHLY FOR THE YOUTH OF THE SOUTH!

This Magazine commenced on the first day of May, 1860, and every effort will be put forth to make it second to none, but rather superior to all.

It has heretofore been known as the "CHILDREN'S BOOK," but as the Publishers concluded to enlarge it with the commencement of the volume, they concluded also to change its name.

The MAGAZINE contains *eight* pages more than the "Children's Book," and is filled with matter calculated to interest the whole family circle, from the parent to the little one who just begins to look for the "purty picters." The editors will pay strict attention to the selection of the *most* interesting matter.

This is the only publication of the kind in the SOUTH. Will not Southern parents patronize it? What more delightful visitor can be received monthly than the YOUTH'S MAGAZINE? Send $1, and receive it for one year. At least send for a specimen copy.

III. Quarterly.

THE SOUTHERN BAPTIST REVIEW.

EDITORS:

J. R. GRAVES.
J. M. PENDLETON,

Professor of Theology in Union University, Tenn.

Terms.—$2 per Annum, strictly in Advance.

This work is quarterly; each issue 160 pages; making a volume of 640 royal octavo pages each year. Subscription price $2 a year, *in advance.*

It has won the reputation of being the *strongest Baptist Quarterly*

PERIODICAL PUBLICATIONS.

in the Union. The best writers in the South contribute to its pages. It is, in itself, a Theological Library. No minister or reading Baptist should be without it. Its exceedingly low terms place it within the reach of all. Any minister sending three new subscribers for the Review, will receive his copy gratis. A specimen number sent, if desired.

The following notices reflect the opinion of the Baptist press, South:

The work is decidedly a Baptist work: it sets forth and defends their views of scriptural doctrine with a clearness, pungency, and power which we have seldom seen equalled. We most heartily recommend this *Review* as an able exposition of Baptist orthodoxy.—*Biblical Recorder, N. C.*

SOUTHERN BAPTIST REVIEW.—We have received No. 1 of Vol. II. of this *Review*, Graves, Marks & Co., Publishers. Nashville—Elder J. R. Graves, J. M. Pendleton, and A. C. Dayton, Editors. It is much more Baptistic than the *Christian Review*, being devoted more exclusively to Baptist literature, to the maintenance of our tenets and practice, and to refuting the objections of gainsayers. It is an able and practical work, is doing good service, and ought to receive a liberal patronage.—*Religious Herald, Richmond, Va.*

IV. Annual.

THE SOUTHERN BAPTIST ALMANAC AND REGISTER.

This will be a beautifully illustrated work of sixty pages, issued on or before the first of October of each year. It will contain the most perfect statistics of Baptists throughout the South of any similar work issued in this country. Price 10 cents.

NOTICES TO CLERKS OF ASSOCIATIONS.

Minutes are published to impart denominational and statistical information. A great many are worthless. A minute should have a table containing a list of churches and delegates and post-office, number baptized, received by letter, Res., Dis. excluded, deceased, number whites, number blacks. THESE COLUMNS SHOULD BE ADDED UP. Besides this table, there should be a table containing the names of ordained ministers and their post-offices, licentiates and their post-offices, and the clerk and moderator of the association. It should contain an abstract of the church letters.

☞ Let each clerk, without fail, send, *in writing, the statistics of his Association, so soon as his Association adjourns;* also a copy of his minutes, as soon as published, to the "Southern Baptist Register," Nashville, Tenn., and he will receive a copy of the Register in return.

TO ADVERTISERS.

WE WOULD MOST RESPECTFULLY CALL ATTENTION TO
THE FACT THAT

THE TENNESSEE BAPTIST

Visits nearly 15,000 Families Weekly!

IN EVERY SOUTHERN, SOUTH-WESTERN, AND WESTERN STATE.

BY FAR THE BEST
ADVERTISING MEDIUM IN THE SOUTH OR SOUTH-WEST.

Advertisements strictly limited to Eight Columns.

TERMS.

For one square or less—ten lines, or the space occupied by them—for the first insertion, $1; for each subsequent insertion, 75 cents.

For three months, per square	$ 8 00
For six months, "	15 00
For twelve months, "	25 00

Special notice will be called to your advertisement as often as changed.

Advertisements, to secure attention, and editorial notice, must be paid for in advance.

To TRUSTEES AND TEACHERS OF SCHOOLS. — All Baptist schools will be charged one-fourth of these rates, if *prepaid*—not otherwise.

Articles written to advertise schools will be charged same as advertisements. When facts are furnished they will be noticed editorially, if the school is advertised in this paper.

To PUBLISHERS.—All books advertised in this paper, approved by its editors, are purchased and sold by the South-Western Publishing House. All publishers of good books find it to their interest to advertise in its columns.

These being our established rates for the year 1861, it is hoped that no one will ask us to recede from them.

CATALOGUE

SOUTHERN BAPTIST

SABBATH-SCHOOL UNION,

CONTAINING A LIST OF ITS PUBLICATIONS
SO FAR AS ISSUED.

NASHVILLE, TENN.:
SOUTHERN BAPTIST SABBATH-SCHOOL UNION,
59 NORTH MARKET STREET.
1861.

SOUTHERN BAPTIST S. S. UNION.

EXECUTIVE BOARD LOCATED AT NASHVILLE, TENN.

A. C. Dayton, *Cor. Sec'y.* | H. G. Scovel, *Treasurer.*
Geo. C. Connor, *Travelling Agent and Missionary.*

THE CHILDREN'S FRIEND.

This beautiful Monthly serial for Sabbath Schools and Families is edited by
A. C. Dayton, and published under the direction of the *Executive Board* of the
Southern Baptist Sabbath School Union, on the following

TERMS:

When postage is paid at the office of publication, the *following* will be the
rates:

15 copies to one address,	$1 88	Postage, 54	$2 42 per year.
20 " " "	2 50	" 72	3 22 "
30 " " "	3 75	" 1 08	4 83 "
40 " " "	4 00	" 1 44	5 44 "
50 " " "	4 50	" 1 68	6 18 "
60 " " "	5 40	" 2 16	7 56 "
70 " " "	6 30	" 2 40	8 70 "
80 " " "	7 20	" 2 88	10 08 "
90 " " "	7 75	" 3 12	10 87 "
100 " " "	8 00	" 2 36	11 36 "

No advantage can be derived by prepaying a less number than fifteen copies,
nor even those directed within the State where published.

All matters for publication should be addressed to A. C. Dayton, Editor, and
all matters of business to Graves, Marks & Co., Depository Agents, Nashville,
Tenn:

HYMN BOOKS and MUSIC BOOKS.

The "ARIOLA," a delightful little Music and Song Book for Sabbath
  Schools ....
  Per copy ....
  Per dozen copies...

The SABBATH SCHOOL SONGSTER, a smaller book of much
  merit, by L. B. Fish..
  Per copy...0 15
  Per dozen copies...1 50

b

SOUTHERN BAPTIST S. S. UNION.

READING LIBRARY.

	Boxed.	By Mail.
Training of Children	16 cents.	19 cents.
English Bible, Vol. I	18 "	23 "
" " " II	16 "	20 "
Stories for Children	14 "	17 "
Weaver of Naumburg	22 "	27 "
David the Scholar	14 "	17 "
Reward of Integrity	14 "	18 "
Mignella	14 "	17 "
Knife Grinder's Son	20 "	25 "
Buds and Blossoms	16 '	20 "
Little City	18 "	23 "
Stories about Jesus	20 "	25 "
Nobleman Laborer	16 "	19 "
Carrie's Pony	14 "	18 "
Moss Side	18 "	22 "
Melodies of Heart and Home	16 "	20 "
Christopher Columbus	20 "	25 "
Model Family	16 "	20 "
Snowy Fleece	14 "	17 "
Ellen Manning	18 "	22 "
Stories of the Apostles	16 "	20 "
Beautiful Queen	16 "	20 "
Child to be Saved	22 "	27 "
Bible, No. I	16 "	20 "
Green on Gambling	20 "	26 "
Saul of Tarsus	18 "	23 "
Emanuel	14 "	17 "
Elijah the Prophet	14 "	17 "
Norwegian Boy	14 "	17 "
Pilgrim's Progress, Vol. I	18 "	23 "
" " " II	18 "	22 "
Angel Lilly	14 "	17 "
Short Stories	14 "	17 "
The Worsted Thread	14 "	17 "
Life of Moses	18 "	23 "
Gems	14 "	17 "
Nellie Wentworth	18 "	22 "

C

SOUTHERN BAPTIST S. S. UNION.

	Boxed.	By Mail.
King's Messenger...	12 cents.	17 cents.
City of Palm Trees...	16 "	20 "
Life of Cyrus...	16 "	20 "
James Stanley...	24 "	30 "
A Sermon..	14 "	18 "
Miguel Servede..	18 "	22 "
Aunt Abbey's Stories..	18 "	22 "
Will it do ?..	14 "	17 "
Life of Daniel..	16 "	19 "
The Bible, No. II...	16 "	20 "
Charles Stone...	16 "	20 "
Secret of Happiness...	16 "	20 "
Mother's Influence..	17 "	20 "
Visions of Daniel...	16 "	20 "
Memoir of I. Teasdale..	19 "	23 "
City of Rivers..	16 "	20 "
Objection to Baptists, (Prize Essay.).....................	24 "	30 "
Virginia Wallace...	18 "	22 "

Besides its own publications the *Union* is prepared to furnish those of all other Baptist Publication Societies.

QUESTION BOOKS.

DAYTON'S QUESTION BOOK, Vol. I. per copy.......................0. 15
"   "   "   " per dozen copies............1 50
DAYTON'S QUESTION BOOK, Vol. II, per copy.......................0 15
"   "   "   " per dozen copies............1 50
CATECHISM IN RHYME, by Mrs. Graves, per copy....................0 10
"   "   "   "   " per dozen copies..........1 00
CATECHISMS, HISTORICAL, series for children, (Preparing).....
"   DOCTRINAL,   "   "   "   "

CARDS,

On each of which is a verse of Scripture, teaching some important truth, intended to be given to Pupils for *early attendance*, and *good recitations*.
Per set...0 20

TESTAMENTS

Of a small and convenient size, with clear type, intended for Testament classes, per dozen..1 00

PRIMERS

Adapted to Sabbath School instruction, and permanently bound
Per copy...0 10
Per dozen copies..1 00

d